# *THREATCON*

## ASSAULT ON THE PENTAGON

A novel by David Alexander

# *DELTA*

Triumvirate

Publications
New York • London • Sydney

# THREATCON DELTA

This is a work of fiction. Names, characters, places and incidents are either the product of the author's imagination or are used fictitiously, and any resemblance to actual persons, living or dead, business establishments, events or locales, is entirely coincidental.

A Triumvirate Publications International thriller novel. Published by arrangement with the author.

For more about David Alexander:
www.davidalexanderbooks.com.

ISBN-10: 0-9977810-4-1
ISBN-13: 978-0-9977810-4-5

Triumvirate Publications International
2001 Madison Avenue
New York NY 10035

DAVID ALEXANDER

# Threatcon Delta
# Assault on the Pentagon

**A Global Thriller**
By David Alexander

When an ousted mogul and his Russian partner
team up to take over the US government,
America's first woman president tackles the first
major strategic challenge of her administration.
Threatcon Delta: Assault on the Pentagon tells the
story of how terrorism, treason and global
organized crime converge to place the most potent
symbol of American military power under the
control of a determined and ruthless group of
heavily armed and extremely dangerous men who
can't be stopped, yet who must be stopped.

This global superthriller is based both on author
David Alexander's extensive and detailed research
into the history of the Pentagon, combined with
first-hand knowledge of the Pentagon's most
closely held secrets by this veteran defense
insider, all of which has been artfully woven into a
masterpiece of high-concept suspense fiction.
In fact, the combined impact of accuracy and
authenticity blended with superb storytelling may

find some readers asking themselves if perhaps some parts of the story shouldn't have been made public, for fear that terrorists or global criminals might some day use it as a basis for an actual plan of attack.

Yet the assault on the Pentagon portrayed in the book is no standard terrorist martyrdom mission either. Those who've taken over the headquarters of the United States military have an exit strategy that has been brilliantly devised to shuttle them to safety and provide for the enjoyment of their ill-gotten profits -- a scam on a global scale that promises to net the Puzzle Palace's hijackers a considerable fortune.

By any standard, Threatcon Delta: Assault on the Pentagon is action thriller fiction at its boldest and best. It's one of the achievements that have earned David Alexander a secure place at the top of the list of the world's masters of the game.

Liberty begins as the aspiration of the individual, and sovereignty is the measure of the absolute power of the state. As we look around us today, we see an erosion of this fundamentals of international society ... Since sovereignty is priceless and must be inviolate, it is fundamental that no nation has the right to do that which if every other nation did likewise, would destroy this fragile fabric of civilization...

-- Senator William Fulbright / The Arrogance of Power

To save the country, we had to destroy it.
-- General William Westmoreland

# THREATCON DELTA

## Author's Note:

Prior to the institution of color alert codes after 911, Threatcon, or Threat Condition Delta, was the highest threat level recognized by the US government and military service branches. Like Condition Red it was to be invoked when a terrorist attack had occurred or when intelligence indicated terrorist action was likely. The invocation of Threatcon Delta always implied that the situation was extremely grave and that the most stringent measures might be taken to combat it. Though this condition code is no longer in official use, I have retained it for this book as it seems less of a cliché than its present equivalent, and seems to have an aura of gravity about that makes it, in my opinion, a more fitting title for this book and the fictional action, characters, locales, histories and situations that unfold in its pages.

DAVID ALEXANDER

*DAY ZERO:*
*MONDAY, DECEMBER 2ND*

**BEFORE**

# THREATCON DELTA

*Prolog*
## CLEARANCE

*T*he secret National Security Council white paper lay atop the desk of outgoing Defense Secretary Robert Battle, the same enormous Pershing desk that had originally belonged to James V. Forrestal when he'd become the first occupant of the Pentagon's fourth floor E-Ring office that would soon be occupied by the new administration's candidate.

The report was headed NSC-G-04578 and bore Top Secret Restricted Data headings indicating that its bigot list was substantively restricted and tightly controlled. The report, titled, Non Operational Contract Operations in the War Against the Global Terror Nexus, was a study undertaken by the secret planning cell, codenamed Garnet, convened by the NSC at Battle's behest. Its aim had been to assess the success record of the joint Pentagon-CIA NOC teams deployed throughout the world under the code name of Operation Janus Hinge. Among its tasks were assassination, rescue and recovery, technical surveillance, intelligence collection, counter-WMD operations and other related missions, including the secret rendition program that shuttled suspected terrorists to worldwide black sites, which were prisons and killing centers for clandestine executions.

So far the program, reinstituted several years earlier, had met with mixed results. While some operations had proven to be spectacular, albeit covert, successes, others had failed dismally, while the results of still others were problematic, and in fact raised more questions than they had answered and had stirred up more problems than they had addressed.

Under the panoptic umbrella of Homeland Security Act legislation, squeamishness about sanctioned elimination of enemy personnel had far less impact on public morale than in the past. This, thought Battle, was one good thing to come out of the troubles of the last few years. In Battle's opinion the US had for too long been hamstrung by an inability to employ direct lethal intervention to eliminate key opposition players. Leaving wet jobs in the hands of surrogates such as the Israelis, French or British, and even, on occasion, the

Russians, posed several operational problems. Tasking the operatives out of your own shop was the way to go ... at least on paper.

Out in the world, though, it had proven another thing entirely. There had been high-profile successes, such as in the terminations of Osama bin Laden and Abdul Qadeer, but there had also been notable problems and failures. Too much cowboying, too little positive control exacted by mission commanders too far removed from the field, too little oversight, too few clearly defined goals. In the SecDef's opinion Janus Hinge had proven a fiasco, much as the secret Black Box Project that it had been based upon many decades before, and in which Battle had played a part as a far younger man, had also ended in a similar debacle. The risks were simply too high, and so was the price for failure, even for small ones.

Battle settled his horn rim glasses on the bridge of his nose and picked up the thick blue-striped report, rifling through its many pages before slipping it into his briefcase. He had made his decision. At the secret meeting of the NSC scheduled for later that morning in the cramped meeting room one hundred feet beneath the Oval Office, he would cast his vote for the elimination of Janus Hinge.

Battle had little doubt that all but CIA Director for Special Operations Ulysses Napletano, and perhaps the Secretary of State, former four-star Army general Jack Albright, would demur, but Battle was still confident that the motion would pass. The Chairman of the Joint Chiefs, General Truscott G. Bailey, who like Battle was a presidential appointee and who shared lame-duck President Tyler Johnson's views on policy, hewed to the DOD party line -- so would back the Defense Secretary -- and the combination of DOD and the Joint Chiefs would form a powerful voting block.

Yes, Battle's resolution would at least this time stand a chance of ratification. And so might the recommendations of the planning cell within the Defense Deputies Committee that Battle had set to the task of crafting a bold new initiative in counter-asymmetric warfare and counter-terrorist operations. It was a radical plan and it held its own attendant risks, but Battle knew he could massage the sticking points and sell it to the president.

As for the personnel involved in Janus Hinge, by the end of the day they could all be defunct and need to be eliminated. No getting around that. If left alive they would be ticking time bombs, waiting to explode. These were dangerous people, far too dangerous to be left alive after Janus Hinge was terminated. Fortunately, most of them, including the operation's CINC, General Saint, had already been snatched and placed aboard secret rendition flights to nowhere. All of them were now languishing in the black holes of the black world, hidden away in foreign prisons with masks on their faces and sanitary napkins in place of johns.

The thought made Battle cringe, but only for a moment. Fortunes of war were brutal, and men like General Saint had known the score when they had gotten into the game. Sometimes even the best, like Saint, were sacrificed in the name of the higher logic and the greater good. The only part Battle couldn't stomach was the mass secret executions that would be carried out, starting with Saint, within a matter of hours.

Cold-blooded killing had never been his style. Fortunately there were surrogates for that kind of thing ... the Israelis, the French, the British, and some of our new friends from Baghdad and Tehran, just to name five examples.

Battle removed his glasses, rolled down his shirt cuffs, slipped on his jacket and tightened the knot in his tie. Both the president and president-elect, who would be present at the meeting, hated tardiness, and Battle didn't want to be late, even if his presence there was largely to brief his successor who was waiting for Battle to reach legal retirement age and collect full retirement benefits.

# DAVID ALEXANDER

The SecDef tapped the three-inch thick stack of manila file folders even against the top of the Pershing desk, dropped them into the black leather attaché case that lay open atop the desk where they fitted close beside a small Uzi submachinegun which he kept both as a precaution against what had happened on Strike Day and as a permanent way out, should events in the offing lead to the worst-case scenarios he dreaded.

Battle closed and latched the cover and left the outer, E-Ring office, emerging from the complex of fourth floor rooms that formed the Office of the Secretary of Defense into the carpeted corridor beyond. He headed toward the elevators, and the Pentagon's River Entrance below. An official limo waited to take him across the Potomac River to the White House.

*DAY ONE:*
*SUNDAY, SEPTEMBER 11TH*
**NOW**

## UNDER ATTACK

One
## Arrivals and Departures

*B*y the time Rommel Krieger reached the Building's River Entrance parking lot early that Sunday morning, the Pentagon's western facade was mottled by the chill September rain. You could watch the weather marching overhead as you drove through the winding Virginia countryside; thunderheads, rain and skies the color of a bad bruise rolling in with the storm front. Krieger liked it, and he liked the emptiness of the immense North Parking lot before most of the Building's thousands of daily occupants arrived for work.

Krieger pulled into his parking space, one of those reserved for the fortunate few bearing V.I.P. status and marked with a blue rectangle, rolled up the windows of the late-model Toyota, killed the engine and got out, affixing the photo ID tag to the breast pocket of his black blazer. Krieger passed through the security checkpoint behind the

15

River Entrance doors and walked through the Pentagon mall toward a Hotties kiosk. He nodded a curt hello to some passersby but otherwise said nothing, nor did anyone seem anxious to speak to him. Not, that is, until Krieger stepped into the fast food concession.

"Props to da Blitz Man! Waddup pimp? Yo' boy Shuggie's got what you need this morning to shake them cobwebs. El Blendo Supremo for ma dog da Blitz. Hotties' fi-nest Columbian coffee beans. Bitchin' hot. Good to the last drop. Gotta be tasted to be believed."

Shuggie slid the flat-bottomed cone that was capped with a thin white plastic half-shell, and wore a ring of heavy brown paper, across the top of the counter.

"Next, da Blitz gets his bagel. Lightly toasted by my special posse of munchkins from da 'hood. Schmear of Philly -- not too heavy -- on each delectable golden section. Loo-kin' good! Be tastin' even better. And you just know it go down with El Blendo Supremo smooth as a ho' when she get dat bling."

Krieger watched the uniformed Hotties counterman wrap up the bagel in waxed deli paper and put it in a white bag emblazoned with the Hotties stylized coffee-mug-and-steam logo. Krieger laid a bill on top of the glass display, and collected his breakfast. He didn't wait for any change and Shuggie didn't expect him to.

"Yo! All ma homeez! Put yo' blunts up for da Blitz. He bold, he cold. Give ma homes here his props. He da G of defense. Ma pimp here be saving da world and nobody know it. Every day in every way da Blitz be on the job. Yeah, he da dog of da hour, 'cause he gots da power...."

Krieger wondered, for just a second, why people like Shuggie found him an irresistible target for the kind of familiarity that he considered an affront to show anyone but his most intimate friends and associates. It was a supreme irony that the ultra-reserved Krieger, who rarely spoke, who never tried to make friends, who shunned most conventions by which the rest of humanity lived, never ceased to attract the attentions of the same kind of people who once thronged Jesus to kiss the hem of his robes.

It never failed. The underdogs of the world loved him. Vicious and hated pets became tame in his presence. Crotchety old ladies smiled like love-struck schoolgirls when he was around. The opposite was also the case. The powerful loathed him. The corrupt smelled their primeval antagonist and sharpened their pitchforks. Krieger's very presence was as irritating to them as chlorine gas.

# THREATCON DELTA

He was tolerated, he had survived, he continued, only because he had never been wrong and his opponents -- when it came to challenging him -- had never been right. Krieger had been right too many times to be flushed down the organizational toilet. He had been right about the Soviets three years before the Berlin Wall had fallen. He had been right before that about the Mahdi six years before Strike Day. And in the months following the attacks, he had been right about the Chinese eight years before the nuclear confrontation in the Sea of Japan that had marked the start of the century's third decade.

Krieger was shunned because he had been right when the others had been wrong, because he had been strong when the rest had been weak, because he had seen the truth when the rest had been too timid to face up to it. His fate was that of the boy who cried out that the emperor was naked as the procession of pious frauds passed in stately review. His sin was to speak truth to power, but doing so was also Krieger's sworn duty in the two presidential administrations in which he had served at cabinet level rank, and as an officer in the joint Special Operations Command, USSOCOM, before that, and he considered it dishonorable to bow and scrape when danger threatened the republic and menaced the world.

# DAVID ALEXANDER

Rommel Krieger had been bred for the Army. A West Point graduate, he had risen to commanding general of US forces in Japan, headquartered in Okinawa. At the age of thirty-five he was the youngest officer ever to serve at that post. He began his civilian career at the White House soon after that. Before Krieger's fiftieth birthday he had served as national security advisor to two presidential administrations. Now, at the age of fifty, Krieger was far too young to retire and far too old to take any more shit. His position in the political maze of Foggy Bottom was precarious. His present job was at best a compromise.

An under-assistant to the Secretary of Defense, speaking on behalf of his boss -- to whom Krieger was now a Washington non-person and political untouchable -- had made Krieger an offer and he had reluctantly accepted it: prepare high-technology white papers that comprised sections of the annual Defense Department Guidance, the blueprint for military acquisitions, force-sizing and cutbacks.

Otherwise, stay hull-down and keep well out of sight.

■

Krieger negotiated the corridors of the Pentagon like the insider that he was. The Pentagon had originally been built with no elevators, only stairs. There were elevators now, but reaching them sometimes required navigating through a maze of rings and intersecting corridors. Krieger checked his tablet's digital clock as he sipped the still-steaming El Supremo blend and the burnished steel doors lurched shut with a faint hiss. Not yet seven. Enough time for a workout before meeting the new round of bullshit that blessed each wonderful new day.

Ten minutes later Krieger was in the Pentagon's fourth floor gymnasium, stripped to his waist and wearing a pair of black boxing shorts that read "Gleason's Gym, Brooklyn, New York" in conspicuous, inch-high, white letters. He had a pair of black teak nunchaku in his hands, a legacy of the martial arts training that had become a minor obsession while serving in Asia among karate-ka, aikido masters, and later, practitioners of guje gongji and the arts of the ninja. The bag was taking a beating, but like Rommel Krieger himself, it couldn't complain.

DAVID ALEXANDER

Two
**A Drive to the Office**

*T*he security teams guarding General Truscott Bailey, Chairman of the Joint Chiefs of Staff, were in position amid the shrubbery along the roadside and in the scrubby woods behind Quarters One, the restored Victorian mansion that was the official billet of each serving CJCS and family. The general was at breakfast. The ten-inch square of liquid crystal display panel hanging underneath the kitchen cabinet above the aluminum sink was lit up with the talking heads of the Early News Hour.

Bailey ignored it. The TV was for his wife, Mary, not him. The general preferred getting his news from the Washington Post, the front page of whose morning edition he now scanned as he spread room temperature Philadelphia cream cheese on a toasted bagel half. By a not uncommon convergence, the story he was reading was the same as the one his wife was watching on the morning news.

"...so far they've been able to move around the area like ghosts. Unseen, unheard, unknown. Until they strike and another person dies. News Hour anchor Vince Ho Minh is on the scene at this most recent shooting incident that took place only about a half hour ago. Vince?"

The general turned his head. Images shifted across the flat surface of the small plastic rectangle. Official vans emblazoned with the shield, dragon and wreath of the Washington DC Metro police department formed the backdrop as strobe flashes of red and white hazard lights punched through the fogbound gloom of a drizzly Sunday morning. The camera panned left, then zoomed into tight focus on the face of a familiar local news personality. Media ethnics, thought Bailey. Just the right trace of foreign accent too; light as a feather, but unmistakably there.

"Right, Jim," said Ho Minh. "It's another grisly shooting incident like the ones that have shocked and sickened us for months on end. This morning yet another fatality's been chalked up to the Beltway shooter. Today's victim was a 37-year-old Falls Church, Virginia, elementary school teacher on her way to do charity work for the elderly at a local hospital."

# DAVID ALEXANDER

The camera panned across yellow crime scene hazard tape to a wrecked black SUV that had smashed into the highway median, then zoomed in on the left-hand side of the windshield that resembled a spider web with a hole in its center through which part of the steering wheel was visible.

"Police say it happened at about 5:20 AM. A single shot, according to FBI ballistics experts here at the scene, from the same high-powered rifle that fired the other lethal bullets that have claimed victims all around the Beltway. Sheriff Sloan Baker, in charge of the case, told me that the victim probably died instantly. She'd been shot clean through the center of the forehead by what was apparently an expert marksman."

"Vince, were there any witnesses to this latest tragic, terrible shooting?"

"No, Jim, as in all the other cases, no one saw a thing, or at least no witnesses who might have seen anything have so far stepped forward with information for the police. I should add here that the police have asked that anyone who has observed anything – anything at all – should call the special Metro Major Crime Squad hotline number that's been specially set up to help track down the shooter. Again, that's 1-800-555-COPS. All calls will be treated in strictest confidence.

# THREATCON DELTA

This is Vince Ho Minh reporting live from the scene of the shooting."

"Thanks Vince. You'll continue to keep us posted on this tragic story, won't you?"

"You bet, Jim."

The picture segued back to the News Hour set where the two studio anchors made some idiotic back-and-forth commentary, then the show cut to a commercial for a revolutionary disposable kitchen mop whose phallus-shaped handle vibrated to massage housewives' overworked hands. The general checked his watch and chewed his burnt bagel half as his wife brought him a thermal aluminum coffee mug. He'd drink the hot coffee as he rode to work as was his daily custom. He glanced at his watch. Five minutes after the hour. Time he got a move on.

Danny, his driver, would already be in front of the two story Victorian house, the engine of the Lincoln running, the flag of the CJCS atop the aerial fluttering in the morning breeze.

The Chairman pushed up from his chair and pecked his wife on the lips as he tucked the Post under his left arm and held the soft-sided thermal mug in his right hand. He stooped to pat the family schnauzer, Brownie, as he went to the door of Quarters One and stepped outside. The morning air was invigorating. It was a classic fall day. The West Virginia hills were riotous with autumnal color. Then he felt the cold droplets on his face and looked up, realizing there was weather ahead. He opened the rear door of the car and got in.

"Morning, general," said the driver.

"Good morning to you, Danny."

"Nice morning. Finally feels like autumn. Nothing like this air."

"Forget it, Danny. I'm not listening. I'm a summer person. You can keep it. Besides – " he glanced at the window to his left that was beginning to show specks of wetness – "rain's coming."

Danny laughed. That was the general; crusty on top but golden inside. He gunned the ignition, shifted into drive and made a k-turn toward the road.

"Sounds smoother, right?"

"I can hear it. You changed that cylinder with the bad piston ring?"

"Yeah. Did it last night. Replaced the cam too, and another one that also looked worn out. Couldn't sleep, so I went into the garage and worked on her a little, then I drove around some. She's running smooth as our new president's ass now."

Bailey chose not to reply to Danny's remark, though he felt no remark was too crude when it concerned that bitch in the White House. Her positions on defense were well known in advance, and despite campaign promises that she favored increased funding for military programs, the same Linda Halifax who'd been soft on defense as a senator from liberal-infested eastern Connecticut was showing every inclination to do the same as the nation's commander-in-chief.

Bailey himself was a holdover from the previous administration. Like Colin Powell long ago, his tenure as CJCS had lasted well into the incoming president's first year in office, and while the media wondered aloud if the CINC who'd led the nation to victory in Iran and North Korea would remain at the Pentagon, Bailey was under no such illusions.

Like many of his predecessors, including Powell, Bailey had lasted so long due to a combination of the Army's mandatory retirement regulations and political infighting over his successor. The appointee to the office of Secretary of Defense, Hubbard "Hubby" Smith, was a Halifax crony. He had chaired the House Armed Services Committee for the last five years, and his defense acquisitions policies had earned him the cognomen of the King of Cutbacks. Unquestionably there was bad weather ahead for the Pentagon; heavy rains would fall. Bailey was glad he would be getting out.

Danny drove on awhile and turned from the state route onto the federal highway. The

Chairman eyed the loose leaf binder lying beside him on the seat. It was the agenda for that morning's Tank briefing. He studied it on the forty-five minute drive to the Pentagon's immense South Parking from Quarters One, though he was conversant with all the issues on the table.

Most of them concerned two major programs, one of them being Vindicator, the USAF's pet project, the other Speedball, which the Navy wanted but probably wouldn't get, especially with new and colder winds poised to blow down from the power centers of DOD's fourth floor E-Ring domain.

There was one other project: Northern Cross. Bailey had pushed for its cancellation over the protests of the Chiefs. He'd fight tooth and nail to slay that particular dragon before they pushed him out of the Office of the JCS. Bailey considered killing the program his personal responsibility. Northern Cross was bad news. He was determined to see it go before he himself went.

"Let me know when you want the music, general."

The general looked up and saw Danny's eyes reflected in the rearview mirror, only then realizing that the driver had been speaking to him for several seconds while he'd been absorbed in his thoughts.

# THREATCON DELTA

Bailey said, "It might as well be now," and Danny raised the specially outfitted and heavily armored Lincoln Town Car's sound- and bulletproof glass partition separating front and rear compartments as he flipped the switch to pipe classical music into the rear compartment. He knew the general's habits. Bailey always studied his Tank brief notes on the ride to work, and he liked as few distractions as possible in the process.

Danny drove on, noting that eastbound traffic along Shirley Highway was light at this point, even though they were blasting a new road through the hills a few miles ahead, which usually slowed things down. The rain was now a hard, steady drizzle and flashes of lightning lit up the rolling, gray belly of the sky from time to time. Danny didn't think it would last, though.

The construction worker in the dirt-stained yellow hard hat and reflective orange rain parka stood astride the highway median divider strip waving a red flag and gesturing toward his right. A detour sign had been placed in the median where two eighteen-wheel trailer trucks were locked in a deadly embrace, like prehistoric beasts that had slaughtered each other in mortal combat. There was a West Virginia State Police black-and-white parked with its hazard lights turning in the rain and a slickered trooper in a Smokie hat talking to the two parties to the collision. A police tow truck was parked nearby, the light cubes atop its roof sending revolving luminous spokes of intense red and white knifing through the pelting early rain.

The general was engrossed in his briefing notes and hadn't noticed that the limo was slowing to a halt at the roadside detour. He'd been in the midst of reading about the Northern Cross program cancellation. The Project, as he'd privately called it, had enjoyed the backing of retiring Defense Secretary Robert Battle and the covert backing of the NSA and CIA, as well as most of the seven members of the National Security Council, which included President Halifax and Vice-President Toussant Lumumba.

The two spy agencies had insured that Northern Cross was funded through the last two presidential administrations, even though one occupant of the Oval Office was a predatory hawk and the other a confirmed dove. The CJCS had opposed it and had made its cancellation a priority on his appointment. The almost simultaneous appointment of new SecDef, Hubbard Smith, who also opposed Northern Cross, had turned the tide of opinion. The project simply presented too many risks. Technological risks, political risks, military risks ... among others.

"General."

# THREATCON DELTA

It was his driver's voice over the intercom. For the second time the CJCS looked up from his Tank briefing notes and took in the scene outside. The hard hat waving the red hazard flag. The worsened rain. The two crashed eighteen-wheelers. The strobe lights revolving in the cocoon of silvering wetness.

"Sorry, Danny. I wasn't paying attention."

"No problem, sir. There's a detour just ahead."

"I see that. Ask him what's going on."

The driver rolled down the window and eased the limo toward the construction worker.

"Hey, what's happening up ahead, buddy?"

"Two trucks crashed earlier today. The fuckin' Beltway Sniper shot one of 'em – you can see the hole in the windshield of the white truck. An EMS team's on the way to get the driver out. He's dead – took a bullet right here."

He pointed a stubby forefinger at the center of his forehead.

"One truck's carrying a load of toxic waste. The detour takes you around to Route 16. It's about fifteen minutes, more or less. It'll be hours before this mess is cleared away."

"Right. We'll have to wait for clearance first."

The hard hat shrugged and waved them over to the shoulder.

Danny turned to the CJCS.

"You heard him, general."

"Alert our watchdogs of the change in itinerary and proceed."

"You got it, general."

The driver keyed the secure radio on intercom mode and notified the DIA agents in the car a half mile behind them about the detour. The agent who took the call opened the notebook computer on his lap, flipping it on. It was uplinked to a remote imaging satellite parked in a geostationary orbit above the eastern seaboard.

The downlooking view from fifty miles overhead was crystal clear despite the dense cloud cover and heavy rain. The satellite's multispectral imaging sensors, including all-weather synthetic aperture radar, and high-speed, massively parallel onboard processors, insured bulletproof functionality. The agent scanned the road network in the vicinity of the detour route and saw no visual indication of threats. He switched to threat evaluation mode and let the system make its own decisions using fuzzy logic algorithms. The results were negative.

The agent shut the large black razor clam on his lap and keyed his throat mike.

"Affirmative. The route appears clean. Cleared to proceed."

The general's driver rogered that and told the CJCS that they were okayed to take the detour. The general told him to go ahead and returned to his notes with a final glance out the window. In that instant his glance caught the expression on the workman's face before he had a chance to control his features. The old soldier's instinctive reactions to danger were suddenly triggered. Bailey turned his head as the car passed the detour point and saw the hard hat staring at him.

*Something was wrong*, he thought at that moment. But he didn't know what.

The general delayed a split second too long in telling his driver to stop and turn the vehicle around. Once on the local route, two huge trucks swung out and blocked the limo's path. The Lincoln Town Car had been specially equipped with run-flat tires, bulletproof windows and polylaminate windshields, a chassis lined with Kevlar padding, and an armored undercarriage, and Danny had been specially trained to use the Uzi Micro machinepistol that was capable of firing three-round bursts of Teflon-coated ammunition from the standard thirty-shot clip loaded in its magazine well and the two high-capacity seventy-five round mags he carried in his jacket pockets.

None of this was effective against the twin walls of rolling plate steel that now pinned the car between the two trucks, nor was polylaminate bulletproof glass much of a barrier against cobalt-tempered titanium-tipped rounds fired by a

Kalashnikov AK-47 at nearly point-blank range. In the hands of the Corsican Mafia the Russian-made assault rifle had proven itself time and again as an effective weapon against bulletproof glass, and thus a favorite tool in the lethal moving ambushes known as *assassino della moto* in which the Corsican mob specialized.

Three rounds of the Avtomat-Kalashnikova's 7.62 millimeter specially tempered ammo, fired in rapid succession into the same spot on a windshield, were guaranteed to first weaken, then penetrate, then punch right through any type of security glass in existence, no matter what its composition and regardless of its thickness or density. The present case was no exception; the third round plugged through ten thousand dollars worth of polylaminate security windshield leaving a spiderweb-ringed hole. Fired at nearly point-blank range, the bullet, though badly deformed, still had plenty of kinetic energy left to blow apart Danny's head.

Fourth, fifth and sixth shots made sure the general was also dead before he even had a chance to react.

Equally important to the shooter was that the rapid rate of fire, close range, and special ammunition, reduced the visible signs of physical damage to the CJCS and his personal effects, including the Tank briefings he'd been reading while en route.

The security vehicle that had trailed the general's staff car didn't require such subtleties of the lethal arts, being of no tactical consequence to the rest of the operation, and so other, faster, and more brutally efficient methods were used to dispose of it and its passengers.

The SMAW/HE rocket is a shoulder-fire weapon developed to destroy heavy armored vehicles, such as tanks and armored personnel carriers on the battlefield. It had proven its worth to Marine units barreling into Baghdad in Strykers and Bradleys after the Shock and Awe campaign that had opened the war in Iraq, turning Iraqi APCs into Baudelairian daisy chains of smoldering garbage. If deployed against a passenger vehicle, such as the Town Car trailing the CJCS's limo – even a heavily armored one – the target doesn't stand a chance in hell.

Crouched on the downslope of the culvert lining the shoulder of the federal highway, the shooter lay concealed behind mottled strips of camouflage Ghillie cover, and the SMAW firing tube projecting into space from the shadows of the culvert was similarly camouflaged. At the approach of the vehicle the shooter's scope lit up with a flashing green triangle that indicated the laser ranging sight had acquired a solid lock on the weapon's target. The shooter fired the round and ducked – the round didn't have far to travel and the explosion would be horrendous at such close range.

Instants later the security vehicle had been disintegrated right down to its under-chassis, which was engulfed in a broiling, black-orange goblin's face that ballooned quickly upward on a grotesque pedestal of churning smoke and crackling flame.

The SMAW shooter keyed his SINCGARS comms twice. The signal indicated that the initial phase of the operation had been successfully accomplished. He was out of the action now. He had earned both his danger pay and a five-figure completion bonus that, with some high-stakes drug smuggling on the side, would set him up in southern Mexico for years to come.

### Three
**Ghosts and Coasts**

Six hours out of the Baton Rouge docks, and making three knots on a northwesterly course along the serpentine Atlantic Intracoastal Waterway, the coastal freighter Vista Charger now lay two miles off the South Carolina shoreline. Off to starboard, an uneven line of yellow-white lights that marked the port of Charlestown twinkled in the dense fog that lay heavily across the sea and the land.

The Intracoastal stretched north from New Orleans to a point on the coast below Philadelphia, Pennsylvania, crossing eight states and linking the rivers and canals that lay between them, such as the five hundred mile New York State Barge Canal and the Welland Canal between Lakes Ontario and Erie. Every year eighty million tons of coastwise cargo moved along this mainly inland waterway network, a tonnage exceeding that which was carried along the nation's highway system by heavy trucks, while also including foreign goods from transatlantic ports of call.

The Vista Charger was a twenty-five thousand ton cargo liner sailing under US charter. Lashed to her deck she carried a full load of six hundred twenty-by-thirty-foot corrugated steel shipping containers. In the container ship's vast hold the Vista Charger also carried row upon row of fifty-foot truck trailers as well as railway cars. Most of the trailers would be offloaded by the coastwise freighter's crew when it put in later that morning at the sprawling Susquehanna River dockside facilities that lined the east side of Baltimore.

Three trailers would be offloaded at a destination a few miles to the north. These trailers were not on the ship's manifest, although they were very much on the mind of a man who stood on deck as the Vista Charger, riding low in the water and laden down to her winter load line with dead weight tonnage, slid into the rolling gray mists beyond Port Charlestown on its coast-hugging route.

The man leaned out over the side of the ship and watched the lights of civilization recede on the vessel's coastward side.

His name was Casper Saint. For the last fifteen years, since the promotion that went with his appointment to theater CINC of CENTCOM's war in Syria, the title "general" had preceded it and four shiny gold stars had adorned it. Saint was returning home, or at least so it felt to go back to where he was headed. He had been away for almost two years. For most of that time Saint had meticulously planned the events that were to commence later this morning and draw to a conclusion some three days hence. Saint had lived for this moment. Its anticipation had become an obsession, but it was always more than that; it was also a reason to go on living.

The general checked his watch, a Tag-Huer wrist chronometer that had accompanied him into battle for years, suddenly becoming aware of the dim red and blue glow of lights off the vessel's stern, on the Atlantic side of the freighter. The dim outline of another ship began to materialize. The Vista Charger sounded its foghorn and the other vessel did the same.

The two vessels drew closer. The time, according to Saint's wrist chronometer, was zero-six-zero-nine hours. A grim smile broke across the lower half of Saint's hard, angular face, a face resembling a mask fashioned of dark, basaltic stone, as the vessels neared one another and crewmen on each ship tossed hawser lines across to be made fast to the cleat-topped iron bollards studding either deck.

The maneuver had been practiced to perfection. Within minutes men dressed in paramilitary fatigues and fully armed with automatic weapons were crossing from the other ship onto the rain-lashed deck of the Vista Charger. The men formed up and saluted Saint as the thick lengths of braided multi-filament mooring cable were stowed and the ghost vessel vanished into the darkness, the drizzle and the fog. The general dismissed his troops and they went below. Saint remained on deck, watching the new lights of a new port loom into view as the ship plied the dark waters of the Intracoastal to its final destination.

■

Rommel Krieger emerged from his morning gym workout and took one of the River Entrance-side elevators down -- all the way down.

At the Pentagon's ground floor Concourse level -- technically the Building's second floor, but to all intents and purposes the main floor of the sprawling edifice -- he, as usual, found himself the only occupant of the rapidly descending steel cage. This was not surprising. Krieger's office was located one level beneath the subbasement of the immense government office building. While some of Pentagon staffers recognized Krieger on sight, few except for the CJCS, the SecDef and their miscellaneous deputies, actually knew of his existence, let alone what function he might perform. Those who did know about him had invented a less than flattering nickname. They called Krieger "Quasimodo."

Krieger's inverted belfry was an office at the extreme end of a dimly lighted corridor lined with heating and electrical conduits -- exposed parts of the "ductbank" that wound around the five sides of the Building -- accessed by navigating a maze of tunnel-like hallways that connected with the bare concrete-walled chamber that marked the sub-sub-basement elevator stop. The steel door bore a number and a black and white picture of old-time film actor Lon Chaney Jr. as the Hunchback of Notre Dame that Krieger had downloaded from a movie website and printed out on a self-stick label sheet.

Krieger had installed a proximity entry system that opened the door at the pass of a key dongle containing a coded microchip. Krieger waved the dongle and heard the latch click open. He was momentarily surprised to find the office lights on. He hadn't recalled leaving them on when he'd quit work the night before. Nor did he recall anyone else having access rights to his office. Yet apparently that's what had happened. Somebody had invaded his private domain and turned on the lights.

Krieger suddenly flashed back to an email message from the SecDef of at least a week previous. The memo from the E-Ring -- as quickly trashed as it had been scanned -- had said something about an assistant being sent him and that no argument would be brooked this time.

Now, an inner door opened and nemesis in human form emerged into Krieger's presence.

"Sir, Ensign Henrietta Sabio reporting for duty."

The young woman in Navy dress blues actually saluted him.

"First: stop saluting," Krieger told her. "Second: get lost, Ensign Scabies, or whatever your name is."

"Sir, I can't do that. I've been assigned to this duty by the office of the JCS pursuant to orders from the Third Floor. If you feel you have a problem, you will need to submit form T-789-Z-14 in triplicate through the Office of the Secretary of Defense, Room E-32453-7, before C.O.B. Mondays and Thursdays. Until approval for your request is granted -- my doubt of which outcome I must respectfully express, sir -- I regret that, at least for the time being, I am your new assistant."

Krieger stared at her, glowering.

"Sir, are you all right."

Krieger stared at her harder.

"Sir --"

Krieger put up his hand.

"Ensign Scabies, I am trying to control myself. Thus, the silence and the ruby flush that you may have momentarily noticed on my cheeks. Now, kindly shut up and listen --"

Krieger repeated himself but it did no good, not even telling the intruder to get lost again. He was a veteran of the Pentagon bureaucracy. A wolf among wolves, he had seen four Secretaries of Defense and five Chairmen of the Joint Chiefs, as well as numerous Assistant Secretaries, Under-Assistant Secretaries, Deputy Secretaries and Assistant Deputy Secretaries, get flayed alive as the gears of Pentagon machinery ground their careers to hamburger and ripped their guts to garters. And now it just happened that the wolf pack had deemed it fit to send a fair lamb dressed in Navy dress blues into Krieger's subbasement lair.

Well, he wasn't about to buy it. Not as a coincidence, anyway. As a plot, yes. As a coincidence, no.

She had to be a wolf too, all right, and one in sheep's clothing at that, in this case the smart blue uniform of a Navy ensign. Yet Krieger, veteran of the Building's bureaucratic mazes, also knew he was stuck with Sabio. For the moment, at least.

Still, he wouldn't take this lying down. Ensign Sabio hadn't the slightest idea of what she'd let herself in for. Krieger would relish the infliction of infinite indignities upon his new assistant.

Krieger studied her closely. She was about twenty-seven years old by his guess. Black hair, straight, like that of a Chicana. She had a pronounced Spanish accent. Cute. But a bitch when she held the upper hand he'd bet.

"Level with me, Ensign Sabio, you've been sent here to spy on me, haven't you?"

"Sir, that's not the case, I assure you. As I've said, I was --"

Krieger held up his hand.

"Enough, Ensign Sabio. I wouldn't believe anything you told me anyway. You're a spy. From the SecDef's office."

Krieger's eyes lit up. He'd been struck by inspiration. "That bastard Gerber. He's behind it, isn't he?"

"I don't know what you mean sir."

"Ensign Sabio," Krieger said, changing tack, "it's time to level again. What did they tell you about me?"

"Frankly, sir?" she asked.

"Yes, Ensign Sabio. Please be as candid as you're able."

"Well, sir," she began. "I was frankly told that you were a mental case and that you were only down here in the subbasement because you were at one time the president's personal friend and also because you served with former Chairman, General Winters, in Afghanistan and Iraq."

43

"What else were you told? That I ripped the living hearts from sacrificial victims with my teeth and chewed their bloody entrails on the River Entrance Parade Ground? That I prowl Pentagon City looking for little children to bake for my bread? That I breathe fire and belch smoke? Any of those things sound familiar, Ensign Sabio?"

"Honestly, sir?" She paused a moment. "Something like that."

"You're smiling Ensign Sabio, did you know that? I didn't think it was possible. You know it's against regulations, don't you, ensign?"

"Really, sir?"

"Yeah, but don't worry, I won't tell on you."

Before she could answer, Krieger said, "OK. You're here and I can't do anything about it -- yet. So let's put you to work."

"Yes, sir. That's what I'm here for."

Krieger went to a steel supply closet bolted to a wall, unlocked it and rummaged around.

"Okay. Then take these."

He handed her a mop and a rusty metal slop bucket. Ensign Sabio looked crestfallen. That was good. Krieger permitted himself a smile.

"The bathroom needs cleaning, Ensign Sabio," he told her.

"Sir, I --"

"Sir, nothing," he admonished. "You're my assistant. Fine. I can't get rid of you. Fine. But since I'm your boss, then I get to boss you, so I'm bossing you. The toilet, which is full of nasty, crusty, algae, needs cleaning. That's an order, Ensign Sabio. Got that?"

She hesitated.

"Yes Sir," she ultimately said.

"Now get to it. And don't hurt my pet alligator."

"Alligator, sir?"

"Just kidding."

Krieger watched her go. Now it was his turn to smile. This might be fun after all.

He sat back down in front of his workstation and prepared to draft an email on the Pentagon's internal system protesting this intrusion into his private domain and interference with his sacrosanct work on behalf of the nation's defense in peace and in war.

He knew who was behind it, of course. His arch nemesis, Jack Fuckin' Albright.

Once the present Secretary of State and Krieger had been associates. Then had come the election, and Albright showed his true colors. Albright had hitched his wagon to the rising star that was then Connecticut Senator Linda Halifax.

When Halifax became president, Krieger had been her first pick for State, but Albright, head of the Halifax administration's transition team, had outmaneuvered him. Krieger was forced to write an endless white paper on next generation stealth robotics that was to be included in the next fiscal year's Defense Policy Guidance, the annual blueprint for force sizing, acquisitions and doctrine that determined, among other things, the defense budget expenditures that the Pentagon would propose to Congress and the President.

Krieger was given a toilet-sized office in the Pentagon's basement, an old computer and a beat-up steel desk that was probably secondhand during the War in Vietnam, and six months to complete the job. After that, Krieger knew, he'd be history. Some excuse would come down from the E-Ring to fire him, and unlike the high-echelon political players who'd depart their comfortable DOD billets with golden parachutes for the plush boardrooms of corporation-land, Krieger would doubtless have to print up new resumes and canvas second-string colleges for a berth as a junior professor.

That had been two years ago. Somewhere in between, Krieger had vanished from the bureaucracy's radar screen. Miraculously or otherwise, the expected axe had never fallen. Instead of getting the guillotine, he'd gotten the hunchback's belfry. He had become a legend, a ghost, a Quasimodo of the Pentagon's version of the Underworld. Actually there was no reason on earth why Krieger needed to come to work at all at this point. He could have telecommuted or taken a permanent vacation for all anyone cared.

Now, apparently, someone had remembered he was down there and sent in a spy -- a spy in the house of love, Krieger suddenly thought. Where was that from? He knew the answer somewhere in the back of his mind but couldn't place it yet. It might come eventually. It might come to him yet, he thought. Not that it mattered.

Anyway, the last thing Quasimodo needed was a pert, efficient, young assistant-spy, house of love spy or any other kind of spy. This meant Ensign Sabio had to go. Sooner was better than later. Krieger didn't like writing interoffice memos, but this time he had to play the bureaucratic scribe.

He sat down and drafted one that was polite yet firm. Its subject line read: Who Will Rid Me of

This Bothersome Ensign? That was like another line from somewhere he'd have to remember, Krieger reflected, as he sent the message winging on its emailed way.

■

The Vista Charger negotiated the last of the Intracoastal's meandering watercourse. The cargo vessel now reached a point within Chesapeake Bay that put its position within three nautical miles of Washington, DC.

The ship was now a short distance from the mouth of the Potomac River, and from the scattered port facilities along the Potomac's broad lower reaches.

Inside the hold of the vessel, powerful arc lights illuminated a portion, toward the freighter's stern, of the huge parking area where its cargo of fifty-foot truck trailers was parked.

In this section of the Vista Charger's cargo hold, there was now a great deal of activity. The troops that recently embarked were carefully checking their weapons and inspecting their gear. Two of the trailers were being hitched to diesel rigs, while a third awaited the diesel that was rolling toward it across the parking area. The rear loading ramps of all three trailers were in the process of being lowered. Men in combat fatigues climbed the ramps and switched on the interior lights, while powerful arc lamps were positioned to better illuminate the trailers' internal spaces.

Inside the now brilliantly lit innards of the elongated steel rectangles were arrayed an assortment of military vehicles whose types ranged from Bradley armored personnel carriers to military-grade Humvees equipped with antiarmor rocket launchers and .50-caliber machineguns.

While the paramilitary-garbed technical specialists began making final checks on the vehicles inside, the captain of the ship consulted the final GPS waypoints to his destination. Despite the dense fog and pelting rain that severely hindered visibility, the digital map display clearly showed that the vessel had now entered the reaches of the lower Potomac and was only minutes away from its offloading point.

The captain turned and gestured to Casper Saint, who like the men below, was now dressed for battle and wore a nine-millimeter Glock semiautomatic pistol as a sidearm. Saint merely nodded assent, his gaze fixed on the swirling gray coils of fog beyond the windows of the ship's bridge, and did not return the captain's glance.

Four
**The Value of Training**

*T*he staff car of the CJCS rolled across Washington Boulevard toward the Pentagon's southwest-facing South Parking lot, its windshield wipers beating a furious counterpoint to the increasing tempo of the driving autumn rain drumming against intact and inviolate safety glass. South Parking, which bordered the two giant cloverleaves of Washington Boulevard to the West and Shirley Highway to the South, and big as two football fields placed end-to-end, was one of the three main parking areas that served the approximate twenty thousand occupants of the Building on any given weekday.

The boat basin beyond had been the unintentional result of the two million cubic tons of river mud dredged from the Potomac's bottom to make the cement that fashioned the Pentagon's steel-reinforced concrete walls and the piles and caissons that anchored those walls and the foundation beneath them to the former swampland that had been drained to make room for it. The original builders of the Pentagon had made decisions as they went along -- the boat basin had been one of many such ad hoc decisions as the Building had gone up wedge by wedge in the fall of 1941.

The black Lincoln Town Car continued across the expanse of the South Parking facility, paralleling the Building's West Facade, toward the Pentagon's Concourse Entrance. The enormous walls of the Building -- appearing alternately gray or white, depending on the time of day and weather conditions -- gray now in the rain, loomed up on either side of the entrance doorway, stained here and there in the midst of the drizzle and creeping gray fog by irregular dark patches of wetness, the windows lining each of the four stories reflecting the cloud-driven darkness outside, except for those few in which lights in the offices beyond could be seen glowing. The largest government office building in the world, the Pentagon never closed, never slept. Even on weekends work went on behind its walls.

"Inform security of the attack. Threatcon level will be determined subject to advisory from Deputy Chairman Rogers," the occupant in Army green in the back seat of the Town Car informed the driver. "Also request a medical team. I don't think I need it, but just in case."

The driver affirmed his instructions and did as he was ordered.

# THREATCON DELTA

The Chairman next pulled out his cell phone and fingered down a key that called a number in an E-Ring office adjacent to his own spacious fourth floor suite. Deputy Chairman of the Joint Chiefs of Staff, Army General Clayton Rogers, answered on the first ring.

"Clay, you've undoubtedly heard what happened by now," said the soldier, then paused. "Yeah, it was a close call. Anyway, you're in charge till I get there, which won't be long, but just so you know the score." Another pause.

"No, Clay, I'm okay, really. They fucked up, thankfully. Good job on the security and medical teams. Tell 'em an ETA of about fifteen minutes."

The Deputy Chairman asked his chief about the remaining security arrangements on the contingency checklist. Pursuant to new regulations in place after the Strike Day terrorist attacks, the Pentagon's entire security apparatus had been overhauled. First and foremost was the assignment of a threat condition. These ranged from Alpha to Delta, which was the security level of highest alert.

"I've already taken the initiative of setting the Threat Condition to Delta, sir," the deputy told his chief.

"Affirmative on Threatcon Delta. We'll remain at that level until such time as a conditional downgrade is warranted."

"Yes, sir. Understood."

Security procedures attendant on the various threat conditions were, to all intents and purposes, automated. Computers at the National Military Command Center on the Pentagon's third floor had been programmed with an extensive database of contingency options.

Depending on the actual threat condition declared, linkages to the vast infrastructure of the US military and political establishments and to the national and global newsmedia could be immediately activated. The decision matrix was under the initial command and control of the office of the CJCS, subject to countermanding or emendation by the secretary of defense on the orders of the president.

Of immediate consequence was the activation of security procedures under the top-level threatcon that was now in force. Agencies and departments on the federal, state and local levels, ranging from Homeland Security to the FBI to the D.C. Metro Police, were all to be placed on alert.

In particular, two special security detachments had been given the task of rapid reaction to a crisis affecting the Pentagon.

One of these was the Pentagon's internal security detail, responsible for protecting the interior of the building. The second and much larger and heavier response force was the First

# THREATCON DELTA

Mobile Security Detachment, a rapid response unit of the Sixth Infantry Battalion, based at nearby Camp Peary, an Army base approximately twenty miles to the southwest. Unless its commander had received countermanding orders, the upgrading of the emergency alert level to Threatcon Delta had already sent the mobile unit into action.

Both the CJCS and his deputy were well-versed in the procedural intricacies existing under the four threat conditions that ranged from alpha to delta, but it was the CJCS who had priority to change or cancel any or all of them based on his appraisal of the prevailing state of national security.

"Any changes you want implemented on security procedures under the threatcon?" Rogers asked his boss.

"None. All security procedures and linkages normally in effect under Threatcon Delta are a go -- repeat, go. My ETA's now about ten minutes or under."

"Affirmative, sir."

The Chairman of the Joint Chiefs signed off and disconnected. He permitted himself a smile of satisfaction as, through the winding sheets of rain and fog, he saw the flashing lights of Defense Department security and emergency vehicles rushing to meet the bullet-pocked Town Car as it drew closer to the Pentagon's River Entrance.

Yet his hands betrayed the nervousness he felt. They were shaking. Not much, but enough to be noticed.

The man riding in the back seat of the Town Car took a white plastic Vicks inhaler from the side pocket of his olive drab Army tunic and raised it to his left nostril. The cylinder was filled with amyl nitrate. Pinching the right nostril he inhaled sharply and felt the freeze-burn rush of stimulant shoot up his septum and into his brain.

The shaking in his hands instantly abated as the amphetamine took effect. He removed the inhaler and reversed the process, then tucked the inhaler away in his right side pocket and turned to watch the scenery, his mind temporarily a peaceful blank, his nervousness gone.

■

From a well-concealed vantage point some distance away, a vantage point hidden at the top of trees in the wooded verges bordering the state highway route, a figure in military camouflage combat dress trained the scope of a 7.62-millimeter Dragunev SVD sniper rifle at points in an extended field of view. Through the glowing perpendicular green optical crosshair reticles of the digitally amplified monocular gunsight, the sniper saw the Town Car flying the flag of the

Chairman of the Joint Chiefs of Staff race across the Pentagon's South Parking Lot. The banner, emblazoned with the eagle and Shield of the Republic, fluttered in the powerful slipstream.

He jogged the scope a bit to the right, adjusted the digital zoom factor, and the crosshairs framed another portion of the distant tableau that resolved into clear, sharp focus. Security cars were rushing from the River Entrance toward the oncoming vehicle. At 50X magnification it was like he was right there with them, except, that is, for the red death dot of an invisible laser beam that moved with the barrel of the rifle, first marking one vehicle, then another, for a long-range kill.

Still continuing to observe the unfolding events with the dispassionate and detached concentration of a trained soldier, the sniper reached for the button above his left chest and depressed it three times, then two times, then another three times, keying his SINCGARS comms.

A return code sequence of tones in his earbud confirmed that his message had been received onboard the Intracoastal freighter Vista Charger and had been understood. The sniper then moved from his position from the upper branches of the tree. His instructions were to get closer to his new set of targets.

*Harasho*, he thought.

■

The coastwise freighter had tied up on the rusted and weather-beaten iron spiles jutting like the decayed and time-blackened teeth of some prehistoric beast from the dock of an abandoned shipping company's wharf on the Potomac. The guillotine gate on the Vista Charger's rear deck had opened and slid upward, and then a ramp was lowered down to the floor of the pier. There was a loud, sharp thud as the steel end of the steep ramp banged against the macadamized surface.

Three eighteen-wheel trailers had then rolled out of the hold and crew dogs commenced the unloading of the military vehicles that had been contained inside the cargo carriers. The vehicles rolled first across the interior of the wharf, then onto the pockmarked asphalt of the dockside, and then were driven out onto the four-lane blacktop highway that ran on a north-south axis adjacent to the piers.

Minutes later the military convoy was in sight of the immense low-rise building that was its objective.

■

"Are you injured, sir?"

"No. Fortunately I escaped anything except some scrapes and cuts."

The Chairman looked into the young military doctor's wide brown eyes and saw that the lie was taking hold.

One of the security specialists interrupted.

"Sir, we've received a report that a military security detachment from Camp Peary's First Mobile is now en route with an ETA of less than ten minutes. The detachment's commander stated you'd ordered them in."

"Correct. I did," replied the Chairman.

"Sir, the Fifth Armored Infantry Battalion from Fort Henry is the unit that's been tasked with this duty, according to -- "

"Don't argue with me, captain," the Chairman snapped. "That was my decision and I've good reason for it. The detachment will arrive any minute. They're to be afforded complete cooperation by all personnel. Understood?"

"Yes, sir."

"Fine," said the CJCS. "I'll now proceed to my office."

The Marine general broke free of the doctor's grip.

"I can get there under my own steam, soldier. Thank you."

The Chairman stood shakily and brushed off helping hands. He walked stiffly, showing obvious pain, yet moved with dignity toward the elevator. His tall, gaunt form betrayed a slight limp as he entered the car and pressed the fourth floor button. The doors slid closed and the elevator lights flashed toward the third of the Pentagon's five stories. They opened again minutes later and the Chairman negotiated the series of corridor rings with the familiarity that comes with daily use.

Entering his E-Ring office, the Chairman nodded his customary morning greeting to his staff members and brushed aside their chorus of concerns for his safety. He was all right, he assured them all -- it takes more than a few bullets to stop a Marine, he quipped. More important was the security of the Pentagon, if not of the nation itself. And of that being in jeopardy, he had no doubts.

The Chairman picked up the handset of one of the three color-coded console phones on the huge, glass-topped desk, a near duplicate of the enormous eight-and-a-half-foot-long desk that General Black Jack Pershing had originally used as War Secretary and which had served Secretaries of Defense for decades, until its destruction on Strike Day, and punched a lit square button colored red, inside of which was a small white label imprinted with a name.

"Clay, I've got bad news for you -- your moment of glory is past. I'm back in command as of now."

"Damn it, sir. I was beginning to enjoy all the power."

The CJCS laughed.

"Well, maybe next time."

His familiar voice turned gruffly serious again.

"Clay, I want you to set up a command post in the NMCC," Chairman Bailey told his deputy.

"Already done, sir."

"And the rapid response team from Peary, the First Mobile, what about them?"

"ETA's under five minutes. No -- wait, they're already here. I've just gotten a confirmation from my exec."

"Excellent. I'm going to change into a spare uniform and clean up a little. I look like the backside of hell. Give me a situation report in about ten minutes."

"Yes, sir."

The CJCS sat back in the black leather wing chair and put his feet up on the desk of the man he impersonated. The enormous replica desk that, like himself, was an imposter in the spartan office. He closed his aching eyes and rubbed them, feeling the eyeballs roll around beneath the loose flesh of the lids. They felt overheated, like marbles on a stove. He was beginning to develop a splitting headache. He could feel it coming on.

It wouldn't matter, though. The next few minutes would make everything that preceded irrelevant, and besides that, his role would be finished and he'd bail out via his escape line.

For the last sixty days he had lived, breathed and slept the character whom he'd impersonated. He had been selected because of a natural resemblance to Marine General Truscott Bailey -- indeed he looked so much like him that he was almost his double -- and because he was a trained actor. Cosmetic surgery had picked up where nature had left off. The actor had even undergone dangerous surgical procedures to re-graft corneal sections to his eyes in order to defeat biometric identification based on capillary patterns.

His fee had been two million dollars, half of which was already sitting in a numbered account in Liechtenstein, a country that kept the secrets of its depositors far better these days than the Swiss did. The rest would follow via electronic funds transfer upon completion of the operation.

The impersonator felt his headache start to come on full-force. He needed another snort of the inhaler.

"Not dangerous," he told himself. "In another few minutes it won't matter who sees what."

He produced the inhaler from his pocket and placed its conical tip inside his left nostril as the door to his office opened and one of his two administrative assistants entered. Her eyes widened as she caught sight of the general's unaccustomed actions.

"I'm sorry," she apologized, her tone of voice giving away her surprise. "I should have knocked. But in the excitement...." her voice trailed off, and a palms-up gesture completed her sentence.

# THREATCON DELTA

The impersonator smiled and nonchalantly took the inhaler from his nostril, placing it end-up on the glass top of the Pershing desk.

"Not a problem," he replied in dulcet tones. "Come in, please. Shut the door behind you."

The secretary hesitated only the briefest of instants, then did as her boss told her.

"Sir, I just heard --"

The silenced semiautomatic pistol was aimed at her heart and its trigger pulled as the door clicked shut. Two muffled spits, inaudible beyond the soundproof office walls, marked the consecutive bursts of fire. Twin red punctures instantly opened on either side of her chest. The gun spat again. A third puncture shattered her once pretty face, spraying gloppy chunks of it against the wall behind her.

They had trained him in the use of the weapon in case of an event like this. The important thing was not to hesitate. Draw and fire in quick succession. The shock of impact, they'd told him, would silence any cries for help. What was the term they'd used -- hydrostatic shock, he now remembered. It worked, whatever they called it. Worked damned well.

The woman, face shot off, already dead, crumpled to the gray office carpet. The impersonator carefully laid the semiautomatic pistol away in a top desk drawer, then got up and dragged the corpse across the carpet, leaving a messy trail of blood and bone fragments, and stashed it behind the leather office couch.

The important thing was that she'd been silenced. They'd drummed that into his head too, time and time again. It would all be over in a matter of minutes anyway. The Chairman turned and watched the cold mercury rain beat its drum roll against the fourth floor window of the office.

He liked the rain. It always had a soothing effect on his nerves.

Just like money.

■

Crewmen aboard the Vista Charger unfastened and stowed the heavy hawser cables from the big iron cleats that had anchored the coaster to the dockside. The rain had worsened. Their faces were lousy with it and it ran from their brows into the sockets of their eyes, stinging like acid, which, in the smokestack East, it actually was in part. They worked with the haste and determination of those who knew that every moment counted and that the mission timetable was more sacred than any bible.

On the dockside other crewmen were driving the now empty truck trailers back up the ramp and into the yawning hold of the big containership. The last of the military vehicles that the trailers had held within their spacious confines was now disappearing into the gray, wet shroud of the early morning fog, tail lights winking out as the armored, motorized column crossed from the wharf onto the highway.

The crewmen on the deck of the Vista Charger pulled the lines back in and signaled to the helm via high-frequency radio that the ship was ready to shove off from the pier. The diesel engines changed pitch as the screws rotated and the enormous steel hulk began to move, and gather speed, as it launched itself downstream into the Potomac's broadening lower reaches.

The column of military vehicles did not have far to go. Its destination, the Pentagon, was less than a half-mile distant. The vehicles had been altered to reflect the lightning-and-shield insignia of the First Mobile Security Detachment from Camp Peary. Inside the cab of the lead vehicle, General Casper Saint used the radio to transmit on emergency frequencies.

He informed the police that the emergency convoy was en route to the Pentagon and should not be impeded. He found the authorities cooperative. The West Virginia State Police and Highway Patrol had blocked the access road corridors to a squeeze-point where civilian traffic was diverted to allow the military convoy to proceed to its destination unhindered.

Within a matter of minutes the convoy had turned from Washington Boulevard into the North Parking lot of the Pentagon. Looking northward, the sprawling parking area flanked the Boundary Channel with the Potomac and the Arlington Memorial Bridge connecting Arlington to Metro DC visible in the distance. Looking south, was one of the five sharply angled building corners; in this case the one that divided Wedge Three, and the River Entrance, from Wedge Two, and the Mall Entrance. The River Entrance would be the objective of the main force, with a flanking force deployed to the Mall Entrance.

"Everyone knows the parts they're to play," Saint radioed over the secure encrypted SINCGARS frequency used by the commanders of the takeover force. "We're almost at the objective. Good luck."

He broke transmission and, one final time, checked the compact Sites Spectre M4 nine-millimeter submachinegun that was cradled in his lap, removing the full clip, working the bolt action to pump a live round from the breech, then thumbing the bullet back into the top of the staggered fifty-round mag and hammering it into the well at the bottom of the grip with the calloused heel of his big right hand.

Then, as the lead vehicle juddered hard to a screeching full stop directly in front of the

Pentagon's River Entrance, Saint was out the door and up on the running board, his arms waving as he directed the troops that emerged from the armored personnel carriers of the mobile unit and raced pell-mell toward the doors of the River Entrance directly ahead.

Hot blood surged to Saint's head as adrenaline coursed through his veins.

It had begun....

Five
**Offensive Action**

*T*he troops of the assault force began to spread out through the Pentagon's mezzanine level. Other groups made haste to reach the rooftop above the fifth floor and secure both it and the pentangular-shaped plaza between the immense building's five wedges. An Army Apache helicopter flew in low, its IFF transponder chip identifying it as friendly to the safed weapons of defensive ground contingents, and then revealed itself as belonging to the enemy, as it dropped a quad-barreled, automatically belt-fed Oberlikon antiaircraft gun emplacement onto the roof.

"There is no known defense against concentrated Triple-A fire available to assault aircraft flying low envelopes," they recalled Saint as telling them in the pre-op briefing. "That was proved to the Soviets time and again in Afghanistan, and it was a strategic pitfall we avoided as a result. The only effective countermeasure is Stealth. You will take over the Pentagon. It is not the ITT Tower in Baghdad in the Persian Gulf War; Stealth is not an option for the opposition. There is no way in hell that the Pentagon will ever be hit conventionally. If we're ever hit, it'll be with a nuke."

The troops now on the roof quickly made the Triple-A gun secure. The helo flew off on an arcing trajectory toward the deck of the Vista Charger, raking North Parking with rocket and heavy machinegun fire to cover its departure. Once onboard the freighter, it would be lashed to the deck and camouflaged with special coverings impenetrable to satellite or high-altitude UAV imaging sensors.

The Pentagon's internal security detachment immediately went into action. The five-hundred-strong Pentagon Force Protection Agency (PFPA), which had replaced the antecedent Pentagon police, was equipped and trained to deter a hostile takeover. Paramilitary troops armed with H&K MP5 submachineguns and bullpup M4A1 assault rifles met the invasion force head-on. Firefights broke out all over Wedge Three.

The defenders were suppressed quickly, however. For all their rigorous training, the PFPA was a hollow force, while Saint's troops were hardened veterans of the covert battleground in a dozen clandestine combat zones. It was a no-contest match in which Saint's hard-chargers soon mopped up pockets of resistance with grenades and close-in submachinegun bursts. The survivors soon began throwing down their weapons and raising their hands. The invaders got out cable ties and began restraint and sequestration of prisoners.

General Saint saw one of the executive officers of the CJCS's office run toward him.

"Are you General Tidings?"

"No, sir," replied Saint. "I am death. Yours, in fact."

Before the questioner could frame a reply, the Spectre submachinegun in Saint's bunched fist spat a three-round burst of nine millimeter hollowpoint rounds into the questioner's chest at nearly point-blank range. The burst was close enough, at any rate, to char his uniform around the bullet holes that released gouts of arterial blood from his ruptured chest cavity.

"Or at least his dark angel," Saint finished with a smile, pointing the weapon's squat muzzle downward to deliver a two-bullet coup de grâce to the forehead of the fatally injured Army officer.

And now Saint laughed. He felt the adrenaline rush coming on with a vengeance. The familiar combat high that simultaneously made him feel invincible and detached. It was almost like looking at himself in a dream, only it was real. He'd come down from it in time. He could handle it -- no problem. For the moment, though, he would enjoy it to the hilt.

Saint stopped and focused for a moment, trying to take in the scene of unfolding violence all around him. It seemed like chaos, but there was an interior logic to it, a controlled anarchy. He replayed the opening scenario in his mind, reviewing the multiple actions that were taking place simultaneously.

First, he knew, a troop detachment was rushing toward the National Military Command Center. It was necessary to take over the NMCC right away. Another detachment had been given the mission of securing the E-Ring offices of the upper echelons of the Defense Department, rounding up and moving prisoners to the innermost A-Ring which faced the Building's pentangular interior courtyard. Still other elements of the invasion force would now be securing the interior and exterior of Wedge Three with antipersonnel munitions and remote sensing apparatus that would enable the monitoring of the secured area from Saint's earmarked headquarters in the NMCC.

The largest of the detachments was a heavily armed force tasked with staging a fire reconnaissance against any would-be defensive elements at the Pentagon that might hinder the smooth and swift capture of all objectives within the scope of the mission timetable.

In particular, Saint had trained his forces with the objective of successfully and rapidly countering and prevailing against PFPA security forces and Marine Corps military police elements that were on permanent duty at the Pentagon and which had been trained for counterterrorist and police operations. Saint's forces had been trained to countervail against the tactics that these internal security forces used, and had been deliberately equipped to outgun and outmaneuver their opponents. Saint had carefully analyzed all of the strategies -- hell, he'd even originally devised some of them, hadn't he? Saint had no doubt that his force would prevail.

Saint checked his wrist chronometer. The time was 0740 hours. His headset and lip mike were patched into the mission's LandWarNet-based combat information network. Saint monitored the operational chatter of the various mission elements and his lightweight head-mounted display gave him schematic representations of what each assault element was doing.

From the combined mission information available to him Saint realized that the operation was proceeding on track. The timetable called for Wedge Three to be secured by 0800 hours. He believed this objective would be met. In fact, in minutes Saint received confirmation that it had indeed been successfully accomplished.

"St. George, this is Puff."

The disembodied voice that crackled in Saint's right ear belonged to his executive officer.

"Longbow is secure. Repeat -- Longbow secured."

Behind the voice Saint heard a few sporadic bursts of automatic fire, shouts of command and then savage whoops of victory. Longbow was the operational code name for the National Military Command Center, the nerve center of the US defense establishment. It was located almost exactly two stories above his head, on the third and fourth floors in a series of secure rooms extending from Rings E through C and situated within easy walking distance of the office of the Secretary of Defense.

"Congratulations, Puff," Saint replied. "I never doubted your capabilities. You're five minutes ahead of schedule, though."

"I'll slow it down some next time, St. George," his exec answered.

"You do that," Saint answered. "I'm coming home."

"I'll bake some cookies, St. George," said Puff and signed off.

■

# DAVID ALEXANDER

As Saint's strike force was consolidating its gains and securing its objectives throughout the captured Wedge, other actions automatically happened as elsewhere invisible tripwires were pulled. Police emergency and military units received alerts. The alerts pulsed along the nation's emergency channels, reaching out to scattered outposts across the country and around the world.

The Alternate Military Command Center buried inside Raven Rock Mountain, and NORAD, headquartered within another mountain in Colorado, both received the alert. So did the military and political staff of US allies and foes alike. From the UK Ministry of Defense headquarters beneath the streets of London, to the underground bunker complex of the Israeli Keriya, headquarters of the IDF, heightened security was put into effect.

At the White House, emergency Secret Service security procedures automatically went into action. President Halifax, whose workweek customarily began on Sunday, was having coffee at her Oval Office desk. She found her sanctum invaded by a Secret Service security detail and she was unceremoniously summoned from her chair and led through the corridors of the White House toward a waiting limousine discretely parked outside the West Wing gate. She was driven toward Marine One, the presidential helicopter, toward Andrews Air Force Base to the southeast of Washington DC where KNEECAP, the emergency aircraft maintained by Strategic Command, or Stratcom, was to loft her into an airborne command post for the duration of the crisis.

The vice president, given to protest, was merely lifted from his bed at his official quarters at Number One Observatory Circle at the US Naval Observatory, a large, white, brick Victorian mansion on the southeast corner of 34th Street and Massachusetts Avenue, and then hustled in a careening ten-minute drive through the streets of the District to the Executive Mansion and then into the White House Command Center, a buried and reinforced bunker with communications links to the US military and to global political nodes and centers. Subject to what followed, both key White House staff and political VIPs would be taken to the secret underground hideout known only as "Special Facility," a tunnel warren hidden deep within the Catoctin Mountains of Pennsylvania, about two hundred miles south of Washington DC, a facility built to withstand a direct nuclear airburst, followed by months and years of war and aboveground chaos.

Other entities were also on standby alert, especially the Pentagon's two close Beltway neighbors, the Central Intelligence Agency and the National Security Agency. At the CIA's Langley, Virginia, headquarters, in a vaulted room with a cipher lock manned by armed guards, CIA Director Hampton Yee was personally manning the large flat-panel "god" screen at the center of a bank of monitors on the wall above a large command pit that measured an architectural story in depth. The screen showed satellite feed from an imaging platform in a fixed orbit above the eastern seaboard. In a moment, imagery from a high-flying Global Hawk UAV sent by the USAF and cruising at sixty thousand feet, was also contributing real-time imaging to the multispectral displays.

Farther to the south, at its sprawling complex at Fort George G. Meade, Maryland, the NSA's array of megacomputers linked to orbital electronic intelligence satellites was also focused on the rapidly developing crisis at the Pentagon. The NSA's orbital assets included FERRET -- satellites whose enormous trailing antennae could pick up anything from cellular phone transmissions to rocket telemetry and feed it rapidly into the NSA computer farm for rapid deciphering. The NSA was monitoring global communications using keyword priority, searching for anything that connected with the rapidly unfolding events. The computers automatically listed and prioritized the contacts. One by one these appeared as links on monitors at the NSA, where analysts, aided by intelligent machines, assessed each new contact.

Nearly two thousand miles to the west of the Washington DC Metro area, the joint US-Canadian facility buried on spring-loaded steel buildings inside the hollowed out, steel mesh-lined Cheyenne Mountain in Colorado and known as NORAD was also following crisis procedures. Its tracking radars and orbital infrared sensors were scouring orbital space to determine whether hostile launches of missiles were taking place. The data would be calculated and graphically echoed on screens at the NMCC in the Pentagon, and on similar displays at other locations, including the AMCC, or Alternate Military Command Center, at Raven Rock and the White House Command Center. So far there was no indication of intercontinental ballistic or theater nuclear missiles having been launched.

Nevertheless, the domestic alert state of Threatcon Delta was echoed in the upgrading of the Defense Condition, or DEFCON level. The DEFCON level, which runs from one through five, with one being the highest level of alert consistent with a state of war, was upgraded from a peacetime status of five to DEFCON 2, a state that placed US forces around the world on alert one stage short of actual conflict.

Finally, the White House issued a Yellow security alert to the public at large. The nation was in crisis.

Again.

■

One other facility -- a hidden command center -- was alerted, although it was neither in the United States nor in the territory of any of its allies, and located thousands of miles to the east, two time zones distant from the Capital.

In the darkness of the command center, a tall man with a black patch over his right eye watched a series of mammoth screens. The data was the same as that available to the NSA and CIA, augmented by assets of his own. He was the silent partner of the operation. The general was the front man. He had, in the course of his career, supplied logistics and intelligence to General Saint's covert Phoenix Battalion. He had supplied a great deal of other things to global criminal organizations too.

At 1840 hours, local time, the eye patch wearer received a message that flashed on one of the display screens. Thousands of miles away, General Casper Saint, now secure in the NMCC, sat in the catbird seat. He awaited the nod from his chief technical officer, who had patched into the computer system and was manipulating joystick, mouse and keyboard on both a laptop and the keyboard on the instrumentation console.

# THREATCON DELTA

The technical was named Lev Varukoi. He was a former Russian computer systems officer who had worked for the KGB's technical directorate before emigrating to France, where his skills found him employment with the French intelligence service, SDECE. Varukoi had fallen afoul of his new masters at Sedeek as well when he had been discovered using computer crime techniques to pad out what he considered his meager paychecks. He had been an able recruit for the Phoenix Battalion. Saint's covert outfit had been for Varukoi what it had been for many, if not most, of its other members -- a kind of latter-day Foreign Legion, albeit one that fought only in covert battlegrounds, outwardly, at least, without official sanction.

The Battalion had given the outcasts of a dozen nations another chance to live -- and to die. The men Saint had admitted into its ranks had to be prepared for death. They had to be men -- and some women -- for whom life didn't matter anymore, who had nothing else left to lose. They also had to have exceptional skills. Paradoxically, they had to be both the best and the worst at the same time.

Saint demanded the most rigorous standards of excellence from his personnel. Such men and women should by conventional wisdom not have existed; yet they did exist, and in numbers sufficient to staff a battalion-level force. The globalized economy, Saint reflected, had made beggars out of the gifted, the talented, the exceptional and self-motivated, while it rewarded those who, with mechanical obedience, followed orders like good and faithful robots. The global machine's loss had been Saint's gain.

Under his command they had succeeded where conventional troops had utterly failed. They had succeeded in covert operations that would remain locked in Defense Department and CIA vaults for the next century. They had succeeded in missions too dangerous and too demanding for the Seals or Delta, or any other unit in any other army, in fire zones that ranged from the arid wastes of the Kirghiz mountains in the cross-border regions between Afghanistan, Iran and Syria, to remote islands in the Indian Ocean and Arabian sea, where global terrorist strongholds had been established.

They had provided the politicians with cover stories for the failure of North Korea to launch its land-based medium-range nuclear missiles on the US Sixth Fleet, for the supposedly accidental destruction of an Iranian plutonium reactor, for the absurdly "accidental" sinking of an advanced neo-Soviet Akula-class submarine, and for many more incidents that never even made the news.

Saint had earned his troops' unequivocal loyalty.

Now they would get their reward. This was the big one.

The screen before Saint lit up. The eyepatched face appeared. It was Varukoi, communicating under the code-name "Boris."

"We're here, my brother."

"I can see that. Congratulations."

"I'll announce this fact to the world. First, there are the cleanup operations that are being initiated as we speak."

"Alpha is ready, my brother."

"I never doubted it," said Saint, who bit the end off a Cuban cigar, spat it sideways and lit up with an army lighter. "I'll report back to you at the next scheduled sitrep."

"Again, my brother, good luck."

"Fuck luck," said Saint with a laugh. "Luck can go fuck a duck."

He blanked the screen and gestured to his exec as he puffed on the cigar. Crews of black-clad, heavily armed men fanned out through the captured Wedge of the Pentagon, on a search and destroy mission.

Saint turned to his chief technical, Red Dog Juan.

"Can you do Northern Cross within the timetable?"

"Do you have to ask?" Red Dog Juan replied and clicked the keyboard.

Almost simultaneously the words "Northern Cross" took shape on the screen in characters as bold as the plan itself.

Six
## Every Man for Himself

*T*he five-sided Pentagon building is built on a plan of concentric lettered rings intersecting with numbered corridors that radiated outward from an "A-Ring" or central Main Corridor like spokes on an enormous, if misshapen wheel. The wheel itself is further subdivided into five enormous Wedges, each of which might comfortably house a building the size of the US Capitol.

Prior to the Pentagon renovations that came in the wake of Strike Day, only the first two divisions were physically demarcated. Afterward there were actual wedges too, their borders defined by security firewalls, including pneumatically controlled steel blast doors impervious to small arms fire that could, within seconds, close tightly to secure each of the five wedges individually.

Wedge Three was now effectively sealed off from the remaining four Pentagon Wedges. The massive steel guillotine doors that had dropped within seconds of the takeover had blockaded the wedge at two key points, between Corridor 1 to the south and Corridor 2 to the north of the Wedge. On the five floors of this pie-slice of the Building, Rings E through A formed a series of arcs diminishing in size and expanse as they drew closer to the narrowest section of Wedge Three.

Because the Pentagon is so large, comprising a surface area of more than four million square feet, even a single Wedge of the building represents an area of considerable size capable of holding hundreds of offices and thousands of staffers. General Saint's operations platoon had estimated that even on a Sunday morning there could potentially be upwards of two thousand civilian and military personnel trapped inside any single Wedge. So as Saint consolidated control of the National Military Command Center on the third floor, he ordered armed security squads to fan out and round up unfriendlies.

Those captured in the sweeps were to be herded into containment areas set up inside break rooms on the second, third and fourth floors, where they could be more easily watched and more efficiently controlled. Others, primarily members of the vanquished Protection Forces, were kept under guard in the Pentagon's central outdoor courtyard. The hostages were not considered important to the overall plan -- in fact their presence was an unwanted necessity in a takeover, and a Sunday takeover had been planned to produce as few hostages as possible -- but those who were present might play a role as bargaining chips later on, should problems arise.

Saint's XO, Sgt. Nickel Bag, was giving commands to personnel who were setting up the control mechanisms.

Saint checked the prisoners they had taken in the storming of the building. The Secretary of Defense wasn't among them. Doesn't pay to work on Sunday, now does it? The SecDef's absence had been factored into the plan's parameters, though it would have been good to snare him in the net. It was okay, though. Defense Secretary Robert Battle was a well-known power junkie who considered the Pentagon as his private domain. Depriving Battle of the control of his little playhouse would in itself be a powerful bargaining chip.

"Do I have the public address?"

"Yes, sir."

"Attention. Those of you in Wedges One through Four. Within ten minutes these Wedges will be sealed off. The security bulkheads between the Wedges will then be locked down. Be advised that we have the capability to fill them with VX nerve gas at any time we wish. Those who have not evacuated by then will assume the burden of risk for their own safety. Repeat: You have ten minutes to evacuate or risk death or serious injury. That is all."

Saint watched the big screens. As he had expected, the "evacuation" was developing into a riot. They were scrambling, stampeding to leave the Building. In a warped mirror image of society at large, it was every many for himself and devil take the hindmost.

That was good. Let them kill each other. Saint didn't give a damn.

They -- their kind -- had tried to kill him, hadn't they?

■

"Sir, I can report that the bathroom is now free of all pernicious contaminants including disease-causing micro-organisms."

"What?"

"Sir, you ordered me to police the bathroom. The mission has been accomplished. Contaminants to the bathroom facilities have been removed and the bathroom floor is now in a state of positive sanitation. Perhaps you would care to inspect my accomplishments."

Krieger had almost forgotten Ensign Sabio. He was wrapped up in another project, concerning the intricacies of active versus passive Stealth technology. He turned in his chair to face her.

"I'm sure you did a really nice job. Now, please to get lost as Charlie Chan used to say."

He turned back to what he was doing.

"Sir, where is my desk?"

"Your *what*?" Krieger asked. He sounded to Sabio like someone whose religion had just been insulted.

Just then his workstation screen went blank. That was strange. Krieger checked it out. The system appeared to be working, but the internal Pentagon Intranet was down. Other strange things were happening besides this. Krieger got up and decided to investigate.

"Sir, where are you going?"

"To have a *shufti*. You can come too."

"What is a shufti, sir?"

"Whatever you want it to be."

"Sir?"

"That's a *koan*."

"That's a zen term, sir. Are you into zen, sir?"

"You might say that, Ensign Sabio," Krieger replied, "every now and zen."

The subbasement seemed oddly deserted. The elevators weren't working. The doors appeared to be locked down. This wasn't all that unusual, though. The Pentagon redesign that had taken years to implement had barely touched the subbasement.

This level was a warren of tunnels, some of which led to the Potomac River, and to sewer mains and the massive water tunnels that ran beneath Washington DC. It was a tunnel network that rivaled the catacomb networks of shepherds' caves and subterranean irrigation tunnels of Afghanistan or Iran in complexity. Krieger had seen both firsthand.

Only the custodial and maintenance staffs actually ventured down here on a regular basis. Krieger's office was the only one on this level. The arrangement, which had been intended by General Bailey to drive any normal man crazy and contravene the president's direct order that Krieger be accommodated, had actually worked out to Krieger's advantage.

Krieger had outfitted vacant rooms as workspace and gym. He had an office, shared with his partner, at a Beltway consulting firm near Maryland, but he rarely went there. In the bowels of the Building, alone with his computer workstation, he had found a foot of earth from which he could move the world if he wished.

"Wait in my office Ensign Sabio," Krieger told his new assistant. "Do you have a gun by the way?"

"No."

"There's a Glock pistol in the top desk drawer. It's loaded. I'd suggest you get it out while you're waiting. You do know how to use a semiautomatic?"

"Yes, sir, I do," Sabio answered. "I am a qualified ..."

By this time Krieger, who had donned a head-mounted display and wrist-top control panel, was disappearing into a crawlspace between the walls, and wasn't paying attention to Sabio anymore. Maintenance bays built between the Pentagon's walls as part of the ductbank had communications shafts and crawlspaces that ran straight down to the subbasement.

From Bay C-6, Krieger's present position, he could negotiate the crawlspace up and down the length of Wedge Three. Other crawlspaces connected to other Wedges. Since the crawlspaces also offered little mobility to invaders, no special security had been installed inside them. There were other shaftways, bays and hidden rooms throughout the Wedges used for maintenance, in part, for the Pentagon's massive heating and refrigeration system. Krieger had keys and cipher-lock codes for access to locked doors.

His interest now was surveillance. He could plug the system directly into the Building's security net, bypassing safeguards. He keyed real-time video into his HMD using his wrist-top keypad, which included a mini-trackball mouse. Blank screens full of static confronted him as he scrolled through video streams from the banks of surveillance cameras monitoring the Pentagon's vast interior spaces and exterior perimeter. The cams were down.

Yet, purely by persistence, Krieger did find one that was still operational -- third floor, Corridor 2 between A- and B-Rings.

The scene showed assault troops in full battle dress herding Pentagon personnel toward a break room at the end of the corridor. Some resisted and were smashed across the skull with the buttstocks and receivers of the M4A1 assault weapons they ported. The troops had the distinct appearance of professional soldiers. It showed in the way they moved and used their weapons. Who the hell were they? Krieger looked for unit patches on sleeves, but the imagery was too fuzzy to discern details clearly.

A digitized face suddenly swam into focus. A pair of eyes stared into a distant camera lens and seemed to float a few inches from Krieger's field of view. Then a combat rifle's stubby muzzle was raised to point like a threatening finger jabbed in the face. A bright, if silent, burst of flame followed -- no mike to capture sound on this linkage. And then this video feed channel was gone too, replaced by buzzing, crackling static. One more cam down.

# THREATCON DELTA

*Madon'*, Krieger cursed in Sicilian, his favorite language for cursing.

Smart guys, he thought.

Krieger scrolled through the remaining cameras identified by icons in the virtual view-field of his HMD. None were operational. The tactician in him took charge as he assessed the situation. It appeared that only a single Wedge had been taken over -- the Wedge in which he and Sabio were now apparently trapped.

"What the fuck is going on?" Krieger asked at the air.

It was a pointless question. Some shit was shaking, that was clear. Once in combat you never lost that sixth sense. It was clanging like a bell now. Unfriendlies had taken control. Not impossible, Krieger thought. Some of the Pentagon's security holes were gaping, although neither the Office of the Secretary of Defense or the Joint Chiefs would admit such gaps actually existed. Well, thought Krieger, somebody had just danced right through one of those nonexistent holes.

An old Pentagon adage went flitting through his mind. The half-life of a number one priority is exactly three minutes.

Krieger saw no option but one: escape. He would help nobody's cause by staying inside Wedge Three. Should breaching teams run fiber optic cables into maintenance shafts he might even become an obstruction. He'd bet that somebody on the outside was already calling up the Building's blueprints. For all he knew a breaching mission might already be beyond the planning stage and underway.

Krieger crawled back out into the lighted corridor. He found Sabio waiting in his office with his Glock semiauto pointing straight at him. Krieger asked her to lower the gun. There was just enough time to put pre-planned routines into effect. Sensitive files would be destroyed -- the blueprints first, if Krieger could manage it. As to his escape route, Krieger already had its details worked out.

He told Sabio to hustle into the corridor. They were leaving.

But they were a minute too slow.

Suddenly the LED numeric indicator winked on. An elevator was on its way down. Krieger grabbed Ensign Sabio and pulled her into one of the dark recesses between banks of conduit pipes that snaked along the walls.

"Sir, this is most irregular."

"Shut up, Ensign fuckin' Sabio, and don't 'sir' me either. That's an order."

"Understood," Sabio replied smartly, "sir."

■

They watched the elevator doors slide open.

# THREATCON DELTA

Two hard men cautiously emerged, their movements straight out of an Army field manual. They were dressed in woodland-pattern camo fatigues and they brandished M-4 assault weapons. Black balaclavas covered their faces. They waved the autoweapons back and forth, peering into doorways.

What was going on?

The two soldiers walked down the corridor, wordlessly communicating by means of hand signals. They passed the hiding place in which Krieger and Sabio had hastily sought refuge. Krieger heard them kick open the door to his office and rummage around inside.

"Nobody here," he heard one say to the other.

"Let's go back, this area's secure."

"Right."

Krieger huddled deeper into the shadowy recess formed by the gap in the horizontal masses of utility conduits.

"Sir, I suggest we take these operatives out. They're obviously terrorists of some kind. I am fully trained in unarmed combat, competent in three martial arts, including jeet kune do -- "

"Negative. Nobody's taking anybody or anything out. This isn't a fucking Chinese restaurant, Sabio. We'll let them go. When they're gone, we'll try to get our own sorry asses out of this rat trap. You got that?"

"As you say, sir."

Backs pressed against the wall, they waited as the two masked commandos passed their hiding place. Suddenly one of the soldiers stopped in his tracks. Stepped back one pace. A sixth sense was at work, Krieger knew, a combat sense. He knew that one of the pair of killers had detected them somehow, picked up their vibrations; call it what you will. He'd seen it happen before. He steeled himself for what had to come next.

The silhouette of a gun muzzle jerked in shadow across the gap. As the bullpup barrel of the M-4 appeared, Krieger reacted quickly, lashing out with a hapkido sidekick to the man's arm that sent the rifle skidding along the corridor's concrete floor. An upward, flat-palm blow to the windpipe crushed the trooper's larynx and thyroid cartilage. He made gagging sounds and blood trickled from his mouth. As the wounded killer's knees buckled, and he sagged to the concrete, Krieger slammed his heel against the side of his head, caving in his left temple. The merc was dead before he hit the floor.

Krieger heard grunting and whirled in place, prepared to pull Ensign Sabio's fat out of the fire. As he took up a wing chun combat stance, arms splayed, hands open, body balanced, he saw her deftly flip the much larger figure onto his back.

Moments later she had knocked him cold with a single elbow smash to the face.

"Good going, sir," she told Krieger. "Unfriendlies appear to be secured. What now?"

Krieger shook his head in a show of helplessness. Jesus Christ, he thought, today was just not turning out like he'd expected.

Then it struck him.

"Shit, it was The Doors."

"What, sir? What about the doors?"

"'A Spy in the House of Love' was a song by The Doors."

"Sir, I don't follow you. What does that have to do with anything?"

"Forget it, Sabio," Krieger said. "Just let's hustle."

"Are you suggesting we dance?"

"What?"

"The hustle," she began, "is a kind of dance -- "

"Forget it, Sabio. I meant to say let's get out of here quick, okay?"

And hustle they did.

But not before Krieger reached into the side pocket of his pants and pulled out a playing card, which he flipped onto one of the bloodied corpses on the floor.

■

"Sir, a possible problem may have cropped up."

"What?"

Saint swiveled in his command chair, stared up at his XO.

"Timmons and Frazzini have not reported back nor can they be raised on SINCGARS. I sent them down to recce the basement. They've popped off the Soldier 911 map display too."

"How long ago was this?"

"Forty-two minutes exactly, sir."

Again Saint swiveled in his chair. He punched up the monitors in Sector 30, which included portions of the Pentagon subbasement. These showed remote video feed of the basement area adjacent to the elevator bank.

Saint panned the security cameras back and forth. He saw nothing amiss. The corridor was completely vacant except for water and waste mains and cable conduits that snaked along its ceiling and walls. A light glowed at the vanishing point beyond which the camera could not see. Otherwise, nothing.

"Can't raise them on comms, you said?"

"No sir. They don't reply."

"Shit. You know what I think?"

"What, sir?"

"I think somebody drew first blood."

"A possibility, sir."

Saint keyed his terminal, clicking on the icon representing Pegasus' station. Lieutenant Pegasus was the unit's assistant techie. Sub-geek to Red

# THREATCON DELTA

Dog Juan, he was a specialist in hacking large-sized databases. Pegasus should by now have gained access to all personnel records stored in the Pentagon's clustered computer file-servers by this point.

"Pegasus, who's in the vicinity of Sectors 30 to 34?"

"Those are all in the subbasement, right sir?"

"Yep."

"Just a minute. I'm retrieving the map data now."

A few moments passed. Pegasus began to read off names from the personnel roster, all of which belonged to members of the maintenance and custodial staff.

"Martin Anderson, Chief Custodian. Alice C. Medford, Office of Records and War Archives. Rommel Krieger, on leave and reassignment from the National Security... "

"Hold it. That last name. Is it on the hot list?"

"Checking, sir."

Pegasus punched up keys on the console in front of him. Prior to the mission a hot list comprised of individuals of special operational interest -- whether they might make especially good hostages, or posed a particular threat to the mission -- had been compiled in the mission's planning and preparation stages using hacked Defense Department personnel lists, and public-access information from the National Archives and Records Administration.

"Yes, sir. That name is hotlisted."

After a moment's pause and more keystroking, Pegasus went on:

"Sir, Rommel Krieger occupies room 3C101. It is located in the subbasement sector of Wedge Three. Krieger has been issued a level-2 security clearance, giving him unrestricted access to all but security code-word level omega areas. Krieger also has full code-word privileges on the Pentagon intranet, the Defense Department ARPANET and remote computer sites on the Defense global information grid, such as WarSimNet and Future Combat System."

"Who is he, exactly?"

"According to the hotlist, basically, nobody, sir. Just some policy wonk who was part of the incoming Halifax administration's transition team last year. Krieger wound up on the outs with the SecDef and was shouldered out of the State Department post he was promised. But he was a personal friend of the president, had dated her in college, and had also served with the former CJCS in Afghanistan and Iraq. The president wouldn't throw him to the dogs. She gave him the office as a consolation prize, sir."

Pegasus added, "The hotlist has him down as a potential hostage due to his usefulness as a bargaining chip."

"What's he do down there, besides jerk off?"

"Writes some sort of technical white paper, sir. On ... Stealth warfare."

"For the last year?"

"Yes, sir. Apparently that's what he's been doing. It's updated each year as part of the annual DOD Defense Planning Guidance which, as you know, is the blueprint for each fiscal year's defense acquisitions planning and becomes part of the Quadrennial Defense Review. Apparently Krieger's white paper will be in the next QDR which will appear later this month. He's also published some books on the subject, and written adventure novels under a pseudonym."

General Saint paused and steepled his fingers beneath his chin. He mulled over the particulars of the situation while he re-lit his cigar and took a reflective puff.

"A thinker ... a writer ... a dreamer, huh? Can you get into the DIA files?"

"I anticipated you'd ask, general, and am already inside the Defense Intelligence Agency system. Just give me a moment or two more and I ..." Pegasus fell silent, and only the clicking of keys broke the stillness. "Sir, I'm afraid I've temporarily hit a brick wall. The file on Rommel Krieger is restricted at an extremely high security level. This will take a little doing."

"Somehow I half expected you'd say that," Saint replied. "And while you're at it, try getting me the CIA, NSA and NSC files on our newfound subbasement Phantom of the Opera, if they exist, that is."

"If they exist, general, I'll obtain them," replied Pegasus. "You can count on it. Give me a few moments more, if you would." Pegasus keystroked furiously. "I have the Defense Department personnel files on Krieger now from the DIA's secure database."

"Break it down for me."

"The files basically show the same as our hotlist, with some variation as to military service. He apparently served in the Army at one time."

Saint frowned. He shook his head and his eyes swept from side to side.

"That's bullshit. Something about this guy rings a bell. 'Blitz Krieger.' I've heard the name. If it's the same Blitz Krieger I'm thinking about, then he's a bad actor who headed some supershit snake eater team working out of the office of the JCS about ten years ago. Called SLAM -- stood for search, locate, annihilate, missions unit. They did classified commando missions. Used solely for clandestine counter-WMD, the gritty stuff nobody else could do. Very deeply classified. They didn't even tell me about it till the unit's deactivation. You think it's the same guy, lieutenant?"

"Well, I suppose, sir that -- "

"Suppose nothing, Pegasus. That data you got -- it's cooked, probably by this Krieger himself, who I'm really beginning to think is the same guy they called 'Blitz' years ago. If so, then that mother is one dangerous loose end to leave untied.

"You know, Pegasus, I think I want his ass found and killed on the double. You got that?"

"Yes, sir!"

"Now find out what he's really been up to down there -- not Krieger's fucking cover. I want the ground truth -- and let me have the intel on the double. Pegasus, you get inside the NSC computer like a good little hacker, or black hat, or whatever you guys call yourselves and find out for sure."

"Yes sir!"

Saint shut down the video comm link and sat motionlessly for several moments. Then he turned to his XO.

"We got us a problem."

"I heard, sir. But don't sweat it. Kiss his ass goodbye. My men will solve that problem easy. Our friend's as good as history."

"Take care of it."

Sgt. Nickel Bag saluted, then turned smartly on his boot heels and left the command center to pick himself a few good men. He'd relish this job. It would be first blood drawn by his side in battle during the mission.

Sgt. Nickel Bag would lead the squad himself, and he'd do that piece of shit right. He'd use a K-Bar on Mr. Krieger, a K-Bar stropped to an edge so sharp it would slice a falling cunt-hair neatly in half. He'd cut off an ear before his target died. Make him suffer. They called him Blitz, but fuck him. As far as "the Bag" was concerned, his name was Shit.

Sgt. Nickel Bag saluted his CO, walked briskly toward his adjutant, and commenced barking out a chain of rapid-fire orders. He wanted a five-man action squad equipped for close-quarter operations assembled on the double and whipped down to the Pentagon basement.

In a half hour, he knew, this Blitz wouldn't be trouble anymore. Fuck, he thought. He wouldn't be nuthin' anymore.

## Seven
### A Bitch and a Half

The Mount Weather command and control facility sits within a vast complex of enormous granitic rabbit warrens excavated deep into the heart of a mountain with a core of solid iron in the black hills of southwestern Pennsylvania. The top-secret DUF, standing for deep underground facility, lies some two hundred miles from Washington DC, putting it under an hour away by jet-turbine helicopter from the nation's capital.

President Linda Everett Halifax, less than a week from having completed his first hundred days in office, rode an elevator from the helipad on the mountain top down into the innermost depths of the DUF.

With First Husband, and former Connecticut governor, Warren Halifax at her side, she was accompanied by a throng of Secret Service personnel. Also in the queue that left the presidential helicopter, Marine One, was an aide carrying the "football," an armored steel attaché case handcuffed to the president's wrist and primed to explode if the wrong combination was entered more than twice in a row. It contained the nuclear Gold Codes that would enable the president to authorize tactical or strategic nuclear strikes from anywhere in the world she might happen to be.

Only minutes before, en route from the White House from which she had been hustled as the news of the events on the opposite shore of the Potomac broke, Halifax had authorized the continued declaration of Threatcon Delta, the third and highest national security alert.

Threatcon Delta, in which the conventional and nuclear military forces of the United States are primed in a state of readiness for war, is independent of the defense condition, or DEFCON, levels of the SIOP or single integrated operational plan for waging nuclear warfare.

Even with Threatcon level Delta in force, the DEFCON level was still set at two -- a state of national alert verging on war, or DEFCON-1. While the president could override this state it was now set by automated means. The SIOP had been fully automated in the final months of her predecessor's administration by the new COLOSUS alert status system.

The COLOSUS computer cloud network had been designed as a failsafe mechanism to remove the factor of human error from the response loop of the decision matrix.

The computer nodes that controlled COLOSUS were buried in the most secure, and the most secret, facilities available at closely guarded locations around the world. The dispersed arrangement of the redundant systems made COLOSUS virtually impregnable to attack and hostile intervention, whether by direct assault or through computer hacking.

Even if all but a single link were destroyed, the system could still continue to function, directing the nuclear and unconventional weapons arsenal of the United States in the absence of human judgment with the rapid decision-making speed vital to a credible reaction against nuclear attack.

■

President Halifax was shown her temporary office for the duration of the crisis. She was familiar with the layout at the DUF from preparedness drills that she and other administration officials had conducted in secret on several other occasions. The drills had been intended to insure that a smooth transition from the normal working environment of the White House could be made in time of national emergency to preserve what was known to policymakers as COG, or continuity of government.

# DAVID ALEXANDER

The president went straight to her office. Halifax was gratified to note that her key executive staff, which had been evacuated along with her and the First Husband, were already finding their places. They would remain here at Mount Weather until it was firmly established that the developing situation at the Pentagon posed no tangible risk to the person of the US chief executive or the physical safety of the Executive Mansion at 1600 Pennsylvania Avenue.

In the meantime, Halifax took immediate stock of the situation. A CRITICOM link to the White House command center -- another bunker buried beneath the presidential executive mansion with secure links to the national military command structure -- put the president in direct videoconference contact with her Cabinet and her principal aides. These, and the deputies of their respective Cabinet-level chiefs who sat on the National Security Council, were now gathered around the rectangular oak conference table in the White House Situation Room, located two stories beneath the Oval Office.

The deputies made up what was known as the National Security Policy Group or NSPG. It was the NSPG that, on a day-to-day basis, was frequently responsible for most of the nation's national security decisions. The department chiefs themselves were largely political appointees, trusted managers who in turn hired experts as their deputies. The chiefs -- there were seven of them in all, made up of the heads of the CIA, Joint Chiefs, NSA, Homeland Security, and four others including the Office of the Vice President -- might craft policy on the macro level; the deputies were micromanagers. They were the ones who, more often than not, actually ran the show.

"Update me. What's happened since I left? Dan -- you begin."

Halifax unbuttoned her collar and loosened her paisley-pattern silk blouse as she leaned back in the leather swivel chair behind the desk, facing the large, flat panel display mounted on the opposite wall. Daniel Atkins, the DepSec or Deputy Secretary at State, glanced at papers assembled in front of him.

"Ma'am," Atkins began, "It's now clear the Pentagon has been penetrated by a hostile paramilitary force. This force -- we estimate it as about battalion strength -- is now in control of Wedge Three, which, as you know, contains the National Military Command Center, the Office of the Secretary of Defense and the Office of the Chairman of the Joint Chiefs of Staff."

"Are those persons now in the NMCC?" asked Halifax.

"We believe they occupy the NMCC, yes," Atkins confirmed.

"Damn. What about the rest of the building?"

"The situation is currently in a continuous state of flux," Atkins went on. "Reports indicate small arms fire and grenade or similar antipersonnel munitions explosions throughout the building. We can't say for sure just what is happening yet, though, and we've yet to learn what, if anything, the terrorists want."

"Shit." Halifax banged her fist against the side of the desk. She was mad. This should not have happened on her watch. After 911 and Strike Day it was never supposed to have happened again. But that was naive thinking. Anything could happen -- anytime. And it was her job to respond.

"Who's behind it?" asked the president. "Is this possibly one of Massoud Mahdi's ops?"

"We don't believe it is an Islamist terrorist operation, ma'am," Atkins replied, "at least not of the conventional type."

"What the hell does that mean?"

"Madam President, security camera video has been subjected to computer-aided biometric analysis..."

"...You mean face matching."

"Yes, ma'am, face matching. By this means we've established the identity of the person who we believe is the leader of the takeover force. You see, they all wore masks -- ."

"-- but not the leader."

"No, ma'am. The leader was also masked. However ... well, ma'am, the term "face-matching" is kind of antiquated. Today's biometric systems can also accurately match body types, gestural language, even the shapes and proportions of head, limbs and torso, and make reliable matches based on these data."

"I see."

"Here is the biometric matchup," Atkins proceeded.

Immediately a window popped up on the flat panel display. It showed a frontal view of the ebony face of a man with a sickle-shaped scar running down the left cheek from eyebrow to jaw line, and disappearing under the curve of the jaw. The eyes, though cold, burned with a malicious intelligence.

"Lieutenant General Casper F. Saint," Atkins said.

"Yeah, I recognize him," Halifax replied. "Except Saint's supposed to be in prison, correct?"

"Correct, ma'am. General Saint was charged under Homeland Security and PILGRIM Act statutes, and in accordance with extraordinary rendition policies. He was secretly remanded to the custody of secret Detainment Facility Vector in Thailand. Under applicable statutes he was to be held as an enemy combatant without trial until it was deemed suitable to either execute or release him."

"Apparently Saint had other plans."

"Some heads are rolling over in Chang Mai as we speak, ma'am. Saint somehow managed to escape about seven days ago. Right under their noses. And he managed to leave the country and get back to the United States."

"He was a brilliant tactician."

Atkins nodded.

"Apparently he still is, Madam President," he corrected.

White House Chief of Staff, Burton Funk, who had been evacuated to Mount Weather along with other Cabinet-rank White House staff, asked another question.

"What was Saint in for? Funk wanted to know. "For that matter, who exactly was he?"

"Saint originally served as chief of Pentagon security to the Office of the Joint Chiefs of Staff under the direction of the CJCS. After the terrorist attacks, Saint was given the direction of staging tiger team attacks on -- "

"-- Excuse me, Dan, what's that term mean, exactly?" asked Secretary of Agriculture, Scott Helms, who sat in on the meeting as a close personal confidant of the president.

"That means Saint staged what might be called mock attacks to test various security procedures and systems at the Department of Defense and also at various units that were connected with the Pentagon. Saint not only staged infiltration of the Pentagon in order to test national defenses, but his team also staged infiltration of Defense Department computers."

Atkins scrolled through some notes on the laptop screen on the desk in front of him. In the silence there was only the flat, hollow, plastic, tap-tap-tap of the keyboard and the faint click of the built-in mouse button.

"Saint and his people did their jobs too well, though. He made some of the senior brass hats with a lot of clout look bad, so he was given another assignment."

Here the president chimed in.

"Covert operations, wasn't it?"

Atkins nodded.

"Very covert. Deep black operations. Saint assembled a team that operated in the most remote corners of the world and took on the most high-profile of missions. Saint was our avenging sword, to coin a phrase. Then, later, we learned about Saint's connections with Russian organized crime, specifically with an operator known by the code-name Alexai, and the secret military base near a desolate mountain village named Jabal Tuwaiq, and all the rest, which wound Saint up in the never-never-land designed for terrorists."

"Where he was still supposed to be as of this morning?"

"Correct."

"So you might say that General Saint is the one man on earth who knows everything there is to know about the Pentagon, including how to most efficiently take it over?" the president asked by way of summation.

"I'll go further, ma'am," replied Atkins. "Saint is the one man on earth who could conceivably blow it -- and everything inside it -- into a lot of ragged little pieces."

■

President Linda Halifax watched the video on the display fade and the screen saver fill the screen with a moiré pattern of shifting digital colors. She used the desktop console to switch to a grid of picture-in-picture windows that showed all of the major digital newsmedia broadcasts. All were covering the event live with mobile satellite uplink crews already in position on the section of Beltway cleared by security troops including units of the National Guard.

CNN reported that all that was currently known was that at approximately seven o'clock that morning -- somewhat more than an hour previous -- an emergency preparedness exercise was being held at the Pentagon. The purpose of the exercise was to drill Pentagon civilian and military personnel in evacuation and security procedures during a simulated terrorist attack on the Building.

About ten minutes into the exercise, during which smoke dispensers had engulfed the Parade Ground and the North Parking area directly in front of the Pentagon's River Entrance in a dense gray pall, a body of armed and well-trained commando troops had gained access to the ground-floor mezzanine level through the River Entrance. A fire-fight erupted as the attackers stormed through the Pentagon Mall in the main level, heading for elevator and stairway access to Wedge Three.

In the confusion they succeeded in reaching the third and fourth floors. Here, further fire-fights erupted. Plate steel bulkheads were already rumbling into place to seal off the high-security command and control facilities located on the third and fourth floors of Wedge Three, including the NMCC and the JCS briefing room, known as the Tank.

In addition, all access and entry points to these secure facilities were automatically locked down so that a restricted code-word clearance was necessary to gain access, above and beyond the normal cipher lock access codes for these high-priority areas. Somehow these had been bypassed and the attackers had gained entry to the NMCC and other secret sections located in Wedge Three.

# DAVID ALEXANDER

The live video feed cut away to a map of the vicinity, showing Fairfax and Montgomery Counties, Virginia. The Pentagon was located at the base of the triangle formed by Washington Boulevard and Jefferson Davis Highway, which intersected above the Pentagon Remote Delivery Facility a half mile from its northern wing. Two large parking lots flanked the Pentagon, as did a small heliport located near the west-facing River Entrance. The voice over of a live news broadcast commentator suggested that the attack force had staged from a heating and refrigeration plant located about a mile from the Pentagon, then had secretly joined the actual troops staging the exercise.

The reporter summed up by stating that beyond this the situation inside the Pentagon was still unknown. Anything could happen. So stay tuned.

President Halifax popped a gooey-centered breath mint into her mouth and bit down. She had stopped smoking months ago, but the mints would have to keep her going. What the hell was this all about? Terrorism? Extortion? Politics by other means? She would find out before long, she knew. That was the depressing part. She wished there was someone else to face it, but there was only her. Well, face it she would.

The president next did what presidents do. Before making a decision of tremendous import, she dispatched the problem to committee. At least three working groups at the staff and assistant staff level were tasked with considering all the options and preparing a report.

■

A short distance across the Ellipse, and within walking distance of the White House in the Eisenhower Executive Office Building, known more commonly as the OEOB to denizens of the District, an NSPG working group sat in a small white room around a large oak table. The acronym stood for National Security Policy Group, and the group's official title was NSPG-1. Such groups were ad hoc committees established by various offices of the National Security Council's chiefs, generally at the behest of the president or vice-president.

NSPG-1 was such a group, and it had originally been assembled to study a developing political crisis in Iran that had begun the previous week. NSPG-1 had convened early this Sunday morning in order to draft a position paper for the regular Monday morning NSC meeting, but had been sidetracked on orders from National Security Advisor, Ross Conejo, on orders from President Linda Halifax, to study and assess the unfolding crisis at the Pentagon.

Carlton Smith, Deputy Secretary of Defense, chaired the meeting. "What about the other business, the NPIC telemetry? Are the events in Iran and at the Pentagon in any way connected?" Smith had addressed Assistant Director of the NSA Mel Sanchez.

Smith's careworn face was a map of deeply etched lines. Like the others clustered around the table in the National Security Council meeting room, he was in hastily donned casual clothes. He'd been summoned from his home in nearby Falls Church, Virginia, on a clear, cold Sunday morning when he'd normally have done other things.

This morning, for example, Smith had promised to drive his youngest daughter Sissy to Wal-Mart where she could buy new sneakers and where he could also check hardware items off his list for the plumbing and renovation work he was doing in one of the three bathrooms of his two-story home. Well, those plans were now shot for awhile.

Smith's reference was to some disturbing satellite imaging intel that had recently come in to the joint CIA-NSA National Photographic Interpretation Center or NPIC.

"At this point we can't be certain, Cal," Sanchez answered from the NSA's seat at the conference table. "Overhead surveillance and SIGINT intercepts indicate the events are unconnected -- so far anyway."

# THREATCON DELTA

Earlier that Sunday morning, at 0240 hours Washington time, the CIA's NPIC photoanalysis section had received telemetry from an IMPROVED CRYSTAL orbital imaging satellite. The telemetry was routed to a vaulted room behind a cipher-locked door at NPIC headquarters in a nondescript glass-wall building off the Beltway; the intel take was coded as PHANTOM, which in spook circles gave it an importance slightly higher than the stone tablets brought down from the mountain top by Moses.

The Kennan-class satellite, also known as Keyhole, resembled a Volkswagen Minibus with wings, parked in LEO, or low earth orbit, above a selected portion of the earth. The wings of the Minibus were in fact enormous photovoltaic cell arrays that collected, and concentrated, the sun's radiant energy for operation of the satellite's onboard imaging, cryptographic and uplink-downlink systems.

The photoelectric energy did not run these systems directly -- they needed regulated power supplies which did not fluctuate in voltage or amperage -- but powered an array of wet-cell batteries much like conventional automotive batteries, which were linked together in tandem.

At the earthbound-end of the minibus were an assortment of optical imaging sensors that could scan a three hundred mile swath of the earth's surface below with amazing clarity. Despite the advances of foreign satellite systems and the privatization of space, the latest of the IMPROVED CRYSTAL series, continued to place the ability of the US intelligence community to surveil people, places and things on the earth with unsurpassed accuracy remained unchallenged.

The PHOTINT specialists had looked at near-real time telemetry from the IC that had been parked in orbit over the Southwest Asia, and whose omni-eyed purview took in not only the principal Middle Eastern nations, but also much of northeastern Iran, northern Afghanistan and the southern republics of the CIS, including Tadzhikistan and Kazakstan.

They were seeing further evidence of the construction of a deep underground facility in southeastern Iran which analysis indicated might be sufficiently hardened to bounce JDAMs like peas fired from a straw, or to even withstand a direct nuclear strike. There was also, at this stage, little doubt concerning the nature of the use that this facility was to be put to when complete. The regularly spaced clusters of holes in the ground were the first test borings of what would soon become launch silos for long-range missiles. Not even theater ballistic missiles, but true ICBMs.

# THREATCON DELTA

That these would be nuclear-tipped missiles was plain from the PHANTOM data derived from the covert special forces activities in the Kirghiz Bottleneck, that corridor used by the neo-Soviets to fly in war materiel through Iranian airspace undetected by AWACS coverage. The Russian operative with nano-ocular camera implants had transmitted these findings to the US special forces team on the ground. The president had signed a finding authorizing the experimental implantation surgery on the Russian as well as the covert mission by Marine special forces elements.

The Marine snake eaters had brought the report to their chief and he brought it to the respective parties on the National Security Council, who'd in turn brought it to the White House National Security Advisor who'd then brought it straight to the Oval Office. The NSA summarized the recommendation for Halifax, who was known to prefer quick oral briefings containing the key information rather than lengthy reports.

The DepSecDef turned to Randolph Stansworth, CIA liaison to the NSC.

"Randy?"

"HUMINT assets have so far shown no indication of a connection between the events in the Transcaucasus and what's happening across the Potomac."

"I see, then -- "

118

Just then the phone rang. Smith muttered a few words and hung up.

"That was the vice president calling from Mount Weather," he announced. "The Chairman of the Joint Chiefs is still unaccounted for. It's believed General Bailey's somewhere inside the Pentagon. As you know, he was injured in a highway accident while en route to his office."

"Christ almighty!"

One of the deputies shook his head. Others muttered too.

"They've rounded up the remaining Pentagon staff from the other four evacuated Wedges -- stragglers who didn't make it out in time, that is. A command center's being set up in the OEOB."

"The Old Executive Office Building's where the chiefs originally convened."

Smith ignored that uncalled-for piece of military history trivia from Stansworth, who could prove even a match for Churchill in a contest between longwinded bores. He went on.

"Other staff will be housed during the crisis in the Rayburn Building and the Eisenhower Executive Office Building. The CJCS's ranking deputy, Air Force General Lyman Whitcomb, is now acting Chairman, with General Armstrong, Army Chief, as his deputy. Whitcomb has declared the prevailing national emergency level as Threat Condition Delta, per Chairman Bailey's original recommendation."

"Which is what exactly?" asked Tom Ronson, the assistant press secretary, one of the backbenchers seated in the row of chairs behind the table.

Smith nodded at Stansworth, who explained.

"For those of you unfamiliar with the term, a Threatcon, or Threat Condition Delta, is the highest threat level recognized by the national defense command structure, including the Pentagon. For example, it is invoked when a terrorist attack has occurred or when intelligence indicates terrorist action is likely. The invocation of Threatcon Delta always implies that the situation is extremely grave and that the most stringent measures may be taken to combat it."

"Goddamm," Ronson exclaimed and made a notation on the legal pad on his lap.

"Whitcomb is also planning to order the DEFCON level raised from two to one," Smith added.

Advisors around the table nodded. DEFCON level five was peace. One was a state of supreme national emergency. Nobody needed explanation of what this meant. Since its establishment, which dated back to the Cold War era, the DEFCON level had never risen higher than two.

"Well, that's the long and the short of it is so far," Smith announced. "Better get ready for a hard ride." He paused. "And if you know any prayers, you had better say them while you still can."

Eight
### More Decisions

*"H*ere it is, sir," Pegasus said to Saint. "Confirmation on our elusive friend in the basement."

"Give me a quick rundown."

"Yes, sir. Rommel Krieger was a specialist in finding missing things. From lost nuclear submarines to stolen nuclear weapons. After the Gulf Wars ended Krieger operated a Beltway consulting firm called Global Threat Solutions, more commonly known by its acronym GTS.

"The firm's putative reason for existence was accounting for former Soviet ICBMs and nuclear materials and arranging for either their destruction or purchase by the Atomic Energy Commission. GTS performed this service under contract to the Defense Department. Krieger made a lot of money. GTS was also probably a cover for other, more clandestine, work that Krieger did for the CIA's Directorate of Operations.

"Be that as it may, GTS became involved with a company run by the business partner of former Senator Linda Everett Halifax, on whose transition team Krieger played a prominent role as had been promised, but Halifax didn't make good on her commitment. Instead Krieger was given the task of preparing a white paper on Stealth warfare, on which he happens to be an expert, in his office. A year later, he's still technically at work on this same paper."

Saint puffed on his cigar, rolled it around.

"Sounds like a cover."

"Which it almost certainly is, sir," answered Pegasus. "You see, farther back Rommel Krieger earned the name "Blitz" Krieger for his prowess in the dangerous and unpredictable realm of covert operations. If I might make a suggestion, it's my belief that Krieger was placed in the Pentagon basement as a kind of insurance policy, a kind of house detective who was reporting back to our new bitch president on security matters here and at Defense."

"It's got the ring of truth. Is that all?"

"That's the gist of it, yes, sir."

Saint flicked cigar ash. He got on SINCGARS to the active recon unit that was hunting down Krieger in the Pentagon's extensive bowels several floors below the NMCC.

"Have you found him yet?"

"No. Don't sweat it, though, boss."

"If you can avoid killing our friend, then I want him brought here alive. I'd like to ask him some questions."

"Affirmative, sir. We'll try to be gentle. Dragon – out."

Nine
## Zero Foxtail to Big Bear

*"O*kay. You ladies know the drill. Now tell me all about it. Hinch, you first."

Sgt. Nickel Bag squatted over the map printout spread on the corridor floor. On the other side five men in black battle dress, cradling automatic weapons, and with grenades and comms gear clipped to web harnesses, faced him.

On the printout was a diazo blueprint of the subbasement that had come from the Pentagon's hacked computer database.

Hinch was a muscular black guy with a shaven head. He had a gold ring in the lobe of his right ear. He also had a couple of tats, including one of a flaming skull overlapped by the words "Semper Fi" on his biceps, but you couldn't see those now.

"Squad One. Down the north access stairs. On Bedloe's squelch, hit the door and fan out. I'm on point. Tully and My Bitch break left and right. Free-fire rules. We see it, we kill it."

Hinch said this all in a flat, sullen, fuck-you kind of growl, staring down at the map as he spoke, only looking at Sgt. Nickel Bag when he was finished speaking, and then without even moving his head, just rolling his brown eyes to the whites and fixing the sergeant with the cold, fuck-you kind of psychotic stare for which he was well-known, universally feared and justly proud.

The G-3 nodded slowly, and evenly at Hinch, and spat on the floor to one side. Hinch spat too -- onto the ammo clip in his meat-hook fist -- and palmed it up the hole in the receiver with a loud crack.

"Zattrini?"

Zattrini was wiry, his face was young and lean but the sharp, jutting angles of jawbone, nose bone and cranial dome beneath the leathery looking flesh that came with his Sicilian ancestry made him look old beyond his years.

Like Hinch, Zattrini affected a studiedly blasé attitude. Unlike Hinch, Zattrini was a shavetail who'd never seen action outside a combat simulator. Sgt. Nickel Bag knew Zattrini was scared shitless but tried hard not to show it as Zattrini too sounded off for the tough noncom.

"Squad Two. South access stairwell. On squelch, hit the door. I take the point."

"Rules of engagement?" asked the sergeant.

"Rules of engagement -- fuckin' waste 'em all."

This got a slight laugh from the others, mainly from the way Zattrini had said it. Trying to act big....

"I am on point ... I am one bad motherfucker ... and I am good to go," Zattrini added.

Sgt. Nickel Bag nodded, the sage guru pleased with the neophyte's lessons learned, albeit making a mental note to temper Zattrini's loud mouth -- talk was cheap and shit like that got guys killed.

"Very nice, ladies. As for me, I'm taking the elevator down alone. When the doors open, I pitch these two."

He fondled the spherical, black objects hanging from his harness near his shoulders. These were flashbang grenades, intended to stun the team's intended victims and set them up for the knockdown kill. Blinding light and deafening explosions. He'd seen their effects enough times before with Delta Force to know their capabilities firsthand. No deer in the headlights ever was stopped in its tracks as fast or as finally.

Sgt. Nickel Bag had trained the team in rapid interdiction strike or SLAM -- search, locate and annihilate -- operations at their staging area in the West Virginia countryside during the weeks prior to the op's commencement. By now they were as adept at putting two rounds into the heads of their targets in a half-second as the best Delta Force shooters. Sgt. Nickel Bag knew this because he'd spent years with Delta, training shooters to do precisely this thing with accuracy, speed and precision, and do it every time they tried.

"Alright. Let's fuckin' eat some pussy."

"Hoo-yah!" came the response.

His men were psyched. That was good. That was how they were supposed to be. Psyched to kill. Psyched to die. Psyched for every fuckin' thing in between.

Sgt. Nickel Bag rose to his feet, placing the folded-up map in the side pocket of his fatigue pants and donning the black balaclava combat mask. The other five did likewise.

Cradling their H&K MP5 submachineguns they moved silently yet with practiced speed toward the stairwell exits. The team commander watched them file down, nodded with satisfaction, then went into the elevator.

■

The dull gray paint on the basement's cinderblock walls had enough reflectivity to throw off scintillations of bright white light as the flashbangs exploded. Acrid clouds of dense white smoke billowed and swirled through the narrow corridor.

Sgt. Nickel Bag reached across his barrel chest and keyed the comms strapped against his left shoulder. Two clicks on the send button of the compact Motorola SINCGARS-capable unit --

meaning it was of military grade using frequency hopping technology that made it resistant to jamming -- let those on the net, including his squad, know he was in position. Unlike the movies or novels, this was the real world, and talking into little hands-free sets didn't cut it most of the time. He cradled the Heckler & Koch MP5 -- "Hocklers" in merc lingo -- set to three-round burst mode, took a deep breath, counted three seconds to synch him with the two flanking squads, then hustled from the elevator.

To either side, Squads A and B were deploying into position. They moved commando fashion, bodies hunched, weapons cradled at groin level, gun muzzles tracking back and forth, as did the wary eyes in the sockets of every team member.

Each man had a flexible lip mike jacked into their SINCGARS comms, but comms were to be used only in an emergency -- again, chatting on the phone when in combat was for the movies, not real life. In keeping with the fact that talking during an op could get you killed, the two squad leaders used hand signals to direct the men who filed down the long corridor and proceeded to open doors or, if locked, to kick them in.

Hinch, the point man of Squad A, cautiously approached Krieger's office. Its door was ajar.

Signaling to two of his men to cover him, Hinch went in fast on a half-crouch, his Hockler tracking back and forth, ready to blast anything that moved.

The office appeared deserted, though. Hinch relaxed a little and keyed his comms.

"Office is deserted, boss. Am ... ah, what have we got here?" Pause.

"Found a tripwire. Looks like the faggot was fixing to booby trap us."

Hinch looked down at the taut, horizontal length of clear nylon fishing tackle.

"Fucking piss-ant pogue," he cussed, expressing a low opinion for the maker of the booby trap. Hinch's mother could have done a better job. In fact, Hinch knew his mother actually did do a better job -- his mother had been a Marine gunnery sergeant.

Hinch signaled for his squad's ordie to come in and assist. He was already crouching over the almost invisible line of filament stretching diagonally across the office floor. Hinch gently fingered the fine nylon cord and ran his eye along its length.

One end was tied around the handle of a filing cabinet flush against the rear wall, the other vanished behind the battleship-gray regulation office desk. Moving carefully, Hinch found the other end.

Three fragmentation grenades were tied together in a deadly bundle.

## THREATCON DELTA

The cotter pins of each had been removed, indicating that the grenades were all armed. The tackle was tied around the pull rings of all three. A classic example of Booby Trap 101. You tripped the det cord and the grenades went bang. In an enclosed space the blast would rip men apart and shred their limbs like so much sashimi.

Hinch got out his combat knife, a well-stropped K-Bar honed to a wicked slicing edge. He glanced meaningfully at the ordie who nodded confirmation.

"Yeah," Hinch said with an evil grin.

Tightly grasping a section of line, he cut the cord.

"That's it," he added. "That shit's finished."

Fuckin' pogue, he thought. Meaning whoever the pussy was who'd set the shit booby trap.

The filing cabinet drawer flew open, powered by a concealed and heavily compressed, steel spring. Another spring, beneath a second three-grenade bundle of love, catapulted the steel file drawer into the center of the office room.

Hinch and the ordie had only time enough to register the swift progression of events before shrapnel and concussion tore them limb from limb. They were already dead, and bloody pieces of their ripped apart guts were sticking to the walls and ceiling, before their brains had sufficient time to process the information and reach the conclusion that they had been outfoxed by a master.

Krieger had removed the charges from the fragmentation sleeves off all three grenades, and had cut down the fuses to one-second timings. The grenade bundle first spotted by Hinch had merely been a decoy. Bouncing off the walls, amplified by the close quarters of the office, the blast wave boomed out into the corridor, setting off trembler switches Krieger had placed in concealed positions.

These trembler switches, bought at the Falls Church, Virginia, Ace Hardware electrical department for seventy-nine cents apiece, and triggered by globules of mercury that shorted contacts inside the tiny glass enclosures, were wired up to other high explosive antipersonnel charges Krieger had slotted along the corridor. By doing so he had set up a Hogan's Alley, a killing zone of blast and steel ball bearings that tore flesh, sheared-off heads and limbs, and ripped guts from bellies with the greatest of ease.

When Hinch had set off the office booby trap it had been like knocking down a row of dominoes. Krieger had slotted plastic explosive and grenade bundles behind the thin pasteboard plates of the acoustical drop ceiling, as well as along the subbasement corridor. These charges were fused by mercury tilt switches operating similarly to the tremblers; small glass vials containing two electrodes separated from a glob of mercury by a tiny seesaw. When the mercury was disturbed the seesaw moved, shorted the electrical contacts and completed a circuit. The detonation principle was similar to that of trembler-activated explosions and produced similar lethal results.

The force of the initial explosion was enough to trigger the nearest trembler. Its detonation was in turn sufficient to set of the next one in line. The effect was a wall of fire and concussion that raced through the narrow corridor at lightning speed. Those members of Sgt. Nickel Bag's death squads caught in the corridor were almost instantly torn limb from limb, then disintegrated, then incinerated. Those engaged in searching offices and storerooms were spared. As the blast subsided, they emerged, shocked and disoriented, ears ringing like fire alarms.

Sabio jumped from her concealed position, hosing down the shocked survivors with an Uzi standard submachinegun. But behind her back Sgt. Nickel Bag was about to gun her down.

Suddenly the tip of a combat knife stuck out of his chest. He looked down, surprised. Touched the wet, red and dripping knife point. Was this really happening? Had a knife really been rammed through his kidneys and out his stomach?

Blood spurted from his mouth, bubbled and foamed as he tried to speak. Sgt. Nickel Bag collapsed. His last sight was Krieger looking down at him. Sgt. Nickel Bag tried to say something. He didn't quite succeed.

Krieger shoved a death card into his mouth. It was the Ace of Spades, with the Grim Reaper on the face of the card and Krieger's old motto from his snake eater days, Non Omni Moriar -- "Not All of Me Shall Die."

"Let's drag him into the elevator," Krieger told Sabio, and reached into the pocket of his sports jacket. "Now a little something for the boys upstairs."

Krieger produced another mercury tilt switch, two C-cell batteries, an electrically actuated ordnance detonator and a block of C-4 plastic explosive. He broke off an inch-sized piece of plastique, rolled it into a pancake, slid the pancake under the corpse, and wired Sgt. Nickel Bag to explode when touched by any interested parties who might want to handle him for whatever reasons one chooses to handle a bloodied cadaver with a knife in its guts.

Krieger then pressed 4 and sent the elevator up: destination, NMCC.

"That's it, Sabio," Krieger said as the lights winked above the elevator. "We're out of here."

■

# THREATCON DELTA

Preceded by Sabio, Krieger climbed down the rust-covered ladder of iron rungs bolted to the brick wall of the vertical shaft descending from floor-level. He paused to slide the plate back over its mouth and lock it back in place, then followed her down.

The tunnel was a maintenance shaft that dropped thirty feet to the complicated maze underlying the foundation of the Building. The Pentagon boasts the largest total square footage of any government office building on earth. On a daily basis it plays host to some thirty thousand inhabitants. The drainage and sewage requirements of such a structure are simply staggering.

Thirty feet below the foundation level of the Pentagon there is a network of brick-lined casements, municipal water tunnels and maintenance passageways forming a labyrinthine maze. In addition to these there is another, and much broader, tunnel, that of an uncompleted sub-Potomac commuter railway link to the Capitol.

The present Capitol express line connects the Houses of Congress to the White House and the cluster of major government offices on E Street, such as the Eisenhower Executive Office Building and the Russel Senate Building. VIPs and staff can shuttle between any of a dozen such buildings, where America's day-to-day national and international government business is conducted, with exceptional ease.

The transit line was to have originally extended beneath the Potomac and into the Pentagon, but was dropped in favor of the system of shuttle buses, railway links and highway access that currently service the Building. The tunnel, begun in 1947, was sealed off approximately thirty feet from the Potomac's western bank. Nevertheless it could be reached via the storm drainage tunnel system that connected to it at several points.

Krieger and Ensign Sabio climbed down the unlit maintenance shaft with that larger tunnel as their destination. Musky drafts of cold air wafted in from far off, coming from the direction of other shafts in the tunnel complex. Krieger broke the cap off a Cyalume light stick and shook it. Chemical luminescence created by synthetic firefly enzymes filled the tunnel, bright enough by which to navigate.

Krieger handed the light stick to Sabio and unshipped a tablet from the pocket of his leather coat. He powered it on and the screen lit up. A flashing icon indicated their current position, a broken green line connecting to other icons indicated waypoints along their line of movement.

"Anybody ever tell you you're paranoid, sir?"

"Yeah, my wife used to tell me that all the time, as a matter of fact," Krieger replied.

"What happened to her?"

"I chopped her up with a fire axe, roasted the bitch over an open fire and ate her for dinner one night when the pizza place next door went out of business."

"I shouldn't have asked, sir," Sabio answered.

"Any other questions, or do you want to stand here waiting for more evil psychopathic fuckers to come and try to kill us, Ensign Sabio?"

"Just one, sir," Sabio offered. "How do you get GPS coverage down here?"

"Have you ever heard of the *qanats* of central Iran?"

"No, sir, I haven't."

"Well, Ensign Sabio, the qanats are water tunnels, somewhat like those we're in right now. They're all over the place in the region, which is very flat and very arid. They channel runoff water from the Elburz Mountains into the desertified interior to irrigate crops; sometimes they extend for hundreds of miles. You can spot them from the air by long lines of craters; just endless rows of 'em out on the desert. Sometimes they go down pretty deep. My teams used to use them to get from place to place during the War in Iran. Better than traveling on the surface, especially during the day."

"So what, sir?"

"So, Ensign Sabio, the moral of my little story is that just because you assume we're using GPS nav down here, it doesn't necessarily mean we're in fact doing as you imagine," Krieger answered. "The tablet is programmed using inertial navigation software, like Pave Low helicopters use, called Individual Soldier Navigation. I don't need GPS satellites to get us where we're going. DARPA built these units for my teams especially for navigating the qanats in Iran because GPS coverage was unreliable down there, especially with radiation from the blown reactor. I guess I forgot to give mine back.

"Naughty boy, sir."

"Yeah, I'm a little devil when I want to be."

"I've noticed, sir."

"Now let's move. Ensign Sabio, you lead. I'll tell you where we turn."

"Yes, sir."

"And don't call me 'sir" anymore, you got that Ensign Sabio?"

"Yes sir," she said without a pause.

■

Seven hardened killers watched the indicator lights on the top of the elevator shaft doorway flash on and off as the car rose to the fourth and final level. At a nod from Saint they raised their weapons and prepared to flank the slide-open door. The camera inside was not functioning, so the occupant or occupants of the elevator car was an unknown. Comms had been lost, along with Sgt. Nickel Bag's commando squad, some time before.

Saint had instructed the fourth floor welcoming committee to fire on his command. He'd positioned himself behind them from a vantage point that allowed him a good look at the elevator, yet one that afforded secure cover from hostile fires.

The fourth floor LED display winked into numeric mode. The soft whine of the pneumatic lifts ceased. The door slid open.

"Safe those guns," shouted Saint.

The car was empty.

Except for the corpse on the floor.

The corpse lying face-down with the bloodied knife-point protruding from its lower back.

"Sir, I think it's Sgt. Nickel Bag," said the unit leader. "Should I check it out?"

"Negative," Saint countered sharply. "Fall back."

The men did as ordered, and. Saint nodded toward his ordie. Reopening the elevator door, the ordnance expert carefully walked to the corpse and knelt down. He shone a penlight beam on the floor.

"He's wired, sir," the ordie said, continuing to study the lashup. "Probably a trembler bomb setup's my guess."

"Deal with it."

"Yes, sir."

The ordie produced the gear necessary to disarm a trembler lashup. He fed the flexible metal tube gently beneath the body and opened the stopcock on the canister of liquid nitrogen. Filmy clouds and an acrid smell wafted out of the elevator as the ordie worked.

After a few minutes he turned off the stopcock and handed the now ice-cold canister to another team member. The corpse, blood and all, was now frozen solid around its midsection.

More importantly, the mercury filling the half-inch glass tube was hopefully frozen solid, and so could not slosh between the wire electrodes and complete the circuit that would cause the detonator to set off the C-4 charge under the cadaver.

Sweating now, the ordie carefully began rolling the body over. He breathed a sigh of relief when he saw that the mercury was indeed flash-frozen in place. Moving quickly, and with cool competence, he snipped the red and black wires connecting the detonator to the C-4 block.

He did not see the grenade hidden under the dead Sgt. Nickel Bag's helmet, though, until it rolled out onto the floor. He had only a split-instant to register that cotter pin and spoon were missing and to calculate that he had up to four seconds to get beyond the twenty-five foot splinter radius prior to detonation.

Krieger had cut the grenade fuze down, though, so it would explode in just over a second flat. Unable to react, the ordie was ripped apart by the high explosive splinter cone when the charge went off. The blast and splinter cone of the detonating mini-grenade was mostly absorbed by his body.

Saint smiled grimly amid clouds of acrid cordite smoke billowing from the elevator. At least the elevator was still usable. That was his main concern, anyway.

"Clean it out. Burial detail," he ordered the survivors.

All around him his merc force sprang into action.

Turning on his heels Saint strode back toward the Pentagon's command center. His face was set, an unreadable mask, yet his thoughts were black and bent on vengeance.

Somebody would pay big-time for this bullshit, he promised himself.

■

"Left. *Now.*"

Sabio turned on Krieger's instructions. They had been slogging through the dark, damp tunnel for the better part of an hour. The tunnel was part of a network of interconnecting underground passageways, vaults and drainage cisterns.

Had it been later in the year or had there been heavier runoff from the rain or snows of early autumn, these would have made passage impossible as the water level would have been too high. It was often necessary to crawl down ladders into cisterns and take other connection tunnels. Fortunately, the first third of September had been dry and there was only a trickle of water lining the concrete floor. After fifteen minutes both Krieger and Sabio had developed intense claustrophobia and the blinking icon on Krieger's tablet was less and less a consolation.

Finally Krieger told Sabio that it was another hundred yards to the vertical shaft that terminated at street level on a greensward a few hundred yards from the bank of the Potomac. They found the steel access ladder that extended upward to street level. They could smell the change in the air as they mounted it, saw daylight seeping down in a white ring around the circle of the hatch.

Krieger discovered that the hatch wouldn't budge. Its interior handle was frozen shut. It was also badly rusted. Krieger was afraid that if they hit it too hard that the latch would shatter. Finally, though, it budged, then gave, and Krieger raised the lid to expose a circle of blue sky. Cold, clear air poured down on them, blowing through their hair, washing their faces.

"You first, Ensign Sabio," Krieger said, and followed her to the surface, noting in passing, and apropos of nothing, that Sabio had a nice little ass.

Blinking in the unaccustomed brightness Krieger at first thought he was hallucinating.

A phalanx of camo-fatigued soldiers faced them, pointing weapons at them. An Army UH-60A Blackhawk helo, main rotors slowly revolving, was parked by the bank of the river. A soldier with colonel's stars on his epaulettes and black beret cocked sprucely on his head stepped forward.

He saluted them smartly.

"Mr. Krieger, you're wanted at the White House," he informed them.

"How the hell did you know I'd be here?"

"All I know is that the president issued orders for us to come get you, sir. She wants to see you immediately."

"What if I don't want to see her?"

Linda Halifax hadn't wanted to see Krieger since becoming president. The feeling was mutual.

"I have my orders, Mr. Krieger."

He gestured toward the squad of armed soldiers flanking the chopper.

Krieger shrugged and he and Ensign Sabio walked toward the chopper. The rotors were already dishing as they stepped inside the powerful slick and took seats on benches projecting horizontally along the sides of the interior hull.

The colonel had hardly closed the side hatch when the helo rose in a steep vertical ascent, translated at sixty feet, and then sped east across the Potomac toward downtown Washington, DC.

*DAY TWO:*
*MONDAY*
*SEPTEMBER 12*TH

**STOP AT NOTHING**

DAVID ALEXANDER

Ten
**Please Don't Eat the Snake Eaters**

"You want me to what, Linda?"

"The correct form of address is 'Madam President,' Mr. Krieger."

This was from the White House chief of staff Burt Funk who sat in on the meeting.

"Let me ask you something, Percy," Krieger began.

"The name is Burt, sir."

"OK. Let me ask you something, Percy. If you had just spent the last twelve hours in the middle of hell, needed a shower, and then were confronted by a woman who is probably still wearing one of the bras you bought her, would you observe the formalities?"

Halifax interjected before her principal aide could speak up.

"Let's stop this bullshit right now," she ordered. "Krieger, I know full-well you've been through the ringer since the crisis began. And I do understand your personal animosity toward me. If I were in your place I might conceivably feel the same. Nevertheless, the need for your services to your country remains as stated."

"And my answer is still the same. N-O. I will not go back there and conduct recon for the snake eaters. I will not commit suicide in the name of honor or patriotism or anything else, including truth, justice and the American way. Forget it, Mrs. President."

"Krieger," Halifax pressed, "there's no other option and no one else to do it. You alone have the mix of skills and knowledge to bring it off. You know every inch of hidden Pentagon corridor. You've ably demonstrated that the commando skills for which you were decorated in the service of your country have not gone stale. Your country needs you again, Krieger. This is not a time for old grudges to stand in the way."

"I said no."

The president was silent for a long moment.

"Name your price, Krieger," she said. "Whatever it is, we'll pay it."

"I don't want anything from anybody. I just want to leave."

"It's not like you're being asked to play an active role in the battle. That's for the Delta Force people to undertake. Your role would be confined to reconnaissance. All that's asked of you is to be their eyes and ears inside the Pentagon. With the benefit of intelligence from someone on the inside they can accurately pinpoint the targets.

"With you we can apply a surgical scalpel. Without you, it could mean the wrecking ball. Who knows what damage could be done to the Pentagon in the course of an air strike? The devastation could be catastrophic."

"My answer is still no."

"Bring in the colonel," Halifax said, turning to the COS.

An officer in uniform entered the Oval Office, preceded by an announcement, via intercom, from presidential secretary Harriet Rosen, who sat at an Empire desk outside the room. The desk, like most of the furnishings chosen by the new president and her transition team, had been selected from the vast treasure trove of antiques that filled portions of the White House basement; artifacts that had been presented as gifts, as the nation reached its Tricentennial year, for almost three centuries.

The officer, wearing an Army green A-uniform, saluted, then stood at ease.

"This is Colonel Robin Hawk. He'll be leading the Delta Force strike on the Pentagon, with or without your help."

"We could sure use your assistance, Mr. Krieger," Hawk, whose nickname "Red" was based on his less macho-sounding given name, said. "Our operational plan is sound. But we lack good reconnaissance and surveillance intel on what's actually happening on the inside. Sure, we could send in scouts, but they lack your intimate knowledge of the interior landscape. You've got the fingertip feel for the place. Nobody else -- at least nobody else we can lay hands on in a hurry -- has that."

"I'll be happy to spell it all out for you in a debrief," Krieger insisted, "but as to going in, forget it. I'm not suicidal."

Halifax looked from the colonel to Krieger. She nodded, more to confirm some inner train of thought than to acknowledge anything anyone else had said. She then crossed to one side of the desk that fronted the French doors with the Yellow Rose Garden beyond.

"I didn't want to have to do this, Krieger," she said. "But I'm afraid you've forced my hand."

Halifax nodded at her chief of staff.

"Mr. Krieger," he began, producing a sheaf of printouts. "I hold here the results of a secret IRS audit conducted this morning. It shows that you have played fast and loose with your finances while CEO of Global Threat Solutions. I won't mince words. If you don't cooperate, the IRS will be authorized to audit you going back beyond the ordinary three years to a total of ten years. You could stand to lose your business, your home, everything."

Krieger was silent. He cast his eyes from the president to the chief of staff.

"I'm waiting."

"For what?"

"For you to bring out the pictures of me giving blowjobs to gorillas and fucking sheep in the ass."

"Mr. Krieger, I hardly think -- "

"Fuckers, you listen up, all of you," Krieger shouted, voice now risen to a roar. "I won't be bribed or blackmailed. I refuse to risk my life. Period."

He stormed out of the office.

The Yellow Rose Garden that stood behind the West Wing afforded a place to walk. Krieger had enjoyed taking walks here when as White House national security advisor he felt the confines of his office too great to stay at his desk. The blue photo ID badge clipped to his breast pocket visible to the White House guards his passport to fresh air, Krieger sat down on a bench beneath a willow tree. The sun was breaking through the haze of cloud cover over the Capital. The trees were already beginning to show the first turnings of autumn. Krieger thought back on the events that had brought him here. It had only been yesterday, a matter of hours really, but it seemed like it had actually been a year.

The Blackhawk chopper that had lifted off with himself and Sabio onboard had followed

# THREATCON DELTA

Pennsylvania Avenue after crossing the Potomac, had set down on the helipad on the lawn in front of the North Portico of the White House. Krieger and Sabio were escorted by a phalanx of troops into the executive mansion's lobby and up the private elevator to the president's West Wing office complex where the president had awaited their arrival in the Oval Office.

President Linda Halifax had arrived only an hour prior to Krieger and Sabio's touchdown on the White House helipad. She had spent the last two days and nights five hundred feet below the earth's surface, amid the maze of tunnels of the Mount Weather Special Facility that honeycombed the Catoctin Mountains of Pennsylvania where emergency security plans had deposited her. Against the wishes of her chief advisors she decided to return to the White House. It wouldn't look right for the president to be cowering underground when a full-fledged crisis loomed and all Americans found themselves threatened by disaster.

Despite its severity, the national crisis fortunately appeared an isolated incident. It took place against a backdrop of relative international calm. There had been a lull in Russia's more militant activities in the Transcaucasus. The Balkans were calm, as was the Middle East. Nor was there any sign of Chinese aggression against

Taiwan despite the People's Republic's recent saber-rattling in the UN Security Council, nor, for that matter, was the Korean peninsula showing any indications of impending trouble.

The DEFCON level, downgraded from two, would remain at three for the present.

Cabinet hawks had it otherwise. They claimed that the takeover of the symbol of America's military might could not possibly be a mere isolated incident. It therefore had to be linked to an overarching plot, at the worst, an attempt to stage a coup d'état, at the least, yet another attempt to stage a major terrorist assault on the order of the outrages of September 11th, 2001 or of the infamous Strike Day that had followed years later. The president wouldn't buy the "tip of the iceberg" argument pushed by the Cabinet's war groupies, at least not a face value, at least not until more facts were in.

Moreover, she was skeptical of militarists and hardliners in general, and her skepticism extended to those hawks in her own presidential cabinet. Like Roosevelt had done with William Stimson and Clinton had done with William Cohen, Halifax, a democrat, had reached out to republicans in order to build a coalition cabinet. As the first woman president in US history, Halifax was aware that her administration faced unprecedented challenges as well as unique opportunities. She knew above all, that whatever the final outcome of the takeover of the Pentagon, her actions in the face of the crisis would stand as an acid test of her power to govern. Halifax knew that she dared not fail or falter in the face of this test, both for her own political welfare and the country's enduring good.

She'd signed the order for a Delta Force team to be assembled in preparation for a paramilitary assault on the Building, but she didn't want that to happen either. To her mind, scenes of a firefight inside the Pentagon, possibly even more of the kind of highly visible damage to the Building of the type that the 911 attack had produced, could be destructive, win or lose.

The best resolution would be a quick, quiet one. A resolution that tied up all the loose ends, and tied them up fast.

If the terrorists -- or whatever they in fact actually were -- that had gotten control of the Building needed to be dealt with, that was fine. But she wanted a surgical approach, not a bull-in-the-china-shop boondoggle. As soon as she had received word of the Pentagon takeover, Halifax's thoughts had turned to Rommel Krieger.

She had known that Krieger would escape. Somehow she had no doubt about it. Halifax's feelings and emotions about Krieger were hard to define. She had loved him once, but she had also hated him. Krieger was a driven man. He had demons inside him that made him unbearable. He called them his *demonische geist*, that Germanic spirit of combativeness that certain men have. Krieger, she reflected, came from a long line of Germans. The fact that some of them had changed sides in World War Two, become American citizens, and enlisted in the US military to fight against the Nazis didn't change the Teutonic craziness that had come packaged in Krieger's genes.

Halifax knew that Krieger hated her guts for siding with Albright against him for the post of Secretary of State, but Krieger had no place in her administration. He was too coarse, too pugnacious, and he'd had too many enemies on the way in to make him a part of a presidential administration whose goal was to build political bridges across party lines. She'd bowed to the wisdom of cutting him loose. Halifax was pragmatic to the core. She'd had no other recourse if her presidency was to work.

Linda Halifax had stopped being a woman when she'd moved into the White House. As the President of the United States, Rommel Krieger had no place in her life. The political and media repercussions of Krieger's presence at the White House would have raised scandal. The press had already begun dubbing him her "Vincent Foster."

No taint of scandal could touch this administration, she vowed. Besides, brilliant as Krieger was, he could never brook dissent, nor suffer fools in silence.

Yet she also knew that to end this crisis she needed Krieger. He had been inside, at ground zero. He had personally taken out a platoon of killers and escaped. Krieger, and the young Navy ensign who had escaped with him, was the only eyewitness to the goings on inside. His debrief would provide invaluable information, and the team of military and intelligence analysts would question him as soon as Halifax was done.

But the president also had one other task she wanted Krieger to perform on behalf of the country. Halifax knew that she would have to force him into it. But she would do it somehow. They didn't call her the Steel Rose for nothing -- even though, for the moment, it was still behind her back.

■

The East Wing of the White House has traditionally been the First Lady's province. It houses the most splendid salons, such as the Yellow Oval Room, and a large banquet hall. It also contains suites for guests who stay at the executive mansion at the pleasure of the president.

The fact that presidents and kings, to say nothing of queens and princes, had stood under the same shower head that was now firing jets of steaming hot water onto his aching shoulder blades, did nothing to lighten Krieger's dark mood.

The bitch -- and by this he was referring to the president -- had a knack for making the wrong overtures at the wrong times. How she'd managed to win a mandate in the last presidential election was beyond his comprehension. Of course, her highness had enjoyed the services of a brilliant, if deluded person named Rommel Krieger, not only in bed, but as her principal campaign adviser. Said sucker Krieger's strategic manipulations during the hard road of the presidential campaign had certainly helped a great deal.

Krieger stepped from the shower stall, toweled himself off and went into the room. He sat on the edge of the bed and poured himself a shot of bourbon. He had asked for a bottle and some sandwiches and one of the White House staffers had brought it all in on a platter.

Krieger decided he would not be swayed by appeals from the Oval Office, however well-intentioned. National security be damned. National honor be fucked. He had predicted that the bitch would need his advice or help on some critical issue eventually and events had proven him correct. Krieger had sworn a mighty oath to laugh in her face should Halifax ever ask him to pull her chestnuts out of the fire. And now he would do precisely as he'd planned.

Let the snake eaters fire away. That was their job. Let the NSC honchos and their backseaters down in the White House Sit Room worry over it in their fiberglass-lined cubbies two stories below the Great Seal of the Republic emblazoned on the circular carpet of the Oval Office. That was their job too. Krieger was out of it. As to their threats of an IRA audit, let them audit away. They could take it all as far as he cared. House. Car. Office. The whole shebang, lock, stock and barrel. Let them have it.

Krieger lay down. He immediately fell asleep.

■

Krieger awoke to the sound of distant gunfire.

He immediately sat up in bed.

He sensed another presence in the darkness of the bedroom.

"The sniper again," said a familiar voice.

The president laid a hand on Krieger's shoulder.

"He or they simply won't be caught. It's uncanny. Almost like they're ghosts."

Krieger turned and saw Linda Halifax's face in the darkness. He was seized by a strange sense of déjà vu.

"What's a nice girl like you doing in a place like this?"

The president laughed.

"I think we're both in the wrong line of work."

He glanced at the bedside clock. It was a little after three in the morning. She had come to him, as he'd suspected she might, sometime after midnight. It had been over for at least two years now, but he'd known she'd come anyway. He had wanted her to, and he knew that when she'd slipped without a word next to him and he'd taken her in his arms and pressed her warm body against his and found her tongue with his own.

"Just go to sleep, Linda," Krieger said. "We're neither of us virgins to any of this, not anymore. Get some rest."

She drew him toward her. He felt the warmth of her breath against his mouth.

"Not quite yet," she whispered, as the wail of police sirens passed along Pennsylvania Avenue, proceeding toward the Ellipse.

Eleven
**The Sun of Austerlitz**

*B*etter they paid the piper now than messed up on the way out, Saint told himself as he inspected the scene in the Pentagon subbasement.

The aftermath of the kill trap was grisly. Body parts, including dismembered limbs, were strewn across the floor, stuck to the walls, pasted to the ceiling. Some were caught in the most unlikely places. Blood, needless to say, was everywhere.

But that, reflected Saint, is what happened when you subjected the fragile human frame to the effects of blast, overpressure and bursts of shrapnel, especially in enclosed spaces. He couldn't say he was shocked. Saint had seen enough battlefields from 'Nam to Nagorno-Karabakh to have reached the point where it all went with the territory. In his mind the many war zones all blended together into a single battlefield -- the Great Mother of all Battlefields that encompassed the hell of all the wars, large, small and in-between -- that General Casper Saint had ever experienced.

Saint produced a Dutch Masters cheroot, a Perfecto panatela. His new horse handler, Captain Da Gamma, was quick to produce a silver Army-issue lighter on which was engraved "Bob Hope Christmas Show, 1971, Long Binh USO, Vietnam."

He held it up, flicked back the metal cover and spun the flint wheel. Da Gamma had replaced the late Sgt. Nickel Bag. So far, so good.

"Vietnam vintage, sir," Da Gamma said. "My grandfather's. You only get that real smell of combustion from one of these."

Saint nodded.

He'd really have to watch this guy, he thought.

"Your report, captain," Saint asked through clouds of acrid gray smoke as the cheroot's tip flared.

The thought flickered through his mind that some of his former XO might be dripping down the section of wall beside him. It flickered for a moment, then was gone. Madness, Saint knew, lay in the direction of thoughts such as those.

"Yes, sir."

Da Gamma smartly snapped shut the lighter, stowed it in his left BDU trouser pocket and proceeded with his brief, consulting a spiral notepad he had pulled from his right trouser pocket.

"The forensic team reports the kill trap was set up by an experienced hand," Da Gamma began. "From the placement of the charges -- which were makeshift Claymores, incidentally -- they ..."

"Makeshift how?" Saint interjected, blowing a perfect smoke ring toward the ceiling.

"Sir, with your permission I can show you," replied Da Gamma.

At a nod from Saint he turned to a laptop and rapidly stroked some keys. An image sprang into being on the computer display in front of Saint. The accompanying text box read: Mst. Sgt. Ronald Timilty.

"Yes, sir," Timilty's voice came out of the display's speakers via the tactical intranet set up by Saint's technicals.

"Timilty you got anything of that roll-your-own ordnance lying around?"

"Sure, sir. Working on a nice-sized fragment right here."

Timilty wore a pair of lightweight eyephone HMDs that showed him a large virtual display in place of a conventional raster screen.

"Bring it over. On the double."

"Yes, sir."

A few minutes later Sgt. Timilty had trotted from the other end of the subbasement to the section where his CO was located, having learned the location from the cursor position on the digital map projected by his eyephones.

"Here's what I mean by makeshift Claymore, sir," Timilty told Saint, handing a shard of blackened gunmetal to his CO.

"Concave steel plating. Lined with C-4 sheets on the concave business-end. Any kind of junk embedded in the plastic. They found nails, ball bearings, bolts -- just anything that could be turned into shrapnel."

Saint pitched the charred metal fragment to the floor where it fell with a dull clanging thud.

"OK. Proceed with the report, Da Gamma," he barked at his XO.

"Sir, as I was saying, the placement of the charges, and the way they were wired to detonate in precise sequential fashion indicates a sophisticated knowledge of setting up this type of kill trap. We're not dealing with a tyro here, sir. This guy's some kind of pro. Ex-special forces maybe."

"It is the voice of Isaac but the hand of Jacob," Saint replied, blowing another smoke ring at the ceiling.

"Excuse me, sir?"

"Old biblical quote, Da Gamma," Saint replied. "You oughta read the Good Book sometimes."

"Yes, sir."

161

# THREATCON DELTA

Saint flashed back to other times and other places. It was strange how they were coming on, the flashbacks, because he hadn't had them in a while -- yet familiar, because it was the old combat rush that had started to come over him since entering the Building earlier that day. It wasn't the ordinary kind of flashbacks that you got from being in combat -- it was a kind of euphoria, but not what you experienced on the battlefield; not quite.

Saint had found one other reference to what he felt in the history of warfare.

Napoleon Bonaparte and his inner circle of field commanders had known the sort of thing that Saint now experienced. They had called it "the Sun of Austerlitz." It had been a kind of intoxication that had come over them at the battle of Austerlitz. The "Battle of the Three Emperors" as they'd called it back then, that took place on December 2nd, 1805.

French Troops reported that the light that flooded over the battlefield had been a thing of almost supernatural beauty. The light of Austerlitz had filled Napoleon's soldiery, inspiring them, transporting them to a higher plane of being. In that divine light, in that living, almost liquid luminescence, they had fought as gods, or perhaps demigods, but not as mere mortal men. And they had prevailed against all odds to win the day for the fledgling French republic.

The memory of that special light had filled Napoleon and his young lions on that field of battle. It was as if the light had been a living flame that had bonded with the cells of their blood. The Sun of Austerlitz had from that day on become a token of their being favored by fate to win, win again, and keep on winning. And it was when that sun had set and the light had faded that they had begun the downward slide into defeat and desperation that was to end for them on the Russian steppes and for their leader at the barren South Atlantic prison rock called St. Helena.

General Casper Saint had seen that light at the battle of Spin Gar Bor in Afghanistan. His troops had been pinned down by determined Pathan hill fighters. Yet in the cold fastness of the high mountain passes, the sun of Austerlitz had again shone down and illuminated Saint's troops in its strengthening glow.

All had felt it, seen it, sensed it enter inside them like an incubus. They too had become more than men, if less than gods of war. And they had prevailed. Later, Saint had called the men together and told them about Napoleon and his troops. Some of those men were with him now, at the Pentagon.

163

# THREATCON DELTA

Saint too had been to Elba. It was not a physical island in a physical sea, but it was a place of terrible loneliness and isolation that could shatter the human spirit against the rocks of despair. But Saint had escaped from that dark, lonely, spirit-destroying hole in Thailand in which the DIA spooks and their associate mindfuckers in "the intelligence community" had dropped him down to die. And now he lived again. And the Sun of Austerlitz shone again.

Shone from the inside out.

Let it shine, thought Saint. Let it shine forever. A line from Shakespeare's Hamlet came to his mind. That I shall live and tell him to his teeth, "Thus didst thou." And then Saint had another notion. He recalled that Tolstoy, in War and Peace, had written of the Sky of Austerlitz and had made it a symbol of the emptiness and futility and folly of war, all war, those that had been fought and all those still to come.

"I want the burial detail to work double time. The remains of KIAs are to be burned in the main heating furnace. The casualties' names are to be recorded. When this is over their next of kin will receive their back pay with a hazardous duty bonus."

"Yes, sir."

Saint flicked ash from the tip of his now half-smoked cheroot, spun on the heels of his combat boots and headed toward the elevator. He had business to attend to on the Pentagon's fourth floor. No more philosophical bullshit. It was time to get the gears turning. The operational tempo of the mission must be maintained, not permitted to flag. The OPLAN took x-factors, such as pockets of resistance that might result in casualties to his men, into consideration.

It was not so much that this eventuality had materialized that concerned General Saint, but that certain bits of data tended to come together to indicate that the individual behind the slaughter of his men was a potential problem. And that individual was Rommel Krieger.

By now Saint had not a shadow of a doubt that this Krieger was the same a hard-charger by the same name from the past. Blitz Krieger, the SAN Man. Stop-at-Nothing Krieger, they'd called him then, or the "Sandman" most of the time. Arrogant sonofabitch. Boasted of putting all the enemy's bad little boys to sleep -- permanently. Made more than one enemy trooper's shit turn white in those days. This same Krieger had to have been the Sandman. Yeah -- had to be.

Yet he'd heard the Sandman had died on the battlefield years ago. Probably a cover story concocted to smooth Krieger's transition into civilian life. Well, thought Saint, let him inject his unwanted presence into the Pentagon op and the Sandman would be put down permanently.

The digital fourth floor indicator lit up. Acrid gray clouds of pungent cigar smoke announced the CINC's presence as he strode into the NMCC command center. Saint had the world on a string, and the other end of the string was tied to his dick. He had planned this op for years, waited patiently, bided his time. Ever since Thailand, when he'd made up his mind to do it, he'd lived with the dream of its accomplishment. All contingencies had been entered into the planning matrix, all possibilities foreseen and accounted for.

It didn't matter if the Sandman was back, Saint thought. He couldn't do shit, not jack fuckin' shit.

But there was a nagging voice at the back of his mind that Saint couldn't suppress. Because Saint knew this one thing, which was that, like him, the Sun of Austerlitz had once shone on the Sandman too, and that it had bonded with the cells of his blood.

And if that was so, then Blitz Krieger would be back, and Saint, for all his bravado, knew that this meant one thing.

Trouble.

■

The National Military Command Center or NMCC comprises a warren of large and small rooms. These rooms take up most of Wedge Three

-- the northeastern corner of the five roughly triangular sections that further divide the five-cornered Pentagon building into as many parts -- on the fourth and fifth floors between Rings E through C.

The NMCC was now ablaze with activity. Saint's thoughts had returned to current business, which there was a great deal of to transact in a very short span of time. Banquo's ghost in the Pentagon subbasement had vanished, the Quasimodo of the catacombs had flown the coop.

Better for Krieger if he stayed that way. Saint figured it was even money he'd escaped just after Sgt. Nickel Bag's squad stumbled into the kill trap he'd set up. That was the Sandman's way of working. He'd stick around to make sure it went down right, then ghost away.

Having at least two handy ratlines, an alpha and a baker, was also part of his MO. The Sandman was undoubtedly miles away by now. He'd left his calling card -- the IED that had blown away the kill squad's point men. Now he was gone. For Krieger's sake, Saint hoped he wasn't dumb enough to come back again. Not even the sunshine in the blood would keep him alive in that event. No power on earth would remove the doom from the Sandman if he crossed paths with Saint.

Saint's cheroot was smoked down to a dead butt by the time he got down to business. That was okay by the general who liked bogarting the suckers awhile before he lit up fresh ones. He checked the Tag-Huer chronometer banded tight on his left wrist. It was time to get the ball rolling.

The OPLAN called for positive control of COLOSUS by 1100 hours and it was now almost game time.

Red Dog Juan, one of only three noncombatants in Gold Force, was the key to this happening. The Colombian was a cybernetic genius. El Bloque Meta, main successor to the Cali cartel, had paid him well for his services in international money laundering via untraceable cyber-cash networks, but he'd gotten bored with the job.

The grapevine had given Juan the intel that Saint was planning a massively important op and Juan had made Saint an offer he couldn't refuse. One morning, Saint had found an email message from Juan offering him his services. To show good faith, the message contained a hypertext link to a banking website. The link connected Saint with an account into which Juan had deposited half a million dollars. *Por la Causa* he'd written in the email.

Saint now found Red Dog Juan in the catbird seat, hunched over multiple keyboards. Saint thought his chief technical looked frustrated. If so that was bad news. The timetable had to be painstakingly followed for the op to fly. Saint had impressed this on his troops from the word go. It was their first commandment, their catechism of combat, the rule by which they all lived ... and died if they fucked up.

"*Una problema, mi hermano Pero Rojo?*"

"*Si, Jefe*, big fucking problem."

"Would you care to elaborate?"

Saint rolled over a vacant chair and sat close to his chief technical. The smoked-down cheroot in his face suddenly tasted foul. He plucked a fresh one from his fatigues breast pocket, bit off the end, spat, and lit up.

"Jefe, this system, she is plain loco, all fucked up," began Red Dog Juan.

"Explain."

"It's not that I can't hack the ciphers, Jefe," Red Dog Juan elaborated, "but that there is a cipher key that we did not obtain. Without it I am afraid that I cannot promise you control of COLOSUS." Red Dog Juan saw Saint's face redden. "At least not by the time-table."

"You assured me..." Saint let the words trail off.

"Jefe, the cipher key can be obtained. Easily."

"How."

"General Clayton Rogers -- Bailey's second in command -- has the key, probably in his former boss' safe. Jefe, you must, ah, persuade the general to give you the key, then," and now Red Dog Juan smiled, revealing a gleaming gold incisor, "we are back in business, *generale mio*."

Saint nodded. He could do this. The deputy CJCS was in custody, he was certain of it, he'd check of course, but he was fairly sure of it. Saint keyed his comms on Da Gamma's ID tag. His newly minted XO's image came right onto the net.

"Sir."

"Check this out. General Rogers. He's with the prisoners in Wedge Apex 3?"

"Sir, one moment."

It took a little more than that but Da Gamma was back fast with a confirm on Rogers' location and condition.

"The general is currently among the prisoners confined to the holding facility we've established at Wedge Apex 3. What are your orders, sir?"

"Bring him to his office with a security detail. I'll meet you there."

"Yes, sir."

"And bring these other prisoners too…"

Sometime later, General Saint, yet another freshly lit cheroot clenched between his teeth, walked into the office of the chief of operations. This was probably not going to be pretty ... or easy, but it had to be done. The cipher key was necessary to establish the COLOSUS uplink.

Without the uplink there was no hand to play. It was the one variable in the plan that could not have been dealt with prior to the penetration of the Pentagon. It was the one wild card. To be fair, Saint's Colombian technical had warned him of the potential difficulty in hacking the system. So there was plan Baker. Now Baker would need to be put in action in order to cough up the code. Saint was confident that it would.

General Rogers looked disheveled, as expected. He'd been hunkering in a vacant office under armed guard for several hours without even being able to take a leak if he wanted to. Rogers' bladder hadn't been so tortured since the Second War in Somalia.

"I'll make this short, general," Saint began, blowing smoke through his nostrils, "we need the key code."

"I don't know what you mean."

"General, there's no time for bullshit. You have the COLOSUS key code in your office safe. We want the combination."

"Blow the safe if you want it then, I won't give you anything."

"We'd prefer you gave us the combination. If it were my safe it would be booby trapped."

General Rogers said nothing.

Saint drew his sidearm. It was an Uzi micro machinepistol that he wore slantwise across his chest on a breakaway rig. There was a crisp ripping sound and then the muzzle of the automatic weapon was jutting into the bridge of General Rogers' nose, a point directly between his eyes. Saint recalled how other pairs of eyes had rolled to the center of their orbits, focusing on the gun barrel in a predictable reaction.

Mostly these had been Pathan tribesmen. It was at that point that Saint had usually pulled the trigger. "Kill one, discourage a hundred," was a motto that he had lived by in Afghanistan, Nagorno-Karabakh and other godforsaken places where he'd led men into battle.

"One more chance, general," Saint said calmly.

The general didn't answer. His eyes hadn't rolled either. He'd been there too, Saint knew. A tough nut to crack, but all nuts cracked, sooner or later. That was another lesson of war.

"Too bad, general."

Sweat beaded Rogers' brow. His eyes were dilated. Saint bet the fucker was praying as he spun and jerked the trigger. The room exploded in a cacophony of noise, a symphony punctuated by the tinkle of a score of ejecting shells.

Rogers sagged to his knees and vomited.

With the acrid stench of cordite in his nostrils, Rogers realized with horror that he was still alive. The horror came not so much from this revelation but from the sight of the bodies of General Bailey and his adjutant sprawled across the room's disheveled furnishings.

172

The corpses were riddled with bullet holes. Bailey's imposter had drawn first blood earlier in the Pentagon takeover, when he'd shot his inquisitive secretary, and Saint had now shot both the actor and the colonel who was Bailey's aide. The phony Bailey had outlived his usefulness and had needed to be silenced. The aide -- well, that had just been for fun. Besides, a little extra persuasion never hurt, after all.

"Two by two, general," Saint intoned. "Two by two, then three by three; until you give me the combination. I'll kill and kill again. I need what you have."

Saint slammed a fresh clip into the Uzi's mag well. "Their blood'll be on your hands."

"Okay, you bastard. I'll get it."

Bailey's former deputy CJCS went to the safe in his boss's office. Opened it. Reached inside.

Out came a .45-caliber semiautomatic Beretta pistol, hammer uncocked and the red dot on the receiver indicating that a live round sat in the firing chamber. Rogers had been quick, but Saint's bodyguards were faster still, opening fire and shooting away most of Rogers' gun hand. Saint took the code book from the office safe as the general sagged in a moaning, bleeding heap to the carpeted floor.

"Get a medic over here. The general needs help," barked Saint as he turned, leaving the safe door dangling open.

On his way out, Saint added to the figure writhing on the office carpet.

"That wasn't necessary, general. You fought honorably. But I won. It works that way sometimes. See you later. When you feel -- better."

Red Dog Juan was overjoyed. It took him less than five minutes to key in the small code module.

Five minutes after that he announced, "COLOSUS is uplinked. We are in control, Jefe."

A wave of excitement swept the command center. Gold Force erupted into spontaneous cheers and applause.

"We've got a long road still to travel, gentlemen," Saint announced. "So let's get back to work."

Saint had his own job to do now. He had an announcement to make. Red Dog Juan nodded. The secure uplink was open. Saint had an unbreakable channel link to the White House. His message would right many old wrongs and undoubtedly start new hatreds festering. That was the way of the world and the way of warfare.

Wrongs avenged always led to further wrongs in an unending cycle of violent confrontation.

## DAVID ALEXANDER

One day the world would destroy itself, of this Saint had no doubt. But first he would win this one last battle.

Twelve
**Render Unto Chaos What Belongs to Chaos**

General Casper Saint made himself comfortable and faced the tiny webcam. Red Dog Juan had spent hours setting up secure communications links from the NMCC to the outside world. He'd just signaled his CINC that everything was ready.

"President Halifax," Saint began. "How are we feeling today?"

The face that looked back at the general was gray and careworn. Saint understood. He would look the same way if men with assault weapons were holding him hostage, even metaphorically, and at a distance.

President Linda Halifax did not answer Saint's rhetorical question.

"I'll dispense with the pleasantries, Madame President," Saint said, lighting up a fresh Dutch Masters Perfecto. "You understand the situation. I'll cut to the chase. I've taken control of the tactical nerve center of the Pentagon. I'm sitting in the catbird seat, ma'am. From here I have

176

command and control over almost ninety percent of America's nuclear arsenal and access to the orbital MILSATCOM network. A sobering thought, isn't it?"

"What's your point?" asked Halifax.

"Ma'am, I am a loyal American. In part I have taken this action to call attention to the deficiencies in security at this installation. You now know that the Pentagon is highly vulnerable to attack and occupation, more so than anyone would have previously suspected. I would suggest that this knowledge is worth something, call it a ... consulting fee, if you like."

"I won't negotiate," answered the president.

"You haven't heard my terms," Saint replied. "Under the circumstances you'll find them reasonable."

The president was a law-and-order freak, and would need some incentive to cut a deal, but this had been considered by Saint.

"It doesn't matter. This administration will not negotiate with terrorists. Period."

"Ma'am President, I take exception to that remark. I am not a terrorist. As I have said I am a loyal American --"

"-- You're a terrorist sonofabitch and a prison escapee. I suspect you're also insane. But whatever you are or are not, you won't get away with this criminal act that you and your confederates have committed."

"You're distraught, ma'am," Saint calmly suggested. "We won't talk anymore for awhile. Maybe you need a little rest. We can talk later. There's still plenty of time for you to change your mind."

He added, "And you'll have to, Madame President -- in the end."

Saint abruptly severed the communications channel to the White House. The president was a weak link. Steel Rose or not, she would fold in the end.

Saint could afford to play a waiting game.

At least for now.

■

"Well, that confirms our worst fears, I'm afraid."

President Linda Halifax swiveled around in the black leather wingback chair behind the glass-topped, polished maple desk in her circular office in the West Wing of the White House. For the better part of the last half hour she'd been facing the flat panel screen built into the wall near the Oval Office's entrance door.

Halifax now turned to face the five cabinet-level advisors who sat on chairs arranged in a rough semicircle in front of the presidential office's fireplace. The advisors, which included Warren Rutledge, Secretary of State, Melissa Samuels,

National Security Advisor and Burton Funk, White House Chief of Staff, wore looks of shock that were nearly identical to the expression on their boss' face.

It was to have been expected. They had all entered a waking nightmare from which there was no flight. Using the Pentagon's tactical internet real-time multimedia links to the outside world, General Saint had informed them that he was in control of the space-based weapon network code-named COLOSUS, a web of six geostationary platforms encircling the planet.

COLOSUS was to have been destroyed by the previous administration. It had been secretly put in place over the course of two decades using covert payloads on military space plane missions.

President Halifax thought back on the secret intelligence briefing she had been given by the CIA Director Hampton Yee a few days after the Inauguration. Halifax had learned then that the NMD program, standing for National Missile Defense, that was to have created a defensive network of mobile theater-range launchers to defend the continental United States against both conventional and cruise missile attack, had been judged a failure almost from its inception.

Her predecessor had signed a presidential finding authorizing a radical alternate solution in the form of a covert parallel program: placing into orbit -- and building in secure, bombproof caverns situated deep underground -- the only antimissile technology of the also canceled Strategic Defense Initiative program that had actually ever worked.

This technology was code-named COLOSUS for Core Long Range Operating System United States.

National Missile Defense had then itself been relegated to a mere deception campaign to disguise the secret efforts to deploy COLOSUS as the strategic defensive shield of choice. Even so, the program had its critics and detractors. Behind the scenes, protests of the dangers which COLOSUS posed slowly gained momentum, until by the end of the outgoing administration its dismantlement was mandated by closed session of Congress.

The outgoing president had signed an executive order requiring its dismantlement within a six-month time frame. Yet the incoming president's cabinet hawks had turned the tables and rescinded that executive order. COLOSUS would remain in place until a new Defense Department study was completed. Too much money had been spent, they argued. Besides, they claimed, there was no other alternative to protecting the US against surprise nuclear, chemical and biological attack.

Halifax's thoughts returned to the dangers of the moment as she again surveyed the room from a reclining position in her wingback executive chair. Also present in the Oval Office was Rodman Blanks, head of the Defense Policy Review Board. Though the DPRB had no official powers, and Blanks served at the pleasure of the sitting president, Blanks wielded tremendous persuasive power in the administration.

It was Blanks who was adamantly opposed to the dismantlement of COLOSUS, calling such a move a pathetic blunder by "fainthearted appeasers of America's enemies," although able to be no more specific than "terrorists in general" in citing those enemies by name when questioned by the press. Blanks also owned controlling interests in several aerospace defense subcontractors in the US, and their affiliates abroad, that had commercial interests in COLOSUS.

The president now turned to Blanks.

"What do you think of your idea now?" she asked.

Blanks stuttered.

"Madam president, I can say --- "

Halifax cut Blanks off.

"--You can say nothing. Neither can I. In my heart I knew it was madness to keep that ... that abomination up there and automate the SIOP.

"The reasoning was sound -- still is -- "

"-- No, darling," Halifax said to the NSA who'd just piped in, "it was never sound. The concept was to automate the SIOP. It was a concept that had been part of the Pentagon's deep-black studies back during the McNamara days in the sixties, but then those studies had been directed against the Soviet Union. Those earlier conclusions had been rejected as unworkable, potentially leading to the extermination of human life on the planet."

"But this isn't -- " Blanks began, half-rising from his seat.

The president held up her hand.

"Let me finish, Rod, darling. I understand all the whys and wherefores. I understand the inexorable logic, that by doing what we did the terrorists know that if they hit us with another hecatomb their patrons in Indonesia and elsewhere will be utterly destroyed with inhuman speed and computerized precision. Not mutually assured destruction, but unilaterally assured retribution. COLOSUS would control the SIOP and trigger Northern Cross, and hundreds of thousands would die."

"And it's worked, Ma'am," the NSA quickly put in with fervor, seizing a pause in the president's declamation to lean forward and punctuate his outburst with a slam of his right fist into his cupped left palm.

"No, darling. The *threat* of it worked -- the technology itself was far too Draconian to ever be a realistic choice for any sane government. And do you know what else? It's led to the morass that Saint and his private paramilitary army -- an army made up of the cast-off scum of five continents -- has now led us into.

"Ma'am, I disagree -- " Blanks began.

"-- And I don't care whether you disagree or not," she interjected with obvious anger, slamming her hands on the desktop.

"To me it's apparent that there's a direct causal connection between General Saint's takeover of the Pentagon and our failure to dismantle COLOSUS. Saint knows all about COLOSUS. He knows the threat it harbingers for the nation and the world.

Most alarmingly," she concluded, "Saint knows that he can exploit and manipulate us. We've lied to America about COLOSUS. Saint understands this. He grasps this central organizing principle of our national indecisiveness full well. And he furthermore surmises, perhaps with more accuracy than we ourselves yet realize, that we'll have to treat with him in secret eventually."

She glanced from face to face around the room.

"The pathetic part is, my friends, I think Saint's got our number."

*And now I'm paying for my mistake, and Lord help us, we'll all pay the piper before this is over*, she thought as she finished speaking and the room fell silent for a few long seconds.

183

"Madam president -- it's not that bad. There are ... some options."

It was Bill Furst, Assistant National Security Advisor to NSA Melissa Samuels, who had spoken.

"Really? Would you care to enumerate them?"

"Certainly, ma'am."

Furst was young, brash and eager to win himself a prominent place in the annals of US history. He'd already won acclaim for his Defense Department position papers calling for a revival of certain aspects of Cold War nuclear brinkmanship as a practical tool of foreign policy. He was a comer, but he was still way out of his depth when confronting the president.

There were no options, no answers, and Halifax knew it. Hell, everybody in the room knew it, probably including Samuels and Blanks, whatever they might argue, as well as Furst himself. Well, let them all have their say, Halifax thought; this was an open forum. Halifax sat back and gave the deputy NSA her full attention.

"Option one," Furst began. "We get a crack CERT unit into action. Interdict the Pentagon computer cloud -- hack into the server clusters. Regain positive control of the secure COLOSUS uplink channels.

Option two: Prepare Rapid Reaction Teams to take appropriate protective action on the assumption that COLOSUS will be activated and deployed; this could save millions of lives.

Option three: Prepare a multiple Hauler mission to orbitally interdict COLOSUS space platforms and destroy them in place."

The president's already tarnished estimation of Samuels and Furst fell another notch. Halifax respected people who admitted realities, however harsh. Furst was willing to sell a line of bullshit in order to advance his career. He would dance on the corpses of billions if it could save his own skin; that was a harsh assessment, she immediately realized; hyperbole, but not by that much.

"Those options of yours are perfect except for one thing," Halifax replied gamely.

"What's that, ma'am?"

"None of them, darling, are worth a tin shit. We all know they're unworkable."

"But, ma'am -- "

"But nothing. A CERT team's incursions would be spotted instantly and COLOSUS activated. COLOSUS would retaliate by triggering Northern Cross. Nothing could stop it at that point. We all know that many more innocent persons would die than would live, and the Hauler mission -- even if it could be mounted in time -- would never make it into orbit in time to stop the mass killing."

Furst, now silent, sank his head, unable to hold the president's steady gaze.

The silence in the Oval Office was broken by the electronic warbles that signaled the Department of Justice and Homeland Security chiefs coming online. They too weighed in with their suggestions. In the end it was decided to treat the unfolding crisis as a terrorist incident in progress and go by the book in contending with it.

First a negotiator would be put in place to deal with Saint. This effort would have to be played by ear. More exotic strategies could be discussed later on.

FBI Director Stanley Hickman offered five candidates for the negotiator job. The president liked none of them. Halifax had another suggestion.

"There was this fellow Strake who played in the Taiwan airport hijack crisis of last November. Why didn't you mention him?"

Hickman instantly puckered; he looked as if he'd just sucked on a lemon.

"Strake's a loose canon, Madam President. He's ... well, frankly he's got some problems -- with his head, if you know what I mean."

There were grunts of acknowledgment from various individuals present in the advisory crescent, and a ripple of laughter. Many in the room knew about Jackson Strake, if only by reputation.

"The media called him the 'Terrorist Doctor' didn't they?"

"Yeah, they did -- and I believe his cognomen was actually 'Doctor Fear.' But ma'am, Strake's plain bad news. Like I said, he's a head case."

Halifax leaned forward. She fixed Hickman with a determined look.

"Get him. The other candidates won't cut it."

"Look, ma'am, why don't we go with Professor McKinney from Cal Tech? He's got a good record. That incident, the one at Damascus -- "

"-- you call an airport full of corpses 'a good record, darling?'"

"Well, ma'am, all I'm saying --

"-- I want Strake on this job. That's an order. Period."

"Yes, ma'am."

Hickman's puckered expression quickly grew a few more basset folds.

President Halifax turned back to her advisors. This was going to be a long morning, she suspected.

## Thirteen
### CIA-0 Venezia

*T*he throaty putter of the boat's engine echoed off the ochre stone walls of the surrounding Renaissance buildings as it chugged along the narrow canal filled with brackish green water. Two men were in the boat. Both were stonemasons, the man at the prow a master, the one behind, his apprentice. They ferried a load of sand and cinderblock from Dorsudoro to the Ca' Resonica section of Venice. They had turned from the Grand Canal into the Rio della Madonna, a narrow *rio* or side canal that was a shortcut into the sections of Venice lying toward the center of the ancient city.

The younger man in back worked the tiller of the boat's Criss-Craft outboard motor, while the man in front yawned idly and blinked in the early morning sunshine. His eyes spotted a familiar sight on the timeworn stone steps of one of the landing stages on the canal-side frontage of an ancient palazzo flanking the venerable gray marble of the rio's paved banks.

Elsewhere, buildings had driveways. Here, where there were no roads and no cars, and everything besides pedestrian traffic moved along the water, there were docks, or poles at which boats could tie up.

On the wet stone steps was the same large black canal rat that the boatman usually happened on at that hour. He had taken a slingshot with him that morning, expecting to see it again. He was going to get that rat. No reason, really. Just for fun.

At the moment the big water rat was eating a piece of cheese, deftly turning it around in its strangely human-looking, hand-like pink paws as its needle-sharp teeth gnawed it down to a crumb.

The apprentice stonemason in the canal boat's prow licked his lips. A smile crossed his vulpine face as he took careful aim....

At the precise moment when he would have shot the pebble gripped between thumb and forefinger the slingshot leapt from his hand with wrenching force. A moment later he heard the supersonic crack of the bullet that had done it. He turned, looking this way and that, but detected no sign of human presence on the rooftops of the stone *palazzi* fronting the canal or in the blank windows of the ancient buildings, or, for that matter, on the landing stages that many of them were equipped with to receive canal boats a their second floor levels.

The apprentice boatman was left with only a single recourse. He made the sign of the cross as the frightened rat scurried into its hole in the palazzo's foundation wall.

As the stonemasons' boat disappeared around a bend in the curving canal, the rat scurried up the stone steps to the top floor of the palazzo. A man with a silenced Walther semiautomatic fixed to a precision shoulder stock stood on the balcony one story above the canal. As the rat reached him, the gunman was slowly, yet deftly, unscrewing the stubby cylindrical add-on from the pistol's muzzle.

He had waited precisely twenty seconds before touching it, after which he knew it would be cool enough, after a single nine-millimeter round, to handle. Mitch Werbel, who had designed the SIONICs silencer that the shooter now placed in his trouser pocket, had personally assured him of this, at the school for mercenaries in Georgia called Cobray that he'd run decades before.

The rat scurried up the pants leg of the man with the smoking gun who placed the small mammal on his shoulder, making frightened sounds.

"We scared that fucker pretty good, huh, Luigi?" he said to the rat as he stroked its small furry head and its long, pink, almost reptilian tail. "He won't bother us anymore, I think."

The rat squeaked with pleasure. Strake gave it another piece of Swiss cheese and set it down in its play pen which was filled with pine shavings. Far from being a native of the canals, Black Luigi was a hooded rat, the kind used in laboratory testing. Luigi had been awaiting experimentation in the laboratory of a Swiss-Italian cosmetics firm located in an industrial complex in the South Tyrol when Strake had rescued him. At first the sight of a rat had filled him with disgust, but then he saw how clean the creature was, and also how intelligent, Black Luigi had become Strake's dearest friend. Nobody messed with Luigi while Strake was around.

It was time to go out and do some shopping. Strake liked strolling over the Rialto bridge and buying what he needed at the vegetable market on the other side of the humpbacked Renaissance bridge near Fondaco dei Tedeschi, where there'd been a Venetian market for at least the last five hundred years.

Strake stood handling yard tomatoes from nearby Vicenza at one of the stalls. While carefully studying the succulent red flesh of one of the offerings of a gap-toothed *veccia* of a fruit seller, apparently absorbed in contemplating the plump garden vegetable, Strake said to thin air: "The answer is a big, fat, fucking no, Brigham."

"You haven't even heard the question yet, Strake."

"Whatever it is, the answer is no," Strake repeated, turning to face the beefy man in single-breasted black raincoat who stood a foot behind him.

"And you're just as lousy at shadowing now as you were back in that Ankara bazaar three years ago. I spotted your fat Agency ass the minute I left my palazzo. I also smelled your incredibly rancid armpits. I guess you were absent the day they taught the recruits not to fart while tailing surveillance subjects, huh Brigham?"

"Would it help if I told you the president herself requested your help with this matter?" Brigham said evenly, trying to ignore the insults from this very well-known hard-ass and sonofabitch. He'd received orders not to get pushy with Strake, and orders, fortunately or not, were orders.

Besides, Brigham knew from experience pushy wouldn't help. Strake had played merry hell with him not only in Ankara, but also in Damascus and three other places he could name.

Brigham respected Strake. To know Strake, in fact, was to respect Strake, even if it was also to loathe Strake and long to belt him in the mouth.

# DAVID ALEXANDER

"Shit, Brigham, it wouldn't matter if Christ and the holy apostles personally came down off the steeple of that fine old Renaissance cathedral over there and gave you their blessing. The answer would still be -- fuck off."

Strake handed the old hagfish of a proprietress in her worn brown sweater who stood behind the vegetable bins some paper Euros and took the plastic bag of tomatoes, getting some change in coinage and an appreciative *grazie signore* back from her as she smiled, showing the black gap in her yellowed front teeth.

"I'm through saving the world from itself. If it's the end, then it's the end. I don't care anymore."

"There are new laws, Strake," Brigham said, unable to keep the edge out of his voice by this point. "We can cut off your pension."

"As long as you can't cut off my fuckin' pecker, Brigham, it's okay by me. My money supply is airtight. Don't bullshit me, you shit-wit, and don't threaten me or I'll simply kick your fat fart of a pussy ass. You can't touch this, home boy. Deal with it."

Strake walked off in the direction of the nearest stone footbridge, swinging his bag of tomatoes to a jaunty, if silent, rhythm. This time Brigham didn't try to follow him as he disappeared into the crowds thronging the commercial streets of Venice's downtown Merceria.

193

# THREATCON DELTA

Brigham had a fallback plan. It would have been dumb to go in without one, considering Strake. So Brigham had made sure he had a good one.

Yeah, it would work. Brigham was pretty confident about this as he ran the plan over in his head.

■

President Linda Halifax sat at her desk. In front of her lay a black vinyl ring binder bearing the words Top Secret: Umbra which were printed in a hologram across its front on a forty degree angle from the margins of the page. Emblazoned a little lower down in large type were two words.

Option Omega.

The president had dreaded the moment when she would have to sit and review the protocols of the Omega Option. The protocols concerned an act of overwhelming destruction almost too horrifying to contemplate. Nevertheless that is precisely what the president had been doing these last few minutes. Contemplating the unthinkable. Sanely considering the insane. Playing devil's advocate in a burning room.

The Omega Option called for destroying the Pentagon with a nuclear device. In fact the Omega Option called for destroying any national military, government or civilian command center that had fallen into the hands of terrorists and could not be re-secured by negotiation or conventional military forces. It was, as its title implied, an all-or-nothing gambit, a strategy of last resorts for use when everything else had failed.

The Omega Option had been drafted decades before, in secret, following the September 11th, 2001 attacks. It was then realized that should terrorists wrest control of national command centers and negotiations or conventional military options fail, then other, more drastic measures, might need to be taken to successfully end the crisis.

The only measure available then and today was a strike using weapons of mass destruction, both conventional, nuclear and, finally, exotic weapons of a hybrid nature. The Omega Option presented the US chief executive with a checklist of sub-options. The president could use one, all, or a mix of several of them.

Plan Omega's options were listed in descending order of destructiveness.

Option One: A five hundred kiloton nuclear airburst. The airburst would be sufficiently powerful to level the Pentagon, leaving nothing behind except charred foundation rubble. The nuclear explosive was either an air- or sea-launched-cruise missile, and was F-22 Raptor-deliverable.

Option Two: Deployment of a massively powerful MOAB conventional bomb or fuel-air explosive. In this case too, detonation would be by airburst. The blast and shock effects would be similar to a nuclear airburst except for the lack of residual radioactivity and electromagnetic pulse or EMP effect. The option's drawback was that the munitions, which were large and heavy in both case, were only air-to-ground deliverable and not as precisely targetable as were nuclear weapons.

Option Three: Detonation or deployment of an exotic weapon -- an electromagnetic pulse munition, for example. Known generically as an "e-bomb," this munition would generate a flash effect of sufficiently powerful electromagnetic energy to electrify a small city. The enormously strong pulse of electrical current generated in the burst would burn out all the systems in the Pentagon, no matter how protected or "hardened" against EMP they might be.

The danger was heavy blowback -- it could also have unintended consequences for the Washington DC power grid and seriously disrupt national defense and commercial computer systems. Cars and trucks would stall all over the place as their ignition system computers got fried. Planes might conceivably be knocked out of the air as navigational processors went haywire or failed entirely. The consequences were extremely unpredictable, but sure to present significant hazards if the option was implemented.

All of this notwithstanding, Halifax had a decision to make. She'd have to choose one option on the list, and, placing the list of options down on the desktop, she'd resolved on the one she would authorize.

The president signaled the acting deputy CJCS -- who had brought her the restricted folder from the emergency JCS headquarters at the Alternate Military Command Center at Raven Rock -- to hand her the presidential finding prepared by the Office of the Joint Chiefs of Staff. Halifax scanned the set of orders it contained, then quickly scrawled her signature across the bottom. The finding authorized the military to prepare to use Option Three against the terrorist forces holding the Pentagon hostage under security provisions of the Homeland Security Act and to stand by to upgrade the options if necessary should the president deem stronger actions advisable.

The president soon left the Oval Office too for the Map Room in the White House's East Wing. There, television cameras from all the major networks connected to satellite uplink vans parked outside the executive mansion's gates had been set up. The president was about to address the nation on the unfolding crisis and continuing ordeal.

She would reassure her countrymen that everything was in order and that the crisis would be swiftly dealt with and end with everything put right again. The president would not say a word about the Omega Option or the far worse consequences of not striking General Casper Saint and his forces before they could bring still more terrible options of their own into play against the United States.

Halifax had so far only signed an authorization that the Omega Option be prepared for immediate deployment. She'd not yet signed off on the plan's go-orders, but she feared it was only a matter of time before she'd have to do this. Saint was as determined as he was brilliant, and as brilliant as he was mad.

In the core of her being, Halifax was convinced that the endgame had come. The countdown to Armageddon had commenced. She shuddered at what this feared option would mean to the future of the United States and the rest of the world beyond its borders.

DAVID ALEXANDER

Fourteen
**A Small Demonstration**

*T*he National Military Command Center or NMCC comprises a warren of large and small rooms. These rooms take up a significant portion of Wedge Three -- the northeastern corner of the five roughly triangular sections that further divide the five-sided building into as many parts -- on the third and fourth floors between Rings E through C.

Some, set up as dedicated mission control centers and situation rooms, are configured as the need and the mission arises -- equipment and computer networking cables are moved in and set up; semi-permanent walls are hammered or wheeled into place; guards are stationed at entry and exit points. Other parts of the NMCC are designed to play far more permanent roles in the national military command structure.

One of these, the situation room in which the Joint Chiefs assess global military developments of an emergency nature, is built on two levels.

# THREATCON DELTA

The upper level, where the Joint Chiefs convene, is a relatively small chamber dominated by six huge flat-panel display screens high on a wall. They form a semicircle above a round conference table of massive polished oak. The lower level is an immense communications amphitheater resembling the launch control center at Cape Canaveral's Kennedy Space Center.

Here the duty officers making up the NMCC battle staff occupy the length of a large T-shaped table with inset display screens at each station. At the smaller top of the "T" sit the four emergency action officers or EAOs, also with built-in display consoles in front of them on the table. Surrounding them all are numerous personnel attending to banks of rack-mounted command, control and communications equipment linked to the military forces of the United States, United Nations, NATO, Warsaw Pact and other nonaligned forces throughout the world.

It is the job of the four emergency action officers, none below the rank of lieutenant general, to absorb and assess and encapsulate the plethora of cables, satellite imagery, media coverage, and other diverse data that stream in from the field, place them in a coherent context, and brief them to the four-star generals who await their reports in the glass-enclosed room overlooking the pit.

# DAVID ALEXANDER

Today the only one who sat behind the conference table was Casper Saint, his combat-booted feet propped on the table's edge. Saint nodded at the guard and the guard opened the door.

Undersecretary of Defense, Dr. Blaines Markoff, and Deputy Chairman of the Joint Chiefs General Clayton Rogers were ushered in at SMG-point; Markoff's hands cuffed in front of him and Rogers hastily-doctored arm in a cast. Rogers, injected with morphine to ease the pain of severe wounding, was ashen-faced and his knees trembled, but he bore his suffering like a soldier.

"Have a seat, gentlemen," Saint told them. "Make yourselves comfortable."

Neither man moved a muscle.

"Consider that an order, gentlemen," Saint repeated, nodding at the guard who pushed his two unwilling guests into the chairs at muzzle-point of a bullpup autorifle.

"Better. Now, gentlemen," Saint began, "I brought you here not only to have the pleasure of your company, which I cherish, believe me, but also to discuss with you some business of mutual advantage. So far our commander-in-chief has refused to negotiate a ransom. I thought I'd discuss it with you."

"Then you're wasting your time, Saint," Markoff answered. I'm sure I speak for the secretary when

I say we wouldn't pay you a plugged nickel. Besides that, we have no authority to do that even if we wanted to. Nor do our opinions count for jack shit in the current situation"

"Exactly," concurred Rogers, standing erect, though shakily, despite the bruises on his face and the dirt and tears on his uniform.

"That's debatable," Saint challenged. "In any event it could be argued that were the president under house arrest at Camp David the vice president would be in control and empowered to make decisions affecting the nation. He might then want your advice."

"What the hell is this all about, Saint?" asked Markoff." You can't get away with this shit. Anyway, where will you put the ransom money that's safe enough to survive an audit? Even the banks in Liechtenstein won't hide that kind of account anymore."

"That will be my problem, gentlemen," Saint said back. "Now, I don't think we have anything left to discuss. So I'll return your respected but otherwise worthless jackshit asses to your, um, quarters."

Saint nodded to the guards who took the V.I.P. hostages away. He decided he would give everybody a chance to think things over. Saint went back into the NMCC. He instructed Pegasus to open a link to the newsmedia.

"Scrivener at CNN wants to talk to you."

"Let's give the bitch what she wants – other than a big dick to suck on, that is."

Pegasus assigned the communications link to Saint, whose desktop screen sprouted a new window.

"Ms. Scrivener," Saint said smoothly. "A genuine pleasure."

"General Saint," Bonita Scrivener began. "Why are you doing this?"

"I've undertaken this measure to demonstrate to the world the dangers threatening our nation's military command institutions. The Pentagon has always been what is described as a 'soft' target in military operational vernacular. Technically, this simply means it's not hardened against a nuclear strike. But it's also soft because it's open to an assault by terrorists, such as I and my troops have demonstrated today before the entire world."

"You've done this all on your own initiative?" asked Scrivener. "To prove some kind of point? Is that what you're saying, general?"

"In a nutshell, yes, Ms. Scrivener. Myself and a group of dedicated American combat veterans who have risked their lives to identify and expose the manifold weaknesses in our nation's homeland defense system. As we've proven, homeland defense today is more myth than it is reality.

These dedicated soldiers here with me today must share the credit for what's been brought to light."

"Well, General Saint, you've certainly made your point. So what now? Are you planning to leave the building now that you've proven you can take it over and hold people hostage?"

"In time, Ms. Scrivener," Saint admonished. "But not quite yet."

"Why not?"

"Because I've not quite finished with my demonstration," Saint explained. "In fact, one might say I've only just begun."

"Really, general? What else have you got to, ah, demonstrate?"

"Well, Ms. Scrivener," Saint went on in a bland voice that masked a coming ultimatum, "for one thing that terrorists could also take control of America's nuclear arsenal, if they were very smart terrorists, that is.

"As an example -- " he continued glibly, the hint of a smirk tugging at the muscles of his jaw. " -- At this moment I have established command and control over an intercontinental ballistic missile silo located somewhere in the black hills of North Dakota, where lives Rocky Raccoon. In less than sixty seconds that nuclear missile will be launched. Where are you presently located Ms. Scrivener?"

"At our regional office in New York City," Scrivener answered, a sudden catch audible in her well-cultivated anchorperson's voice.

"Good. Then you'll have a ringside seat," Saint told her with the air of a mock nonchalant pleasantry. "The missile will explode over Manhattan in less than ten minutes."

"You're not serious, are you?" Scrivener asked, now clearly panicking. "You don't actually intend to launch a nuke?"

"Do I look like I'm joking to you, Ms. Scrivener? Besides, it's my understanding that you, ah, like explosions."

The CNN correspondent said nothing. Saint was enjoying himself. His smile grew broader.

"The missile has just lifted off," Saint announced after a moment's pause. "I suggest you get yourself to any convenient basement as quickly as possible. Or try the subway. It's probably your safest bet."

Saint blanked the screen and lit a fresh Dutch Masters Perfecto panatela. He smiled with unabashed glee, and chuckled softly, imagining the reporter bolting from her seat and running for the subways. What a way to die, he thought. He was glad he wasn't in her shoes.

Fifteen
## Like In Classical Poetry

*J*ackson Strake sat in the command center in the presidential jetliner, Air Force One. The mammoth jet aircraft had been augmented by a lot of extra staff and a lot more gear since the crisis had materialized. Strake had been whisked from the airport where the USAF military transport plane out of Diego Garcia had landed him on a direct flight from Venice's Marco Polo International airport, which was situated on an island in the Venetian lagoon.

Strake had been briefed en route. He now reflected on what he'd learned as he sipped a Beefeater vodka martini with a pony glass full of pitted green olives to one side.

The spooks had made Strake an offer he couldn't turn down. He had been briefed-in on the plane trip over, sitting in one of the spacious conference rooms onboard the triple-decker 787 superjumbo. A computer presentation had been assembled for him.

# DAVID ALEXANDER

There had been a live exercise at the Pentagon, held on the Parade Ground immediately in front of the westward-facing River Entrance. Broad enough to be used for ceremonial functions with visiting heads of state; the Parade Ground was a natural choice to conduct the exercise.

Its object had been to test the readiness of Pentagon staff and emergency response teams to cope with a terrorist attack using chemical weapons. Elements of the District of Columbia National Guard which had been trained as first responders to terrorist attacks were also to participate in the drill, as was the Pentagon's own security staff, made up of military police supplied by the Marines. Colored smoke canisters would simulate an attack using poison gas. Staff members would lie down to simulate victims stricken during the attack.

Everything had gone smoothly until a truckload of national guardsmen rolled up to the Pentagon's River Entrance. No one expected them to shoot their way inside the building. But that's what they had done. Within minutes another truck had pulled up and the equivalent of a company of determined assault troops were engaged in a firefight with defenders who were ill prepared to stop the well-coordinated assault.

The commando-style invasion force knew precisely where it was going. The soldiery reached the Building's third and fourth floors via the elevators that serviced those levels. After another pitched firefight the National Military Command Center had fallen into their hands. The five Wedges of the Pentagon were immediately sealed off by automatic security mechanisms. Afterward nothing worked, including the elevators outside of Wedge Three.

The attackers had somehow succeeded in gaining control of computerized access control systems throughout the building despite biometric safeguards. Within minutes they had sealed themselves in and taken all personnel on the third and fourth floors of Wedge Three prisoner. Attempts to deploy backup systems control all failed. The attackers were presently in total control of the NMCC and the Wedge that they occupied.

It was believed that General Casper Saint, former CINC of SOCOM, the US Special Operations Command, was in command of the invading force. Faceprints and voiceprints as analyzed by computer and human intelligence specialists all were unanimous in the determination that Saint was at the helm. The fact that his whereabouts for the past year since his escape from Thailand were unknown also tended to confirm that it was him.

Saint had escaped from an offshore penitentiary almost twelve months before to the day where he was serving a twenty-year sentence for treason.

Saint had been imprisoned for aiding and abetting terrorist forces during the attacks on San Francisco and Washington DC after the Petroleum War in Nagorno-Karabakh in the Caucasus. Once the oil fields were recovered by a US-led NATO coalition, the general had gone insane, or so it was generally believed.

The accepted story, at least as reported by the newsmedia, was that Saint had switched sides and gone over to the terrorist Nexus whom he had aided in planning the nearly apocalyptic Strike Day attacks on multiple US cities and on the Capitol itself in which thousands had perished.

Much of this seemed like conjecture to Strake, but that's all that they'd told him -- maybe all that anyone still knew. Truth had always been relative.

More often than not, in a digital world where fiction and fact changed places with sometimes startling rapidity, truth was just another kind of lie.

■

This was the sum total of what was known at the moment that General Saint came back online to the president.

"Decision time's up, President Halifax. I would appreciate your answer now."

"We still have to talk about this," she told him. "However…"

A new face suddenly appeared on Saint's screen. It was Strake's.

"Who the hell are you?"

"Jackson Strake. I'm now official White House negotiator. You can talk to me."

"I want to talk to the president."

"She's unavailable. I'm your sole channel at the moment. You'll get a better deal through me, anyway, general, so it's to your advantage."

"Strake … I know you. Doctor Fucking Fear. You did the terrorists on the plane out of Istanbul. I never would have thought I'd feel sorry for terrorist killers but after the mindfuck shit you pulled on them I almost shed a tear. You're a sick fuck, Strake, but I'm not some camel-humper with a dirty rag tied around his head. You won't play your mind games with me, bro'. Have somebody else call me back or something bad happens. This transmission is terminated."

The communication was severed. Strake sat back and popped a caffeinated breath mint into his mouth. It was strong; the way he liked them.

As Strake expected, Saint soon called back. It took a while but he ultimately did.

"Okay. You win. Let's talk this over."

"Sure. I'm in the air right now. We need to extend the grace period until I get to the White

House. I can't do anything at forty thousand feet. There's no face-to-face with the Oval Office possible here. I'll need another two hours."

"Can't be done."

"That's it."

He hung up and got his two hours when Saint called back.

Strake was hustled by executive helicopter to the landing pad on the East Lawn of the White House. A detachment of Marines flanked him and cleared his passage to the White House command center.

Strake immediately encountered problems in the form of Colonel Red Hawk, commander of the planned combined Delta-USMC rescue mission. Hawk wanted to hard charge right in.

"Let's take him now," Hawk argued. "My warriors are good to go. Their blood's up. They don't give a shit. We have a direct subterranean route into the Pentagon basement via the network of old storm drainage tunnels. We can take this sucker, clean house with him and his rag-tag and bobtail mercenary force. We'll take him as easy as we took Khartoum or Jakarta back in 2019."

"I would argue against moving in now," Strake challenged. "Saint's no fool. He's an old pro with everything but the kitchen sink in his bag of tricks. Besides, I have a feeling he's got somebody on the inside track, a pipeline into secret planning. He might know in advance what's happening."

"Who do you mean?"

"I can't name a name at this particular juncture. But I think it's a possibility."

"Madame President," Hawk continued. "I say let's go in now. My hard chargers are ready to roll. All I need is your order and we're set to move."

The president steepled her palms and looked them over, her eyes moving from Strake to Hawk and back again. But she said nothing for a long time.

"We're not ready yet, darling," she finally pronounced. "Stand down until I order you in. That's all."

Hawk left without another word.

■

Strake sat at his computer console. It had only been a matter of hours since his arrival, but he'd sensed a pronounced change in the direction of the winds of policy.

They weren't telling him anything. A bad sign. Especially this early in the game. Hardly had he started when the atmosphere had begun to freeze around him. It happened, sometimes, though. High-echelon zigzags were a fact of life, and outsiders like Strake often wound up with no hole cards to play. The negotiator knew something was definitely about to go down, and he didn't have to be a mind-reader to know that this was probably a counterattack of some kind.

The White House sit room was thinned of personnel. Strake's internal email traffic had slowed to a trickle. His cell phone wasn't ringing as much. And the Marines outside the door seemed to be looking at him with a strangely bemused look. As always, Strake was the last one to know. Events might simply have superseded him, he thought with a mental shrug.

Well, fuck them all, he told himself. Since when did he ever give a shit what they did? In fact, Strake decided he would pick himself up and head back to Venice.

Nodding to himself at the rightness of this decision he rolled the office chair under the trestle table so he could sit close to the display. Minutes later he had ebooked himself an evening SST flight out of Dulles. It was a direct flight, straight to Marco Polo.

He could have dinner at some high-cock DC restaurant, like the M-Bar, and still have time for a drink at the airport bar before departure time. If they caught a tail wind he'd be back at his house in the San Toma district two hours later and unwind with drinks at the cozy little bar at the Do Pozzi he liked to frequent. Strake was composing an appropriate memo to the powers that be when an incoming message icon blinked at him coyly. It

213

was red-coded, meaning it was from Saint. Strake's fingers stopped on the keys.

"Good morning Mr. Negotiator."

Saint's face filled the large flat panel display on his desk. A smaller window showed Strake's face as it appeared to the general.

"General," Strake replied.

"I haven't heard from you in awhile," Saint went on. "Was getting to kind of miss those little discussions we've been having. You strike me as a decent sort of guy, Strake. Did it ever occur to you that you're being used?"

"General, we're all being used one way or another," Strake answered without a trace of irony. "That's just the way it works on this planet."

"True, Mr. Negotiator, all too true. All of us are pawns in someone else's game. That's the way societies work," Saint replied. "But -- let's get specific. What's the game we're in? Why are we pawns? What's the prize?"

"I don't think I follow you."

"Are you a student of epic poetry, Mr. Strake?"

"Yeah, some."

"Then you must know the Aeneid of Virgil."

"I read it in college."

"Let me refresh your memory a bit, then, Mr. Strake," Saint said. "In the poem, Aeneas, who is the son of Priam, former leader of the Trojans, has voyaged to the island of the Sibyls. There were seven Sibyls in all, each possessing the gift of prophesy.

"The Sybil took Aeneas down into Hades, down into the Underworld, in order to show him the faces of Romans yet to be born. Aeneas was to be the founder of this new and greater race, born from the ashes of Troy. It was a race destined to conquer the Achaeans, or Greeks, who had laid waste to Aeneas' people. Everything would come full circle."

"So what's your point?" asked Strake.

"My point, Mr. Negotiator, is that there are still Sibyls in this world, just as there continues to be a Hades beneath. They can show you things, if you let them, Mr. Strake. They have shown things to me."

The negotiator thought to himself that it would all be over soon anyway, so what was the point in trying? Still, the subject of his brief was right in front of him, so why not try to negotiate, even if it was already in all probability the eleventh hour.

"General, where's all this leading to? I don't think you're as crazy as you make out. Yet you know you can't win. You're at a classic tactical disadvantage. You're cut off. Surrounded. It's only a matter of time. Whatever point you want to prove, whatever message you want to send, let me know, and I'll help you send it. Just let's end this thing before it goes any farther. How about it, general?"

Strake watched the face in front of him, watched it carefully. There was no trace of pressure, no trace of fear on it. General Saint smiled and shook his head.

"I've got to go now, Mr. Negotiator. In a few minutes a special forces commando strike on my position will commence. I want to make certain that my own forces repel it as efficiently -- and, for that matter, as brutally -- as possible. We'll talk later, after the body bags get zipped and the steel caskets are shoved aboard the planes."

The screen blacked out.

Holy shit! Strake thought.

The fucker knows what's coming his way!

Sixteen
## The Fulcrum

*G*eneral Casper Saint strode purposefully through the Pentagon's captive Wedge Three. Though a fallen angel, he was nevertheless the master of all he surveyed. At his side was his executive officer, the jive-talking but otherwise capable Captain Da Gamma. Their destination was a high-security vaulted room on the E-Ring, second floor. The room was guarded by two of Saint's fatigue-clad mercenary troopers.

Saint pushed through the open door, a two-ton portal that would easily have graced the largest of bank vaults. What was contained within the secret room was deemed important enough to be kept under the most stringent security precautions possible.

It was the operational nerve center of COLOSUS.

The control area was now manned by Saint's technicians who were attempting to gain command and control over the computer network. Beyond a glass enclosure a robotic arm moved with machinelike precision, selecting cubes, placing them in keyed sockets, moving on to repeat the motion, incessantly whirling and twisting.

Saint smoked his cheroot and beheld the power behind that conical glass enclosure. It was the power to destroy; ultimately destroy; to break the world to pieces if necessary and shatter the lives of every human being on the planet. Saint pressed his hand against the bulletproof glass.

His reverie was broken by a voice in his ear mike.

"Sir, alert level three," said Pegasus. "Surveillance systems and Satellite Team Three reports indicate imminent attack on the Pentagon by Delta Force contingents."

Well, what a fucking surprise, thought Saint. One thing you could say about the opposition: they were so predictable you could set your watch by them.

"Details."

"A mechanized convoy comprised of APCs, Humvees and HEMPTs carrying infantry is proceeding toward our position along Columbia Pike-State Route 244, that is, in the direction of the Pentagon River Entrance. There is another mechanized convoy of similar configuration approaching along the Shirley Highway, which leads to the Southwest-facing facades of the building."

Armored carriers, Hummers and high-capacity trucks, mused Saint. He didn't need to bother asking about the armament the detachment might be carrying. Since Saint knew the types of weaponry with which he'd equip such a force, it was a given that the force was outfitted with precisely such ordnance.

"ETA."

"I compute an ETA of under ten minutes. As you know, sir, these vehicular routes were built back in the early 1940s with dual capacity as military highway complexes when the Pentagon was first constructed. The system of roads that surrounds the Pentagon can accommodate even the heaviest military vehicles traveling at maximum speeds."

"Options."

"Effective retaliation estimated at ninety-eight percent probability using Dawn Horse orbital platform seven, which has been prepositioned in the event of a surprise attack on our position."

Saint nodded. This looked like a good time for Plan-A.

"Activate and place systems on standby," he ordered.

"Yes, sir."

"We'll take them out. I'll personally supervise. It'll be just like Christmas."

"Yes, sir."

Saint rushed to the command center. Before he'd settled into his catbird seat, the reports of the surprise strike had crystallized. A sortie of Blackhawk helos, armed with air-to-ground missiles and thirty-millimeter Miniguns -- motorized Gatlings that could spit out thousands of rounds per minute -- was now also en route.

An unmanned combat aerial vehicle was also vectoring in at thirty thousand feet -- its presence had been detected via the NSA-CIA-DIA Snake Eye covert orbital imaging platform that Red Dog Juan and his tech team had electronically commandeered and had jockeyed into geosynchronous orbit over the eastern seaboard. It was assumed to be a combatant UCAV and not a non-weaponized reconnaissance drone.

"As you can see, sir, the reverse plot on the you-cav shows that it most likely originated in the Indian Ocean. My best guesstimate is at the remote base identified as FOL Alpha."

Pegasus indicated the glowing wire grid diagram showing the UCAV's position and containing in-flight data such as altitude. FOL-Alpha referred to a forward operational location, a clandestine base established on the leeward side of the island of Nimdas located about fifty miles from the northwestern coast of Sri Lanka's Jaffna Peninsula. This FOL was connected to FARP Bravo, which was a forward area rearmament position, in other words, an island crammed with enough weapons to blow half of Southwest Asia to mango chutney.

Not that it would happen -- the FARP was a storehouse for rapid arming of everything from stealth aircraft to carrier battlegroups in a part of the world had become an important operational zone for military activities overt and covert. It was also the main operational area for the Yokosuka, Japan-based US Seventh Fleet.

Also, Saint noted, the FARP had a huge inventory of unmanned combat aerial vehicles each only slightly smaller than a manned fighter plane and equipped with the same missiles, including air launched cruise missiles. Of more immediate importance was that they were also the platform of choice for firing ASAT Block II missiles from high-altitudes into orbital space.

Saint noted the steady increase in altitude as the UCAV's trajectory neared the airspace in the vicinity of the Pentagon.

"That's correct, sir. The predicted target -- "

" -- is our eye in the sky, isn't it?"

Saint laughed and puffed on his cheroot.

"It's one thing to follow an operational contingency plan," Saint said to no one in particular. "It's another thing to follow a contingency plan I devised. This is straight out of a war game we did back in 2016. Laughable. Simply laughable."

"Shall I kill the you-cav, sir?"

"Affirmative, Pegasus. Blow it to all-fuck."

"Yes, sir."

The technician began to input a series of keystrokes that activated positive control linkages to the Northern Cross platform parked in a LEO -- low earth orbit -- above the US eastern seaboard. Synthetic aperture radar imagery from the orbital weapon -- digitally colored and enhanced to be as sharp as any conventional camera imaging -- was immediately relayed to one of the large flat panels high-up on the wall of the NMCC command center.

The screen quickly resolved into an aerial view showing the trajectory of the UCAV -- which was an advanced Switchblade oblique-wing unmanned vehicle the size of a medium bomber aircraft -- rasterized in color-coded track, velocity and altitude wire-grid vector lines, and the system began tracking the target through the skies.

The Switchblade UCAV was equipped with a variety of offensive weapons and could easily be refitted for a variety of combat roles. In this case, its course, velocity and flight vector all indicated that its target was the imaging satellite that was the multiagency spy satellite code-named Snake Eye, now under control of Saint and his team.

This meant that the UCAV would be carrying an ASAT Block II weapon – an advanced version of the original anti-satellite missile capable of locking onto a target satellite in orbit from a maximum flight ceiling between eighty and ninety thousand feet and speeding at hypersonic velocity to destroy its exo-atmospheric target.

"Northern Cross Three has acquired the you-cav," announced Pegasus. "Initiating particle beam weaponization." Pegasus paused. "Mark, one, two, three."

The silence was broken by the staccato, fingertip-to-plastic cadences of a computer keyboard being worked and a trackball mouse being clicked.

"Discharging particle beam."

The gun camera imaging of the Switchblade was a now-you-see-it, now-you-don't affair.

One instant the UCAV was visible between the satellite-generated crosshair target reticle encompassing it in two green concentric circles pierced by a glowing blue cross -- the next instant a burst of light and smoke, with the most fleeting view of fragmentary matter hurtling through the suddenly nova-esque flare-up in the sky, filled the field of view on the display screen.

# THREATCON DELTA

Then there was nothing but empty space beyond vaporous wisps of cloud that masked a dim, gray suggestion of patchworked urban landscape miles and miles below the downlooking radar's synthetic view from five miles up in near space.

"Target annihilated, sir."

Saint nodded, satisfied with the results.

"Think I'll make a little call," he said almost cheerfully.

DAVID ALEXANDER

Seventeen
**A Corridor to Defeat**
*T*he complex of highways surrounding the Pentagon had been constructed at the time that the largest government office building in the world had begun going up. It was a time immediately before and immediately after Pearl Harbor. The world then, as now, was an uncertain and dangerous place that held an uncertain and bleak future for the United States.

The Pentagon was intended by its builders to be more than just a headquarters for military staff that had been spread out across the District and across the Potomac into Virginia between the two World Wars. It was also the centerpiece of what was to eventually become a bold new national network of superhighways whose construction began at the same time as the Pentagon's.

This development was not coincidental. The massive road building effort that was to ultimately link the nation's East and West Coasts was not only intended to accelerate the flow of commercial and civilian travel, but to enable mechanized military vehicles, from heavy trucks to tanks to armored carriers, to deploy quickly from their bases to potential points of conflict. By the late 1930s, as war in Europe broke out, the prospect of direct attack on the continental United States was a turn of events for which the War Department -- predecessor to the Department of Defense -- had tried to plan.

Secondly, and perhaps most importantly, the new highway network was intended to enable military traffic to entirely bypass major urban areas that might become dangerous, trammeling, cul-de-sacs in time of war, and in the event that war came to the continental United States.

As a case in point, the entire system of major traffic arteries between the Washington Beltway and New York City was built to serve a dual purpose. The road system would not only accommodate commercial and domestic traffic, but also be capable of carrying military traffic. Moreover, it would be so constructed as to bypass the national hubs of major metropolitan areas -- which, like Washington, Chicago or New York, might create nearly impenetrable barriers to columns of troops and mechanized armor -- in the event of enemy attack.

Using these new highway arteries, defense forces could simply roll past and around the big eastern cities and use alternate seaports and airstrips for troop deployment and resupply operations. The highway network was then, and is still today, as much a military road network as it is a civilian superhighway grid, as indeed most of the highway infrastructure in the United States remains to this day. The familiar shields bearing route numbers that motorists encounter in transit are one testament to this fact, but there are others, albeit less visible.

With its five-sided design, the Pentagon's fortress-like appearance was more than accidental as well. The Building had been intended with grave deliberateness to serve as a fortress in the event that Washington, DC had been attacked. The government could be quickly moved along the road network to the Pentagon and business carried on. Other facilities -- like Raven Rock, an iron mountain in Pennsylvania whose interior had been blasted out during the Truman Administration to form a shell housing a clutch of steel buildings set on massive springs containing the Alternate Military Command Center, or a similar deep underground command post inside nearby Mount Weather, or even the reinforced bunker complex beneath Camp David -- were far more secure than the Pentagon.

But none of them were fortresses, and none of them stood at the crossroads of east and west as did the Building. The Pentagon was intended to serve the role of citadel guarding the gateway to the American interior, just as it was built to fulfill the function of government office building for the military's extensive staff and procurement administrations.

But what if the enemy, by stealth, trickery, or by main force of arms, had captured the five-sided concrete fortress?

What if the Pentagon itself fell into the hands of America's adversaries?

History was replete with examples of similar occurrences. More to the point -- was there ever a fortress that, once built, had never fallen under the power of the enemy, or been destroyed? The obvious danger of attack or takeover of the Pentagon had been as much on the minds of the Pentagon's original planners and builders, like Lieutenant General Brehon Somervell, who first conceived it, as it was half a century later when its first major restructuring had commenced.

After the terrorist attacks of 911 and Strike Day, security had been greatly heightened, but still the rapid interdiction by military forces in the event of attack or occupation of the Pentagon weighed on the minds of security planners.

A special task force, code-named Janus Hinge, had been assembled as a result. Technically, and according to the US order of battle, the task force was under the aegis of NORTHCOM, the armed forces' northern command which was responsible for the military administration of the continental United States, or CONUS, in the jargon of the military.

It had both an overt, or white world, and covert, or black, aspect. Janus Hinge was responsible for carrying out military security for the Pentagon in a new world of endless warfare and incessant threats. Based at Fort Meyers, which was situated only six miles along the Beltway from the Pentagon's Arlington, Virginia, location, the task force trained for the moment when the Pentagon was in danger of attack, or already under attack.

Troops specially trained and equipped for the mission were the main, although not the only, component of the task force. It was also charged with conducting regular clandestine probes of all aspects of the security of the Pentagon. The threats these probes sought to detect and defend against ranged from hijacked commercial planes or remote-piloted unmanned aircraft smashing into the Building, to armed and armored forces attempting to shoot the place up, to stealthy attacks by virus or computer sabotage -- "cybotage" -- on the technical infrastructure that was the lifeblood of a digital fighting force.

In fact, Janus Hinge was to be run out of the office of the JCS and its command linkage to

# THREATCON DELTA

NORTHCOM only a fiction of the order of battle maintained for external consumption. Janus Hinge's commander, appointed in secret by the Joint Chiefs, acting on the authority of the Chairman, the Secretary of Defense and the President, had been none other than General Casper Saint, then head of SOCOM, the Special Operations Command.

The general had been appointed shortly after the national outrage over the coordinated Strike Day attacks that had laid waste to large swathes of the United States. As the fires that raged for days in some localities continued to send immense black plumes of smoke surging up into the skies, as the White House stood with smoke-blackened facade and the Oval Office pocked was with shrapnel damage from RPG-strikes, as the newsmedia depicted the halls of Congress emptied of America's elected leadership who had been secretly shuttled to deep underground security bases as scores of thousands of ordinary citizens died and were made permanently sick by the aftermath of the chemical and biological attacks, as hell walked the face of the earth, plans to defend the country, to make it impervious to the future murderous hatred of its opponents, were forged.

# DAVID ALEXANDER

Among the fruits of those plans was Janus Hinge, and it had been deemed too important to be tasked along ordinary lines of engagement.

Therein lay the rub, however, because while the real holders of the reins of power that controlled Janus Hinge were deep national security secrets, the US Army's order of battle had placed overt operational responsibility in the hands of the commander of NORTHCOM, and thus in the person of General Homer P. Bock, who on this brisk Monday morning in September, when clear blue skies had replaced the hard rains of the previous Sunday, happened to be the wrong person in the wrong place at the wrong time.

On paper, the Army order of battle stated that at such time that a Threatcon Delta security alert had been declared -- and subject to the orders of the Joint Chiefs of Staff, the White House, or other legally designated entities -- the commander of NORTHCOM could commence military operations at his sole discretion.

In short, to repeat a phrase used by another general who'd become embroiled in another crisis during the Reagan years, General Homer Bock deemed himself to be "in charge" when the Office of the Joint Chiefs fell to the invaders and the White House failed to provide clear-cut orders.

In fact, history records that the general, on learning that the normal chain of command had been broken, called his exec, one Lieutenant Colonel "Mad" Mike Sanders, into his office.

Sanders and his boss both thought alike. They also looked alike, resembling one another not only in general physical appearance but in mannerisms and speech patterns as well. Like some, though by no means all, commanders, General Bock gave preferment to officers who shared his views and interests. Some called Sanders Bock's clone, others called him "Mini-Bock," but never to his face.

"I'm in control now, Mike. Do we have a consensus?" asked General Bock.

"On the face of it, and for the time being, sir, my view would be that yes, you are certainly in charge."

"In fact, Mike, don't you think it wouldn't be much of a stretch to even state that I was the man of the hour? The hero who rides in on a white Arabian charger to save the day?"

"Sir, if you'll permit me to use the phrase, I'd say you were the Lone Ranger."

"And that would make you Tonto, now wouldn't it, son?"

This might, or might not, be a bit of levity, Sanders knew, considering his boss's atrocious sense of humor, so he instinctively treated it as a serious statement of Bock's sometimes bizarre thinking.

"I always looked up to Tonto, sir. Have I mentioned that I'm part Cherokee?"

"Is that so?"

By now the general had strapped on his personal sidearm and combat helmet. Bock struck a pose, but Sanders noted in passing that his face had a shriveled look beneath the Kevlar dome now perched on his hairless head.

"Issue the orders, Mike," Bock commanded his aide. "The troops are to move out. Within fifteen minutes we're to be on the Shirley Highway rolling toward that five-pointed monstrosity of a building. I want everything we have thrown at the job. Mobilize land and air elements. You remember what Patton said, don't you, son? Attack, attack, attack!"

"Sir, I believe that may have been Marshal Foché."

"After today, son, it won't matter squat-all who said what," declared the general smugly as he marched out the door, hitching up his BDU pants.

"You're correct, sir, pardon my brashness," apologized Sanders before his CO's departure.

"That's all right son, because you and me both are gonna lead the charge that saved the fucking You-Nighted-States of Lord-lovin' America."

"Yes, sir!" Sanders quickly agreed.

■

# THREATCON DELTA

The military column that had set out from Fort Meyers at 0800 hours that Monday morning did indeed have both Maxi-Bock and Mini-Bock at the helm.

Unlike his boss, though, Mini-Bock had sense enough to stay well within the confines of an Abrams tank, while his boss rode with his head thrust up from the protection of the turret and his chin jutting forward like that of a latter-day Patton. Mini-Bock's prudence and caution not only made the crucial difference less than ten minutes out of the unit's tactical base and onto the highway, it later made him acting commander by default.

It was at that point, and after negotiating less than four miles of open highway between the Army base and the Pentagon, that the mobile defense force under the command of NORTHCOM met an untimely and sudden defeat at the hands of weaponry that its commander had never dreamed was tracking the column even from the moment that it had begun to roll out of the confines of the fort.

General Bock had never been briefed on Northern Cross.

In the end this inadequacy would make the critical difference between success and failure, and even between life and death.

Eighteen
**Retargeting**

*B*ob, how are things these days?"

Enlarged by a factor of three, the familiar, media-tested, face of Defense Secretary Robert Battle filled most of the rectangular monitor panel in front of General Saint. It was a face that normally commanded respect, even awe.

Battle, who traced his lineage five generations back to one of the republic's founding families, and one of the first families of Maryland, and would not have seemed out of place in the somber vestments of a Puritan, ran the Defense Department with the same severity with which his forebears had condemned accused witches to the pillory, the rack and the ducking stool.

In like manner Defense Secretary Battle had placed the scarlet letter of disgrace upon the brow of several members of the Joint Chiefs of Staff who had openly opposed his policies. Battle, to say the least, was a name to conjure with in the rings and corridors of the Building.

"I'd like my old office back, general," Battle now said, his voice conveying the request in the form of an order.

"Oh, you'll have it back in time, Bob," Saint replied, puffing on his stogie. "Sooner than you think.

"Of course it doesn't help the situation if you try to shoot down our orbital reconnaissance asset with a fucking ASAT, now does it Bob?" Saint continued, reflecting that Battle had grown to regard the Pentagon as something closer to his private manse on the Potomac than a government institution which he headed by presidential appointment to the post of Defense Secretary.

"I don't understand what the hell it is you mean, Saint," the Secretary of Defense retorted testily.

The face of the SecDef became more pinched than usual, and the jowls on its flanks suddenly more prominent. His dour visage, normally resembling that of a witch-hammering Pilgrim, now took on the look of a penitent Trappist monk, an effect somehow heightened by the round, wire-rimmed glasses that the myopic Battle habitually wore. He looked like a man who had not slept well in days, which was one of the things he in fact was.

"You don't, huh, Bob?" retorted Saint. "You're honestly telling me that you, of all people, fail to understand one of the most basic tenets of the strategic arts?"

"And what would that tenet be?" Battle asked with a patronizing quizzical expression that had become one of his trademark mannerisms.

"A commander needs to see the battlespace at all times. Threatened with the interdiction of his airborne and spaceborne reconnaissance and surveillance assets, a capable commander will take any and all steps necessary to defeat enemy actions that might compromise this all-important tactical capability. Are you telling me you've forgotten this, Bob?"

"Don't hock me, general. You're imagining things. We've done nothing except try to negotiate a stand-down. No offensive measures have been taken or even contemplated, nor are there any plans to proceed along such lines."

"Let me correct you, Bob," Saint retorted. "You're the one who is given to wild imaginings. Your imagination is running rampant if you imagine me to be foolhardy enough to entertain that you're serious about the UCAV attack. Especially when there are ground and air attacks on their way even as we speak."

"There are no attacks in the offing. Let me repeat this, general."

Saint replied: "Bob, I'm through playing pecker poker with you. You're stalling. We both know that. I mean, let's level with each other. I'm sitting in the fucking National Military Command Center, for example. I've got all these big, expensive screens on the wall, and they're all connected to big, shiny satellites orbiting the earth, with all kinds of funny little sensors on them that tell you all kinds of nifty shit, such as the fact that there's a humongous force blowing out of Meyers as we speak, and it's headed right for the Pentagon."

"General, believe me -- "

"Now, now, please don't interrupt, Bob. Let me finish. And please pardon my French. I cuss a little when I get excited, you know. You see, Bob, I happen to be holding a pretty good poker hand, in fact a royal flush, so let me just lay my cards on the table. I'll give you exactly sixty seconds to issue the order for airborne and ground attack elements to halt and proceed to roll back their asses. The countdown has begun. If they don't stand down within a minute, I'll destroy them all. Wipe 'em off the fucking face of the earth."

■

Saint blacked the screen.

Checking the Tag-Huer on his wrist, he waited.

After a little while, Pegasus gave him a situation report.

"The inbound helos have not turned back. Nor has the mobile assault column on the route toward

238

the River Entrance. The convoy approaching the Southwest Corner, however, has come to a sudden halt. Shall we give them more time, sir?"

"Negative. Destroy the helos and all elements of the convoy, including those still in motion and those which have halted. As an old colleague of mine once said, 'We will cut it off, and then we will kill it.'"

He added with a laugh, "And then you know what? We'll let god sort 'em out."

"Yes, sir."

All systems indicated that Northern Cross orbital weapons were ready to discharge and that positive control linkages were securely enabled.

Having now assumed full tactical control, Red Dog Juan used keyboard and trackball mouse to arm the weapon, switching to a special bank of lighted buttons to engage the terminal firing sequence. The godlike power to visit swift annihilation on Saint's foes was about to be tested.

Miles below Northern Cross's orbital position, the convoy of heavy armored vehicles suddenly blew apart in a series of rapid explosions and a flurry of mushrooming puffballs of flame.

In the airspace above the air corridor approaches to the Pentagon, the Army's Blackhawk helos that had been tasked to assault the E-Ring redoubt of Saint's forces in Wedge Three with Sidewinder missile strikes and thirty-millimeter chain gun fire, and to act as platforms to deploy a commando strike force into the Building via windows and rooftop, were themselves blown apart in flight.

■

As for General Homer Bock, riding topside on the lead Abrams main battle tank; he had insured his being one of the strike's first casualties as a fist-sized, white-hot splinter of jagged, cooked-off shrapnel from the tank's exploding ammo magazine ripped his exposed head clean off his shoulders.

Bock's last seconds of life were engaged in the struggle to comprehend the dizzying panorama of blurred scenery and blinding lights as the decapitated head -- still wearing its chin-strapped helmet -- sailed through space, then vaporized in the fireball that engulfed the entire convoy.

By comparison, his exec was phenomenally lucky. Colonel "Mad" Mike Sanders had been thrown clear and somehow survived the explosions and thermal pulse waves of the attack, albeit disfigured forever despite skin grafts over the course of the next two years.

The resounding echoes of the explosions could be heard as far away as Chicago and Pascagoola, Florida, and they blew out windows of the four-star international hotels on Capital Hill.

■

Saint keyed his communications. The face of the SecDef again materialized on screen. Beads of sweat clearly stood out on Battle's deeply furrowed brow. His mouth worked strangely. His eyes, behind the lenses of his glasses, seemed to look inward on the hollow interior of an empty skull.

"Bob -- hey there again, good buddy."
The face said nothing, merely stared blankly. The Defense Secretary's eyes were dark circles of fear sunk in fleshy pink ovals; they resembled little boats filled with shining black tar.

Saint went on.

"That attack I told you about a little while ago, Bob? You remember it, I hope? And do you remember how you told me that I'd been imagining things? That it was probably some bad cells in my brain playing tricks on the good cells -- something like that? Well, apparently the bad brain cells were right this time.

"Your heliborne strike force now lies in burning fragments, and the highways are full of blasted tank hulls and charred corpses. Shit, Bob, I wish I'd brought my bible, then I could really put the fear of god in you, quote some passages on laying waste to Ninevah and Tyre, and other ancient sump holes of iniquity -- stuff like that."

"General, I repeat, I know -- " Battle stammered, " -- know nothing."

241

"Yeah, Bob. Guess what? I believe you know nothing. That's because you're a know-nothing schmuck who got his job by marrying the know-nothing daughter of a know-nothing senator who had pull with our know-nothing cunt of a president.

"So here's what I'm gonna do, Bob. I'm gonna teach all of you little know-nothing shits all a little lesson now, so pay attention. I'm about to choose three targets of opportunity and destroy them -- as in obliterate them -- one by one.

"No more dummy warheads, like that one I sent winging its way to New York before. Yeah, Bob, I know you geniuses thought it was a misfire, but it was deliberate. I didn't arm the warhead. I figured that ten tons of missile casing alone crashing into the top floor of the Global Broadcasting Media Building in Midtown Manhattan would get my message across. But did you guys listen -- noooooo, you fuckers obviously didn't.

"So, guy, here's the way it is. Listen up -- this one's live and in color."

"Now, general -- don't -- please don't do anything -- "

"Fuck you little man."

Saint's voice rose in indignant anger. He struggled to control himself. He didn't like himself when he got mad and he tried to maintain his cool at all times. He managed to check himself now, with difficulty, and went on in a calmer voice.

"Three targets. That is all. We'll talk after that. Shit -- where's a fuckin' bible when you need one?"

He broke communications and the screen went black.

Saint then swiveled in his chair toward Pegasus.

"Prioritize and initialize three random targets."

Smoke rings ascended toward the ceiling as he puffed on his Dutch Masters Perfecto.

"Sir, already done."

"What are they?"

"Target one: a ventilation tower for the Brooklyn Battery Tunnel."

Pegasus keystroked and the target, via orbital imaging, appeared highlighted on one of the NMCC's god screens. The white tower was etched against the tip of a small island in the middle of the Hudson River.

"Possibly. What else?"

"The United Nations General Assembly."

"I like that. Options."

"Options prioritized under three categories. One: total destruction. Two: mid-intensity destruction. Three: low-level EMP burst."

"Results of option three?"

"Massive vehicular failure resulting in random highway crashes and clogging of major urban thoroughfares. Power main explosions. Chaos, but limited collateral damage.

"I love New York, so -- "

Saint lit a fresh stogie.

"Fuck it, let's do it."

Pegasus affirmed the order and implemented the remote strike countdown. Northern Cross Four, positioned over the New York metropolitan area energized and discharged its directed particle beam on low intensity. The first thing urban denizens noticed was reported later as a sharp, nonlocalized, crackling of electrical energy, as though a massive lightning storm had struck.

It was, in fact, what Japanese survivors of the nuclear attacks on Hiroshima and Nagasaki had termed the *pica* effect – a unique nuclear burst of photons produced by the intense emission of light energy of a nuclear airburst. In this case the non-nuclear origin of the emission did not alter the appearance of the pica effect.

The effects of the attack shattered windows in the East Side neighborhood surrounding the United Nations. Passenger cars crashed into each other and city buses slammed headlong into MTA shelters where passengers waited to board. A police helicopter crashed into the United Nations headquarters on First Avenue, causing the chopper to burst into flames and destroying part of the upper story of the glass-paneled building. This was a low-intensity attack.

Ensconced in his NMCC command chair, General Saint checked the god screen on the wall in front of and above him. An emergency national security alert message had suddenly lit up the large rectangular imaging panel.

The alert stated that National Security Directive NSD-767 had been implemented and that further information required a security clearance to access.

The few lines in bold white characters that flashed across the face of the god screen every few minutes ostensibly held no threat, but only to those who were not aware of the significance of NSD-767. The bigot list of those in the know was extremely small, so there were not many who in fact had any inkling of the grave significance of the message. Ignorance was, in this case, bliss, if a type of bliss that would inevitably be short-lived.

Only the handful of those in the secret intelligence loop would realize that the message meant that the world had passed over a threshold and now stood at the vestibule to Armageddon.

Those few knew NSD-767 under the code name Dawn Horse. Among those scant few who knew about Dawn Horse and what it implied to the fate of the world was General Casper Saint.

# THREATCON DELTA

In fact it had been when Saint had stumbled onto the existence of Dawn Horse that he had decided to attack and take the Pentagon over. The takeover plan had followed with an inexorable logic after the discovery of the secret national security directive was made.

The fact that Dawn Horse existed had made the takeover possible. And now, Saint knew, Dawn Horse had been activated. He had known from the start that its activation was inevitable. Indeed, with the three strikes on New York City targets using the Northern Cross weapon system, the activation of Dawn Horse was imminent.

"Let me call Bob back," Saint ruminated aloud, and puffed on his stogie. "He's always a lot of fun." Saint thought a moment. "Better still, let me call my broker."

He nodded at Pegasus who took a long time – for him a minute was a long time, and this took most of sixty seconds – to set up a secure cellular communications link to an overseas number.

What made it take time was in bouncing the signals up into space, down again into a series of foreign proxy servers on the global fiber optic computer network, and then encrypting everything so that interception by the NSA – among other potential spook listeners – and consequent eavesdropping on the conversation were impossible.

DAVID ALEXANDER

"Alexai, you old dog. How's it going?" Saint said when Pegasus nodded to indicate the line was open and clear.

More than five thousand statute miles away, in a dacha outside of Moscow that had first been owned by Party members, then by the organized crime figures who had replaced them as the power brokers of the nation, Lev Varukoi sat in front of a similar bank of large computer screens. It was already snowing. Early, but expectable. No global warming here. Not yet. Maybe never. Here, you could still cut mastodon stakes out of the frozen tundra well into the spring. Well, he thought, that was an exaggeration, but it was pretty damn cold just the same.

Alexai was Varukoi's code name for the duration of the operation.

"You're not supposed to check back yet, Rodney." He pronounced it "Road-Knee."

Rodney was Saint's code name for Varukoi to use in communications.

"Well, Alexai, old bean, I got a little tired of sitting here thinking about you counting all that smelly old money."

"We don't have it yet to count, my friend."

"Soon enough. Things are about to roll."

"It's not like you to want reassurance."

"I'm not myself these days," Saint retorted. He smiled. "I see a vision. I see you sitting in front of those screens watching the numbers on the tickers and thinking clever thoughts about those numbers. So clue me in."

Lev Varukoi chuckled. Saint had a streak of prescience. He'd been doing exactly as the general had imagined.

His role in the mission was not only to be the bankroller, and to supply logistics, but also to be the broker and money man at the end of the logistics chain. His systems had links to every major brokerage house in the world, including the Tokyo and Hong Kong stock exchanges.

There had to be enough bidders, hundreds of them in fact, for the scheme to work. It all had to be precisely coordinated too. That was Varukoi's end. In return he would rake in a hefty cut. He deserved it, though.

"Everything's in place. It all depends on what you make happen within the rest of the duration of the mission," he told Saint.

"It'll happen, don't worry, Alexai. With a little help from my friends. Just make sure you take care of the exit strategy. I want to be in good shape to count my twenty billion."

"You're in the best of hands, Rodney, never fear."

"I always worry, especially when I'm told not to."

Saint reached for a switch to sever the communications link.

"That's all for now, Alexai."

"Good luck, Rodney."

Saint punched another series of buttons on the console in front of him, opening new secure communications channels to other individuals playing their parts, wittingly or unwittingly, in the great game.

"Now I think I'll call back Bob."

*DAY THREE:*
*TUESDAY*
*SEPTEMBER 13*TH

**DAWN HORSE**

## Nineteen
### Talk to Bob

*"B*ob wants to see you."

Rommel Krieger turned over on his side.

"How does he know I'm here?" he asked President Linda Halifax who had the half of the bed facing the door.

"Everybody knows you're here. Or did you think this was a secret?"

"I thought it was a secret," Krieger told her.

"Not after the first five minutes," replied the president.

"It's two-fifteen." He added, "In the morning."

"It's important or Bob wouldn't ask."

"OK. So I guess I'll go see Bob."

Escorted by two female Secret Service agents, Krieger had negotiated the ground floor level of the White House and was in the basement ten minutes later.

# THREATCON DELTA

The president had inaugurated a sterner implementation of gender-neutral hiring for the corps of White House bodyguards, citing figures showing that in the field of close protection men perform no better than women, and in some cases are outperformed by women. But that wasn't the only new thing.

The White House basement had been much improved since the days of Nixon's Plumbers and Ollie and company's secret missions to Iran. It was better lighted and the floors were carpeted, to name two newer amenities. It served much the same purpose, though, affording additional office space and serving as a useful location for conducting especially sensitive state business that required utmost secrecy.

The Oval Office was a fishbowl. The president might close its doors but could not close out the attentions of the world. Conversations and meetings were recorded. Records were kept. Witnesses to decisions made and subjects discussed could provide testimony long after the fact. The same went for the Map Room, Yellow Oval Room, Blue Room, Red Room, and other chambers amid the three stories and one hundred rooms of the White House that were frequently used for purposes of conducting presidential affairs.

# DAVID ALEXANDER

Even the NSC meeting room, that small -- deliberately small, much in the same way that the British Chamber of Parliament has been kept small -- room where the National Security Council meets, chaired by its seven cabinet-rank members.

The White House basement, however, has long been a bastion of secrecy. The already mentioned Plumbers were the most notorious example; so was Colonel Oliver North's unofficial skullduggery during the second Reagan term.

There are other examples, though. For instance, there is a numbered room, bereft of other markings, that is located at the foot of a flight of cement stairs off an unheated, concrete-walled corridor that leads down to the second basement -- there are three beneath the White House, with extensive Federalist Era water tunnels at the very bottom -- that is lined with expensive high-technology equipment.

Despite the fact that its very location makes it impervious to electronic eavesdropping, its walls are lined with the same electromagnetically absorbent materials as are the cockpits of Stealth bombers and its interior is checked daily against bugging attempts by would-be eavesdroppers.

Defense Secretary Robert Richardson Battle, given to classical analogies, and unaware that Casper Saint, poetaster of epic masters, had earlier quoted the Aeneid to negotiator Jackson Strake, had dubbed this subbasement chamber the Room of the Sibyls. It was, after all, a place in which enigmatic prophesies of doom were often made.

It was here that Krieger's Secret Service escorts deposited him, and it was within the room that Krieger found the Secretary of Defense and Ensign Henrietta Sabio awaiting his arrival.

"Coffee?"

"Very black."

"Green figs and yogurt with that too, I suppose?" quipped Bob Battle, his good humor having returned somewhat since his run-ins with Saint earlier that day.

"If you have them."

There was an aluminum-encased caterer's pump carafe on a shelf in the kitchenette in the corner of the room. There was always a kitchenette tucked away somewhere. There were several kitchenettes, Krieger reflected, in the underground bunker complex beneath the streets of London that Churchill used during the Blitz. He, Krieger, had spent hours in the Cabinet War Rooms and the adjacent Churchill Museum, fascinated by the details, such as the Prime Minister's hand-drawn cartoons of Hitler on a large map of Europe spread on the wall of complex's strategic command center. Now he flashed on the kitchenette next door to it, where a tin of coffee was preserved beside a stove where a steel percolator, not used since World War Two, sat next to it.

Krieger poured coffee into a white foam Dixie cup from the caterer's carafe, pleased to see that it was still steaming hot, though not as pleased by the too-familiar and unfortunately expected flavor of stale supermarket canned coffee that followed after he'd taken a tentative sip. He took his coffee back to the area with the equipment consoles, bypassing the danishes and pastries on a large, dull silver-colored tray next to the carafe on the countertop. Since the coffee was bad, the pastries would be stale -- it was almost a law of life in the capital.

"Have a seat," the SecDef told him.

Facing the consoles there was a row of form-fitted wire-mesh Aaron Posturefit chairs that swiveled on steel pedestal mountings. The chairs looked comfortable, and they were; they had to be. They were the kind of chairs designed for users of equipment who needed to sit relatively motionless for long spells without stretching their legs or backs.

Krieger sat in one of them and swiveled to face the SecDef. He drank some more of the lousy coffee and then set the cup down into a receptacle built into the right arm of the chair.

Bob Battle began telling Krieger about Dawn Horse, and how the covert military project

255

connected up with General Casper Saint's takeover of the Pentagon.

The Defense Secretary was earnest in conclusion.

"Saint's operation threatens everything. You can see that now."

Battle glanced aside, thinking.

"Paranoid psychosis coupled with a high IQ can be a dangerous combination," Krieger suggested. "Why was he given the brief he got?"

"An ... oversight."

"Just like failure to take him out."

"We're confronted by the present, not the past," Battle replied, somewhat unconvincingly. "That's why Sabio was placed in your office as your assistant. There was at least a failsafe built in."

"And so now I've got to put it on the line," Krieger retorted indignantly. "For god and country. For mom's apple pie." He leaned forward, his face set in stone. "I don't think I'm ready for that, Bob."

"Saint will fuck it all up. You can see that from what I've just revealed to you. Our rogue general is going for broke. There won't be any place left to hide, no holes to crawl into, after Saint has finished with the Pentagon -- unless you figure on living in a cave somewhere eating broiled shit for the rest of your life."

"I like caves, Bob. Besides, you'll arrange for me to carry one of those plastic VIP cards like the one you've got nestled in your wallet right now. The ones that guarantee express service to Mount Weather or some other deep underground facility to preserve -- what's the phrase again? -- ah yes, 'continuity of government.' You can wait out Armageddon down there while suckers like me will take their chances in the ash heap of your former playground."

"I don't know what you're referring to."

"How about I frisk you and find out if you're carrying one of those supposedly nonexistent VIP cards, Bob?"

"Hypothetically speaking -- and this confirms or denies nothing," Battle said after a pause, "it wouldn't make much difference to those who were provided shelter at deep underground facilities in time of national emergency. There would be nothing left to go back to. It would all just be ... over."

Krieger said nothing in reply. He was studying Battle's face. The thought struck Krieger that for what was conceivably the first time in Battle's life the man was telling it straight.

"Pick your team, Krieger. You're on point," Battle was saying as he raised his eyes again and he went on emphatically. "I'm truly sorry about asking it of you, but that's the way it is, and that's the way it'll have to be. There are zero alternatives."

"Your coffee's lousy, Bob," said Krieger.

"Tell me you'll do it."

"I'll do it, Bob."

Deep below the waters of the Atlantic, Dawn Horse sensed the coming of a new age.

It began to awaken.

Twenty
## Outside Inside

*L*-force's purpose was to act as a cleansing agent.

L-force was to engulf the pathogens that attacked the transplant of new flesh grafted onto the system by the operation commanded by General Casper Saint.

The team had been activated a short time before Brilliant Echo -- the code-name, devised by Saint, for the operation that included, but was not limited to, the seizure and occupation of Wedge Three of the Pentagon by his crack Gold Force commando brigade -- by a single coded email appearing on a computer screen.

When L-force's leader had mouse-clicked the decode icon a single word appeared: activate.

Although for the last five years he'd known that one day such a message would arrive, and although he and his company-strength action team had trained for the operation that would commence upon receipt of the activation code, the reality of imminent action came as an almost physical shock.

Then the moment passed and L-force's leader began to round up his team.

The cell's leader knew just enough about the operation to do his job, but not enough to compromise the mission if captured and interrogated. Just the same, he like the rest of the cell wore L-patches under their heart-side armpits. If captured, finger pressure on the patches would release a fast-acting neurotoxin derived from Japanese puffer fish that would kill painlessly in under twelve seconds.

On activation, the Brilliant Echo operation's mobile team leader drew his paramilitary operators together into the safe house established in the West Virginia countryside, in the Appalachian Highlands a few miles outside of the town of Wheeling. The safe house contained extensive weapons stores in locked gun racks and stockpiles of gear and ammunition carefully and secretly compiled over the course of the last five years while the cell was dormant, its members going about their day-to-day cover activities.

As they drilled with weapons and practiced the deadly tradecraft of the commando arts, they awaited the signal from Martian over secure communication. Martian was General Saint's game name for the op. Upon the media's report of the takeover of the Pentagon, L-force's members all knew that the moment for them to act was close at hand. They had not been told beforehand what the precipitating event would be that would call for their services, but when they saw what had happened they had few doubts that this was it -- that this was show time.

Now, a few hours Brilliant Echo's after-action orders were received, L-force's Squad Zero was in a Hummer rolling across the Washington Beltway toward its mission's initial point. Inside the Hummer the six men methodically checked their weapons, ammo and combat gear. The men were well-equipped for every martial contingency. Few found more than minor problems that needed last-minute correction.

During its long period of dormancy the sleeper cell had staged a snatch-and-grab raid on an automated weapons storage facility near Provo, Utah. The arsenal base, established by Congress under the Arsenal Base Act of 2015, was intended to decentralize storage of sophisticated weapons, including weapons of mass destruction, in order to better keep them from getting into the hands of terrorists. The George W. Bush Arsenal Base, occupying thirty miles of open scrub desert, was honeycombed with surface and underground storage depots built by military contractors with high security clearances.

261

# THREATCON DELTA

While the arsenal facility was enclosed by a perimeter fence monitored by low-light and infrared cameras and encircled by a field-effect alarm sensing system, the security system was also its Achilles' heel. Exploiting holes in the secure socket layer protocols that controlled access via the distributed computer network monitoring the facility, L-force's hackers had opened a window of opportunity for a theft of the most advanced weapons in the US inventory.

Random patrols by robotic APCs equipped with low-light cameras and remote-operated, pintle-mounted M-60 machineguns that were linked to the computerized security network, were evaded as well. Two deuce-and-a-halfs had rolled in empty and rolled out again crammed full of weapons, ammunition and miscellaneous combat gear.

Some of those stolen weapons were in the hands of L-force right now. The members of the cell were not only superbly equipped but were extremely capable commandos.

Each of them had a score to settle with Uncle Sam, and with the world at large, for that matter. Each of them had been paid well, and knew that should they die in combat on what members of the cell termed "the Pentagon op" then their designated next of kin would receive the payments in their stead. They knew little more, but what little they did know was enough.

The force behind the operation was large. This had been an op in the making for a long time. It was a lot more than it seemed on the surface.

The moment to act had arrived.

The Pentagon had been taken.

The consequences of this single bold act would shake the world.

■

Almost at the same time that L-force's mercenary hard cases, each with a hardon to grudge-fuck the US defense establishment, each part of a company that packed the firepower of a regiment, saddled up and secretly moved on their targets in Virginia and Metro DC, Marine Colonel Robin "Red" Hawk conducted a pre-mission inspection of the commando team that he too was about to lead into battle.

Hawk's commandos were the best there were, and Hawk was justly proud of them. They were his personally picked and trained hard chargers. They were the best the Marines had to offer, and that made them the best of the best.

The Red Hawk stood ramrod straight and saluted each of the two strike teams as they filed toward the two waiting V-22 Osprey convertiplanes whose rotors were already tilted upward in vertical ascent mode. The Ospreys would make history today. The problem-plagued aircraft had finally proven its worth in the South Central Asian war zone of Nagorno-Karabakh but that was in conventional combat. Today the Osprey would demonstrate that it was also a highly capable tool for use in the internal security role.

The two squads, one to each convertiplane, had two separate missions.

Squad One would be ferried a short distance to the shore of the Potomac where its personnel would make their way into the Pentagon subbasement via the underground route used by the two escapees from the takeover on day one.

Squad Two would be set down atop the Pentagon roof complex, from which they would deploy downward into the Building via one of the five light wells situated between each of the sub-roofs covering the Pentagon's five ring corridors.

The two teams would act as a hammer and an anvil, slamming down with brutally crushing force to pulverize the takeover forces, but they would do this with surgical accuracy. The hostages that Saint had taken would not come under fire. At the same that Teams Able and Baker would attack the insurgents, a third team, Charlie, would stage a lightning hostage rescue mission.

The single fly in the ointment was that Charlie was a Delta team, and though technically under

Colonel Red Hawk's command, Hawk still had to liaise with his opposite number in the Delta chain of command. Well, you couldn't have everything, and his Marines would show those snake eaters from Bragg a thing or two. There wasn't another kind of soldier in anybody's army that could hold a candle to a jarhead.

Hawk saluted the Ospreys as they lifted off from Hurlburt Field, about fifty miles south of Washington DC. Hawk then climbed aboard a Blackhawk which was to shuttle him directly to the mobile command post that had been discreetly set up a mile west of the Pentagon, on the Pentagon helipad landing field. This would be the base station and command center for all the unfolding operations.

If everything went off without a hitch, the Pentagon would be free of the maggots that infested it by lunchtime. Of this the Red Hawk was supremely confident.

∎

The Blackhawk revved its rotor blades.

Rommel Krieger entered through the helo's side hatch.

He was only partly surprised to find Ensign Sabio seated in military webbing, dressed in camo fatigues.

"What the hell are you doing here, Ensign Sabio?" he asked.

"I volunteered, sir."

"I work alone. So get lost."

"The president ordered me to accompany you, sir. I was instructed to render all assistance. And to keep you out of trouble."

Krieger shook his head.

"Look, Sabio. I've ragged you a lot, I know, but you're a good kid. Get off the chopper if you're smart. You've got too much to live for to go back in there. Take my advice. Get out now before it's too late. You don't owe the bastards anything."

"What about you?"

"That's my business."

"I'm afraid I have to insist that I come along, sir," she repeated.

"Okay. It's your funeral, Ensign Sabio. Just promise me one thing, okay?"

"What would that be, sir?"

"Don't call me 'sir,' again."

"Certainly, sir."

The Blackhawk's main rotors began to spin faster now, the initially drooping blades rising to the horizontal until they dished above the hull of the rotor craft. The pilot pulled back on the cyclical pitch stick and the Blackhawk rose straight into the air like an express elevator going up a shaft.

This time the wrench in the guts Krieger felt had only a little to do with the mechanics of vertical flight.

Twenty-one
## Killing with Unkindness

*N*egotiator Jackson Strake sat idly at his tactical VOIP communications console. They weren't telling him anything anymore. A bad sign. The negotiator knew something was about to go down, and he didn't have to be a mind-reader to suspect that this was probably a counterattack of some kind against Saint's paramilitary forces occupying Wedge Three.

The White House situation room had become increasingly thinned of personnel. What had begun as the crowded nerve center of a behind-the-scenes effort toward a negotiated settlement to the crisis was now a sham office staffed by a skeleton crew. Strake's internal email traffic had slowed to a trickle. His cell phone wasn't ringing as much. And the Marines outside the door seemed to be looking at him with strangely bemused expressions on their faces. As always,

Strake thought, he was the last one to know anything.

Well, fuck them all, he told himself. Fuck the pinstripe suits and the laptop-warriors. Since when had Strake ever given half a shit about the games their kind played? Strake had become an expatriate to get away from them. He could pull up stakes whenever he wanted.

In fact, Strake now decided he would pick himself up and head back to Venice. No more sidetracking. This time it was for real. Nodding to himself at the rightness of this decision, he rolled the office chair under the trestle table so he could sit close to the display panel and began to keystroke and mouse-click himself into the websites of three major international carriers. Minutes later he had ebooked himself an evening flight out of Dulles International Airport. It was a direct SST flight, straight to Marco Polo Airport in Venice, Italy.

Propping his feet on the edge of the table, Strake felt relieved. The ordeal was over for him. He was going back home. Back to Venice, and his little pal Black Luigi, who was hopefully being treated well by a certain Campo San Marco prostitute he'd paid to feed and change the pine-chip bedding in his tank twice a week. Strake checked his watch -- he saw he could still do dinner at the swank DC M-Bar and have time for a drink at the Dulles

# THREATCON DELTA

International departure lounge before flight time. If they caught a tailwind he'd be back at his sixteenth century palazzo in the San Toma district about two hours later by a British Airways SST flight.

Strake was composing an appropriate memo of resignation to the Powers That Be when an incoming message made the display screen come back to life. It was red-coded, meaning it was from Casper Saint. Strake's fingers stopped on the keyboard in mid-stroke.

"Hello again, Mr. Negotiator."

Casper Saint's angular ebony face filled the large flat panel display on his desk. As usual, a thin cigar was jutting from the corner of Saint's mouth and the black patch over the general's left eye lent the face a sinister aspect.

A smaller window showed Strake's face as it appeared to the general. It was a study in contrasts. Strake's blond hair, so light in hue that it appeared as almost a shade of gray, his pale blue eyes and light complexion, all combined to give him an appearance of youth, except for the longitudinal scar on his right jaw where the bullet of a would-be killer had creased his face ten years before. No one who saw that scar and looked into Strake's eyes had any doubts that Strake was a bad guy to cross.

"General," Strake replied, sounding professionally cheerful despite the circumstances.

"I haven't heard from you in hours," Saint went on. "Was getting to kind of miss those little discussions we've been having. You strike me as a decent sort of guy, Strake. Did it ever occur to you that you're being used?"

"General, we're all being used one way or another," Strake answered without a trace of irony. "That's just the way it works on this planet. Everybody's a pawn sooner or later."

"True, Mr. Negotiator, all too true. All of us are pawns in someone else's game. That's the way societies work," Saint replied. "But -- let's get specific. What's the game we're in? Why are we pawns? What's the prize?"

"I don't think I follow you."

"As I recall, Mr. Strake, we're both students of epic poetry."

"I think we've already discussed Virgil, general."

"Yes, Virgil. But do you know your Milton, Mr. Strake? I believe every soldier should."

"Well, I liked the part about the devil."

"Yes, Milton's Satan was one of the great characters in literature. A warrior, if you recall, Mr. Strake, cast down from heaven; a former bright angel who had stood at the right hand of the divine throne, thrown down into the foulest depths of hell."

"Like you, general? Is that the comparison you're making?"

"That should be obvious," Saint answered. "But I wasn't thinking of Milton's Paradise Lost at the moment. Instead it was his other great epic Samson Agonistes that came to mind."

"I didn't read that one."

"A pity, Mr. Strake," Saint retorted. "Let me give you the Cliffs Notes version. The story concerns the biblical hero Samson, another warrior, who is brought in chains to the mighty temple of the Philistines. Although shorn of his locks by Delilah, he is still in possession of great strength, and for that reason his captors have bound him with chains of iron to the pillars that support their mighty temple. The Philistines have blinded Samson as well. His eyes are gone. He can't see.

"Do you know, Mr. Strake, to precisely which kind of temple the Philistines had brought their captive?"

"I don't know, general. I'll take a wild-ass guess and say to their gods."

"Yes, to their god Dagon," Saint replied. "But do you know what kind of god Dagon was, Mr. Strake? Dagon was the Philistines' god of war. And the temple to which they had brought Samson in chains was their temple of war, their house of war. 'Blind among enemies. Oh, worse than chains,' the poet wrote, 'In power of others, never my own.' What a plight for the mightiest warrior of myth to find himself in. Wouldn't you agree, Mr. Strake?"

"So what's your point?"

"Here, as in our earlier discussion concerning the penetrating vision of the Sibyls, we have an example of what might be termed the value of tactical reconnaissance and surveillance. The force that possesses this beyond the horizon of its battlefield competitors usually prevails."

Strake figured that the military operation he surmised was in progress was about to commence. It was more than intuition. You developed an operational feel for such things, and his internal clock told Strake that the op would certainly go down soon. Still, the subject of his brief was right in front of him, so why not try to negotiate, even if it was the eleventh hour.

"General, what's the point of these analogies from Augustus Caesar's favorite poet and Milton, who as I recall wrote those epics after the failure of Oliver Cromwell's Glorious Revolution while half-blind and cast out of the centers of power by the restored Stuart monarchy. I know a lot more history, especially military history, than I do poetry. And if history's any guide, you've set yourself up for a classic siege offensive. You're cut off and surrounded, but you've definitely made your point. The nation has heard you. I think it's time all this ended. Don't you?"

Strake watched the face in front of him, regarded it carefully. It showed no trace of concern, no sign of inner conflict. General Saint smiled and shook his head.

"We'll talk later, Mr. Negotiator. In a relatively short time a multi-tiered assault using a mix of conventional forces and unconventional weapons will be used against the Pentagon in an effort to break my forces."

Saint hesitated before breaking contact.

"One final thought. About Samson. You see, the great biblical warrior had been blinded and chained, but still had heavenly eyes, one might say orbital eyes, to which he connected. Those links to high-altitude surveillance, in Samson's case divine surveillance, were invisible to his enemies, but not to Samson. And with his second sight returned the power of his mighty limbs ... power he used to pull down the pillars to which he'd been chained and bring the Philistines' house of war crashing down to rubble."

"General – "

"A three-pronged strike on my position will commence. I want to make certain that my forces repel it as efficiently as possible. We'll talk later --

after I've repulsed or do to the Pentagon what Samson did to the temple of Dagon."

The screen blanked.

Well, shit; foiled again, thought Strake, although he wasn't surprised, somehow. He opened his cell phone and speed-dialed all the White House and CIA numbers he'd programmed into it in order to warn them. He reached no Powers That Be, however. He only managed to get through to a low-level staffer. She promised to do whatever she could. He knew she probably couldn't do shit. Strake sat for a moment, pondering his existing options.

Then he did something he'd never thought he'd end up doing. Strake canceled his express flight back to Venice. After that he picked up the chair, hurled it at the display screen, and, feeling somewhat better, went looking for a weapon as the computer short-circuited and blew apart in a brief spark and flame-out. Too much face-time and too little direct action, thought Strake. That was the problem.

■

L-force tracked the sortie of tilt-rotor Osprey convertiplanes as they approached the Pentagon, shuttling Red Hawk's commando teams into combat to retake the occupied Building's critical Wedge Three.

# THREATCON DELTA

Saint's covert backup team, led by decommissioned Spetsnaz *vasaltniki*, special assault troops, supplied by Varukoi, and kept inactive for years, was now spread out on the Jefferson Davis and Shirley Highways, the two major highway arteries that bracketed the Pentagon's northwest and southern approaches.

One two-man squad, equipped with Strela-18 man-portable missile launchers, was positioned under cover.

The Osprey came into view as a black dot from the south as it flew a north-pointing vector from Andrews Air Force Base six miles south of Washington DC. The Stinger crews were ready. They tracked the Osprey as it approached the roof of the Pentagon and translated to helicopter flight above the River Entrance.

"Targets acquired," the first of the two commandos with the Strela-18 rocket launchers said into the lip mike positioned close to his mouth on a flexible mounting.

"*Otpizdit!* -- waste the fuckers!"

Each of the two Strela shooters pressed the trigger of their weapons. The shoulder-mounted launchers bucked and kicked like little mules. A back-blast of hot, white, acrid-smelling smoke belched from the rear of the launcher tubes. The L-force shooters continued tracking the heat-seeking missiles as they sped toward their targets through the launchers' integrated scopes.

Moments later both warheads impacted.

Fireballs blossomed.

The Osprey shattered outward in a million fragments. These spinning shards were also engulfed by coronas of flame. The main rotor snapped off and broke into jagged, whirling scythes, the ripped-apart blades flying outward in every direction, shattering glass, decapitating the unlucky.

The troops inside the Osprey were killed instantly. Their bodies were shattered by the blast effect and ripped apart by fragments of the aircraft's punctured bulkheads that had been blown inward by the explosion and turned into shrapnel.

Soon only a puff of smoke remained to mark the place in the blue skies overhead where the helo had last been seen.

■

At almost the same time, the second group of rescuers had reached the mission insertion point inside the Pentagon. They were oblivious so far to the fate of the team that was supposed to have gone in from the roof: the squads were operating comms-out, observing radio silence until the attack had commenced and was underway with primary mission objectives achieved.

They were also unaware that Saint had set up an effective tactical perimeter warning system. Portable field-effect sensors had been placed at potential soft points everywhere there was likely to be an offensive breach in the perimeter. The network was monitored through a central hub linked to computers in the captive NMCC.

"Our guests have arrived, Jefe," Red Dog Juan announced.

"Then roll out the welcome mat," Saint replied.

"Si, Jefe. At once," Red Dog Juan acknowledged.

He keyed in commands at the multiple keyboards he'd set up, keeping his eyes on the screen. One by one the antipersonnel ordnance was activated.

"Welcome mat's out, Jefe," Red Dog Juan reported. "Our guests, they will be well cared for."

Moments later the assault platoon of Marines walked into the trap that had been prepared for them.

Robotic sentinels opened fire with automatic weapons. Poison gas escaped in invisible jets from concealed ports in the walls.

Steel bulkheads sped downward from their concealed niches in the ceiling, penning in the dying men who fell as they succumbed to flying steel and corrosive, toxic gases.

The killing machinery was as fast as it was efficient. All the attackers were dead within a matter of minutes.

"Status report," Saint calmly demanded.

Red Dog Juan monitored the bank of video terminals, scrolling from one window on his workstation to another as he checked the real-time feed from individual surveillance cams.

"*Todos muertos*, Jefe," Red Dog Juan said, with undisguised satisfaction in his voice.

"Send a detail after the other two," Saint ordered his XO.

"Yes, sir," Captain Da Gamma replied crisply.

■

Krieger and Sabio were moving back along the municipal water tunnel through which Krieger had led them both out of the Pentagon two days before as Saint's takeover bid was in progress.

Navigating by the INS icons on their HMD displays using a transitioned version of the tablet-based Individual Soldier Navigation app that had assisted Krieger in their escape, they saw that they were approaching their first waypoint of their return to the subbasement of the Building.

Suddenly an explosion rocked the earth causing the tunnel to shake violently.

"Hawk, what the hell is that?" Krieger asked over SINCGARS.

There was no answer.

279

"Hawk, what the hell's going on?"

"There's been a counterstrike. The teams have been hit. Get the hell out of there."

"How bad?"

"We don't know yet, Krieger," Hawk shouted. "But it's none of your affair. Just get out. We'll handle the rest."

Krieger looked hard at Sabio.

"I know what you're thinking, Ensign Sabio," Krieger said to her. "Don't think it. There's nothing the two of us can do. We're not even armed."

"You're right, sir," Sabio replied. "I was just -- "

"Quiet!"

Krieger had heard something. Footfalls. There was no doubt about it when he listened again. There were troops moving towards them. Double-time. A squad by the sound of it, he judged.

"Trouble's on its way, ensign," Krieger announced. "I make it a squad. Somehow they know we're in here. That means that they know about this tunnel."

But a few moments later it was too late for talk. Saint's active reconnaissance patrol had breached the tunnel and was now approaching their position. The members of the patrol were equipped with night vision capable head-mounted displays and could see clearly in the darkness of the tunnel network.

Sighting the intruders, Saint's men opened fire with automatic weapons. Krieger and Sabio took cover but were cornered by the sustained fusillade from multiple gun muzzles.

Sabio pitched a high-explosive antipersonnel fragmentation grenade. The APERS blast killed several of the attackers and forced the rest to tuck their heads down.

Then a gun muzzle spat blue-white flame and Krieger saw Sabio crumple to the concrete floor of the tunnel. He ran toward her but was cut off and pinned down by a wall of automatic weapons fire.

"Sabio!" he shouted from cover.

There was no answer. Krieger called to her again. She didn't sing out this time either.

Krieger was forced to face the realization that Sabio was dead. He'd seen her get hit and go down. Now, she wasn't answering. If that didn't add up to dead, nothing did. There was no point in lingering, not if he wanted to stay alive himself.

Krieger drew enemy fire by pitching an empty jar that he found lying within arm's reach, and broke from cover. A zigzagging run with ricochets spanging and sparking at his heels brought him out through a side tunnel.

"Hawk, you there."

"What is it?"

"Sabio's down. Hit by fire. I think she's bought it. I'm extracting."

"That's too bad, Krieger," Hawk commiserated. "You should have moved when I ordered you to do so, maybe she'd still be alive."

"Watch it, you sonofabitch, or -- "

Suddenly Krieger heard a sound in his SINCGARS headset. It was Sabio's voice. Faint, but she was still alive.

"I'm hit," she was saying. "Can't move yet."

There was no doubt about it. Sabio was indeed alive.

Krieger told her to hang on. He'd be back to get her.

"Hawk, I'm going back in. I want a resupply of weapons at the RV point. Send in a Marine detail."

"No you're not going back in. You're extracting. That's an order. She had her orders and she knew the risks, just like you."

"Orders? You don't give me orders, Hawk," Krieger replied. "I'm not one of your jarheads. Either give me the gear or I'll go back without it. What'll it be?"

"You'll get your gear, but just let's get it straight that you're contravening my direct order to extract."

Hawk was pissed off but Krieger was right.

"Understood."

"I've already issued the orders. The gear will be at the RV point by the time you get there. Out."

## DAVID ALEXANDER

And the comms net went dead.

Twenty-two
## Man-Machine Interface

Saint dreamed he was getting a blowjob in a swank Manhattan hotel. It was his favorite suite at the old Millennium Hilton, the one on the fifty-third floor that had overlooked the World Trade Center on the north side and the tip of lower Manhattan on its southern exposure. The woman resembled Ginger, who he used to take there, except she wasn't quite enough Ginger-like to be the genuine article, and she wore a white bra with a floral weave that had two holes for her nipples and a pair of tight satin pants with no crotch.

Saint's phallus was in her mouth and both in the dream and for some time afterward, the general retained a vivid impression of the intricate weave of the bra and the alternating sensations of the fabric and nipples rubbing against his distended organ as he watched her minister to him.

Although Saint preferred his women completely bare-breasted during sex, her fellatio proved so

284

arousing that Saint was about to erupt in her mouth. He might have done so too, he later thought, except for a knock on the door and its sudden opening that reenacted a real-life occurrence when a female hotel employee had accidentally let herself into the suite while Saint was getting that special blowjob long ago.

"Sorry sir," the voice said, "but you asked to be awakened if anything important happened."

Saint had heard himself grunt something incoherently as he woke up. He felt a moment's disorientation as he came back to his senses.

"Do you see any wings, soldier?"

"What sir?"

"Wings?"

"No, sir. I don't."

"Then I'm not a butterfly dreaming I was a man," Saint told him. "I'm but a man who'd dreamt his butter was about to fly."

"Yes, sir."

If the soldier was perplexed, he didn't show it. The general, after all, was a tactical genius, and sometimes given to saying strange things. "Black Napoleon" was what they called him behind his back. Saint knew all about the cognomen, and was secretly proud of it. Not even Colin Powell had been dubbed with such an exalted nickname.

Saint sat up and flicked on the flight. The room was an office that he'd converted into a makeshift billet. Saint had used it for grabbing what sleep he could during the approximate last sixty hours he'd spent in the Pentagon's NMCC.

He'd issued himself uppers -- go pills -- along with the other members of his battalion-sized assault unit, but Saint preferred to catch some shuteye whenever he could and forego their use.

The drugs tended to cloud thinking, and above all precise, accurate framing of ideas was critical not only to the success of this bold operation, but to Saint's personal survival as well. So Saint slept when he could, as he'd done now, retiring at around oh-one-thirty hours for a catnap, mission contingencies permitting.

A glance at his digital Tag-Huer chronometer told him he'd slept for almost two hours straight. It was now a little past oh-three-thirty hours.

Saint blinked in the flood of light and ran his hands across his close-cropped hair as he strode into the command center. Da Gamma was at his station as Saint took occupancy of the catbird seat on the level above the NMCC's battle pit.

"What's the problem?"

"Sir, we seem to have lost positive control over Northern Cross orbital weapon platform number three. I believe there's reason to suspect that it's been taken out of action by an ASAT strike."

Saint, bending slightly, tapped out a series of instructions on a nearby keyboard, and the wide flat-panel screen at the console in front of him showed him the data. Another series of wire-grid diagrams in windows on the command center's large main screen echoed the view.

The computer system executed a global keyword search of Defense Department surveillance satellites using a knowledge-based expert systems software program that autonomously assigned keywords to remote imaging and signal processing intelligence.

These data could range from a piece of softball-sized space debris -- in which case the user could simply input "softball-sized space debris" or variations on the search term that included "softball-sized space debris striking Keyhole-class satellite" -- and get a return of search results. Even an entry like "spas debri" would work because the search engine employed a fuzzy logic algorithm.

Saint's search returned an icon with a description marked "Classified, Code-word Clearance Required to View."

However Pegasus had hacked into the computer system and Saint simply clicked on the icon. A runtime video in a pop-up window showed the real-time image of a missile track in vertical ascent, followed by its eruption into an exo-atmospheric fireball whose brilliance lit up a shrapnel cloud of exploding fragments -- the disintegrated wreckage, no doubt, of Saint's missing orbital weapon platform, Northern Cross Three.

"So ... looks like the fuckers snuck a leaker past us, huh?"

"I'm afraid it does look like a leaker, sir," Da Gamma replied, acknowledging the military term for a missile that managed to somehow penetrate a defensive envelope.

"Any other indications of trouble?"

"Unfortunately, yes," acknowledged Pegasus, fielding the question. "Here are other orbital surveillance data."

He opened the visuals and graphics from military observation satellite and high-altitude, long-endurance UAV feeds on the three central screens on the wall fronting the amphitheater below. Using a large, arrow-shaped pointing cursor, Pegasus proceeded to brief the general.

"As you can see, sir, there is activity at Strategic Command and US Space Command bases in CONUS, which concerns us. But there is also suspicious activity at known staging areas for clandestine deployment, such as FOL-Alpha and FOL-Gamma in Sri Lanka and Dubai, respectively.

"At the Dubai base, here at Jebel al-Dhanna, a few klicks to the southwest of the large US air base at al-Minhad -- "

# DAVID ALEXANDER

Pegasus indicated the photographically enhanced synthetic aperture radar image of a spike-shaped promontory jutting into the Straits of Hormuz at the Persian Gulf's narrowest point.

" -- the imagery seems to show a sortie of F-22 Raptor aircraft being armed by maintenance personnel with advanced, antisatellite missiles."

The continental landmasses depicted on the large display panel revolved clockwise in the digital equivalent of a human hand spinning a globe of the earth, and now portions of Southwest Asia and the Indian Ocean regions swam into focus.

Pegasus went on:

"Here, at FOL-Delta, just outside Djibouti, in the Horn of Africa, you can see that a strategic Boeing 747-400F jet aircraft equipped with a tactical high-energy laser weapon is being prepared for takeoff. There are other signs that retaliation is imminent, but these latter may be feints."

"The conclusion being that Northern Cross's orbital sensors are the objective of the coordinated tactical strikes that are assumed to be in the preparation stages?" opined Saint as he mulled the data.

"That's correct, sir."

"Even though they must be aware that taking out those imaging satellites will in itself constitute a breach of security that will automatically escalate the SIOP up to the level of DEFCON 1?"

"The opposition may have reasoned that taking such grave risks might prove beneficial in the end. Perhaps they've concluded, rightly or wrongly, that with the target imaging capabilities of Northern Cross weapon platforms blinded or disabled, they could more effectively stage an interdiction mission against our operation here at the Pentagon."

"It's got the ring of truth," Saint affirmed with a nod.

He leaned back and took a few puffs on a fresh Dutch Masters Perfecto.

"What do we need in order to trigger a Dawn Horse intervention?"

"Having assumed you would want to know, sir, I've already worked up a series of retaliatory options," Pegasus replied without a pause.

Pegasus keystroked and mouse-clicked and the list of retaliatory options appeared on Saint's tactical display screen.

Saint scanned his available choices. All of them would have the effect of triggering the Single Integrated Operational Plan, or SIOP, that had been automated under the COLOSUS program, and thereby activating the triad of stealth Dawn Horse unmanned underwater vehicles into launching cruise missile attacks on their global pre-designated targets.

The choices were arranged on an ascending scale of destructive magnitude that began with localized damage on the theater, or tactical, level and ended with strategic options that would result in regional damage on a massive scale.

The cruise missiles capable of being launched by Dawn Horse carried a mix of warhead types and megatonnage. Some were extremely "clean" nukes that, at least in theory, would result in only minimal radioactive contamination, while others were MIRVed weapons carrying multiple warheads.

Only COLOSUS could launch these weapons, but COLOSUS would do so with inhuman speed based upon the SIOP's prioritization of damage from terrorist action to preprogrammed targets around the world.

Saint studied the battle tasking order list and made his choice.

"I'm not fucking around, and this will demonstrate it clearly to those idiots," he growled.

"The next nuclear launch will be made by the SAAE-SIOP, not by me, and the warheads won't be duds. If they thought fifty tons worth of unarmed missile warhead and propulsion section blowing up a block of prime Midtown Manhattan real estate was bad, wait till they see what real destruction looks like. From now on, no dummy warheads. Make a note of it."

"Yes, sir," agreed Da Gamma.

Saint had selected three global targets. They were located at various points on the planet and on three continents, but all of them were considered vital enough to US interests to have been programmed into the automated SIOP as objects of retaliation for terrorist attacks.

The first was the US embassy in Rome. The second was the Rotterdam Oil Jetty, a platform jutting out from the coast of lower Holland equipped for filling oil tankers from refineries inland. The third and final target of the remaining two Northern Cross particle beam weapons was FOL-Delta, the clandestine military base and forward staging area that served US and allied commands in the Indian Ocean.

The general announced his intentions to Pegasus and Red Dog Juan, who cleared all security procedures and confirmed that the space-based weapons were ready to discharge. Saint then keystroked in the commands to acquire the ground-based targets and destroy them.

"Eenie, meenie and mynie mo," Saint intoned. "You're all as good as history, bro'."

The three central screens above the NMCC battle cab shifted to space-based views of the targets being struck. It was a twofold process.

## DAVID ALEXANDER

First the targets were hit by the Dawn Horse particle beam weaponry. The screens showed little in the way of the beam itself, which was largely invisible, only a trace of luminous energy, like Saint Elmo's fire, lancing downward from space.

The effects were startling and spectacular, though. Each of the three targets erupted into fireballs and violent explosions. There was no sound output, as the imagery was recorded from space-based sensors, but the mind supplied all the audio effects that the visuals lacked.

Suddenly COLOSUS flashed a warning on the screens. Via its phalanx of multispectral sensor platforms ringing the planet, the automated Single Integrated Operations Plan or SIOP, which was controlled by COLOSUS, calculated that the coordinated strike represented a valid terrorist attack on vital US security interests.

The SAAE-SIOP's programming was clear on the next step. Dawn Horse was to be activated to retaliate for the strikes.

Secure telemetry insured that positive control of the wholly machine-actuated loop took place seamlessly. The orders to the UUVs were instantaneous. Dawn Horse cruise missiles were loaded into special launchers and sent rocketing up through the surface of the ocean from its depths, into which the Dawn Horse triad immediately lost itself in a series of jinks, turns and dives designed to evade hostile sensors and pursuit systems.

The cruise missiles flew stealthy tracks to reach their inland targets. Their nuclear warheads detonated as airbursts fifty feet above ground. There was no warning, only the telltale flash followed by heat and blast waves that obliterated everything within the circumference of the blast radius in triple nuclear fireballs.

"Yeah -- we bad, we baaaad," Saint chortled as the destruction was mirrored on the tactical screens. "We bad to the fuckin' bone."

An incoming channel buzzed to life.

The face on the screen was that of the presidentially appointed negotiator, Strake.

"What the hell have you done?"

"Pre-empted your side's plans to take out my eyes," said Saint matter-of-factly.

"What plans?"

"Plans that you probably weren't even aware of because they didn't place you in the decision loop, Strake," Saint retorted with venom. "Face it, Strake, you're just a pawn. The power brokers play their games and invent the rules as they go along. They don't carbon copy the little people."

Saint told Strake about the conclusive intelligence concerning an imminent attempt to interdict the orbital Snake Eye sensor satellite array. The general told Strake that he needed to act now.

"You didn't have to use nuclear weapons. You've killed thousands. You've ... don't you see?"

"No, Strake," said Saint. "It's you who refuse to comprehend what's taking place. If you saw clearly you wouldn't ask that question. You'd understand that by having automated the SIOP two years ago, by secret presidential directive, on the plans of DARPA drawn up by that lunatic Jenkins and championed by Tyler when he was president -- that on that precise date and that exact moment what has just happened today was as good as ordained by holy writ, inscribed in letters of fire on tablets of stone."

"You're wrong, Saint. Your case for inevitability falls short of reality. You're missing a few points, general." Since Strake wasn't negotiating anymore, he added, "and a few cogs in your wheels."

"Not so. I repeat: it was all inevitable. I didn't nuke anybody. COLOSUS gave the order and the Dawn Horse triad executed the strike."

"You initiated the chain of events by launching a directed energy weapon attack on three strategic targets. You conveniently left that part out, Saint."

"Sure I did. But the supposed linkage of cause and effect is a figment of your imagination. If anything, I've proven the insane folly of having set up a system as brutal and inhuman as COLOSUS. Besides, if the logic behind the automation of the SIOP is as true as those who placed Northern Cross in orbit and Dawn Horse in the oceans to patrol the sub-seas would like us to believe, then terrorists would eventually have done the same anyway."

"You know what that makes you, general?"

"Yeah, a fucking hero."

"No, Saint, it makes you a classic paranoid psychotic. I'll get back to you."

This time it was Strake who severed contact. The general stared at a blacked-out screen.

"Well, fuck you too," he said and re-lit his cigar.

■

Saint's next action was to contact Alexai.

"The heat's on," he told the Russian. "It's time we discussed the exit strategy. Have we reached the agreed-on breakout point?"

Saint checked his wrist chronometer. It was Strike Day plus two, the third day of the operation, and already nearly oh-four-hundred-hours. Late in the game.

"We're getting close," Alexai told him.

Alexai was intently watching the glowing jagged lines of a cascade graph crawl upward along a grid-patterned square. Each of the rows of the grids represented a million dollars. The spiked graph represented the earnings of the disaster futures that Alexai had invested in across the global stock markets.

"But not there yet."

"You need to score another home run," Alexai reproved Saint, "to make it a grand slam. One more. Then we're all set up for life."

"Yeah," Saint came back. "One more. I think I can arrange that."

He broke off comms and began thinking of the near wet dream he'd recently had. A broad smile broke across his face.

"I'm going to catch some more shuteye. Wake me if anything comes up."

Twenty-three
## Past the Point of No Return

It seemed like part of a circular nightmare where the abhorrent outcome of a monstrous ordeal is replayed over and over. Again, President Linda Halifax spread the unopened binder on the glass top of the desk in the Oval Office. And once again she saw its hologram-encoded identifier bearing the words Top Secret: Umbra, and beneath this stern warning, the same two words were emblazoned.

Option Omega.

She had put the matter aside for as long as possible, but the endgame had come. The presidential finding bearing her signature authorized the preparation of Option Three for use against terrorist forces holding the Pentagon hostage under Homeland Security Act provisions including the PILGRIM Act amendments of 2015. However she had yet to sign off on the final go-order to proceed, and she could still amend or cancel if she wished. But the moment to act had arrived. One way or another, a final decision had to be made, and Halifax was on point.

The dreaded moment when she had to sit and finally review the protocols of the Omega Option had arrived. Yet as before, the protocols concerned an act of overwhelming destruction almost too horrifying to contemplate. Nevertheless, that is precisely what Halifax had been doing these last few minutes. Contemplating the unthinkable; again.

The president opened the black vinyl covered ring binder and flipped back the cover exposing the cover sheet with additional warnings and an index of the tabbed dividers that separated the individual pages between them. Each of the tabbed dividers laid out, in stark detail, the list of doomsday options available within the overall framework of the Omega Option.

The plan, she well knew, called for destroying the Pentagon with one or several apocalyptic weapons, including a low-yield nuclear device. But she was also well aware that the Omega Option had far broader implications for national security. The plan had been originally drafted as a secret operational plan for the destruction of any national military, government or civilian command center that had fallen into the hands of terrorists, and could not be re-secured by negotiation or conventional military action.

Its origin lay in the dark days of turmoil that followed the September 11th, 2001 attacks and preparation for the War in Iraq. It was then realized that should terrorists take control of national command centers and negotiations or conventional military options fail to reach a resolution, then other measures might need to be taken to end the crisis.

Final measures: a strike using weapons of mass destruction, both conventional, nuclear and hybrid. The Omega Option presented the US chief executive with a checklist of scenarios. The president could use one, all, or a mix of several. Plan Omega's sub-options were listed in descending order of destructive magnitude.

She knew them by heart already, but she reviewed them again one last time before she was forced to act in order to impress their consequences in her mind as clearly as possible.

A five hundred kiloton nuclear airburst was the first option. The airburst would be sufficiently powerful to level the Pentagon, leaving little behind except charred foundation rubble. The nuclear explosive was deliverable as either a Tomahawk cruise missile, fired from standoff range from air of naval platforms, or dropped on the Pentagon as an air-to-ground munition by B-2 Spirit bomber aircraft.

Deployment of a MOAB conventional bomb or fuel-air explosive was option two. Detonation here too would be by airburst. The blast and shock effects would be similar to a nuclear airburst, except for the lack of residual radioactivity and electromagnetic pulse, or EMP, effect. The drawback was that the munitions, which were large and heavy in both cases, were only air-to-ground deliverable and not as precisely targetable as were nuclear weapons.

The third Omega option called for detonation of a non-nuclear electromagnetic pulse weapon. Known generically as an "e-bomb," such a weapon would generate a flash effect of sufficient electromagnetic energy to power as small city. The multi-megawatt burst of electrical current, or electromagnetic pulse (EMP) would burn out all the systems in the Pentagon, no matter how protected or "hardened" against EMP they might be. The danger was that it could also have unintended consequences for the Washington DC power grid and seriously disrupt national defense and commercial computer systems.

The president signaled the acting Deputy CJCS, who again awaited her instructions, to hand her the presidential finding, which she re-read, initialed and dated in her own hand. She then took a second document, a codicil to the finding, which instructed that Option Three be immediately implemented, and signed it as well.

The USAF, which like other military arms, was now operating from the Alternate Military Command Center at Raven Rock, was now authorized to carry out Option Three against the terrorist forces holding the Pentagon hostage under security provisions of the Homeland Security Act. As before, Air Force operational planning groups were to stand by to upgrade the options if necessary should the president deem stronger measures were warranted by events.

After her visitor from Defense had left the Oval Office, the president went into the nearby Map Room in the White House's West Wing. It was the central location for newsmedia interviews and announcements from the White House press secretary and the nation's chief nation's executive herself, and it would serve that purpose again.

Television cameras from all the major networks had been set up with uplinks to commercial communications satellites capable of real-time global broadcast. The president was about to address the nation on the crisis, and by extension, address the world.

She would once more reassure the citizens of the United States that government continued to function smoothly, that the crisis at the Pentagon would be handled expeditiously, and that all would soon be as it had been before the assault and takeover.

As in her previous televised address, the president would say nothing concerning the still secret Omega Option or the far worse consequences of not striking down General Saint and his forces before they could bring still more terrible designs of their own into play against the United States.

But the nation had reached and already passed the point of no return, and the countdown to a drastic act, the full consequences of which no one could presently gauge, was well underway. President Halifax prayed that some higher power would intervene. She feared that, if left to fallible human beings, all would be lost.

■

Strake had just ordered his second one-way airline ticket black to Venice. He'd done so in the midst of the president's emergency address, chilled by the realization that Halifax was lying, and that the fact she was lying meant that something truly abominable was in the offing.

Strake had no intention of being around when whatever would next happen took place, especially because he had a fairly good inkling of what form the next step would take -- the doomsday option. Strake knew how the fuckers who ran things thought. There was always the doomsday option waiting in the wings when all else, including sanity itself, failed to win the day.

And, Strake was well aware, everything, including sanity, had just hit the surrealist canvas. Strake's one hope was that his plane would reach international airspace before the doomsday plan -- whatever shape or form it took -- went down. One thing was for sure: his services as a negotiator were no longer needed.

By way of resignation, the negotiator called for a White House limo to take him to the airport. It was one of the few perks that went with the short-lived job. The receptionist was cordial and efficient.

"A car will be waiting at the North Portico Entrance in ten minutes," she promised Strake.

He had brought nothing with him. He would take nothing away.

Strake was soon ensconced inside the comfortably padded leather back seat of the black Lincoln Continental that had pulled in front of the White House North Portico.

"Dulles," said Strake.

"I know," said the driver, a Secret Service agent.

"Fast," said Strake.

"That's the way they always want it, brother."

The driver stepped on the gas.

Suddenly a Marine came running of the door beneath the ornately porticoed nineteenth century facade of the executive mansion. He jumped in front of the car and raised one hand. He held a service pistol in the other.

"Stop!" he shouted.

The driver came to an abrupt, screeching halt.

"Sir," the Marine said to Strake. "You're wanted in the command center."

"Fuck the command center. I've got a plane to catch, soldier boy."

"Sir, I am ordered to inform you that there's been a new development. I can't tell you more. Please come with me."

The Marine tried to open the passenger door but it was locked.

Strake mulled this fresh contretemps over for a minute, then unlocked the door and pushed it open.

The negotiator stepped out of the limo whose door the Marine held open for him. Minutes later he was once again back to where he had started. And he now understood why.

General Saint's face filled the large flat panel screen. He looked considerably more grim than he had looked before.

"Mr. Strake," he said. "Don't leave just yet. Venice is like a dream, but we still have a lot left to discuss."

Twenty-four
**Zones of Deepest Vulnerability**

"*U*nfriendlies."

A flashing red triangle encompassing a bright green numeral three lit up on the right corner of Krieger's HMD display. The system was set on sensor-to-shooter mode. Sabio and Krieger aimed their weapons and automatically raked the three-commando squad with bullets and grenade canisters.

"Fox, what just happened?"

It was Hawk at one of the decimated assault teams' operational sectors calling.

"Engaged the enemy," Krieger said back over SINCGARS.

"What's your position?"

Krieger tapped a key on his wrist-top controller. A map display window enlarged to fill the view field. It showed their position as a blinking red square. Numeric data indicated their present location was a half mile from Krieger's subbasement office.

Krieger gave Hawk a position brief and an ETA.

"That's good, Fox," Hawk advised. "We've got some trouble on our end, but nothing too serious."

Krieger smiled at that. In his ear mike he could hear the clamor of what to all intents was an hellacious fire-fight in progress, with Hawk's wounded survivors standing off fresh, mobile troops. Sharp, rapid crump-crump-crumps that sounded like grenade bursts punctuated the staccato pulsations of sustained heavy machinegun fire being poured into entrenched, well-defended targets. The shouts of combatants laced through the chaos like a leitmotif in an opera from hell.

The devil was back on stage, declared the sounds of war.

"We're proceeding toward our first marked waypoint. Will update when we arrive."

"Roger. Good luck."

"The same, Fox. Out."

Krieger nodded to Sabio and both moved warily from their positions of concealment in alcoves set in the tunnel wall.

The concrete beneath their feet was moist with stagnant rivulets of waste water. The old brick walls of the drainage tunnel were perfectly square. The tunnel, which had been excavated to connect with the District water tunnel system during the original Pentagon renovations, was extremely large. It had been constructed with a dual purpose

-- to enable troops of up to company-level strength to gain fast access to the Pentagon via the building's lowermost under-level in time of emergency.

Krieger cradled his weapon -- a lightweight Spectre M4 nine-millimeter subgun, the same type favored by the opposition -- at his hip as he and Sabio negotiated the dimly illuminated underground passageway. The low-light amplification capability of the tactical HMDs they wore gave them a processor-enhanced false-color view of the terrain in front of them. As Krieger walked, he thought back on the events that had preceded their reinsertion into the tunnel, events that had gotten their start when Krieger had been called into the meeting in the numbered room in the White House subbasement.

Dawn Horse. They had told Krieger about it just after the abortive attack by the combined interdiction teams and before he'd been given his final clearance. Artificial intelligence coupled with the most destructive weaponry known to mankind.

Worse than this: weaponry so destructive that to use it at all, even part of it, even under conditions of limited warfare, was unthinkable. And finally, that Dawn Horse held implicit the fact that this weaponry would be used; that there was in fact no way to turn off Dawn Horse once activated, no way to prevent the massive retaliation that was to follow in train.

Ensign Sabio, Krieger had been told, held the key to decoupling Dawn Horse from Northern Cross. Sabio's assignment to his office by the office of the Secretary of Defense had been part of the fallback plan to neutralize the automated SIOP if it activated what was thought of as the doomsday scenario.

When outgoing president Tyler had pushed his anti-terror defense plan through Congress it had become the subject of a House subcommittee convened by the minority leader. Senator Jason Talbot had opposed the automation plan, calling it, on the Senate floor, "a monstrosity and an abomination that should never be allowed to happen."

Talbot's coalition had fallen short of critical votes, though, and the motion to automate had passed with few meaningful changes. Among these changes, however, was a clause that had been inserted by the committee at the last minute as a rider to the SIOP Automation Authorization Enactment, or SAAE, bill. The clause in the rider had authorized "such entities as may be designated by Congress to examine and oversee the installation of systems relevant to maintenance of the SAAE."

# THREATCON DELTA

Yet another element of the SAAE initiative insured that the space-based system was to be built with the capability of locating, targeting and striking targets with accuracy and speed, even beneath the ocean. Here too, Talbot's committee managed to insert a rider to the bill that would have important consequences down the line.

Talbot and his few supporters had stretched the meaning of this clause to orchestrate a plan to interdict and shut down the automated SIOP if events began to spin out of control, such as they were now doing. The plan was founded on the premise that by decoupling the two components of the new SAAE-based SIOP, the space-based Northern Cross and the undersea nuclear capability of Dawn Horse, then Northern Cross could be turned against, and consequently used to kill, Dawn Horse.

Talbot and his supporters went still further. Unknown to the Defense Department they had built COLOSUS so that a digitally encrypted code sequence, contained on a chip, and called a DCM (Deconfliction Module), could decouple the two striking arms of the SAAE.

That module, more commonly called a "key," containing the integrated circuit chip that held the viral program that would sever the two arms of the SIOP like the heads of a Gorgon, would take effect within seconds of insertion into COLOSUS.

# DAVID ALEXANDER

Once the two SIOP-controlled weapons were separated, Northern Cross EMP weapons in orbit could be reprogrammed to hunt down and kill all of the three Dawn Horse missile launcher UUVs.

The key module had been hidden in Rommel Krieger's office without his knowledge by Talbot's secret faction. Krieger had been chosen with the consent of incoming President Linda Halifax who was opposed to the radical anti-terrorist policies that had led to the automation of the SIOP. Krieger was to be the unwitting sleeper agent of the White House at the Pentagon.

In fact, Krieger had been given little choice. Either pit himself against COLOSUS and General Saint's Pentagon takeover force, or take his chances in a world that had been ravaged by the destructive power of the SAAE-SIOP. There was no alternative: both the key to COLOSUS, and the access controls that would need to be bypassed in order to get into the computer's electromagnetically secure vaulted room, were biometrically coded for Rommel Krieger's metric signatures. Only Krieger's palm prints and retinal capillary patterns would enable an interloper to gain entrance to the facilities and utilize the key. Like it or not, Krieger was once again on point as the Sandman.

Krieger knew there was more, though. The menagerie of intelligence officials, administration

311

policymakers and evicted Pentagon brass who'd briefed him in on the op hadn't told him everything. That much was a given. The familiar if vitriolic redolence of spookery filled the air, and it tainted every aspect of the mission. Krieger recognized the hand of the Medusa, that secret empire that connected global organized crime, legitimate governments and secret intelligence agencies.

"Black minds" -- covert minds -- had dreamed up the Northern Cross-COLOSUS-Dawn Horse triad of the newly automated Single Integrated Operations Plan. Their forebears in covert planning and secret military action before had devised other triads in the past.

The trinity theme ran through the history of covert warfare like a recurring nightmare, just as it ran through the religions of mankind. There was the trinity of the Cold War nuclear triad, symbolized by the Trident, the ballistic missile with intercontinental range bearing the name of Poseidon's weapon, that rode in clusters of twenty-four aboard the fleet of nuclear submarines. Before that there was Trinity, the code name for the first test of the atomic bomb at Alamogordo, New Mexico near the end of World War Two. Long before that there were the criminal Triads of China, the earliest known organized crime syndicates in history.

All of these triads were dark counterparts and distorted mirrors of the religious linkage of man, earth and heaven that formed the core of the religious triads that had preceded those devised by the Medusa. And in the nature of the triad lay one of the secrets of what was taking place here and now, for Krieger was sure that another triad had been formed: of Saint, SIOP and Krieger himself.

Here was the isosceles triangle hidden within the circle, and the circle was the loop of Washington power with its tie-lines to global power nodes. The martial artist in Krieger knew the implications and ramifications of this arrangement full well. It was the hidden triangles within the circular forms of the martial arts that produced the deadliest striking power, their points attacking one's opponent's zones of deepest vulnerability. But there might be other triangles to watch out for, triads of whose existence Krieger as yet had no inkling.

Krieger and Sabio continued to navigate by the virtual screens of their GPS-linked head mounted display panels, moving stealthily through the tunnel and working back toward the concealed entrance to the Pentagon basement.

Suddenly there was an inbound message in their ear mikes. Krieger immediately recognized the familiar voice.

It was Saint's.

"Your side stopped a patrol but you didn't get all the sensors," Saint bragged. "I've been watching you two amateurs. Dumb luck. I've been sitting here counting the ways I can squash you on my fingers."

"Then why didn't you do it already?" Krieger asked.

"Because I've deduced that you weren't sent back in to pick up your lunch box, Blitz old bean. Therefore I'm going to offer you an ass-saving option: Explain why this is happening and you can turn back and leave."

"I'll tell you when I take you prisoner, Saint," Krieger challenged.

"Funny, coming from a guy with absolutely no cards to play. You know my people have killed a lot of your friends."

"There's enough left to do you, Saint. Don't worry."

"There are stragglers, repeat -- stragglers. The assault force was chewed down to the fag-end by my troops. One more time, Krieger."

"No deal, Saint. By the way, how do you feel about the color orange?"

Saint chuckled.

"How do you feel about the color black? Hint: it's the same color as body bags. I'll give you pogues five more minutes. Out."

Saint severed communications.

Krieger looked at Sabio.

Suddenly their threat warning sensors engaged. The head-mounted displays began to flash warning messages.

"I think that fucker's watch is fast," Krieger opined.

Sabio nodded as the shock wave of an incendiary munition exploded with a blindingly brilliant flash at the other end of the tunnel.

Krieger shoved Sabio down on the hard concrete floor as a churning, rolling, black, yellow and red mass of boiling flame spread toward them along the rock-walled throat of the tunnel. Thermobaric detonation, Krieger thought. The sub-nuclear heat of the thermal pulse wave singed their hair and their combat fatigues.

Krieger dragged Sabio toward the protection of a lateral communicating chamber, a square-walled vault that opened on a perpendicular axis to the main tunnel. As soon as they were in the connecting chamber Krieger pushed Sabio along the walls, yelling at her to take cover immediately.

From the opposite end of the main tunnel a secondary explosion followed within heartbeats of the primary detonation. Like the primary, the secondary detonation raked the tubular confines of the tunnel with a rapidly spiraling gyre of broiling flame. When the fireballs collided they shot incendiary spirals off into the communicating chambers. The entire underground cavern structure thundered and shook as the titanic blasts canceled each other out.

"A two-way break," Krieger called out.

"What?"

"Stuff they don't tell you in the Navy, Ensign," Krieger replied. "It's a kill trap. A variation on it, anyway, using higher-yield charges. In a six-way break you've got munitions at both ends of a rectangular death zone and Claymores spaced at intervals on each of the two long sides. Detonation is phased so that the targets are blown back, then slammed from both ends of the box. It totally chops them up."

A two-note squelch chime sounded in Krieger and Sabio's ear mikes. Saint again.

"Since this link is still alive it means you are too. Congratulations. Not many are good enough to stand a chance at surviving that. You know, Blitz, like in the commercial -- say hello to Raid, say goodbye to roaches."

Krieger didn't answer.

"Anyway, I don't expect to hear back from you," Saint said without waiting for a reply. "So just listen up: There will be a ten minute moratorium on further attack in order to give you enough time to voluntarily surrender your fucked-up, sorry asses to my men. After that I'm through playing nice guy. Hint: surrendering is more fun than dying. Saint out."

They moved through the side tunnel leapfrog fashion. This connecting passageway had been constructed for some reason known only to the builders who'd excavated the underground cavern network in the midst of WW II.

The plans logged into the navigational system showed that this passageway made one perpendicular bend, ran straight, and then made another L-turn, forming a U-shaped detour that reconnected with the main tunnel shaft approximately two hundred feet ahead. It had probably been built to allow construction crew to stow heavy earth-moving and construction machinery in the main tunnel, a temporary structure that had never been closed off when the project was completed.

As they navigated in the darkness of the tunnel branch by means of their HMDs' night-vision capability, Sabio tried to contact Red Hawk's team repeatedly but got no reply. They had heard the sounds of a firefight earlier and now feared that the ragtag survivors of Hawk's teams might have all been captured or killed by now, including the colonel himself.

Krieger considered Saint's next move. What was the rogue general planning? Would there be a heavily armed squad of Saint's mercs waiting for them at the connecting point where the far leg of the U-shaped corridor met the main tunnel? Another thermobaric kill trap? Inundation by water diverted from drainage cisterns linked to the tunnel complex?

"Hold up. What's this?"

Sabio had halted. She played an infrared penlight over the space across a section of bare concrete wall. Increasing the brightness and magnification of his HMD Krieger saw that it was obviously a door. A door of dull gray steel whose frame was mortised into the wall and no doubt secured by a ring of steel pegs driven far into the concrete.

"It's not in the building plans," Krieger said, using his wrist-top keypad and trackball to scroll through the digitized blueprints displayed on his HMD. He next tried the door handle. It wouldn't budge.

"It could just be a side room for equipment storage."

Sabio said, "We'll find out" as she affixed a three-inch-long cylindrical plastic explosive squib to the handle and kneaded it down over the lock plate. With an electronic detonator now inserted into the puttylike substance, both Sabio and Krieger took cover. A few seconds later, a muffled report had blown the door clean off its hinges.

They shone their infrared torches into the vault that now gaped through the ragged hole blown in the wall.

"Hell, it's a stairway," Krieger said with surprise, as the cloud of dust raised by the explosion began to clear.

A flight of metal stairs the same battleship gray color as the paint on the steel door led upward toward a shadowed landing a story above. Krieger ducked around and shone up his torch. The stairs seemed to go up at least another story.

"Where do you think it goes?"

"Well, it's not like this is a stairway to heaven," Krieger said. "The whole building's only five stories high and directly above us is the Pentagon subbasement. Offhand, I'd say the stairway leads to one of the three or four unused rooms in the vicinity of my office. I was the only one down there. The rest of the rooms were always kept locked by the custodial staff."

"You never went in there?"

"I said the rooms were locked, didn't I?" Krieger retorted. "Besides, who cares about a locked room in the Pentagon basement? It's not like I needed any more office space."

"Okay, don't get tense," Sabio retorted. "I was just asking."

"Well, that's my answer. Unless Saint's deliberately led us to this room, then he doesn't know these stairs exist, so we can use them for a shortcut."

"What about the basement? What if Saint's got his soldiers covering it?"

"Like you said before, we'll find out, won't we?" Krieger answered.

Turning, he cradled his Spectre SMG and began climbing the stairs.

The doorway at the top of the landing was also locked. After listening carefully for external sounds and hearing nothing, Krieger applied another PE squib to the knob and hinges. Before he could insert the timer, a two-note chime sounded.

Saint again.

"Time's up assholes," Saint warned. "I can't see you two girl scout cookies, but it doesn't matter. You're in the tunnel, so you're dead. You should have taken my offer more seriously. Bye, now -- *forever.*"

Four stories above them, Saint puffed on his stogie as he bent forward and thumbed back the translucent red hood of a silver toggle switch on the instrumentation console in front of him. A slight forward motion of his thumb pushed its ball against the bulb end of the toggle. There was an audible click as the switch latched and completed a small electric circuit.

320

Deep below Saint in the bowel's of the Pentagon, the tiny click in the NMCC command center was magnified a million times into the deafening roar of a terrific explosion as a phased cluster of incendiary charges ignited. The entire tunnel system rocked as the shock front of the explosion traveled at speeds approaching that of sound along the concrete corridor and vented into the side passage where Krieger and Sabio had sought refuge. Its force was so severe that its impact blew both of them against the locked steel door with crushing impact sufficient to detach its lock from the frame. Krieger and Sabio were flung into the room beyond.

"Well, we're here anyway," Krieger said as they both picked themselves up from the floor of the Pentagon basement. They were inside a locked storage chamber. It had apparently not been used since some supplies had been stored away there years before. A fine film of dust covered an assortment of cardboard cartons and unopened crates.

"Let's hope Saint thinks he's vaporized us. It'll give us enough time to get to my office and find the COLOSUS biometric crypto key."

Krieger tried the inner doorknob. The lock was a low-security Qwikset type which was only keyed from the outside. A twist of the knob and the door opened easily into the corridor beyond. Krieger checked cautiously. The lights in the basement were still functional. Blast debris littered the floor.

Sabio spontaneously removed her HMD, keeping her earmike in place. Those things were as uncomfortable as hell, Krieger thought as he removed his own gear and stowed the lightweight and compact headset in his ruck. He was back on familiar turf again and didn't need navigational aids. Since the only access to the basement was via either the two service elevators or up the way they'd just come, Krieger guessed that if no troops were currently stationed in the vicinity they'd have ample warning of their approach.

"My office is this way," Krieger advised, and led the way along the basement corridor with his bullpup automatic weapon cradled in his arms.

Several stories above him, General Saint received the word from the four-man reconnaissance squad he'd sent down to the disused tunnel to check for survivors that there was no indication of remains, in whole or in part.

"They might have been vaporized, boss," the squad leader reported via SINCGARS.

"Yeah, maybe," Saint submitted skeptically. "Check again and then return topside."

"That's a roger, boss," said the squad leader, as he trod cautiously along the charred concrete floor of the blast-damaged tunnel, his combat-trained eyes scanning the terrain ahead of him with

practiced efficiency. If there was anything left of
Blitz Krieger and his little Navy sidekick to find --
even a scrap or two -- he'd find it.

Twenty-five
**No Way in Hell**

*T*he sortie of Switchblade UCAVs was already en route to its designated primary target. Although the target, which was the Pentagon, was at that stage of the mission still at least one thousand miles to the west, the you-cavs would reach their ordnance release points on the eastern bank of the Potomac river in under two hours.

The unmanned remote-piloted vehicles were the stealthiest aircraft currently in the weapon inventory of the US order of battle. They were equipped to deliver nuclear-tipped AMRAAM missiles -- long range cruise missiles that were precision-guided to their targets via secure links to military global positioning satellites in geostationary low earth orbits that formed a network grid surrounding the globe.

Positive control of the airborne weapons was maintained from a secure room in the nearby headquarters of the National Security Agency at

# DAVID ALEXANDER

Fort George Meade, about twenty-five highway miles along the Washington Beltway, across the border in Maryland. Here the operators, on loan from the Air Force, could watch the progress of the UCAVs on banks of panoramic screens receiving real-time visuals from advanced orbital imaging satellites tracking the armed drones. The UCAVs were in a three-airframe sortie -- another of the mysterious triadic functions found so often in espionage and military usage -- thus the attack's code name "Three Party."

In the White House Command Center, the secure bunker system buried in the basement of the executive mansion, President Linda Halifax presided over the executive action group that had quickly gotten to be called Halifax's Eleven since it had been established by Executive Order 1111 as the crisis deepened and it had become apparent that General Casper Saint's negotiations were only a blind to cover his actual plans.

There is nothing -- not a word -- in the Constitution of the United States that inherently endows presidents with the power to make decrees that have the force of law from the Oval Office, and to unilaterally use the military forces of the United States to wage war without the prior consent of Congress. In fact the War Powers Resolution, which calls for "collective judgment" between the White House and Congress prior to taking military actions overt or covert, expressly reserves that right to Congress. Presidents have, nevertheless, made carte blanche use of executive orders throughout the institution of the presidency, citing rights of "executive power," "authority as commander-in-chief" or "constitutional reason of state," and Congress has generally gone along with them -- up to a point.

The Eleven Group had been convened by the Oval Office in order to manage the steadily building and rapidly deepening global crisis. General Saint had undertaken to commit an act of treason unparalleled in the nation's history. All symbolism aside, all outrage over lost national prestige to the contrary, Saint's takeover operation had been as much a supreme act of international terrorism as it had been an act of conspiratorial crime and high treason.

To allow Saint to prevail would be to sanction kidnapping, mass-murder and extortion on a never-before-seen scale and to set a criminal precedent that would invite other, and probably worse, instances of the same in the future. To successfully interdict Saint's operation would require the use of massive force -- nuclear force -- that would destroy the Pentagon along with its occupiers and Saint's many hostages, for there were still thousands of Pentagon staff held prisoner in the four Wedges not under the direct control of Saint's troops.

It was assumed that Saint had an exit strategy -- the general was no suicidal terrorist bent on a mission of martyrdom -- and that if the exit strategy succeeded, then Saint would emerge from the crisis intact and probably disappear forever. There was no other way that Saint could enjoy the billions he had illegally gained by his takeover and subsequent blackmail. The CIA's liaison with the Treasury Department had conducted an assessment audit, and it was believed that Saint's demands for hostage ransom payment might only be a smokescreen -- that he was actually working a sophisticated computer crime scam under its cover.

Should Saint carry the momentum of the operation and successfully exit the occupied Pentagon, he would not only have scored a personal criminal victory -- Saint would in effect have dragged the world across the line between government by legally sanctioned representation and government by mega-criminal cartels who have seized power by force majeure. These, collectively making up the tentacles of the Medusa, formed a global shadow government that would then rise to a new level of worldwide dominance.

# THREATCON DELTA

A secret study commissioned under the same presidential executive order that had established the Eleven Group had shown the president the hows, whys and wherefores of such a catastrophic development. Since the end of the Cold War, criminal empires had reaped untold trillions of dollars from the chaos left in the wake of the Soviet Union's collapse.

Covert arms sales, illicit technology transfers and contraband drugs, had built the foundation of this illegitimate power; a torrent of hidden wealth had flowed into the coffers of international organized crime. The ruling echelons of the former KGB and the East German Staatspolizei or Stasi had merged with the ancient Chinese heroin triads and the Sicilian and American Mafias, including the outlaw factions of the Italian Stidda and the Corsican cartels.

An international coordinating committee -- something like the criminal Commission established by Lucky Luciano at Appalachia, New York, early in the history of the American Mafia -- was required to prevent chaos, divide the spoils and increase power. The result was the Medusa, and the Medusa was nothing less than the world-spanning criminal cartel's shadow United Nations.

The Medusa, the world shadow government, the nexus of international criminal conspiracies, the clearinghouse for death, the underground river through which hidden wealth flowed in a dark and turbid stream, had bankrolled Saint's operation. Saint and the Medusa were conclusively linked. The UCAVs carrying nuclear warheads were the only way to oust the rogue general and his troops, and scalpel out the neoplastic malignancy that had lodged itself into the heart muscle of American national strength.

The president had put the two alternatives to a vote by the Eleven Group -- the first: permit the crisis to play itself out and then pursue Saint around the world and capture him, even if it was years later. Like Saddam Hussein, the outlaw could be publicly humiliated, his assets seized, his lieutenants captured and dehumanized in extraterritorial prisons with carefully orchestrated media coverage to show how they had been disgraced and punished.

Or would it be the second alternative -- the force option, in the form of a shock-and-awe attack strategy? Use any measure of force, nuclear if necessary, to destroy the command and control center that Saint had established in Wedge Three of the Pentagon and hopefully kill Saint and his lieutenants in the process.

The second alternative, if successfully carried out, had the advantage of ending the crisis in one fell swoop. The single bold stroke would eliminate Saint, quash his operation before he exited, and score a bold, media-worthy victory. If the strike was surgical -- using conventional aerially delivered munitions such as MOAB or cruise missiles such as AMRAAM, then collateral damage could be limited to acceptable levels.

Much of the western facade of the Pentagon would be destroyed in the processes, but that had happened before, and rebuilding had been swift. There would be civilian casualties among the hostages known to be held in the captive Wedge Three, but civilian casualties had occurred in the past as well, and the nation had healed its psychic wounds.

Halifax had already tasked White House intelligence czar, Chesley Porcaro, with the task of preparing the public with a steadily growing exposure to media footage of the Strike Day terrorist attack on the Pentagon. Since the start of the Pentagon takeover crisis, that footage -- played regularly and relentlessly on media and Internet news channels -- had built to a crescendo.

Indeed, at that morning's regularly convened National Security Council meeting, representatives of the Central Intelligence and the National Security Agencies had reported that the covert psychological operations campaign to prepare the public for a missile or bomb strike on the Pentagon had begun to reap dividends.

Secret polls conducted by media research firms under covert contract to the CIA brought the welcome news that if the Pentagon were struck by a counterattack and partially destroyed, most Americans would react with relief and support the Administration as long as the public was convinced that Saint and his men had died in the attack. This would likely hold true, the intelligence report added confidently, even with "more than average" collateral damage and loss of innocent lives.

Halifax had taken the initiative when the Eleven were deadlocked on the issue of which course of action to take. She had declared herself in favor of option two, the force option, and had signed another executive order authorizing the preparation and launch of the nuclear UCAV mission.

The covert mission inside the Pentagon itself of Halifax's former lover, Rommel Krieger, was primarily a backstop operation should the tactical UAV strike need to be aborted. The executive decision to re-prioritize for the conventional commando assault in progress, or give the nuclear option the final go-order, would be taken when the you-cav sortie had reached its last critical waypoint prior to ordnance detonation a few miles from the Pentagon.

# THREATCON DELTA

If contingencies warranted, Rommel Krieger would be sacrificed. A greater good was at stake. The Steel Rose had made her choice. Now the president waited for the final games to play themselves out.

∎

Krieger felt the weight of the millions of cubic tons of the Pentagon above him pressing against the blades of his shoulders as he stepped carefully across the corridor floor. He felt like Atlas, propping the earth on his torso as he walked as carefully as a cat on a high tension cable, eyes sweeping back and forth, scanning everything, alert to the signs of killers waiting in the concealment of ambush and to the telltales of thin, fine wires across his path that might be linked to the triggers of deadly booby traps. The pressure of immense weight was purely psychological, but the threat of death was all too real.

Saint was no amateur and neither were his troops. The general had read the manuals of military deception; others he had written himself. He was skilled at techniques of stealth warfare and the Russian military's counterpart art of strategic camouflage and concealment, *maskirovka*. When you dealt with the likes of Saint, you expected everything and anything to happen.

Maybe Saint believed that Krieger and Sabio had bought it in the thermobaric kill trap in the service tunnel, and maybe not. Even if Saint did accept their deaths as accomplished facts, Krieger knew the acceptance would only be conditional, not final till confirmed -- Saint would send out a security and reconnaissance detachment to check it out, look for human remains, physical evidence that they'd actually died.

If his hunting dogs didn't scent on the telltale smell of butchery, then Saint would come looking for them. He might be looking already, in fact, Krieger was well aware.

Krieger stopped short as the basement corridor rounded a sudden bend. He raised a hand silently behind him to Sabio who was bringing up the rear, working security, Spectre subgun tracking for signs of threat. Both stopped and beheld the problem they faced.

The corridor was blocked with fallen debris. Part of the ceiling had given way. Explosive strikes from the original battle that had seen the Pentagon fall to Saint, and the security teams that had spread through the Wedges to take hostages, and that had led to Krieger's escape, might have been responsible for the damage.

Be that as it may, the path was blocked. There was no other way to reach Krieger's office.

Krieger sat down, his back against the rubble heap. Sabio squatted beside him.

"What now, boss?" she asked.

"Don't call me boss," Krieger snapped.

He glanced up toward the ceiling and touched a stud on his digital chronometer. Time was running out.

"Here's what happens. We're going to crawl the rest of the way through the ventilation ducting. The register is right up there. See it?"

He gestured at the grilled rectangle mounted high on the wall.

"I figure it's only another hundred, maybe two hundred yards to reach my office, more or less."

Krieger got to his feet and walked toward the wall. He glanced up at the ventilation register.

"You think you're strong enough to lift me up high enough for about five minutes so I can unscrew the retaining bolts that hold the register in place?"

"I qualify as a Marine Corps physical training instructor. I can cut it, boss."

"Don't call me that."

"Sorry, boss."

Krieger ignored Sabio and went on, "You scrunch down and lift me up on your shoulders. I've got to go first because I don't think you can haul me up, but I can haul you up once I'm in there, no offense."

"None taken, boss."

They set to it. Both had put the HMDs back on and had reactivated their night vision capability.

# DAVID ALEXANDER

There was the potential for booby traps in the ventilation ducting, but they'd have to chance it. There was no other recourse or options at this stage, not if Krieger were to retrieve the COLOSUS crypto key module.

And so Krieger pulled Sabio up after she'd given him a lift to remove the duct's register panel, then Sabio used her fingers to clumsily replace the four retaining screws in their sockets in case a security team happened by, and she and Krieger began to crawl along the aluminum floor of the flattened toroid of the snaky ventilation ducting.

Krieger shone his infrared torch down its length. The ducting ran horizontally as far as the eye could see, broken by faint glimmers of light as it rounded the next bend in the basement corridor. That light, Krieger was aware, belonged to the next register, the one located directly outside and a few feet adjacent to his former office.

It grew hot quickly in the confines of the ductway but they ignored the discomfort and began moving along its galvanized aluminum bottom, crawling as quietly and as fast as possible. Krieger had briefed Sabio that they were to proceed along in spurts, pausing every few seconds to listen for signs of hostile activity. Sounds traveled far in the metal ducting. Discovery would mean death.

# THREATCON DELTA

The ductway was a natural amplification tube -- the sound of a rifle barrel striking the side of the aluminum crawlspace too heavily could resound up through the ducting and be heard on the floor above. Faint though the sounds might be, it could well be enough to alert a trained commando to the presence of interlopers sequestered in the vast building's guts. Krieger wished he'd brought along a roll of masking tape with which to wrap weapon handgrips, receivers and clips, in order to muffle sounds made by contact between gunmetal and aluminum walls, but he hadn't done it.

And so Krieger and Sabio moved like rats in a maze, elbows and shins, toes and heels, pushing them slowly, painfully forward. The distance was short. But the risks were great and multiplied by their vulnerability in the enclosed confines of the ducting. Silence was the thread on which their lives might hang.

■

"What the fuck was that?"

Younger, the squad leader, had heard a faint rasping sound. He thought it had come from the ventilation register.

"You hear that Sikes?"

Sikes, on point, looked toward where Younger's raised index finger was directing. He shook his head. Negative.

"Didn't hear nothing."

Younger wasn't so sure. He told Sikes to squat down and give him a leg-up so he could take a quick look inside the ventilation ductway. Sikes cursed and did as the team leader had ordered, and Younger shone his Mag Light into the crawlspace beyond the checkerboard pattern of crisscrossing metal bars inside the rectangle of the register's gridded facing. He saw nothing, but put his ear to the register just to make sure.

"Sarge, my shoulder blades are fuckin' numb," Sikes protested.

"Shut up, Sikes. I'm listening."

Sikes again did as he was ordered, though mentally shouting everything that his silenced vocal chords were prevented from uttering as he felt the ripple soles of Younger's combat boots grinding into the protesting musculature of his aching shoulders and pain-lashed neck.

Younger was simultaneously grinding his ear into the iron meshwork of the register face but he heard nothing concrete -- faint sounds of machinery, vague rumblings of the ventilation and heating system, the assorted smells of mechanical lubricants and dust that had been sucked into the system over the course of time -- nothing else.

"That's it, hunker on down," Younger told Sikes, and the trooper gratefully lowered his burden within hop-off distance of the floor. Younger alighted from his wobbly perch and wiped his hands on the sides of his camouflage fatigue pants while gesturing to Sikes to hand him his short-barreled M4A1 assault rifle.

Sikes rejoined the rest of the squad which stood awaiting their leader's next command.

"Let's get to it," Younger said, and with a nod of his chin, sent the squad to continue down the basement corridor. "The sooner we check it all out, the sooner we can get the fuck out of here."

Less than twenty feet above their heads, Krieger and Sabio were approaching the faint dusting of yellowish-white light that marked their exit point from the ductway.

Twenty-six
## A Decision Postponed

*"M*a'am, the you-cavs have reached their first waypoint," the president was informed by speakerphone.

Halifax sat in the Oval Office, stroking her pet tiger-striped tabby cat Waldo.

"Do nothing yet."

"Yes Ma'am."

The cat hissed and she tossed it down to the carpeted floor. It ran to the French doors of the presidential office and scratched fitfully at the glass, intent on finding a way out.

Twenty-seven
**War by Other Means**

*"T*his whole goddamn place is a mess," said Krieger.

Minutes before, listening at the back of the ventilation grid-work, hearing no sounds in the basement corridor outside.

Just stillness. Emptiness beyond.

Working the machine screws loose from their sockets and carefully removing, turning and pulling in the steel mesh, trying not to inhale the dust that came off the metal. Then, sliding down, Krieger's belly against the wall, while Sabio held his feet by the necks of his combat boots. Squatting, turning to scope out the corridor for signs of danger, then turning again, flashing the all-clear to Sabio and pulling her down to the floor.

Krieger's office was a shambles. File cabinet drawers had been torn from their tracks and their contents indiscriminately dumped onto the floor.

The desk was overturned and lay at an angle against a wall. Computer gear, including Krieger's laptop, actually pieces of it all, were scattered in lacerated shards of mangled plastic across the wads and mounds of papers and file folders dumped from cabinets. The scene was pure chaos. Saint's mercs had put the place through a meatgrinder.

"Were they just going balls-out, throwing a shit-fit, or was there a purpose behind tossing my office?" Krieger asked -- pointlessly, he realized, as the words came out. "Were they after the crypto key."

"They couldn't have known about the key," Sabio told him.

"Really? I'm not that certain. Saint seems to know everything about everything, doesn't he?"

"The initiative to counter the SIOP automation was tightly compartmentalized. There were no leaks."

"Rule one, Ensign Sabio," Krieger disagreed. "There can always be leaks. Usually from the top down instead of the bottom up."

"You're not suggesting that the secretary of defense -- "

"I'm not suggesting anything, ensign," Krieger retorted. "But I'm not discounting anything either. Now where do I look for this holy grail you buried in my office?"

"Permit me to correct you, boss. I buried nothing. As I said, the key was placed secretly by a team -- "

"Just tell me where it is, Sabio."

"I don't know where they put it."

"Is this a guessing game, ensign?" Krieger asked. "Are we going to play twenty questions now?"

"There will be no guesswork needed, boss," said Sabio. "I was about to add that although I was not briefed on the location of the key I was in fact provided with the means of finding it."

"You're gonna wave your magic wand now?"

"Something like that," Sabio answered.

Krieger watched as Sabio began to move around the office. She seemed to be scanning the office interior. Near a corner of the room she stopped and placed her hand on the wall. Krieger heard a faint latching sound from inside and a section popped out. Sabio extracted a small black cylinder, apparently of some hard, injection-molded plastic, and handed it to him.

Krieger stared at her, his eyes moving from her face to the object held in the open palm of Sabio's outstretched right hand.

"I'm beginning to see ..." he paused as it became clear. "...you're a cyborg ... or something like it. Were you cloned from Barbarella or something, ensign?"

"I'm as human as you are, boss," Sabio said. "I was part of a DARPA project. It including a special training regimen and biometric implantation. What is Barbarella?"

"An old movie about a girl and a computer."

"I never heard of it."

"You're too young."

"Will you take the key?"

Krieger scowled and accepted the DCM key from Sabio's open palm. He inspected it for a few moments. It looked no different from conventional hot-pluggable computer storage device containing a memory chip. In fact it obviously was a mass produced, commercially available hot-pluggable memory module.

"Are you sure this is the key? You can buy one like this at K-Mart."

"It's not the envelope, boss, but the message inside it," Sabio replied. "The program contains the instructions to COLOSUS to unlock the two global strike components of the SAAE-SIOP. You plug it in, let the system scan your biometrics, and the program loads."

"Getting there's half the fun," Krieger added.

"Fun? I don't see anything funny here, boss," Sabio replied.

"Forget I mentioned it," Krieger told her.

"Do we use the ventilation ductway again to reach the next level?"

"We'll take the elevator."

"Is that really wise, boss?"

"We'll see, ensign," Krieger told her.

Stepping over heaps of garbage, Krieger led the way out of the office, both of them automatically going into combat mode, crab-walking sideways, back to back, with the muzzles of their SMGs cradled in their arms for quick-triggered autofire.

They reached the elevator just as the red-LED basement floor indicator flashed descending numbers, a chime sounded, and the steel door slid rapidly open. The movement took them by surprise.

It was too late to move or break for cover, so they positioned themselves at either side of the elevator and pointed their subguns at the opening door.

Troops in tactical vests and camouflage fatigues were inside the car, and they had guns in their hands too.

■

Saint talked to the face in the tactical display screen in front of him. The face belonged to someone he'd never seen before. Young, fresh. Who in the fuck was this?"

"Who the fuck are you?"

"My name is James Bond," said the face. He wasn't smiling.

344

"Holy shit! James Bond. I'm really impressed. I always wanted to meet you, Mr. Bond," Saint mocked. "But where's Strake, Mr. Bond? Did you dispose of him with some fiendish gizmo M gave you?"

"Sorry, sir, but Mr. Strake left unexpectedly," said the face. "I've been ordered to take his place as negotiator."

"And you are with...?"

"I work for National Security Advisor Samuels, who personally appointed me as her deputy. My credentials include deputy crisis negotiator during the Syria-Azerbaijan missile confrontation, and assistant to the deputy assistant negotiator on the recent transit strike here in the District. You may have read about it."

"Oh, yes, I certainly read about it, Mr. Bond," Saint replied. "By the way, is that your real name or a clever alias you've decided to use."

"Well, sir," replied the face with some abashment, "I'm frequently asked that question. Actually the name is my real name, however please feel free to call me 'Jim' if you like."

"Okay, Jim," answered the general with feigned politeness.

"What can I do for you, sir?" asked Bond. "I am empowered to negotiate on behalf of the president. We would like to end this episode as quickly as possible and with minimum further damage to vital national infrastructure, and, of course, loss of life."

"I'm sure you do," said Saint, who glanced downward across the darkened battle pit below his balcony level perch in the command center catbird seat. "That probably means that somebody else -- maybe the guy from a pizzeria in Alexandria, for instance -- has sent a sortie of unmanned combat aerial vehicles on an attack trajectory for the Pentagon.

"I mean, heaven forbid that I should think even for a moment that you'd be trying to bullshit me, Mr. Bond," Saint concluded with a pleasant smile.

The three large flat-panel god screens Saint watched showed the trajectories of incoming UCAVs, with a digital clock in a side window ticking down their ETA to slam the Pentagon. The feed originated from a variety of orbital strategic imaging assets under Saint's direct command and control. They included not only Northern Cross target acquisition imaging, but also included three other satellites -- two military and one civilian -- into which Saint's hardware and software specialist, Pegasus, had deftly hacked.

The combined imagery and wire grid data was a product of data fusion using the high-speed, massively parallel Toshiba-IBM cloud computer system that the Pentagon claimed it didn't have but actually did, though on paper it belonged to the

NSA, which also, on paper, was run by the Defense Department, which it actually wasn't.

"Sir, let me assure you that no hostile action has been taken or even contemplated. There is no attack in progress. We are interested in resolving this crisis by negotiation, not by further bloodshed."

Saint nodded, looking at the face. Maybe the mutt actually believes this shit, Saint thought.

"Yeah," he said after puffing on his cigar, "yeah, Mr. Bond, I really believe you mean it."

Saint flicked ash and went on, "You poor little schmuck. You're just a pawn in the game. You're not even in the loop. You're just a little-bitty mushroom blinded by a ton of gorilla shit. Well, listen up, Mr. Bond, you tell that bitch at 1600 Pennsylvania Avenue that she's in for one mutherfuckin' helluva surprise."

Saint terminated the transmission as Bond was framing a reply. The screen blanked to black. Saint reached across the desktop for the gooseneck mike, seeing an afterimage of the stunned Bond's thin-lipped open mouth.

"Vector Section, situation report on Squad Zero."

Down in the darkened battle pit, the Vector Section consulted their dedicated command screens. Another face appeared on the display that seemed to float in the darkness in front of Saint.

"Squad Zero in position. Good to go. Will commence operation at your signal, sir."

Again Saint scanned his bank of god screens. The ETA readout numbers showed that the incoming messengers of death had inched forward on the display, but at the supersonic speeds the UCAVs were traveling, the distance they had thus far traversed could be still be reckoned in scores of miles. There was still time left to act. Time aplenty.

"Order Squad Zero to attack its primary objective. Wish them good luck."

"Roger, sir."

Saint eased back in his formfit military-issue Aerons chair. He keystroked in a command sequence. A now familiar face appeared.

"Hello Mr. Bond."

"Yes, sir?"

"Mr. Bond, do you remember that part in the movie *Thunderball* where the top of Emilio Largo's yacht, the Disco Volante, opens up and exposes this big, fat, humungous fuckin' missile?"

Bond thought that over a minute.

"Yes, I think I might have seen that particular film at one time, sir."

"Well, you're about to see the sequel, Mr. Jim Fuckin' Bond," roared Saint.

## Twenty-eight
## Parallel Operations

*T*heir fingers eased back on the triggers of their Spectre submachineguns. A heartbeat more and the weapons would have discharged their lethal nine-millimeter bursts into the elevator. Friendlies would have died on both sides. Inside the elevator car were Colonel Red Hawk and the five survivors of his original team. Plus one other.

A thin brown ghost. Shuggie from the Hotties kiosk in the Pentagon mall.

"Yo, Blitz Man, what up, ma dog?"

"Shuggie! Man, I am glad to see you. I thought you might have bought it when Saint hit the mall on his way in."

"The G from the Pentagon 'hood, MC Shugmeister almost did get whacked, Blitz Man," Shuggie replied. "But I happened to be getting ready to mop the floor. When I saw what be goin' down I hid my black ass in the utility closet. It was close, ma dog. But I still mackin'."

# THREATCON DELTA

Hawk clapped Shuggie on the shoulder.

"We found your friend hiding in the elevator shaft in Wedge Two. It was just luck. We'd run out of rations but Shuggie had stuffed a rucksack full of food from Hotties and hidden it there. It kept us alive."

"You've been to the other Wedges?"

"Wedges Four and Five," Hawk told Krieger. "We basically used them as hiding places. The Wedges are locked down. Saint's troops emptied them out but they're kept under remote surveillance from the NMCC command post set up by Saint."

Hawk used hand signals and a nod of his chin to send two of his hard chargers down the corridor on perimeter patrol while the other three commandos and the deputized Shuggie unslung their gear and sat down against the walls. Hawk did the same, along with Krieger and Sabio.

To Krieger, the unexpected appearance of the remnants of Hawk's interdiction force was a favorable turn of events. This new development meant that Krieger had a squad-strength detail to back up his play.

Krieger sketched out the events that had taken place since radio communications with Hawk had been lost almost twenty hours previous. He told Hawk about the key to COLOSUS ("It stands for Core Long Range Operating System United

States," he explained) and how Sabio had been entrusted with the mission of briefing Krieger about it as a last ditch failsafe measure if the worst ever happened. Krieger explained the mission he and Sabio were about to undertake solely on their own -- to enter the COLOSUS data well and insert the DCM, or deconfliction module, the crypto key that was now in Krieger's possession.

Colonel Red Hawk took counsel of his thoughts for a few long minutes, while his eyes strayed around the area to take in his troops. The two troopers had returned to report that the corridor was secure, and now all his men were either resting or inspecting and cleaning their weapons.

His force was dog-tired and his men were not at their best. Before running into Krieger and Sabio, Hawk's mission had been escape and evasion only. He did not look favorably on now leading his people back into potential combat; more than potential really, because the chances of engaging Saint's troops in a firefight were, in his opinion, extremely high.

"My men are tired, hell, they're plain worn out," Hawk told Krieger. "On the other hand I don't see how you two can possibly succeed on your own hook." Hawk thought a moment more. "There's no possibility of reinforcements being sent in. Politically, and operationally, that's out too. In fairness to my men I'll have to put the matter to a vote."

Hawk told his troops to listen up and briefed them on the situation, explaining the risks and options as best he could. In the end they all volunteered.

"Okay, then let's saddle up and move out," Hawk ordered. "We've got ourselves one last job to do before we're home."

∎

The attack on the National Security Agency's Fort George G. Meade headquarters commenced within minutes of Squad Zero's receiving its orders to strike, and while the nuclear-tipped three-UCAV sortie was still en route to destroy the Pentagon.

The NSA's headquarters is reached by an access road that connects to the Washington Beltway near Mardela Springs, Maryland. A sign conspicuously posted at the turnoff warns that unauthorized access is prohibited and apprises those who would still take the turnoff that a security checkpoint lies just around the next bend.

A convoy of Humvees that had been augmented with TOW and Viper missile launchers and multibarrel heavy machineguns paid no heed to the warning sign. The Hummers also ignored the security checkpoint, in fact showed it violent disdain, by launching a TOW missile strike at the diagonally striped, steel-reinforced blade barrier barring their path, coordinated by Minigun salvos.

The electrically driven feed belt mechanism of the Minigun fired thousands of rounds of heavy caliber, 7.62x51 millimeter bullets at the security station. Standard ammo was interspersed with green tracers every fifth round which made sighting on the close-range targets child's play for the shooters inside the heavily armored Humvees. The effect of the withering rocket strikes and rapid machinegun enfilade was to chew up the emplacement and effortlessly kill the three uniformed security guards who came running out porting M4A1 automatic rifles before they could fire off a shot.

The Humvees roared through a fireball amid the still flying debris of the blown-away security checkpoint into the parking area of the NSA. In front of them loomed the large, glass fronted office buildings that housed the largest and most secret intelligence agency on the face of the planet. The NSA had been established, along with the CIA, by the first National Security Act of 1947 and successive codicils and amendments to the Act throughout the late forties and early fifties. Nominally, it was part of the Defense Department. Nevertheless its charter was secret and the agency was accountable to no one, except the president, which it consulted only when necessary, and often as an afterthought.

The gleaming glass buildings housed not only the largest collection of supercomputers in the world, but also the living quarters, offices, shops and restaurants that served the day-to-day needs of the thousands of NSA employees who lived in this self-contained world of secret intelligence and rarely left its confines. The small city was the modern-day realm of what in the ancient past would have been a select priesthood that controlled the levers of secret power from which many other forms of power flowed. More to the point, part of that secret power was now directing the sortie of nuclear-armed UCAVs that neared their final waypoint before their ordnance release points that would destroy Wedge Three with a low-yield nuclear strike using Plywood munitions.

The secret city of the NSA also had its own private police force, and this security force was rushing with sirens blaring and dome lights revolving red and blue as the four Hummers breached the checkpoint and barreled toward the glass-and-steel Central Administration Facility headquarters building. More rocket strikes and machinegun fire destroyed the police vehicles and killed the would-be defenders, sending fireballs and dense black smoke billowing from the burning, overturned vehicles ballooning up into the air past the rooftops of the multistory glass office buildings.

Inside one of the rooms on an upper floor of the NSA headquarters building, the crew controlling the UCAV sortie watched orbital imagery of the UCAVS while other screens showed a variety of flight data including moving map displays and estimated time of arrival to their ordnance release point. The chief flight control officer was seated at the console wearing a head-mounted display and whole-hand haptic exoskeleton that enabled the operator to maneuver the UCAV by manipulating controls that existed only in the virtual environment generated by the computers wirelessly linked to the command and control architecture of the system.

Because the UCAV was programmed for autonomous maneuvers, which included long-range, long-endurance navigation and combat operations, such as dropping munitions and firing missiles, the flight controller normally didn't have to take over very often, and it was no exaggeration to say that the UCAV practically flew itself. Nevertheless, security regulations mandated his presence in the man-machine loop, and there were a few critical operations for which a human operator was a necessary evil.

In addition to the HMD, which showed the remote UCAV operator the same data as were shown on the large wall-mounted displays, and the whole-hand haptic exoskeleton, the chief flight controller also had access to a side-stick controller that was similar to the type used by jet fighter pilots. The control stick had numerous buttons on it by which the controller could direct the UCAVs in flight and control the targeting and firing of onboard weapons should such manual control prove necessary at any time.

The control center was an ultra-secure facility. The room -- lined with radar-absorbent composite material, RAM, was impervious to penetration by external signals intelligence and completely soundproof. The only indication of impending trouble was a suddenly coruscating and intense red strobe, a shrill, repeating electronic chime, and a security warning indication that popped up as a Windows dialog box on both the control center's wall screens and the HMD worn by the flight control officer.

One of the members of the control center crew immediately picked up an in-house phone and was connected to security which informed him of the attack unfolding outside the building. It was to be the last act the man performed, and nearly the last activity that any of the five persons in the command center performed too.

Inside the lead Humvee, a member of Squad Zero also wore a head-mounted display and had his hands on twin control mechanisms resembling the backup joystick controller for the civilian NSA flight control officer bearing the mission code designation Number One twelve stories above him in the secure upper floors of the glass tower. The Squad Zero team leader and chief technical officer saw in the HMD display that command of the Viper missile launchers onboard the three Hummers was now under his control.

In a matter of moments his target was acquired -- a glowing red and blue crosshair reticle encompassed the real-time image of the tactical objective. The crosshairs encircled the suite of rooms in the tall, dark glass-walled building above the attack force at whose core was the darkened control room in which Number One remotely piloted the autonomous UCAV en route to deliver a nuclear strike on the Pentagon.

The Squad Zero team leader was also connected by networked real-time communications to General Casper Saint in the Pentagon's NMCC. Saint was about to observe every facet of the operation on multiple display screens that showed him not only a satellite view of the Blue Man team's penetration of the NSC compound, but also showed him the approach of the UCAVs sent to destroy him and his men and end his control of the Pentagon.

"Target acquired. Weapons are go," Saint heard the Squad Zero leader say in his ear mike. "Awaiting your orders, sir."

"Launch weapon," Saint directed him. "Kill those fuckers. Kill the birds."

"Yes, sir," replied Squad Zero mission commander and depressed the silver toggle beneath a red hood flicked by his thumb to jointly release the three Viper missiles from the launchers on each of the Hummers.

An instant later, all three missiles were in flight. They didn't have very far to travel. Their billowing white exhaust contrails snaked upward to the upper stories and their warheads effortlessly penetrated the glass-walled building, and then they disappeared inside. A heartbeat later the warheads reached the structural core and detonated in tandem within the control center. Those inside the center lived long enough to fleetingly glimpse the blurred images of something penetrating the walls of the secure room, and a sudden blinding incandescence.

They did not hear the sound of the tremendous explosion that ripped the entire top three floors off the glass tower. They were already dead by then, already vaporized by the shock waves and thermal pulse of the detonating high explosive.

Outside the walls of the NSA tower, the building's roof section suddenly blew apart into a million glittering shards as a fireball, orange and black, resembling a toadstool or puffball or similar tumescent growth blasting from the trunk of a blighted tree, suddenly ballooned outward into space. Yellow flame, gouts of it, like dragon's breath, shot out against the clear blue sky. Multiple explosions echoed off the low, rolling stands of hills that surrounded Fort Meade.

"Mission accomplished, sir," reported the Squad Zero mission commander.

"The objective is completely destroyed."

From the balcony level overlooking the battle pit of the National Military Command Center, Saint watched the result of the strike on the NSA play itself out on the central large screen display. The real-time feed from orbital space showed the UCAVs that had been under the positive control of Number One suddenly zigzag drunkenly as positive control was lost.

Moments later the UCAVs' fallback programming was activated by their onboard computers. The instruction set called for each of the unmanned killer drones to self-destruct in the absence of positive control. Each of the UCAVs independently tried to reconnect to the control signal telemetry feed, but failed.

After a successive number of retries, their onboard processors defaulted to self-destruct sequences. A countdown commenced as they changed course and soared skyward. They were committing robotic suicide.

Saint smiled as each of the three killer robot aircraft exploded harmlessly at eighty thousand feet, their nuclear weapons consumed in the incendiary detonations that destroyed them, the thermal pulse destroying all residual radioactivity.

"Extract now," Saint ordered the Squad Zero team's ramrod, still at the NSA compound and watching the building burn. "Return to Escape and Evasion Plan Baker."

"Understood, sir," the Squad Zero mission commander acknowledged.

Amid the fire and smoke of destruction the Humvees turned around and roared away from the decapitated glass tower, whose ruptured upper section now belched a plume of spreading black smoke into the cloudless blue sky. It soon became a pall that drifted across the Maryland countryside and across the Potomac river into Washington DC. It was soon visible from the Oval Office of the White House itself.

Saint broke communications with Squad Zero and punched in another series that connected him with Alexai.

"Your stock has risen," Alexai informed him.

"How much."

"A billion more on the plus side."

"They're panicking. That's it. Make me richer."

"That's what they're doing. Dawn Horse strikes just hit Istanbul, Baku on the Black Sea and downtown Beirut. Low yield nuclear strikes."

"We can't push this thing too much further."

"Yes, we're nearing the GIP (or GI Point, Goldberg Instability Point)," Alexai agreed. "Maybe one more group of strikes."

"That means it's almost time to exit. Get it all ready, Alexai. I'm growing hemorrhoids big as Concord grapes sitting here. I want to count that fucking money so bad I can feel it in my hip pocket."

"Understood," said Alexai. "I'll be back to you."

Across the Potomac river, President Halifax heard the rolling after-reports of the explosions that had partially destroyed the NSA headquarters and saw the pall of pitch-black smoke blow slowly across 1600 Pennsylvania Avenue.

She closed the French doors to the Oval Office and turned to see the National Security Advisor seated in a chair in front of her desk.

"I suppose this means it's Rommel Krieger's show now," Halifax said to the NSA.

"In that case, Ms. President," frowned the NSA from her seat, "I don't know which is the worse alternative -- the end of the world, or Blitz Krieger sent to rescue it."

Twenty-nine
## Some Surprise Moves

COLOSUS, the core processor cluster of the automated SAAE-SIOP, was housed in an air-conditioned, shock-absorbent service tunnel, known as a data well, located between the third and first floors of Wedge Three, between Corridors Six and Seven. The shaftway was somewhat broader in circumference than a water tower; broad enough to drive a car through, if the shaftway had been horizontal instead of vertical.

A numbered steel door set in the wall in C-Ring, midway between the two corridors, opened to a catwalk some eight feet down from the top of the shaft, but first a short vaulted room, lined with electromagnetic absorbent materials used in Stealth and scanned by arrays of biometric, thermal and acoustic sensors, had to be traversed. The doors were automatic as well as keyless. They opened and closed subject to authorization being granted or denied.

# DAVID ALEXANDER

Saint had detailed a security squad to guard the corridors and section of ring that led to the first access point. The squad used a nearby, now vacant, office as its command center where a trooper continuously monitored a laptop linked to surveillance cams set up in the corridors, elevators and adjacent areas.

Two sentries, armed with bullpup AKS rifles, the short-barreled Krinkov type that Saint had learned to treasure in the rugged Kirghiz highlands for their reliability and striking power, were posted at the hatch of the COLOSUS data well. They had orders to shoot on sight and shoot to kill.

The main linkages to COLOSUS terminated in the NMCC battle cab, where a dedicated high-speed server cluster in a data center housing the NMCC's network node, kept routine tabs on the performance of the enormously powerful and formidably enabled supercomputer array in the data well. This network array, which was configured on the network by the name of Cerberus, also served as the firewall for COLOSUS, defending against intrusion attacks and screening for viruses and other forms of malicious code and cyberattack.

The Cerberus computer array was autonomous from COLOSUS; it kept the much larger computer system in the data well under constant observation, thus its name for a watchdog of the Greek god of the underworld.

Cerberus was in turn normally monitored round-the-clock by technicians at both the NMCC and facilities remote from the Pentagon, including the Alternate National Military Command Center at nearby Raven Rock, and StratCom, at NORAD's steel-cube city thousands of miles across the continental US inside the hollowed out shell of Cheyenne Mountain, Colorado.

Once Saint had taken over the Pentagon's critical Wedge Three, he had cut off all external links to COLOSUS. Saint had then placed the globe-spanning supercomputer solely under his personal command and control.

In the early hours of Tuesday, September 13th, a few hours after the UCAV mission was aborted by Colonel Yuri's domestic Spetsnaz strike, under the Squad Zero code-name, on the National Security Agency's Fort Meade headquarters; as firefighters using high-pressure hoses were still trying to put out the fires that continued to rage high atop the multistory glass tower at Fort Meade, and as huge craters of low-yield nuclear strikes on Dawn Horse cruise missile targets around the world were still smoldering -- something unexpected began to occur.

■

"Sir, Cerberus' systems monitoring has detected a potential processor malfunction that's just cropped up."

"What is it?" Saint asked Pegasus.

"Cerberus is monitoring extensive CPU usage and reallocation of software services in COLOSUS consistent with reprogramming of its artificial intelligence sublayer."

"Tell me again -- in plain English."

"It appears, sir, that COLOSUS is reprogramming itself."

"Doesn't it do that normally?" Saint asked.

The general had made it his business to know all there was to know about the mission; this included briefings on all aspects of Northern Cross, Dawn Horse and COLOSUS.

"It's supposed to run diagnostic routines. Correct?"

"Yes, that's technically correct, sir," the technician confirmed, "but what I'm seeing isn't diagnostics. The system is processing sophisticated Mandlebrot algorithms that are, in effect, denying positive control from outside the system."

"Is it taking control autonomously?"

"That could be the case, sir."

"Can we shut it down if we need to?"

"No sir. We can't. Not even by disconnecting its power supply feed. It has emergency backup power supplies. It can keep itself going indefinitely."

Saint saw no alternatives to sitting tight.

"Keep me posted," he instructed Pegasus.

"Roger, sir."

■

"Yo' -- it ain't the Artist Formerly Known as Prince, but it's da shit, yo'."

The sentries posted at the access door to COLOSUS were startled by the sight of Shuggie sliding across the floor, executing splits not seen since James Brown played the Apollo Theater. They raised their bullpup autorifles and pointed it at the skinny dreadlocked figure that was sliding along the floor.

"Don't pull dem triggas, ma dogs," Shuggie shouted, edging closer, "or you gonna blow away the magnificent shit that my man -- and our muthafuckin' fearless commander -- General Saint -- be sending yo' way."

Shuggie did a series of somersaults, edging closer to the sentries who continued to hold their fire. Then he got to his feet, jutted out his hands. They now clutched wads of money.

"Do yo' eyes deceive you, ma bruthas?" Shuggie asked as he waved the money back and forth. They could clearly see crisp, fresh hundred dollar bills. They could practically smell the printer's ink.

"No, they definitely not fooling you. Like a Roman Caesar, General Saint's giving all his good little soldier boys a tiny bling-bling of his appreciation today."

Shuggie jutted out both arms and held the tempting wads of bills close to the two sentries. Then he threw the money in their faces and hit the deck.

Bullets spanged off the walls as a salvo of hip-level heavy caliber machinegun fire raked the sentries and made them dance like marionettes viciously jerked by a mad puppeteer. Blood spattered the walls as Colonel Hawk's squad chattered away with bullpup M4A1 automatic rifle and Heckler & Koch MP5 submachinegun fire.

A second two-man buddy team simultaneously attacked the antechamber beyond the doorway, firing two forty-millimeter grenade canisters from the undermounted M203 launchers attached to the barrels of their stub-snouted Colt assault weapons in rapid succession. They ducked for cover as the high-explosive rounds discharged into the room.

The grenades, canisters color-coded black, were designed for antipersonnel offensive fire. At point-blank range the two detonations merged into a single, deafening concussion, pelting every living thing in the room not only with the razor-sharp splinter fragments of the burst outer casing, but adding to the carnage with a death cloud of hundreds of tiny, yet razor-sharp steel flechettes that had surrounded the shell's explosive charge.

Flattening against the sides of the doorway, the buddy team hugged the walls with their backsides as a blast front of smoke and spinning debris blew out the doorway, then, nodding at each other, quickly pivoted on their boot heels to shove the barrels of their M4A1s into the still smoking room and rake the interior with sustained, close-range 5.56 millimeter bursts that ricocheted around the room as a guarantee of death.

Shrill, two-note alarms were now klaxoning across the corridor, insanely shrieking out their twin notes of danger. Hawk's crew paid them no heed as they went through the corridor killing any and all unfriendlies they found and shooting out the prying eyes of surveillance cams wherever they appeared. The whine and spang of bullets and the thuds and booms of grenade explosions interspersed with the shrieking of the alarms until, one by one, each of the siren horns positioned behind protective ceiling grilles had been destroyed by M4A1 burst fires.

When the corridor was cleared of unfriendlies, one of Hawk's troopers squatted down and aimed a SMAW man-portable rocket launcher at the blast door. There was no time for niceties such as access codes at this stage. The high-explosive warhead struck home and blew the heavy armored steel door clean off its hinges. The huge metal slab crashed against the walls, bounced off, then tobogganed down the floor of the corridor, raising sparks as it skidded along, hitting finally with a crash that seemed to shake the building.

"Good luck," Hawk called out to Krieger and turned aside, to race down the passage with his hard-chargers in train.

Sabio joined Hawk's troopers in hustling away from the strike sector. They had other jobs to do elsewhere, throughout Wedge Three, in fact.

While Krieger entered the data well attempting to gain operative control of COLOSUS and decouple Northern Cross orbital weapons from Dawn Horse submersible missile platforms, Hawk's team would strike at Saint's stronghold in the National Military Command Center.

The last-ditch offensive would be balls-out. There would be no quarter given and no turning back.

■

"Damn!" Casper Saint cursed sotto voce.

Running man-figures aimed weapons at him. Fire blazed and there was darkness on the face of the waters.

In other words, bovine excrement was again hitting the whirling blades.

It was fortunate that it was only the remote feed from the surveillance cams that Hawk's troops

369

were destroying with automatic fire as they spread out across Wedge Three.

The rogue general had thought those soldier boys sent by Halifax were long gone, but Saint now realized he'd been wrong. They were apparently still alive. There couldn't be many of them left, though. He'd calculated the body count himself. The human remains pouches were neatly stacked under ice in the makeshift mortuary they'd set up in the basement.

Nope, he was dealing with stragglers here, no more.

Saint figured it was the ragtag remnants -- a squad, maybe, or a little more than a squad -- of the commando force that had been sent in to oust him the previous day. Where they'd been holing up and how they'd evaded death and capture, Saint didn't know. What was important was that his own force enjoyed a huge superiority of numbers and arms.

The survivors now attacking were really as good as dead. Saint figured he could relax about that part of the experience.

Nevertheless, there were bigger problems that Saint saw were rearing their dangerous heads.

From his catbird seat on the balcony above the darkened battle pit, Saint saw the dental work breaking loose from the jaws of perdition. A soldier had to know when to withdraw and a gambler when to quit; Saint was both, and all the signs pointed to now being the right moment to begin pulling up stakes and folding up tents.

A wide-screen panel flashed to life in the semi-darkness. A face appeared in a window at the display's upper-left corner. The face wore a perplexed look beneath the black beret with the laughing skull insignia perched on its shaven head.

"Sir, there has been a Dawn Horse interdiction at the target sectors that now appear on the central tactical display."

The central god screen showed the flashing tracks of incoming cruise missile rounds while its satellite screens depicted orbital imagery of the actual strikes. A reactor in Israel was now a mass of glowing embers.

A second strike wreaked havoc at a large factory complex only a few scant highway miles outside of Moscow. An accompanying feed label identified the factory as the Khrunichev National Space Center research facility, a government think tank.

As Saint watched the displays, two more incoming warheads riding incandescent vapor trails arced from the skies on trajectories toward other targets located elsewhere across the surface of the globe.

# THREATCON DELTA

The international petroleum jetty facility at Trondheim, Norway, which offloaded North Sea oil into tanker vessels, was struck by a tactical nuclear airburst, sending a mushrooming fireball soaring high into the stratosphere. On the island of Honshu, one of the four main Japanese home islands, another missile strike caused massive destruction as it obliterated a sizable stretch of high-speed commuter railway between Tokyo and Osaka in a blinding nuclear detonation.

"Don't tell me, let me guess -- it's COLOSUS."

"Highly probable, general," Pegasus retorted, seeing no humor in Saint's pose of bravado under fire. "The system has isolated itself from all external links. It does seem to have taken control of itself."

"How did this happen?"

"We don't know, sir," Pegasus replied. "It's completely unexpected."

"What can we do about it?" Saint asked, but he already knew the answer -- bail out.

Pegasus had little to add to that assessment. Saint told him to keep him posted.

Meanwhile he called Alexai via encrypted Internet phone. Saint quickly outlined the rapidly deteriorating situation to his ex-Russian Mafiya confederate. Both of them concurred that it was time to extract. The money count had mounted with the body count. No reason to take more heat.

"What about the malfunctioning computer?" the Russian asked Saint.

"When I set the charges," Saint informed him, "I'll blow it to hell along with the rest. It's just another few bricks of C-4 to add to all the other shit that's happened, that's all."

"You think it'll work?"

"If it doesn't, what do you expect me to do about it? Run a fucking virus scan? Maybe you want me to run out and buy the Norton Utilities, huh?"

"Okay -- don't get excited. It sounds like a plan, my brother," Alexai approved. "The extraction countdown now commences. We'll use timetable B just to make sure."

They'd previously agreed on four fallback, or emergency, timetables. A was the green timetable. B was the yellow timetable, which was to be used in case of unforeseen contingencies cropping up. C and D were amber and red timetables, respectively, but they were the dogs in the manger and not to be used unless Saint's dick was really and truly caught in the wringer.

"Packing up my old kit bag," Saint said to Alexai, his cheerful self again.

The screen went black.

To Pegasus and Da Gamma, he said, "As you've heard, extraction procedures commence as of now.

It's been a real pleasure working with you gentlemen. See you all in Acapulco sometime."

The general rose from his catbird seat and left his post at the captured National Military Command Center for the last time -- without so much as a backward glance.

DAVID ALEXANDER

Thirty
**In Through the Out Door**
*T*he entire array of global military power was now tasked with the destruction of the two lethal arms of the automated SAAE-SIOP. Coalition peacekeeping operations under US command attempted to bring relief to devastated areas while the undersea hunt for the stealthy Dawn Horse UUVs increased in tempo and grew to include an array of international military forces.

The nuclear strikes rained down by Dawn Horse were still not hitting at the cardinal centers of global politics, business and culture, but they were getting closer to the heart of global civilization with each new missile sortie.

Under presidential emergency authorization, the surviving outposts of the US military made the full specifications of the Northern Cross directed energy weapon satellites and Dawn Horse undersea robots available to the Kremlin and to its European allies alike. The entire world now had a stake in the speedy destruction of the automated killing machinery that seemed intent on dismantling civilization piece by piece.

Chaos ruled at the captured Pentagon, from which COLOSUS coordinated the operations of the two striking arms of the SAAE-SIOP, yet whose deactivation or destruction, though a matter of vital importance, was impossible until the Pentagon was cleared of its occupiers. Unknown to the White House and the world at large, those occupiers were now in the process of preparing to vacate the Building as fast as possible. Saint's troops were busily slotting explosive charges as part of their exit strategy. Saint himself was changing from the combat fatigues he'd worn throughout the mission into nondescript street clothes.

While the intruder-occupants of Wedge Three were bent on escape and destruction, one figure moved alone in a sterile world of glass, plastic and steel. Rommel Krieger had entered the COLOSUS data well.

The instant he did, he heard a synthetic voice, neither female nor male, say, "Welcome."

Krieger heard the pneumatically actuated armored steel door slide shut behind him with a soft, yet final, whisper of closure.

He was alone inside the lair of COLOSUS.

Red shafts of intense, coherent light played out from above him, enveloped him, ran along his body, along his limbs, up his midsection and then finally wrapped themselves around the contours of his skull.

"Rommel Krieger," the synthetic, unisex voice went on, identifying the trespasser.

Then: "I have been expecting you."

Suddenly there was another light, one that came in an abrupt, blinding flash, and Krieger felt something strike him a solid, punishing blow squarely in the center of his chest.

He felt himself plummet headlong into a vertical tunnel of darkness as his senses fled him and he seemed to die.

Thirty-one
**Comes the Payoff**

*K*rieger came back to his senses, and as consciousness returned, like air filling a balloon, he realized, with a sudden horrified awareness, that he didn't remember where he was or how he'd gotten to be here. Somehow a small mammal with very sharp teeth had gotten into his head and was gnawing at his eyes from the inside out, or at least it felt like something like that was causing the intense, painful throbbing in his cranium.

Still dazed and disoriented, he became aware that something large, with curvilinear contours, so familiar, yet now impossible for his shattered mind to grasp, was blocking his frontal view. Framing this form was a circle, again familiar, yet for the moment, at least, incomprehensible to Krieger's powers of observation and identification and far removed from his frame of reference.

A dot pulsed orange high up on the thing, moved side to side, faded, leaving behind the stale odor of smoke, then flared again. Somehow the odor was a sign to Krieger that he was in grave danger, but the reason for this, like everything else, somehow eluded him. Then a light flashed on, smaller and dimmer than the one that had knocked him cold, yet bright enough to make him wince all the same.

The round object slid sideways, revealing a jumbled view of lighted screens and blinking multicolored LEDs against a background of almost seamless black.

"Get up."

Krieger just lay there. He had no intention of obeying the order. Then he was seized by the shirt collar and felt himself rising upward despite his own inertia. Dumped unceremoniously into a chair in front of liquid matrix display monitors. The voice was familiar. It took a second or two to place it, but Krieger was coming back to himself. Then he knew instantly why the smoke-smell had signaled danger.

"Saint," he said, choking out the word.

"Wish I could say it's good seeing you again, Blitz, but I'd be lying," Saint told Krieger.

Saint was in the company of two of his mercenary troopers dressed in camo fatigues, both of them armed with Spectre M4 submachineguns. The duo was positioned at corners of the huge cylindrical data well. The general, cigar clenched

379

in the side of his mouth, tip glowing as he drew in smoke, wheeled over a desk chair and sat down on it backwards, his hands dangling carelessly over its back.

"I've got a plane to catch in a little while," Saint told Krieger. "So we've got to do this fast. It's just blind chance that we both wound up here at the same time. But," he added, re-igniting his cigar tip by drawing another lungful of smoke, "fate works in strange and miraculous ways sometimes."

Saint held up his hand and curled back his fingers. Cupped in his palm was the DCM dongle, the plastic cylinder containing the COLOSUS crypto chip.

"Tell me what this is," Saint demanded.

Krieger tried to fit the puzzle pieces together while Saint spoke. Adrenaline now coursed through his veins and his head was clearing rapidly.

As his mental machinery began to turn, Krieger reasoned that if Saint was in the data well ahead of him, it was likely he was there to destroy COLOSUS, since there was no way to reprogram the massively parallel computer -- no disk drives, ports or connectors of any kind were available in the well, and the keyboard was only for human operators to input requests, not enter programming. There was no way for code to be input via keyboard; the operating system wouldn't recognize keyboard commands.

"That's my homework," said Krieger. "I need it back."

Saint nodded to one side and a tactical-gloved fist clutching a gun struck Krieger a savage blow against the side of his head, making him see stars. He felt himself about to black out and fought to stay conscious.

"Blitz, we just don't have time to fuck around playing word games. Not today."

Saint was in a grim mood. He was worried. Krieger suddenly realized why that might be. Saint's operation had succeeded. Saint was on a running timetable, because all military operations followed a timetable, usually a strict one, and his op would be no exception. But something had gone wrong with COLOSUS, and Saint's timetable was in jeopardy.

Saint held up small the plastic cylinder.

"Again, what's this?"

If Krieger had set up an operation like Saint's, an operation that involved taking control of and securing a building as large and as important as the Pentagon, then that timetable would not only be tightly organized, but it would be severely limited. Krieger would set it up for two or three days at the maximum, then put his exit strategy in place, probably with diversionary strategies built into the overall plan.

Saint shouldn't be here, deep in the guts of COLOSUS -- he should be extracting, surmised Krieger.

Saint wasn't extracting, though.

This meant Saint had a problem and wanted to correct it, if he was able, before he pulled out. And in another second or two Krieger thought he'd guessed the nature and scope of Saint's problem.

"You're in deep shit, general," Krieger declared, and out the corner of his eye saw the trooper who'd pistol-whipped him before advance two steps, only to be stopped short by a shake of Saint's head.

"You opened Pandora's box, and now you're looking for a way to shut it again, aren't you, Saint?" Krieger went on, as the soldier lowered his weapon and backpedaled. Well, there's no way to do it. That data stick won't solve your problem."

"Why not?"

"The DCM can reprogram the COLOSUS CPU, decouple Northern Cross from Dawn Horse, then use the particle beam weapons to destroy the robot submersibles along with the remaining unlaunched nuclear weapons. After that, Northern Cross is told to end its own existence. The system commits suicide."

"So where's my problem?" Saint questioned.

"Only I can use the dongle."

"Assuming that's true, there are no sockets in this well -- we checked," Saint told him. "Where would you insert the dongle?"

"It's proximity activated, just point it anywhere and the code is transferred, but you need the right biometrics, and those are mine. Handprints, retinal patterns, the whole enchilada."

For a few moments Saint pondered what Krieger had told him. Then he shook his head. Krieger understood then that Saint had realized that decoupling the orbital weapons from the subsurface missile launcher submersibles would not help his case. It would only spell the destruction of the automated SIOP. The mass-killing mechanisms would still be active, and in place.

"I think I'd just as soon blow the thing up," Saint concluded. He gestured to his men who continued slotting the demo charges around the circular perimeter of the data well.

Saint tossed the crypto key into Krieger's lap.

"You can keep this, Ace."

Saint then reached across his midsection with his right hand and pulled out a nine millimeter semiautomatic handgun, a Sig P230 with a stubby silencer attached to its muzzle. Krieger's eyes focused on the load indicator on one side of the weapon's receiver. The tiny dot of red paint showed that a bullet was chambered and ready to fire. Krieger also noted that the pistol's safety catch was off.

Condition zero. A trigger pull away from eternity.

Saint pushed the stub-end of the silencer into Krieger's forehead.

"Nice try, Blitz," he said, "But -- unfortunately -- no cigar."

A muffled spit marked the exit of the silenced bullet from the suppressor-fitted gun muzzle. Groaning with the shock of ballistic wounding, the mortally injured man keeled over sideways, blood gushing from the destroyed remnants of the shattered head.

Krieger was still alive. It was one of Saint's troopers who'd been hit. Automatic fire now raked the room, sending sparks flying as ricochets rattled around the data well. The fire ceased and Krieger heard a voice shout his name from the catwalk above, on the lip of the circular pit.

He didn't answer. There was no time. The shock of sudden gunfire had caused Saint to glance aside just before pulling the trigger. Saint's outstretched hand had wavered for a split instant. Now, in slow motion, through a perceptual tunnel, Krieger saw Saint's head begin pivoting toward him again. Time snapped back into synchronization as Krieger put every ounce of physical strength into his calves and forearms. Propelling himself from the chair as if on springs, he swept aside Saint's outstretched gun hand.

Reflex action sent a silenced bullet hissing like an angry rattler close by Krieger's ear. A second -- then a third -- death-spit followed as the heat of ignited powder singed Krieger's hair and cheek. The force of Krieger's movements would have bowled over a lesser man, but Saint still stood on his feet, and his hand still firmly gripped the silenced handgun. There was steel in that arm, as in the rest of his body.

Saint smiled a Reaper's grin and tried to shove Krieger backward. Krieger smashed him hard across the head with the knobby point of his elbow. The gun dropped with a clatter, and Saint lost his footing, but as Saint went down, he pulled Krieger on top of him. Now both antagonists rolled on the floor, grappling, heaving, locked in a primal contest for supremacy.

Krieger freed his right arm long enough to land a punch at Saint's battered face, and Saint's hold was broken. With both arms now suddenly freed, Krieger balled both fists together into a spiked mace of protruding knuckles and bone, and began to bring it smashing down, only to be sent sprawling onto his back as Saint booted him in the midriff.

Then Saint was up again, the silenced Sig P230 in his hand, breathing hard and bleeding from the side of his head as he staggered and leveled the semiautomatic pistol.

"That's enough!"

Sabio was pointing a Spectre SMG at Saint's head. The general reeled like a drunk and panted for breath, but he nodded acceptance, dropped the gun and kicked it across the floor. Though Saint was winded, his eyes blazed; he still had plenty of fight left in him. Krieger scooped up the Sig that Saint had dropped.

Sabio and two of Colonel Red Hawk's troopers in the data well with Krieger and Saint. The general's two troopers were sprawled at catacorners. Neither mercenary moved. Or breathed.

Krieger also retrieved the crypto key. The small plastic cylinder seemed intact. Krieger found the biometric station and placed his face against the binocular retinal scanner and his hands flat on the palm print analyzer. Lights glowed. A screen display indicated that he was granted access privileges to the system. Krieger pointed the DCM toward the banks of strangely illuminated computer processing units. Nothing happened.

Suddenly the display flashed a message confirming that the decoupling had occurred. Now Sabio got in front of the terminal. As Krieger watched she began to keystroke in sequences of commands that were echoed on the display in graphic and alphanumeric format.

"This could now be done elsewhere, but since we're here, I think I can command the orbital components of the SIOP to attack and kill the Dawn Horse elements using Northern Cross weaponry."

She hit the return key, executing the program, adding, "As you can see, commands to the system can now be input. That was a bonus of using the DCM."

The screen reported that the system was about to do just this.

"There it goes," said Sabio. "It's done, boss."

Automatic fire raked the data well.

The rapid cadence of dozens of rounds was deafening, and the ricocheting bullets forced Krieger, Sabio and the two troopers that Red Hawk had lent her to take immediate cover.

As they tucked in their heads to duck the incoming fire, there was a spurt of dark motion, and a sprinting figure streaked past them.

It was Saint, making for the access ladder to the doorway above. Saint had a pistol in his hand and was snapping off covering fire as he broke for freedom. Krieger didn't know how he'd gotten the gun, but he sensed it had something to do with one of Saint's guards firing SMG bursts from one knee, and the empty holster on his belt. Saint had either managed to extract the pistol from the soldier's apparent corpse, or the shot-up mercenary had thrown it to him as he summoned his last remaining ounce of strength to make a final play.

Whatever Saint's fate, the badly wounded trooper hadn't long left to live. He was holding himself up and firing his Spectre submachinegun by an intense effort of will. His effort to cover his chief's escape succeeded. Saint managed to mount the short steel-runged ladder flush with the wall and reach the data well's overhead catwalk.

Snapping off a volley of rapid fire from the snatched-up pistol, the general ran through the door to freedom. It might have been coincidence that at least one of the bullets he fired mortally struck the trooper with the submachinegun who'd covered his escape, but the effect was to kill him instantly.

As the soldier fell heavily sideways and lay completely still, Krieger, Sabio and Hawk's men were on their feet and in pursuit of the fleeing fugitive.

When they reached the C-Ring corridor, though, Saint was gone without a trace. The elevator at the end of the ring showed a red floor-level indicator LED glowing above a cluster of pixels on a black matrix. The pixels formed the number one.

# DAVID ALEXANDER

■

A moment later, the entire building seemed to violently shake. A succession of fearsome explosions rocked the floor and made the walls tremble. It felt like the entire Wedge was about to crumble to pieces and fall crashing to the ground.

■

Saint had been in tighter places. But he'd never had more riding on his successful escape and evasion. Now it was up to Alexai and the Spetznaz specialists in the Washington-Virginian-based L-Force team that had, by prearranged plan, been sent in to extract him from the Pentagon. The things the Spetsnaz had learned in the weeks of their posing as the so-called Beltway Sniper had helped prepare them for the precision driving that lay ahead as the mission ended and extraction ops commenced.

The explosions now rocking the Pentagon came off exactly as planned, timed to the exact minute and precise second. Saint checked his Tag-Huer wrist chronometer as the phased, sequential detonations continued going off in rapid succession. His troops were following his orders to perfection. The charges would cycle around the low-rise star-shaped building, round-robin fashion, Wedge by Wedge from Wedge Five to Wedge One.

# THREATCON DELTA

Each explosive charge had been calculated to produce several specific effects.

One of these effects -- and the primary one -- would be to blow the blast doors that prevented access and egress to and from the five Wedges of the Pentagon clean off the massive locking bolts that secured them in place. Announcements would already have been made informing the hundreds of captives -- the takeover op had commenced on a Sunday morning, and the number of weekend hostages had carefully weighed in the planning -- that they were to prepare themselves to make a hasty exit from the Pentagon.

The main anticipated consequence of the first effect would be to free the captives and cause massive pandemonium as they broke free, helter-skelter, desperate to escape their long confinement without adequate food, sanitary facilities or ventilation, and in fear of their lives.

The second consequence flowed from the first -- the chaos created by the sudden shock of the explosions and the even greater shock of the hundreds of captives rushing pell-mell to freedom outside the Pentagon would create a perfect diversion to enable not only Saint, but the scores of surviving mercenaries who had joined him in the operation, to also make their getaways in the confusion that ensued.

## DAVID ALEXANDER

The mass exit strategy had been based on a careful study of newsmedia footage of the aftermath of the 911 and later Strike Day attacks on the Pentagon. The analysis had shown conclusively that even with police, national guard and emergency services personnel standing by, the huge outpouring of a frenzied human mass made effective crowd control impossible.

Panicked Pentagon staffers spilling out of the burning building, coughing and vomiting amid dense clouds of smoke -- clouds like the ones that again now poured from the Pentagon -- presented a stampede that defied the best efforts of authorities. Among the many reasons was the innate sympathy of those stationed outside that would spare the escapees further hardship by using harsh measures to halt them or herd them into a manageable group.

Of course, if the crowd was known to be hostile -- or that among them were interspersed groups of rogue soldiers known to be heavily armed and determined to escape -- that would present a different set of circumstances. In such a case the police or the national guard would certainly use tear gas, high-pressure water jets, or wade in with shields and batons, at the very least. But this wouldn't be the case now.

Like Saint himself, his men were trained to make their escapes in civilian clothes. Their uniforms and larger caliber weapons -- everything excluding compact handguns which they could conceal during the Tuesday exit part of the op -- were cast down in heaps inside the Pentagon.

With disheveled clothes and hair, with faces blackened and streaked by camouflage paint to mimic the grime of smoke soot, with hands held up to mouths as they emerged coughing and gagging from the burning, smoldering building amid the hordes of fleeing innocents, his men were to make their way to pre-planned escape corridors. Most, if not all, would get themselves successfully to safety and live to spend the tens of thousands of dollars that each had earned in the operation. As for the rest, who didn't, provisions had been made to provide for the next of kin that survived them.

As the explosions continued to detonate and shake the foundations of the immense five-sided building, Saint ran with the crowd of escapees who stampeded blindly, herd-fashion, bent on nothing else except running from their terrible three-days confinement.

Saint found it hard to suppress a smile -- the hostages had behaved exactly as pre-mission analysis had predicted; one reason why a three-day op had been planned was because psychological studies showed forty-eight hours wasn't quite enough to drive them wild enough, while more than sixty hours tended to weaken captives too much for the final stages of the exit strategy to prove completely effective.

Saint kept his expression as grim as possible, hiding the excitement and elation he felt as he ran with the rest of the escapees toward the Pentagon's River Entrance-side North Parking lot.

He had survived! And moreover, he had won!

The op had netted him at least six billion dollars that were now sitting in untraceable numbered bank accounts in a variety of offshore banking havens that would never be reachable by the US government.

Homeland Security could go fuck itself. So could the IRS. Nobody -- nothing -- could touch that wealth; that almost incalculable wealth that was now his. Try as he might, Saint could not even envision a billion dollars, let alone twenty. He'd have fun trying, though. That was for shit and sure.

He was wealthy beyond his wildest dreams. All he had to do now, Saint knew, was keep running and not look back.

And if there was any trouble ...

His right hand clutched the compact parabellum semiautomatic pistol in the pocket of his torn suit jacket, his index finger wrapped around its trigger, his thumb tightened around its grip.

# THREATCON DELTA

Thirty-two
## An Unfinished Sentence

Saint feigned injury and sickness, but loped purposively across the vast, football stadium-sized North Parking lot. The location of the parking space where one of the two crash cars was kept stashed -- thirty rows down, twenty rows across -- was etched in his mind. Saint saw the black Mercedes S-600 town car parked precisely where it was expected to be, and two men, one in the back seat, the other behind the wheel, sitting unobtrusively inside the vehicle.

Both carried police identification that would stand any test, and the car -- which was as heavily armored as any presidential limo -- bore a DC Metro shield above its front and rear bumpers. At the press of a button its headlights and taillights were also programmed to flash like that of a genuine police vehicle.

A car like that, racing through the panic ensuing the catastrophe at the Pentagon with lights flashing, would certainly attract attention, but chances are it would not be stopped, or if stopped, permitted to continue on its way.

The general risked a glance over his shoulder and took heart. Other escapees were pouring out across the vast parking lot, heading for their vehicles, bent on getting as far away as quickly as possible. The Pentagon's River Entrance, the front facade of Wedge Three, was gloriously engulfed in flames, and continuing to belch enormous, billowing quantities of dense, black smoke, despite the desperate efforts of firefighters to put out the inferno.

His escape vehicle was only a few score yards away from him now.

Saint controlled himself, and loped forward, limping slightly from his injuries. He was on his way to freedom now, and he didn't want to blow the game at the final scrimmage.

■

Rommel Krieger pushed the Army medic away as she tried to attach the sticky electrode pads of a monitoring device to his bloodied head. He'd already had large band aids stuck on his face, and that was enough for the moment.

This wasn't over, yet. Not till Saint had been conclusively dealt with. The general had made it a personal contest and Krieger was not about to let his final chances for settling accounts with the rogue soldier pass him by.

# THREATCON DELTA

The Pentagon was a house of pandemonium as the mass of former hostages escaped its burning confines. Krieger was obsessed with the notion that somewhere in that unruly, terrified multitude was Saint, getting clean away under cover of sweeping hysteria and wholesale confusion.

Krieger watched a civilian Bell Scout helo suddenly traverse the River Entrance Parade Ground and set down near the knot of Army ambulances that included the one where he was being treated. He stared at the light, observation helo for a long minute, and suddenly had a BFO, Pentagonese for a blinding flash of the obvious.

Using his cell he contacted Hawk at the temporary operational command post that had been set up on the perimeter of the burning building. Krieger wanted to use the Scout to hunt for Saint. Hawk made speedy arrangements for Krieger to get a ride on the chopper.

"Can you circle the parking lot, low enough so I can see faces?" Krieger asked the helo's pilot, a civilian security contractor, after painfully loping across the greensward to the Bell.

The pilot, who'd been doing an aerial security survey of what DOD calls the "Pentagon domain," a term including adjacent highway interchanges and building complexes, handed Krieger a pair of binoculars.

"Sure. These'll help."

## DAVID ALEXANDER

They strapped in and the helo pilot lifted off.

■

The Vista Charger slid down the Potomac.

Laden with its cargo of truck trailers, the containership had sailed the Atlantic Intracoastal Waterway to its destination at the cargo docks of Portland, Maine. It was now on its way back down the East Coast on a southbound journey that would see it crossing the Panama Canal in roughly two days' time.

The containership would slow to a stop a little farther down the Potomac, but it would not weigh anchor. It would wait ten minutes and no more, before resuming its outbound journey.

Its captain was on a timetable.

Within hours the Vista Charger was to leave American waters behind and become a speck of steel hidden within the vast expansive reaches of the global seas.

■

Krieger alternated between scanning through the clear thermoplastic dome of the Bell Scout with his naked eyes and using the binoculars to zoom in on targets on the highway complex below.

His head throbbed where he'd been pistol whipped, and if he leaned over too far, he began to feel as if he was blacking out. He was afraid he might have suffered a concussion and cursed himself for breaking away from the rescue personnel, but there had been no choice. Any further delay and his already dwindling chances of apprehending Saint shrank still further.

They might already have dwindled to nothing, Krieger realized. So far there was no sign of Saint. In the pandemonium below, it was an infernal chaos of smoke, flares, lights, racing vehicles, and running people, with newsmedia hanging around the edges of the tragedy like a flight of scavenger buzzards.

"Wait a minute."

Krieger saw the black Mercedes limo suddenly wheel around and tear out of the Pentagon's North Parking lot onto the Jefferson Davis Highway. Through the binoculars he thought he caught a glimpse of something metallic, gleaming dully in a flash as sunlight glanced off ... a weapon -- yes, it might be a weapon.

"That car," he pointed downward.

"I see it," said the pilot, and manipulated cyclic rotor pitch and collective pitch controls, angling the main rotor downward and sideways to spin the chopper around on a horizontal axis. Moving the hand-controlled pitch stick with deft precision, the pilot sent the small, light, reconnaissance helo shooting downward and forward on its new trajectory.

Krieger tried to focus the binoculars on the rear of the speeding vehicle below. He was able to make out the official looking police shield, but not all the numbers on the license tag.

The unmarked limo's front- and rear-mounted hazard lights were flashing as it roared onto the Jefferson Davis Highway beyond the Pentagon's Potomac-side parking lot. Traffic was gridlocked as Metro police struggled to detour the Tuesday rush hour traffic into Virginia and toward the 14th Street Bridge complex into the District, but the swollen river of moving metal was too much for them to effectively handle.

The official vehicle was making progress, though. Using the horn and flashing its emergency lights, the limo was forcing other motorists to make way for it as it fought its way out of the mess of tangled commuter traffic in the vicinity of the burning Pentagon.

Krieger put down the binoculars and rubbed his smoke-burned and reddened eyes. That car probably was a police vehicle, after all, which would explain the object that might have been a weapon. Dismayed, he told the pilot to swing the Bell back around and have another look at the Pentagon River Entrance-side parking lot, but Krieger's hopes were sinking. At this stage he held out as much expectation of locating the rogue general as finding a needle in the proverbial haystack.

Then suddenly, Krieger realized what was wrong about the car on the highway below, and he knew they weren't police.

"Hold it."

The pilot was already swinging the helo around when the realization struck Krieger.

The vehicle was moving away from the Pentagon, not toward it. Maybe they were cops -- but they were acting just like fleeing felons.

"There a loudhailer on this thing?"

"Got a bullhorn in the storage locker behind the seat," replied the pilot.

"Get me in close, right over the roof of that limo down there," Krieger shouted above the deafening racket of the spinning rotor blades. "But be ready to move this thing out of harm's way if they fire on us."

The pilot nodded as he rotated the helo, but Krieger could see that he was scared.

■

"That chopper started turning and now it's right behind us," said the man with the high-powered automatic rifle, sitting behind the general and to his right in the back seat of the Mercedes sedan. "I don't like it."

They waited and saw the chopper single them out. Then a figure clutching a bullhorn leaned out its bubble cockpit's right side hatch.

"Identify yourselves. Stop the vehicle. Repeat. Stop the vehicle and identify yourselves."

The helo hovered low above the getaway car, and the noise made by its churning main rotors was almost deafening, but the bullhorn amplified Krieger's voice to leave no doubt of what he wanted the car's occupants to do.

"If I can get through this last piece of shit gridlock here," cussed the wheelman with a gesture of one hand, though a glimpse at his face told Saint he was sweating with fear, "it's smooth going to the drop-off point."

The general whipped out the compact Heckler & Koch MP5/10 submachinegun which, unlike standard H&K SMGs, came bore-sighted and chambered to accommodate heavy caliber ten millimeter rounds instead of the standard nines. The SMG lying slanted across Saint's lap was also loaded with a nonstandard hundred-round ammo magazine, with spares on the floor within convenient reach.

The general snapped back the cocking lever, arming the compact, yet powerful and deadly submachinegun.

"Let's do the fucker," he said.

■

A hail of automatic fire rotored up from the vehicle below as the driver applied maximum engine torque and slammed the front end of the heavy limousine into the rear ends of two compact cars ahead of him. The desperate maneuver forced them out of the way and cleared a path for the escape vehicle to bull free and out into the open.

It wasn't called a "crash car" for nothing. Apart from its armoring and other augmentation, the Mercedes had been outfitted with a specially modified front end that was made of a light yet extremely hard titanium-steel alloy, while the rugged transmission and engine were better suited to a Mac truck or Abrams tank than a mere passenger vehicle.

The result was that while the Mercedes' front-end was hardly scratched, the vehicles in its way were tossed aside like so many crumpled chewing gum wrappers. Its tires spinning, screaming, and throwing up clouds of burning black rubber smoke, the crash car broke from its impasse and turned off the Beltway onto a secondary artery that took it through the forested suburban enclaves in the vicinity of Falls Church , Virginia.

Bullets spanged and whined off the sides of the Bell, and cracked its Plexiglas bubble, but the pilot to his credit seemed more stubbornly intent to pursue the car the more they were fired on. Krieger snapped off fire from his handgun, wishing he'd taken the precaution of properly arming himself with a heavier weapon. Finally the pistol's hammer snapped with a hollow click on an empty firing chamber.

"Fuck. It's dry," Krieger cursed.

"There's a SPAS-12 behind the seat. It's loaded."

"Next thing you'll tell me you got a whorehouse full of midget Siamese twins somewhere in this thing."

"Yeah. Got that too," deadpanned the pilot and kept pace with the car. "I'll radio the cops on the emergency channel."

Krieger nodded and leaned out the open side hatch in the glass bubble surrounding the crew cabin, angling the weapon downward.

The wind shear was fierce, but he sighted the combat shotgun on the back of the car, hoping to "squirrel" the rear tires with a lucky ricochet. He thought he'd hit it after pumping off a few blasts of .30-ought shot, but the car kept going, even as the automatic fire, marked by rapid muzzle flashes, kept erupting from its sides. The limo was obviously equipped with run-flat tires, and probably bulletproof windshields and an armored chassis too. Leave it to the general.

Out in the open now, the car was making good time, moving fast on the straightaway along a stretch that paralleled embanked railroad tracks that emerged into the open from behind an undulating, tree-studded ridge of low-lying hills.

403

Up ahead, Krieger saw, was the entrance to a rail tunnel. You'd have to be crazy to run a car off the highway and try for the tunnel, but in his guts Krieger knew that was just what the driver would do.

Sure enough, to Krieger's chagrin the getaway car driver swung the Mercedes onto the railroad right of way and drove it right along the tracks. The Mercedes swerved wildly, and the tracks slowed it somewhat, but it didn't stop, not for a second. Then, with a final, disdainful burst of automatic fire aimed upward at the pursuing helo, the car disappeared into the tunnel's gaping black mouth.

"Shit -- you see what they just did?" asked the pilot.

"It got eyes the same as you," Krieger answered.

"Man, I hope there's a train coming. That would fix their asses. Fuckin' train..." he let the unfinished sentence hang in the air.

"Don't count on it," Krieger told him. "Any idea where this tunnel lets them out?"

"Yeah, I know the area pretty well. It's kind of a long tunnel, though, runs for about a mile or so in the direction of the river. It's a cargo route. Takes railway cars to sidings on the lower Potomac docks where they onload and offload onto freighters on the Intracoastal."

"Is that right?" Krieger asked, musing.

"What do you want me to do?" the pilot asked after a brief pause.

"Get us over there," Krieger decided. "To the end of the tunnel as fast as this crate can make it."

The pilot nodded and pushed the Bell for every ounce of speed its engines could deliver. It took them longer than it took the car because the helo had to fly around the mountain that contained the tunnel, while the car only had to cut straight across from end to end. Yet when they reached the opposite mouth of the tunnel, there was no indication of a car or a train. Krieger told the pilot to take the chopper down close to the tunnel exit so he could peer inside.

The pilot descended and hovered at the mouth of the tunnel. Just then a Lexington-bound express freight train rocketed out, sounding its horn. The chopper pilot just managed to avoid them being dashed to pieces against the mountainside as the diesel locomotive, trailing a line of containerized flatcars, streaked past at high speed. There was no sign of the Mercedes.

"Shit. That was a close one."

Krieger thought a few moments.

"You said the tracks led to the river. That there were cargo sidings on the docks, right?"

"Uh-huh."

"Let's go there."

"We're real low on fuel, man."

405

# THREATCON DELTA

"Just humor me, okay?"

The pilot nodded and they swung fast toward the river. As they breached a forested stand on some high hills, they saw the river water sparkling below in the reflected rays of the late afternoon sun. It was growing dark, but the huge, steel bulk of an Intracoastal containership anchored near the deserted dock was clearly visible through the binocs that Krieger held up to his eyes. So was the vehicle that was parked next to it.

It was the Mercedes.

Krieger drew in breath. As he continued to scope out the scene below, he saw Saint exit the vehicle and clamber aboard the freighter. Krieger grasped the SPAS-12 and raised the combat shotgun toward the Bell's open hatchway -- still out of range, he knew. Tense moments passed, and now the chopper had almost come abreast of the siding. Krieger again leveled the weapon, and sighted down, now confident that he was in range of a money shot.

Suddenly a figure turned from the back seat of the parked vehicle below and spun out the door he'd shoved open. There was a flash from the front end of the cylindrical object in the outstretched hands of the partially crouched man-form. The flame belching from the mouth of the Dragon launch tube lit up the finned TOW projectile that streaked up toward the Bell, trailing a wire behind it, and also illuminated the snaking white contrail of exhaust smoke that followed it as it sped toward them on its deadly trajectory.

"Incoming!" Krieger shouted as the TOW missile's warhead detonated.

There came another flash and a sickening pinwheeling sense of spinning crazily in space, and Krieger knew the Bell's tail rotor had been blown off by the missile from the man-portable launcher. The world turned upside down as a second high-explosive warhead struck the damaged helicopter, and with a sickening lurch as the machine blew completely apart, Rommel Krieger began to fall to earth.

Thirty-three
**First the Darkness, Then the Light**
*D*azed from the fall, Krieger realized he was in danger of drowning amid the fuel-soaked, flaming wreckage and the cascade of jagged metal debris that showered down from the shattered chopper. He'd landed in the water. Looming in front of him was the amidships hull of the vessel. Further toward the stern, a row of steel cleats in the boilerplate stretched in a vertical line between deck and keel, disappearing below the waterline.

Daylight was fading, but in the shadow of the ship it was already fully dark.

Reacting, rather than thinking, Krieger reached out, grabbed hold of the nearest cleat, and hung on tight, letting the retreating vessel carry him along through the murky waters. He considered his predicament and his options, his mind dazed. He realized that if he let go of the cleat that he'd probably drown. The water was cold, too cold.

The shore was close, but in his condition he might not reach it before severe hypothermia took its toll.

Catching his breath, steeling himself for what lay ahead, Krieger began to pull himself up out of the water. His left foot found purchase on another ladder cleat. He pushed down against the steel staple and reached for a handhold on the one above it. His grip held steady. Krieger began painfully, slowly, to inch himself up toward the deck of the containership.

At least, he thought, at least I'm alive.

■

In the East Wing of the White House, media crews had set up in the Yellow Oval Room, the large hall customarily used for those state banquets and conferences that did not demand the higher security of the basement-level National Security Council meeting chamber.

Other presidents had preferred the Map Room for addressing the nation, but Linda Halifax found the Yellow Oval Room more to her liking. It was the room favored by Jackie Kennedy as First Lady and still bore something of her unique decorative élan; her remodeling touches were still in evidence and had remained largely intact through successive presidential administrations. While the Map Room was a man's bastion, the Yellow Oval Room bore a woman's distinctive emblems of style, and while president, Halifax also remained a woman.

The presidential address she was about to make was planned to quell the public's fears concerning the new crisis resulting from a surprise attack that had again struck the nation. The trauma of Strike Day was still fresh in the collective mind of America. The hostile seizure of the Pentagon; the taking, and cold-blooded murder, of hostages -- no one yet knew how many -- the subsequent explosion that for the second time in recent history had torn apart the Pentagon, the revelations that squads of heavily armed Spetsnaz commandos, trained in the black arts of sabotage, murder and mass destruction behind enemy lines, had been responsible for the heretofore unexplained highway sniper attacks and a host of other violent acts, had all had a devastating effect on national morale.

There was a fine line separating order from anarchy and the public perception of a nation besieged by enemies who struck, time and time again, without warning against a government powerless to defend its citizens, could unravel the minds of Americans everywhere.

The stunning blows had sent the stock market reeling. The Dow, NASDAQ and Standard & Poor Indexes had all hit record declines for a bull market. Having consulted her economic, military, and policy advisors, the president had been presented with a grim overall picture. The national social fabric was beginning to fall apart. Her address to the nation was intended to begin to knit the raveled ends back together as the first step to national healing and readjustment.

Despite the shocks and the dangers, Halifax had good news to give the nation this evening. The doomsday machinery of COLOSUS had been permanently deactivated. The foolhardiness -- indeed the madness -- of having automated the nuclear SIOP had been conclusively rectified. She would inform the nation that the SIOP's computers and global sensors -- and therefore the weapons of mass destruction at the system's delivery end -- were once again under the direct control of human beings, and that she had convened a special presidential advisory panel to liaise with Congress toward a thorough overhaul of the nation's defense infrastructure to insure that such an atrocity would never happen again.

The president would also advise the country and the world that the two components of SAAE-SIOP had been destroyed. Dawn Horse, the triad of unmanned underwater vehicles carrying sophisticated cruise missiles too stealthy to be shot down in flight had been attacked and destroyed by SAAE-SIOP's space-based element,

411

the network of high-energy particle beam weapons in orbit code-named Northern Cross.

She would assure the millions who watched the live media address that NORAD and global counterparts -- including the Soviet Division of Missile Attack Warning complex based at Solnechnogorsk near Moscow -- had confirmed that nothing but space debris was left of Northern Cross; the orbital particle beam weapons had themselves been ordered to self-destruct. Halifax would assure viewers of the broadcast address that the small nuclear reactors that powered both Northern Cross and Dawn Horse had been completely vaporized by explosives and the plunge through earth's atmosphere, and that there was no danger of nuclear contamination of the world's air or oceans.

There was much the president would omit too. Halifax would not mention the fact that the whereabouts of rogue ex-US Special Forces Command chief, General Casper Saint, were still unknown, nor would she respond to direct questions from the press concerning Saint. The whereabouts of Defense Department military analyst and Stealth warfare specialist Rommel Krieger, too, were presently unknown. By now the media's unofficial concordat with the White House tacitly disavowing knowledge of Krieger's intimate relationship with Halifax was dissolving in the potent acid of crisis and the white heat of national peril.

Press Secretary Evan Crawford had been told by his sources that the Washington Post was about to devote sizable editorial space to the Krieger-Halifax connection in its coverage of the crisis, not the least of the press allegations being that Halifax had used Krieger as a covert agent of national policy, one whose life the president had been as ready to sacrifice to political and operational expediency as she'd been disposed to take Krieger into her White House bed. Needless to say, neither Crawford nor Halifax would entertain questions from the media concerning Krieger either.

Halifax now went from the Oval Office where she'd studied the final text of the address written for her by White House speechwriters Caroline White and Jesse Rogan; the final draft, still warm from the printer, contained Halifax's final line edits and last-minute additions. Halifax was mostly pleased at the way White-Rogan had subtly changed her remarks to make them read better on camera, but some of them she felt were just a little too literary for her liking, and weren't the way she'd actually say them. Rather than send the text back for another round of copyediting, Halifax had simply red-penciled out the White-Rogan changes and penciled her own back in.

# THREATCON DELTA

She was on her way to the Yellow Oval Room, dodging media remote uplink crews, blinking in the hot glare of pole-mounted helium-argon Klieg lights and stepping carefully over the huge masses of coiled black coaxial cable that snaked their way across the corridor and into the large chamber where camera personnel were making test footage of the desk, backdrop, and visual props that were to be part of the presidential address.

"Ten minutes," said Crawford, running up to chaperone the president through the busy chaos inside the large, media-crowded room.

"You're late. We've barely enough time to do the test shot."

"Do we need to?" she asked, "I'm not Michael Jackson exactly."

"Don't argue with me Ms. President," Crawford said, helping Halifax into the chair behind the desk where cameramen, technicians and cosmetic personnel immediately surrounded her in a buzz of activity. "Just for once don't give me problems ... Ma'am."

"Okay, Evan," she said. "You're the boss," adding, sotto voce, "here, anyway."

The president subjected herself to the ministrations of the dozen-odd individuals who closely encircled her, including the several men and women with newscams perched on their shoulders, their lenses and lights pointed at her face like the threatening muzzles of shotguns ... which, in a way, they were

No one, let alone the president, was aware that one of those cameras, though not a gun itself, was sending its real-time video and audio feed to hidden vasaltniki shooters skilled in the tactical art of maskirovka who were preparing to make this presidential address the last one that this president would ever live to make.

■

"Get up."

A light shone in his eyes.

A stinging sensation. A kick or a slap. He groaned and awoke. He had been asleep or unconscious.

"Get up, damn you."

It began coming back to him.

He had pulled himself up, slowly, painfully, reaching the gunnels of the departing freighter. He'd rested, gathering what strength he could for the final act of raising himself over the edge of the stern and gaining the quarterdeck that lay beyond the gunnel. While he'd hung there his eyes swept the shadowed expanse of the vessel's uppermost cargo deck area.

He'd seen no sign of activity or movement, but that could have been deceptive -- there might, he knew, be sentries equipped with night vision-capable head mounted displays and silenced weapons walking deck patrol.

He'd listened, hearing nothing, but that meant nothing either. A killer with a gun could be watching him in the darkness at that moment, smiling mordantly as he waited for Krieger to haul himself up. Then, letting his victim relish the fleeting moments of false hope remaining to him, squeeze off a burst of autofire and send a faceless corpse splashing into the cold river thirty feet below.

Krieger had moved, flinching inwardly in anticipation of the imaginary bullet in his spine or his ribs or to the side of his head as he bit back the grunts of pain, aching muscles protesting to be further punished, begging to be released from suffering; and then he'd reached the apex of his ascent, and let himself slide down to the hard plates of the ship's main cargo deck.

He'd lain there, soaked to the skin, chilled to the bone, exhausted to the core of his being, amazed simply to be still alive -- and listened. Seconds elapsed -- they had felt like eternities, but they were only instants -- and then he rose to a half-squat, looked around, and broke for the nearest cover.

Krieger had no plan. He had only instinct and anger as guides to action. He was determined that Saint would not be allowed to escape accountability for his high crimes. Saint held all the cards, but that would not help him in the end. It was clear that Saint had been engaged in something bigger than even massive criminal extortion. Saint clearly had high-level support.

What Saint had engineered had been a coup d'état, perhaps one that had failed in the end, but a coup nonetheless. What had happened had been the application of violent force at a key national pressure point, a final hammer blow in the wake of Strike Day's terrorist attacks, contrived to blast away the final underpinnings of the social structure and send it all crashing down, as first the two towers, and next the Capitol dome, had been shattered to rubble. Strike Day had sown the seeds of anarchy, and Saint had watered those seeds with blood and fire and death.

Krieger sensed it all in a flash of metanoia, that state of supreme intuition that transcends all barriers to knowledge. He also knew that capturing or killing Saint was the key to stopping the momentum of whatever insidious, serpentine conspiracy had been set in motion by the Pentagon takeover and the burning of Wedge Three.

There was more. There was more than only the Pentagon -- more than only the stolen billions -- more than even crushing blow struck against the United States. This was the end game, a global coup de main in the offing. The unspeakable conclusion of decades of preparation, the culmination of waves of attack on multiple levels and by means of a multiplicity of militant forms.

Saint held the key.

Perhaps Saint in some ways was the key.

"Get up or I'll kill you."

Krieger obeyed the voice. He raised himself to his feet, fighting back searing waves of pain and fatigue that hulked on the margins of his senses, and strange white lights that danced at the corners of his visual field.

"Shut up," he told the voice. "I'm good to go."

He suddenly realized there was no one in the darkness of the deck of the moving ship. The voice had been Krieger's own.

By the pale light cast by the moon and stars in the night sky above, he made his way along the afterdeck to the bows of the freighter.

He needed to get his hands on a gun.

He knew there were guns onboard.

He'd find a way.

DAVID ALEXANDER

Thirty-four
**Gun and Run**

*I*t was a ghost ship. A ghost ship on a mystery voyage in the moon-silvered darkness and the sudden, pelting rain.

The fine droplets had begun falling, glazing the deck and reflecting the full moon as the brief shower passed and Krieger roused himself to action. The bitingly cold hypodermic needles of rain and ice had revived Krieger as he crouch-walked toward the bow of the vessel, breaking stride at intervals, taking cover to watch and to listen.

Containerized and palletized cargo was lashed to the deck, row upon row of heavy cargo skids and corrugated steel shipping containers. The containers were standard shipping cubicles marked by the familiar logos of international business conglomerates. There was still no sign of human presence. Aside from the keening of the wind and distant traffic noises on far-off West

# THREATCON DELTA

Virginia roads, the ship was eerily silent. Krieger was grateful for the presence of the shipping containers. Their dark bulks, piled high across the cargo deck, sheltered his movements toward the Vista Charger's bow. If not for them he would have been dangerously exposed.

Krieger had no way of knowing how many crew members were onboard the freighter, yet this much stood out in his mind: so far he had encountered no sign of deck patrols. This was a relief, yet oddly disturbing. If Saint were making his getaway aboard the Vista Charger, where were his protectors? Saint's kind never played solitaire, the operational term for a solo agent's tradecraft. Saint's modus operandi was to assemble groups and give them orders. Others always did the killing and dying for individuals like Saint.

Yet there were indisputably no patrols on the deck of the Vista Charger, nor any sign of them on any raised vantage points that overlooked the open deck -- Krieger had scoped them all out.

Unless Krieger was himself being scoped out by hidden shooters -- framed in the perpendicular crosshair reticles of night-scopes riding atop long-barreled sniper rifles -- unless Krieger was already a target, and his unseen, unsensed, unknown killer was merely awaiting Saint's execution order, or timing the fatal trigger-pull on some secret homicidal whim of a brilliant, yet sadistic mind,

420

then something was wrong, because pieces seemed missing from the puzzle.

Taking a few minutes to watch, listen, and gather his strength, Krieger broke from the cover of a cluster of corrugated steel cargo containers and moved on a careful, loping crouch toward the bridge that rose some two stories athwart the freighter's bows. Rain had started falling again, this time more heavily and considerably colder -- the ratio of icy needles to frigid droplets had increased to the point where the downpour was just shy of a full-fledged ice-storm. The mercury colored bullets pelted the ship in a desultory manner at first, but within minutes had set up a crackling din that was loud enough to drown out even the steady throb of engine sounds rising up from below decks.

Krieger was now only a few hundred yards from the Vista Charger's bridge in the forecastle, a wall-like structure with windows front and back across the topmost ten feet that rose some twenty-five feet above the surface of the vessel. Light glowed dimly from within the central windows of the topmost row of lighted squares. The Vista Charger's control room, Krieger knew, was directly between the rear and front top windows. The bridge had weather radar, GPS, satellite-television and long-range communications antennae bristling across its roof. Two steel ladders -- one at port and at starboard -- gave access to both the control room and the section below. Krieger decided to make for the lower level and reconnoiter before proceeding to the top.

With the rattle of the worsening ice storm affording him partial cover, Krieger broke free of the last cluster of shipping containers and sprinted for the rightmost steel access ladder. The now icebound deck was slippery beneath his feet. He almost lost his footing as he neared the ladder.

Grasping its handrail, he half-expected to feel the heavy thud of a hollow-nose bullet striking the base of his spine. Nothing happened, except that his hands and feet found purchase on the freezing, ice-fettered rungs, and he pulled himself up toward the steel door five feet above him. A yank on the handle and the unlocked door easily swung open.

Inside the bridge, Krieger hugged the steel bulkhead and tried to get his bearings and allow his eyes to adjust to the semi-darkness of the interior. It was considerably warmer in here, and he rested, allowing the heated air to thaw his cold, rain-pelted body. Krieger realized now that he'd been dancing on the tightrope edge of hypothermia. His fingertips and toes felt numb and there was a vague tinge of vertigo circling the corners of his thoughts.

422

# DAVID ALEXANDER

A sudden surge of mindless panic seized hold of him for a moment. What was he doing here? Why was he doing this? A voice shouted for him to break and run. Krieger silenced the voice. Forced himself calm.

He'd heard those voices before, heard them for the first time during Army Ranger selection, running a three-day wilderness course through the Rockies that was designed to make applicants give up and quit. The more fatigued his body and mind, the more strident and mocking those inner voices became, the more they cursed him for a fool who should give it up and go back home. In order to stay on the course and reach his objective, Krieger had fought to silence those contentious voices. It was not the first time in his life that he'd heard them.

Now, again, he was hearing them. Now, again, he silenced them, cut them off, listened to a deeper, truer voice that told him to go on, no matter what, to prevail against whatever odds.

Krieger prepared to traverse the final few yards' distance. He wished there was a gun in his hands. With a gun he would stand a far better chance of meeting whatever situation came his way. But he didn't have a gun, just the cards he'd been dealt, and he'd have to use them as best he could. He mounted the interior stairway, two short flights of metal steps confined in a boxy, steel-walled well.

# THREATCON DELTA

A sudden light flashed. A blurred, flailing man-shape hurtled toward him from a corner hidden beyond the next bend in the staircase. Something sinister caught the light. Near his head. A long shape, flashing in the yellow gleam of a bare, low-wattage bulb.

Knife, Krieger thought and spun toward the attacker, his blurred senses snapping together like the crazy patterns of a kaleidoscope suddenly resolved into sharp focus by a turn of the hand to reveal a clear image at the end of the perceptual tunnel.

The image of danger.

The image of a man, face contorted, lunging at Krieger with a big, serrated-edged combat knife.

Krieger was all adrenaline now. It coursed through his arteries, lighting up his nervous system, helping him swiftly react. Hands, elbows, forearms, spine, legs -- all launched into concerted movement.

The attacker had knife training, but it was military. In military knife fighting, the soldier is taught to grasp the combat knife blade-downward, with the haft clutched firmly in the clenched fist of the stronger hand. Military training holds that this is the most stable method of grasping the knife.

Street fighting, however, holds the exactly opposite view; that the blade be pointed upward, that the arm is flexible, lunging and sweeping into the attack, and that the military method leaves the attacker employing its techniques vulnerably open to successful counterattack.

As Krieger's attacker tried to close, stabbing as he charged, hoping for a quick kill, cutting the large arteries on the sides of the throat or plunging the knife into Krieger's heart, Krieger sidestepped, pivoted, swept up his left arm in a hard, guje gongji block to the killer's knife arm.

Yin and yang began to turn in a circle. Krieger's sifu had told him of circles, and of the deadly triangles concealed within them. Mastering circles and triangles was one of the secrets of guje gongji, the art of destroying an attacker by methodically breaking bones. Krieger's blocking arm began to describe a circle as it first pushed the attacker's knife arm down to shoulder height, then became a triangle with dagger-like elbow pointed toward the bladesman's face, as Krieger's hand slid down to grasp the killer's knife-hand by the wrist.

At the same time Krieger pivoted on his hips, consciousness focused in the tan-tien region an inch below the navel, describing another semicircle and triangle with his right arm that delivered a crushing elbow smash to the attacker's face. Krieger felt his would-be killer's nose break and crumple, felt the upper cheek bones splinter as hot blood spurted from the smashed-in visage.

425

The attacker let out an animal's mortal yell of pain and Krieger felt the beefy body start to go limp.

Now Krieger's right hand was on the attacker's knife arm, just above the elbow, while his left hand continued to grasp the wrist of the hand still clutching the knife. Guge gongji was the art of levers, the science of the application of precise force at precise points to break the human skeleton in precise places to useless shards and shattered fragments.

Using the killer's forearm as a fulcrum, Krieger pushed hard on the thick wrist clutched in his right hand. The wrist snapped with a wet, pulpy sound. The knife clattered to the deck. Krieger then broke man's the elbow joint. Easily tossing the now semiconscious killer to the steel deck, Krieger finished him with a heel stomp to the nape of his neck, breaking apart the upper spinal vertebra and ending his life.

He picked up the killer's knife. It had all taken under a minute. But now a door above was open and, in the spill of light from higher up, Krieger faced two hard men with drawn submachineguns.

One of them was Saint.

The other, in sailor's grungies, was probably another crewman. More light spilled out around Saint as the hatch to the control room yawned wide.

The guns convinced Krieger to drop the combat knife he'd taken from his would-be killer. It clattered to the deck.

The second sailor hustled down the stairs and checked his fallen partner. He looked up at Saint and shook his head once. Saint made a sideward motion of his head. The crewman shoved the barrel of his submachinegun into the small of Krieger's back.

Smelling stinking breath, he heard the rasp of the gunman's voice in his ears as Saint's underling force-marched him up the flight of metal stairs at gunpoint.

The sailor told Krieger he was going to kill him, that Krieger was going to die. He sounded happy about it too.

■

"You've made my associate very upset, Mr. Krieger," Saint told him. "The man you killed was like a brother to him."

They were on the bridge, in the control room of the Vista Charger. Krieger was seated in a chair facing the front row of slit-windows. Black sky and occasional flashes, like long silver needles, of bulleting rain caught in the glare of ship's lights, was visible through the storm; nothing else.

Krieger looked from Saint to the sailor who kept him covered with the small, black machinegun, an Uzi Micro with a fifty-round high-capacity clip jutting from its magazine well. The sailor stared at Krieger and moved his lips soundlessly.

"What's his name?" Krieger asked.

"We call him 'Bruno,'" Saint said. "I don't think he's ever told anyone his real name. Right, Bruno?"

Bruno didn't answer, just shook his head, then turned back to stare at Krieger, mouthing silent things that were probably dire threats and almost lasciviously cradling his weapon. Krieger told Bruno that he was sorry for having killed his boyfriend, but that Bruno shouldn't have gone around playing with pointy objects either. Bruno stopped twitching at the mouth and rushed at Krieger, rearing back his right arm to prime it for a savage, head-breaking thrust of the Uzi's heavy machined-steel receiver against the flat of Krieger's skull.

A burst of gunfire stopped Bruno in his tracks. The bloodied sailor had just enough strength left to turn his head toward the source of the automatic fire that had stitched him across the midsection, opening up his sternum and releasing jets of spurting arterial blood amid a hot, slimy belch of gored viscera. The Uzi clattered to the deck and went skittering toward Krieger.

As Bruno died swaying on his feet, his last earthly sight was of Casper Saint clutching a still smoking Heckler & Koch MP5 subgun at bellybutton level, a wisp of smoke curling from its muzzle. He was no longer conscious as a final three-round burst blew most of his head off and sent the sailor's corpse spinning to final, if undignified, rest against a nearby bulkhead.

"Uh-uh, Mr. Krieger," Saint said, now directing the gun muzzle at him as he watched Krieger's eyes turn toward the bloodied Uzi lying near his feet. "Don't even think about grabbing Bruno's weapon. It wouldn't be too healthy."

Saint kicked the Uzi aside. Then, keeping his SMG trained on Krieger, picked it up and placed it on the freighter's control console far out of the reach of his captive.

"That's better," Saint said.

Reaching into an inside pocket of his brown leather jacket, Saint pulled out a fresh Dutch Masters panatela, bit one end off, spat it out, and with the virgin stogie clenched between his teeth, used a lighter to get it going.

Engraved on the Army-issue Zippo was "Bob Hope Christmas Show, 1971, Long Binh USO, Vietnam." This meant nothing to Krieger, but the general recalled how his XO Da Gamma had gone wide in the eyes as he'd shot him on the way out of the Pentagon's NMCC. Da Gamma, who'd been lighting a cigarette when he died, had known far too much for his own continued good.

# THREATCON DELTA

Saint's eyes flicked to the digital clock high on the control room's wall. He told Krieger there was still time for a little talk between too old pros -- but then they'd both have to leave.

DAVID ALEXANDER

Thirty-five
**Brave New Times**

*I* suppose I should thank you for having disposed of Bruno," Saint began, a cloud of gray smoke rising from the stogie set in his mouth. "That meant one less sloppy job for me to do."

"Yeah, two less witnesses at your trial for capital murder, extortion and high treason," Krieger told him.

"More correctly, and somewhat less hysterically, two fewer inept and untrustworthy loose ends with whom to contend. I would argue with your premonition of a trial in the offing. Maybe you've forgotten that a person vanished and presumed dead can't be put on trial."

"You're planning to disappear."

"More or less," Saint told Krieger. "But that was hardly a major deduction on your part."

"My unstated question was where -- where do you go in a globalized, digitized, paved-over world, Saint? Where can you hide and still spend all that money you've stolen? That's what it's all been really about -- money, and nothing else."

Saint dragged on his cigar and smiled.

"Look around you, my friend," Saint told him, spitting out a piece of Alabama-grown tobacco leaf. "What do you see? You see a massive robot, a vessel whose every operation, from the functioning of its power plant to the navigational course it follows, is directed by computers linked to equipment control mechanisms of every kind.

"The Vista Charger is a metaphor for our brave, new times. The ship is owned and operated by the Medusa, a global criminal cartel begun by the former Soviet KGB hierarchy and the ousted *vlasti* or oligarchs of the post-Soviet Commonwealth. It operates solely by digital processors and robotic servomechanisms. The ship, in short, represents the wedding of high-technology and covert intelligence in the sweaty bed of global organized crime.

"So complete the circle, Mr. Krieger. Tell me what that means."

"Well, Saint," Krieger shot back, with a half-grin that wasn't as forced as he thought he'd have to make it under the circumstances, "it probably means that cigar you're smoking's got a little more in it than just tobacco."

"Amusing, Mr. Krieger, very amusing," bantered Saint, "but you're wrong, you know.

What the ship represents can be communicated in a single word: the future.

"Things have changed," Saint went on. "The Pentagon was also a symbol. Among other things, it stood for national government -- and governments, for that matter nation-states, are now utterly obsolete. They're as obsolete as the outmoded, shopworn concepts that they enshrine. Concepts like freedom, democracy, representation by the people --"

" -- Laws."

"Correct, Mr. Krieger," Saint snapped, not too graciously accepting his captive's interruption. "Laws too. Especially laws. The rule of law has always been a fiction, hasn't it? One which always has catered to the privileged few who occupy the exalted pinnacle of the broad-based social pyramid."

"For a murderer and extortionist you almost sound like a radical."

"No, Blitz," Saint said, almost sadly. "The old world order has burned itself out, just like the Roman Empire did long before our own perilous times. We're merely delivering the coup de grace to a dying hulk of outmoded history, a woolly mammoth, down on its knees, freezing to death in the Ice Age snows. The twenty-first century has seen the world cross the line between the old order and the new one to follow. I'm just one of the barbarians at the gate. Or an emissary of that future. Take your pick.

"For years already, what was once called crime has become business, at the same time machines have grown dominant while human beings have become their subservient drones. Computers run themselves -- in fact, they run the world. Human beings have become little more than machines' servants.

"The Pentagon op was only the first of the final shock waves that will ultimately end the old world order," Saint told Krieger.

"The wealth that its capture generated will enrich me, but also fill the coffers of the Medusa. The hammer blow I struck in executing the operation will be followed up by aftershocks in rapid succession that will smash the United States to rubble as surely as an asteroid from interplanetary space might have done, or to use another metaphor, as definitively as the forces of the Gothic chieftain Alaric smashed the gates of Rome to end its thousand-year reign."

Saint told Krieger what those hammer blows would be. As smoke still billowed from the charred wreckage of the Pentagon, the White House was to be blown apart and the president killed. It was set to happen within the next thirty minutes as Linda Halifax gave her televised State of the Nation Address from the Yellow Oval Room.

While the horror of the president's execution and the destruction of the executive mansion was still fresh, Spetsnaz vasaltniki teams, acting under Blue Man cover designation, remaining hidden in the vicinity of Washington D.C., would strike at other targets -- while other teams, freshly activated from their dormant, sleeper, states in other major urban areas, such as New York and Los Angeles, would activate and unleash a carnage as barbaric as that which any ancient invader had ever visited on Rome.

And then the final sleepers would activate. The Medusa's hidden servants who had been placed in government positions, who held high military posts, would emerge from deep cover.

They would assume power, declare the US Constitution and the Bill of Rights null and void and announce the inauguration of a new police state in which hundreds of millions of excess human beings would no longer have a place or be necessary to the functioning of society, except as slaves. The whereabouts -- names, addresses, ethnicity, finances -- of millions of initial out-culls from society's ranks were already programmed into massive computerized databases.

That had been one of the purposes of Strike Day and the 911 attacks that had proceeded it -- to set the apparatus of mass surveillance and control in motion, to spur on and to legitimize the compilation of massive databases on the citizenry of the United States and to develop larger and better computer systems to utilize the data and to build and run more powerful machines against the day when humans became utterly obsolete.

Saint had only one question for Krieger.

"I've always wondered," asked the general with a strange look in his eyes, "how it feels to fuck that bitch in the same bed Lincoln died in."

As Saint concluded, Krieger realized that whether or not Saint's rantings were true, Saint was mad.

"Spoken like a true paranoid psychotic, Saint," Krieger told the general. "Besides, he did free the slaves."

A muscle twitched on the side of Saint's face and a cold gleam of latent, uncoiling ferocity came into his eyes. For a moment Krieger thought Saint would shoot him dead on the spot.

"Don't make me kill you -- yet," he told Krieger. "I want you to live long enough to see your girlfriend and that fucking white shithouse she lives in blown right off the face of the earth."

Gesturing with the muzzle of the Uzi, Saint ordered Krieger onto his feet.

DAVID ALEXANDER

Thirty-six
**Hammer Down**

*T*he aircraft was a surprise.

Krieger had suspected that the Vista Charger was not to be Saint's escape vehicle, that it was merely a platform for something else, a helicopter or light plane. He had in mind something like a Harrier or Marine JSF, a VSTOL aircraft that could take off vertically from the deck of a ship and land the same way.

He had not suspected what Saint actually had ready.

Pelting ice-rain fell hard on the deck; both Saint and Krieger were soon wet with it.

Saint stopped at a point in the deck amidships, said "Open. Saint. Authorization Code oh-seven-two-nine-bravo."

There was the sudden whine of powerful pneumatic servo-actuators engaging below their feet. A section of the decking slid aside. Something began to emerge from the darkness of the hold below. The pelting ice needles rapped and tinkled on its metallic hull as it was raised upward to deck level.

It was an aircraft with cantilevered main wings and two stub wings -- canards -- in front and just below the cockpit. Too large to be a fighter plane, it was about the size of a Learjet. Krieger had seen nothing like it, though it resembled some sort of immense, metallic bird of prey. Saint ordered Krieger to wheel over the steel access stairs that would enable them to enter the vulturine aircraft.

Cautioning Krieger not to do anything stupid, Saint mounted toward the cabin with Krieger in the lead, his weapon jammed into the hollows between his ribcage and pelvis.

The aircraft's interior was spacious and luxuriously appointed, very much like a Lear's at that. The plane differed in that the seats were form-fitted, and they had special contours for legs and head and arms. The seats were obviously designed for withstanding high-G maneuvers and high acceleration rates that would produce the artificially high gravitational forces like those in a spacecraft rocketing into orbit.

"We'll take our cabin seats soon," Saint promised, "but the cockpit's the place where our adventure begins."

A prod of the gun barrel in Krieger's ribs propelled him towards the cockpit hatch, which

438

was apparently sealed tight by a sliding panel now retracted and concealed in the doorway bulkhead.

Beyond was a spacious control center with pilot and copilot's seats facing a horseshoe-shaped console, flush with flat-panel displays and lighted pushbuttons. Beyond the console the bubble Plexiglas windshield sloped down toward the sharply tapered nose of the aircraft. Various control stirrups and sticks depended from the ceiling and rose from the floor within easy reach of the two chairs.

Saint told Krieger to sit in the copilot's seat and waited until his captive was ensconced in the form-fit chair. He then pressed one of the glowing buttons on the panel.

Automatically controlled clamps immediately latched themselves around Krieger's arms and legs, imprisoning him in the right-side chair and immobilizing his hands so that they could not reach out to manipulate the aircraft's controls.

Only then did Saint slide the compact SMG into the military-issue pit holster slung across his barrel chest and seat himself in the pilot's chair.

"On the screen in front of you is a digitally enhanced thermal imaging view of the deck of the Vista Charger," said Saint as, with manipulations of buttons and keys on the small console-mounted keyboard, he began preflight engine diagnostics and oriented the navigational system to a cluster of satellites in orbit.

"There are thermal sensors placed across the vessel's deck, by the way," he explained. "That's how we saw you coming."

"You're not the only one with remote sensors," Krieger told Saint. "We're undoubtedly under satellite observation at this moment. That should be obvious to you."

"Yes, it's obvious, I'm not an idiot," Saint replied evenly. "But it doesn't matter. I'm getting a little ahead of myself. Bear with me, my friend -- that is if you want to keep on living somewhat longer."

"It's your show, Saint," Krieger challenged.

"Then I'll get on with it. As I was saying, the Vista's cams are showing us a digitally enhanced real-time view of a portion of the afterdeck. Keep your eyes on the container cluster in the center of the view screen."

Saint manipulated joystick controls and input security codes and passwords into the console keyboard. The screen showed one of the shipping containers raising up on pneumatic actuators.

It stopped with a sudden robotic lurch, then its front hatch slid open and something made of a dull silvery metal extended from the interior. Lights winked on it as sequences of numbers flashed across the top of the screen, giving systems diagnostics data.

"What we're looking at is one of the Northern Cross weapons that didn't make it into orbit. Like the space-based particle beam and directed energy weapons that finally went on-station, the early Strategic Defense Initiative -- what they called 'Star Wars' during the Reagan years -- also developed kinetic energy weapons.

"This is one of them. Technically known as a rail gun. It fires two pound titanium bullets propelled by reverse magnetism at hypersonic velocities, in this case at Mach four. With computer targeting, the bullets are highly accurate."

Saint needed to explain no further. Krieger knew all about rail guns, and he also knew without Saint telling him what the target of this one would be -- the White House. Striking their objective at multi-Mach velocities, the combined impact of a volley of those puck-sized titanium blocks would unleash the equivalent in kinetic energy of a subkiloton nuclear blast. A salvo from the rail gun would be enough to smash the White House to smithereens.

Krieger knew that after SDI had been canceled, and Cold War geopolitical realities changed, KE weapons technology had shifted to space-based and ground-based applications. Kinetic energy weapons weren't much use as weapons that could reach the planet's surface from space, which is why the Northern Cross program had only put particle beam weapons into orbit.

"Targeting, like the navigation of this aircraft, and for that matter, that of the remaining course of the Vista Charger, is controlled via a secure network of orbital, ground-based, and onboard computer systems. They're foolproof. Unlike humans, They don't make mistakes."

Saint reacted to a series of coded electronic beeps and input new data into the aircraft console. He studied the tactical displays in front of them, nodded in satisfaction and continued his explanation.

"We'll lift off the containership in a few minutes," he said to Krieger. "After we're gone, the Vista Charger will continue on her pre-configured route. The containership will reach a point in the broad region of the lower basin of the Potomac river which will, for a few fleeting minutes, give the rail gun on its deck a clear shot at the White House, which would then be approximately three miles distant.

"That will be enough time for the system to acquire the target and fire a multiple-round salvo, which at hyper-Mach velocities will strike its target in under four seconds. At that point you and I will be in a position for a ringside seat for this gala history-making event."

# DAVID ALEXANDER

The aircraft, Saint explained, was a hypersonic shuttle plane developed jointly by the Air Force, DARPA and the deep-cover spook sections of NASA, which had begun as a Defense Department agency tasked with beating the Russian military into space, and which had always had secret intelligence and military components. The plane was designed for small runway takeoff and could reach any destination on earth in two hours or less. It was a prototype that was stolen by Saint's L-Force commandos under cover of the Janus Hinge operations to pinpoint weaknesses in Pentagon security almost a decade before.

Saint chuckled as he added that an aircraft that had never officially existed could hardly be considered stolen. After all, since the plane was a myth instead of a reality, how in the wide, sweet world could anybody ever steal it?

"To complete this momentous evening, the Vista Charger herself will detonate. You see, Blitz, many of those 'shipping' containers actually contain powerful tactical nuclear charges in the submegaton range. Once out at sea, yet close enough to the shoreline to have a crippling effect on inbound and Intracoastal traffic for some time to come -- well, in a word: 'bang.'"

"You've thought of everything, Saint," Krieger acknowledged.

"Yes, everything."

"But not how to function as a man."

Saint glared at Krieger. This time the full impact of the hatred was obvious, the malice open and malignant.

"Your kind is impotent, Saint. Like Hitler. Like bin Laden. Like Xiang Hoon or Tench, for that matter, when they failed in Indonesia. You can't function as a man so you compensate by blowing things up. You're nothing, Saint. Just another dirty little shit --"

Saint's face began to convulse and a large muscle twitched like a serpent beneath his right ear.

"-- shut the fuck ... up!"

"-- Just a dirty impotent little black boy from Tremont Avenue in the South Bronx who wanted to fuck whitey, fuck his women, but couldn't get it on. What did you call Halifax, Saint? That 'white bitch.'"

Krieger shouted his taunts straight into Saint's face.

Saint drew his SMG. He aimed its stub-muzzle point-blank at the bridge of Krieger's nose.

"I told you to shut ... the fuck ... up."

He intoned the words, slowly, but his gun hand and his head quivered with barely suppressed rage. Krieger realized then that he stood only a trigger pull away from death.

"What's the matter Saint, did I strike a nerve?"

444

Krieger spoke more softly now, but the effect of his words was profound. A change had come over the general. A switch had been pulled in his inner mental machinery. A decision had been reached.

"I want to do you now," he spat, his words a venomous hiss, "but at close range all the blood and fuckin' guts spilling out of you when the bullets tear you up will fuck up the cockpit controls."

Saint unlocked Krieger's fastenings to the cockpit chair. He jammed the Micro-Uzi's muzzle into the side of Krieger's head, pressing it painfully hard into the parietal bone below the earlobe.

"Get the fuck up, bitch. We're going outside."

Saint's powerful arm hauled Krieger bodily from his seat. Saint pushed his captive forward, shoving him with the meaty palm of his free hand between the shoulder blades as he jabbed the SMG barrel into the nape of his neck. The two enemies marched quickly through the aircraft cabin, reaching the plane's still open access doorway in under a minute after leaving the cockpit.

Saint moved the gun, positioning the barrel precisely between the two bony lobes dividing the rear of Krieger's skull.

"Fuck you."

He squeezed the trigger.

Nothing happened.

# THREATCON DELTA

Krieger spun, pushed -- not knocked, but moved with deft precision -- the weapon aside, twisted it out of the larger, heavier man's reach, but he couldn't hold onto the weapon as Saint reacted with a balled, ham-sized, bunch-fisted right to the point of Krieger's jaw. The fight sent both antagonists sprawling onto the cold, hard deck of the Vista Charger, as the frigid ice rain battered them alike.

A head blow sent Saint rolling aside, and Krieger used the interval to stagger to his feet, quickly followed by Saint, each combatant trying to gain solid footing before the other man rose and assumed a fighting stance.

Saint was up a fraction of an instant before Krieger. With a howl of insane anger he charged, lashing out with a savage karate giri, a snap-kick to Krieger's chest delivered with all the force of the pelvis, and attacking thigh musculature, behind the punishing blow.

Krieger sidestepped and the martial arts foot strike snapped past him, missing his heart zone by less than an inch. Countering on the follow-through, as Saint turned back to face him, Krieger launched a punishing sidekick to Saint's rib cage that would have crippled him had Saint not fended it off with a fast downward-sweeping arm block that deflected the kick and bled off most of its ballistic power.

# DAVID ALEXANDER

Krieger countered with a roundhouse right to Saint's head that forced the general to react, raising his arms and crossing his wrists against Krieger's accurate hand blows. Both opponents were evenly matched, and both knew that the contest would continue until one man wore his antagonist down sufficiently to get inside his defenses, or until one man got lucky -- and it was luck that decided the contest in the end when, landing on the balls of his feet from a glancing foot-blow from Krieger, the deck of the containership rolled slightly in the worsening squall.

The freighter slanted far enough, and its icy deck was slippery enough, to send the Uzi SMG that had dropped from Saint's grasp at the door of the hyperplane to the steel deck plates below as he'd prepared to drop the hammer on Krieger -- sent the subgun sliding a foot or two. The Uzi came to a final stop against Saint's combat boots. In another second it was clutched in a two-handed shooter's grip as the general rose shakily to his feet.

"You were good, you might have won," Casper Saint acknowledged, breathing heavily as he extending his arms straight out from the shoulders, aiming across the SMG's twin open sights, and prepared to finally end the contest.

"I just got lucky."

# THREATCON DELTA

Saint squeezed the trigger as bratting tongues of blue-white flame lit up the rain-swept darkness.

With an amazed look the stricken man gaped down at the row of red punctures that had almost magically opened up in a ragged line across his abdomen, his eyes widening in amazement and fear as the blood began to spurt from them in dense, multiply fountaining jets.

Then his knees gave out and Saint crumpled to the cold, ice-slippery deck of the containership. His eyes were already dead and sightless as Sabio ran to Krieger and helped him to his feet.

"What took you?" Krieger asked as he staggered shakily to a standing position.

"The weather for one thing, boss," she told him. "Not very good for flying."

"I wasn't being serious, ensign," Krieger told her, reaching into a side pocket of his pants and extracting something that flashed for a moment as he flicked it into space.

The death card came to rest on Saint's chest, and quickly became covered with cold rain and warm blood.

Now he saw the Marine-piloted Seahawk helos landing on the deck, the devil-dog hard-chargers fast-roping down from them, bullpup assault weapons at the ready. He heard their shouts and the rapid cadence of a hundred boots pounding hell out of the freighter's deck.

He didn't have a chance to say anything else. Krieger heard the whine of jet turbines only a few feet away and saw the general's escape aircraft begin to lift vertically off the cargo deck.

"Get in!" he shouted into Sabio's ear at the top of his lungs as the turbine wail increased, and pushed her ahead of him. They tumbled into the cabin of the robot aircraft as the hatchway automatically trundled closed and the plane lurched into rain-lashed vertical flight.

Krieger took Sabio into the cockpit and climbed into the pilot's chair while Sabio took the copilot's station. As the VSTOL aircraft began to rise higher from the containership's deck, Krieger briefed Sabio on the devastating events that Saint had warned him were about to happen, telling her to brief Red Hawk via mobile SINCGARS.

Sabio keyed her ear mike and was on the satcom-enabled LandWarNet to Hawk as the VSTOL lifted to a transitional altitude of thirty feet and began to fly horizontally toward the District through the howling center of the storm cell.

"Boss, you just heard me tell Hawk about the kinetic energy weapon launcher and how the Vista Charger is set for nuclear detonation. What about the plane? You don't seem to have it under control."

"Don't rub it in," Krieger told Sabio.

449

# THREATCON DELTA

Krieger tried everything he knew to get the aircraft under human guidance, but the console displays still showed that the plane was flying on automatic. The digital countdown toward translation to hypersonic flight was ticking rapidly toward mark zero. In a matter of minutes the plane would point its nose up, activate its scramjet thrusters and rocket into the upper atmosphere.

"What will happen if we can't get control of the aircraft, boss?" asked Sabio.

"Let me put it this way, Ensign Sabio," Krieger replied acidly. "The Java Sea coast of Sumatra, Indonesia has very big, very hungry mosquitoes this time of year and probably a reception committee at whatever remote airstrip this baby's programmed to land at that would be more than happy to gun us down the minute we stepped out of the cabin."

"I see, boss," Sabio replied, as Krieger continued to struggle with the controls, getting nowhere.

"Sabio, I'm afraid we'll have to ditch. Have you got any C-4 on you, by any chance? There must be parachutes around somewhere."

Sabio's eyes went over the console.

"If you'll permit me, boss," she said, "I'd like to try something."

"Try what, ensign?" Krieger retorted testily. "What could you possibly try that would --"

By this time Sabio had reached across and had rapidly input a series of keystrokes into the small keyboard mounted on the console.

"Authorization sequence accepted. Awaiting instructions."

The voice came from somewhere in the cockpit overhead. It was a robotic voice, asexual; neither male nor female. The voice of the plane, Krieger realized.

"Instructions: immediate landing on deck of containership Vista Charger," Sabio told the plane.

"Authorization approved. Resetting navigational data. Turning and revectoring aircraft. Preparing to land."

Krieger stared daggers at Sabio.

"For once I'm at a loss for words with you, ensign," he said.

"Boss, I am trained in counter-technical intervention warfare operations. In this case, access codes which might -- and in this instance, actually did -- override the V-77X hypervelocity scramjet aircraft prototype were supplied to me prior to commencement of the mission. Fortunately the codes have successfully overridden the plane's original programming."

"In other words, you cheated."

"Does it really matter, boss?" she asked.

Krieger didn't answer. His eye had caught sight of something on the cockpit floor. It was a virgin

Dutch Masters Perfecto, apparently one from Saint's personal stash.

Krieger picked it up and bit one end off.

As he turned back in his seat, Sabio had produced a lighter from somewhere. Krieger held the tip to the flame she offered and lit the stogie up. Suddenly he noticed that engraved on the Army-issue Zippo was "Bob Hope Christmas Show, 1971, Long Binh USO, Vietnam."

"Thanks, ensign," he said.

"Don't mention it, boss."

"By the way, ensign, where'd that lighter come from?"

"Ask me no questions, boss," Sabio told him, deadpan, "and I'll tell you no lies."

The whine of the engines diminished as the plane neared the deck of the Vista Charger and proceeded to land.

# *TWO HOURS LATER: TUESDAY, SEPTEMBER 13TH*

## EXECUTIVE PRIVILEGE

## Epilog

*P*resident Linda Halifax faced the battle-arrayed camera lenses of the global mass media. She was relieved by what had just been whispered in her ear, but she was also profoundly shaken.

They had all come a hairsbreadth close to the end -- the end of everything. But she couldn't ponder the implications now, she couldn't even begin to. That would come later. Much later, she hoped. In the meantime the president had a speech to give, an address to the nation that now would have to be made on the fly, without referring to the carefully worded and edited prepared speech.

Halifax looked straight into the camera. She drew in her breath and began.

"My fellow Americans," she said, surprised at how steady her voice seemed to carry. "Our nation has weathered one of the worst storms in its history. But winds of destruction that had threatened to uproot the tree of liberty and tear it root and branch from the soil of democracy blow no longer.

"Rest assured, my countrymen, the nation is safe, the storm passed. Let me tell you what has happened...."

"Hey, where was that in the speech," the assistant press secretary asked his boss, but got no answer.

All eyes were on the president in what the assemblage sensed was history in the making.

■

A few days after the president's emergency broadcast, Lev Varukoi was driving his custom-built Lamborghini Diablo along the corniche of Spain's Costa Del Sol, the 238-mile Sunshine Coast of Andalucia. The town of Puerto Banus, with its picturesque rows of pastel-walled cafes and its pleasure craft moored in the private marinas that flanked the corniche that was the Russian's destination, was as unimportant as any of the other details of his stay in Nerja, the ancient hill town overlooking the white sand beach at El Capistrano.

Business was the last thing on Varukoi's mind. He had taken out a long-term rental on the villa for two reasons; the first being an immediate, pressing need to go to ground quickly after the Pentagon operation's failure, the second being that Nerja, as the old saying went, was good earth for foxes. It was this because the region along the Andalusian coast was one of the few places on earth where the orbital surveillance assets of the US and American intel gathering partners in Europe, Asia and Australia, had scattered and inadequate coverage.

Covert hit teams and long-range weapons alike required dependable reconnaissance and surveillance intel in order to be effective. Such intel could most easily be provided from space via imaging satellites, and, with somewhat more difficulty, from high-altitude reconnaissance aircraft and UAVs. The least efficient means would be a spotter team on the ground, because little was known about Varukoi besides his game-name Alexai, if indeed as much as even that.

The Russian had been meticulously careful, as always. The rogue US general, Saint, had known no more about him than was necessary, and Saint had been Varukoi's single point of contact on the mission's operational side. At the moment, Varukoi felt he had little to fear from the Americans. He was considerably more concerned about the client-side, for the Medusa was somewhat better informed about him, had already paid a nonreturnable retainer for his services, and were far more unstable and ruthless when their aims were thwarted. But he had stealthed them too, and was confident that even the global terror nexus had as little to go on as did the Americans.

The drive along the sinuously winding coast highway to Puerto Banus was a relaxation mechanism, and it usually worked. Ignoring the custom-built car's superb Bose sound system, the Russian drove without music, but enjoyed a non-filter Turkish cigarette as the breathtaking scenery below was revealed in striking glimpses along each new bend in the two-lane mountain road. The Diablo handled exquisitely, and Varukoi was confident that behind the wheel of the high-performance sports car he was more than a match for any ambush attempt, especially with the motorized Plamya offensive systems hidden beneath each headlight.

The electric-motor grenade launchers could be activated by voice command and fire multiple-round bursts of forty millimeter explosive canisters that would rip hell out of any other vehicle -- no matter how large or heavy -- attempting to block the road, and the Armscor Viper MGL, a grenade-firing shotgun that fired forty-millimeter shells from a six-round drum magazine -- that lay within easy reach on the passenger seat, would help him finish off any survivors. Varukoi was well prepared for ambush, and a cell call to a certain local police official who was the regular beneficiary of serious cash payments under the table -- even for the high-rolling crowd that inhabited this jet-set mecca -- could be counted on to discreetly clean up the mess and contain the situation long enough for Varukoi to depart for his secondary hideout location.

Not that any of this would prove necessary. Though taking detailed and prudent precautions, the Russian was confident that his stay on the Costa Del Sol would continue without mishap until he was ready to move on. Varukoi's tracks were well-covered, and in addition to Senor Mendoza, Chief of Police, Varukoi had bought the services of several other individuals well-positioned to note and report on any activities of concern to him. And since most, if not virtually all, of the denizens of Nerja and its environs were involved in shady business of one kind or another, and also added to the police chief's retirement fund with regular payoffs, Varukoi would hardly stand out amid the den of high-class swindlers, thieves, whores and shysters that lived here.

Varukoi began to feel relaxed as Puerto Banus came into view along a certain switchback on the mountain road that afforded a particularly breathtaking vista of the whitewashed buildings and marinas of the chic seaside resort town. The road also straightened out for a half mile or so, giving Varukoi the chance to gun the Diablo flat-out at high-speed, and the Russian reveled in the feeling of naked power as the Lamborghini's high-performance in-line tri-turbo V-8 engine roared tigerishly and bulleted the sports car forward until the next series of hairpin turns, just before entering the outskirts of Puerto Banus forced him to slow down to a somewhat more reasonable velocity.

Exhilarated from the late-night drive, Varukoi angle-parked the Diablo in an available space on the corniche close to a waterfront stretch that was well-situated for people-watching and yacht-spotting at any of the several cafes on the town's landward side. Evening had deepened from violet into black, and the stars that had shone dimly overhead on his ride in were now glittering blue-white pinpoints across the velveteen night skies of southern Spain.

Helped by a small gratuity, the maître d'hotel of one of the trendiest cafe-bars on the corniche found Varukoi a choice table with a pleasing view, enhanced by the first glass of vintage Malaga chilled in a salver of ice -- and not uncouth refrigeration -- to a precise temperature of thirty-five degrees Fahrenheit per Varukoi's exacting instructions. At this temperature the full, robust flavor of the tart mountain wine was brought out, and it was also the best temperature at which to drink the wine with a hearty plate of tapas and mariscos.

With the second bottle of Malaga now uncorked by the wine steward, Varukoi's attentions turned to the superb views of the well-rounded apple-asses of the chic women passing him on the corniche. Everything, he knew, was for sale here, and many of the prettier girls were whores of one kind or another, whatever they chose to call themselves. It had always been that way, and would always continue to be that way, like it or not. As he finished the second bottle, Varukoi again summoned the maître d'hotel and arranged for two exceptionally gifted French hookers to be available in fifteen minutes for a session at one of the *cabinets privée* maintained for such entertainments on the upper level of the swank eatery.

Such private rooms had also been a traditional amenity provided for special clients in Europe since at least the late Renaissance. The practice was time-honored and its rules were well-established, and called for complete privacy and secrecy, and the door to a cabinet privée would not be opened unless a discreet knock was answered with a summons to enter.

Varukoi was not disappointed in the two women who joined him there a short time later. They had come equipped not only with the ancient beguilements of the practiced concubine, but with the more modern equipage of snortable Viagra in pocket-sized inhalators, and an assortment of condoms in various colors, sizes and textures. It was understood, however, that the rubbers were purely discretionary on the part of the client -- at the staggering rates these girls charged, anything, and everything, short of outright mutilation, was permitted.

It was much later when Varukoi returned to his villa along the high coastal road. In the flashes of multiple orgasms he'd enjoyed, thanks to modern pharmaceuticals and the timeless ministrations of the two accomplished trollops, the Russian had devised a bold new strategy.

It was actually quite simple. He would hit the Pentagon again, from an entirely new perspective. He could arrange the strike within ninety days, from anywhere in the world. This time it would work. His clients would be satisfied, and Varukoi would receive payment in full, to say nothing of having saved his own skin from the merciless retribution of the Medusa.

Now unbent and fully relaxed, Varukoi looked forward to further unwinding in the villa's hot tub with a bucket containing a bottle or two of brut champagne while he mentally fine-tuned the emerging plan. Nothing like a come or two to clear the mental passageways for thinking; it

461

never failed to work for him. The realization that his enemies might have struck at any time, that the two women whose full-lipped mouths, exquisitely tight vaginas and firm, plump-nippled breasts had teased him to such increasing heights of ecstasy, might themselves have been trained assassins, only increased his determination. What better proof that Varukoi was invisible to all potential pursuers than this?

The Diablo purred like a kitten as the Russian idled down for the final turn in the road to Nerja and smoothly nosed the car into the villa's driveway. He was still a little high from the evening's delightful encounters, but not so much that he would ignore one final precaution before entering the house.

His smart phone was uplinked to a reliable commercial security service providing real-time tracking data on all known satellite orbits, which could be accessed regionally or globally via a handy app.

A fact well-known to astronomers, amateur and professional alike, but little known otherwise, is that most satellites are visible to the naked eye, especially in areas located far from large urban areas, such as the mountain country flanking the Andalusian coast. Considering orbital surveillance satellites key to any attempts to find and kill him, Varukoi had made it a habit to check the current orbital tracks of satellites several times daily, especially when entering and leaving the villa. He did this now after emerging from the car, noting that only the US-Russian space station Freedom was passing overhead, and was reassured because Freedom was a research station without any surveillance and reconnaissance imaging capabilities.

Using the coordinates from his cell's display screen, Varukoi found the quadrant of the night sky across which Freedom would shortly pass. In a minute or two, he was able to conclusively match the increasingly bright speck of yellow-white light that crept slowly across the constellation of Sagittarius to the orbital profile of Freedom. After some minutes more of strategic sky-gazing, his practiced eyes detected nothing else that resembled a manmade satellite or other airborne surveillance asset, and Varukoi contentedly went inside.

Less than an hour later, while polishing off his second bottle of well-iced brut champagne as he watched a subtitled cable broadcast of Bunuel's film "Paris by Night," Varukoi heard a sudden whistling sound that grew steadily louder as, with a start, the Russian realized that whatever was causing the sound was heading right for the roof of the villa. In a split-instant the whistling had become a resounding boom that shattered the stillness of the Andalusian night and set off a chorus of wildly barking dogs in villas throughout the coastal hills, but Varukoi was no longer among the living, and so didn't hear it -- while high above, winking in the black velvet heavens above Andalusia, the space station Freedom passed silently onward to a vanishing point below the broad curvature of the far horizon.

■

Three time zones away, and less than a half-hour later, Rommel Krieger sat at the big Pershing desk that had come with the office of the Secretary of Defense. The EuroHawk UAV that had made the high-altitude surveillance run at ninety-thousand feet across southern Spain from the joint US-UK forward operational location at Diego Garcia had transmitted back the imaging data in real-time.

The series of photos on the wide display screen in front of Krieger showed the catastrophic damage to the Spanish villa, and vindicated the novel approach to the termination with extreme prejudice that had ended Varukoi's sinister life of extortion, murder and other miscellaneous crimes. The two-ton block of ice that had struck the Spanish villa squarely in its center had stamped the villa out of existence more thoroughly than as if it had been struck with an aerially delivered munition from a fighter plane, yet without collateral damage of any kind, and conveniently providing a ready-made cover story along with everything else.

As newly appointed defense secretary with a hands-on management style, Krieger had personally chaired the select covert planning committee convened under a secret executive order from the Oval Office and signed by President Halifax authorizing the use of lethal force and the covert force option in the aftermath of the attack on the Pentagon. While the civilian crew of Freedom had been evacuated by earthbound Space Shuttle, a commando team under the direction of Colonel Robin Hawk had enacted an attack plan carefully crafted by supercomputers at the National Security Agency, itself now undergoing emergency rebuilding.

The plan called for the entire water reserves, including waste water, of Freedom to be pumped into orbital space, at a precise point above the earth where, in the shadow of the earth's night side, it would instantly freeze into a solid block of approximately ten tons weight. Commandos equipped for extravehicular activities would then attach a thruster pack to the miniature iceberg. The thruster, with a self-contained inertial guidance system, would place the ice block into a trans-atmospheric trajectory that had been carefully calculated using supercomputer simulations to bring the two-ton mass remaining after atmospheric friction had melted away most of the iceberg -- and all evidence of the thruster pack -- and bring it smashing down onto the villa where the Russian fox had gone to ground. The two hired girls from Puerto Banus had helped finger Varukoi as well as insure he had no house guests when the ice block struck the villa.

Krieger put the display panel into standby mode and buzzed his secretary to summon the armored limo that was the SecDef's prerogative. The destination, as often at this hour, was a familiar one to Krieger's driver.

As the National Security Acts mandate, the Secretary of Defense serves at the pleasure of the President, nor was the double meaning of the phrase lost on anyone knowledgeable about Washington affairs as the limo slid into the White House via the very private North Gate entrance, adjacent to Lafayette Park, a short time later, below the lighted bedroom window of the presidential suite.

# DAVID ALEXANDER

The editors at Triumvirate Publishing
International hope you have enjoyed Threatcon
Delta: Assault on the Pentagon.

Also by David Alexander:
Snake Handlers
Habu Patch
Under Attack
Under Attack II: Kill Chain
Chain Reaction
I Kinda Spy
Trainjack
War Pigs
Sword of the Mahdi
Death Pulse
Brooklynese
Bloodbath
Puzzle Palace (nonfiction)
Military-Industrial Complex (nonfiction)

Bonus Preview Excerpt
**Brothers of the Gun**

3. Buccaneers of the Spanish Main

*B*rilliant streaks of aquamarine, strange flashes of dull purple and lancing rays of scintillating gold lit up the churning, dull-gray waters of the Spanish Main, a region of ocean, shoreline and islands situated between the east coast of Florida and the north coasts of Colombia and Venezuela below the Lesser Antilles with the Caribbean and Gulf coasts lying in between.

This name was first given to it by the Spanish plunderers who'd prized it as a route by which to gather and move the pillaged gold, silver, precious gems, the hides and furs of rare native beasts, and other valuables of the conquered civilizations of the New World, as well as a transshipment point from which the booty of Spain's colonies in the Orient could be shipped back to the overflowing royal treasuries in old Madrid.

Later on, long after the old Spanish hegemony had been forever lost when Nelson won at the

## DAVID ALEXANDER

Battle of Trafalgar, the coastlines and waters of the region became favorite haunts for cut-throats and buccaneers to lie in wait for merchant vessels flying European flags, whose holds full of rich plunder would fetch high prices in the black markets and crowded kasbahs of exotic ports of call.

Such was now the case as a new day dawned in the spring of the year 1883.

■

The pirate raider was a two-masted warship, her hull sheathed in nearly five inch thick iron belt armor amidships, tapering to half the thickness at prow and bow. The jacketing of iron, intended mainly to gird the vessel -- whose name was Courageous -- for battle against ships of the line also served double duty against the predations of the foot-long wood-eating teredo worm and sundry other similar pests abounding in the warm tropical waters in these southern latitudes.

The Courageous had been built as a blockade runner, fleet -- her 1500 horsepower, four-boiler steam engine made for a top speed of almost 15 knots -- and difficult to see until another vessel was abeam of her, thanks to her low draft which displaced less than 1200 long tons yet allowed her to slide through the water quiet as a whisper.

And she was deadly too.

# THREATCON DELTA

Amidships, behind the prow and before the bow, were positioned twin pillbox turrets, each one clad in armor of five inch thickness, and each one of them containing powerful main guns.

Inside the forward turret were mounted twin Armstrong guns -- 254 millimeter cannons capable of fire that was both rapid and accurate at long range -- and one of the newest compressed air powered Gatlings firing belt-fed .44 caliber ammunition.

The aft turret contained a single Armstrong -- a 40 pounder with a smaller bore, firing 120 millimeter rounds, but was also outfitted with a 12 pound cannon and a second Gatling machinegun, this one gas-driven. A third Gatling was the sole armament of a smaller iron turret positioned atop the aft brigantine mast, while a fourth and final Gatling, also gas-driven, could be fitted to mounts amidships at port and starboard, as the need might arise.

These same mounts could also accommodate Cosgrove rockets with explosive warheads which could be used at longer ranges than the ship's guns.

And if neither guns nor rockets failed to do their bloody work well enough (or if circumstances favored it) the Courageous was also outfitted with an iron armored ram bow that could stave in the timbers of an enemy vessel and send her straight to the bottom.

She had been wrighted in England by the Lairds, whose boatyard had supplied both Confederate and Union with ironclads and blockade runners during the turmoil of the Civil War. Decades earlier, the same boatyard had built the special ship that President Tom Jefferson had ordered constructed to serve as a decoy in the war against the pirates of the Barbary Coast who had been preying on American shipping in the waters of the Indian Ocean. Disguised as an unarmed merchant ship, she would bare her guns behind concealed panels to port and starboard as the pirates got within range and blast them out of the waters.

So too was the Courageous equipped, but she also had the new Gatling guns bolted to her decks and launchers for Cosgrove rockets positions on her masts in addition to the cannons above and below as well as heavier armaments than Jefferson's warship carried.

Ably manned by a crew of twenty rough though capable seamen, the Courageous was more than a match for any ship that sailed the seas, and the fact that she was equipped with condensing apparatus capable of extracting fresh drinking water from the sea, meant that the Courageous needed few stops at bases and could prowl the seas independent of land for long periods of time.

# THREATCON DELTA

And while the Courageous was herself a pirate vessel, she was an American privateer, and like her predecessor she too sailed with the secret blessings of the current administration of President Chester Arthur.

She too had a mission, which was to throw a spanner into the well-laid plans of first, the Spanish and French to gain new footholds in the southern reaches of the Americas, and second, the Ukase in Moscow to do the same in the colder reaches of the north. For this purpose the Monroe Doctrine -- officially American, tacitly British as well -- had been promulgated against further attempts to colonize the Americas by the powers of Europe.

While British and American ships of the line policed the open seas, other actions against foreign interlopers would remain secret and never be made known. Such actions included those for which Snakeskin Blake and his Anglo-American crew of larcenous cutthroats were paid in the pillaged buccaneer's booty that they were able to recover from the ships they sent plunging straight down to the muddy bottom.

■

On this particular morning, the Courageous lay at anchor leeward of the reefs guarding the approaches to Two Rocks Island, a rough and broken wind-scoured rock in the ocean that did not appear on any navigational maps, and was thus as much stranger to the seas upon which it lay as it was a welcome and much sought out refuge for freebooters who plied the Spanish Main between the Caribbean Coast and the Gulf of Mexico.

Centrally positioned in the Caribbean midway between Port Au Prince in Haiti and Cartagena on the northwest coast of Colombia, Two Rocks Island was a sharp sliver of stone cast off the skeleton bones of the Greater Antilles which lay scattered across the Caribbean's uppermost reaches in a messy jumble that was the bane of merchantmen and sworn friend of pirates.

As far as islands went, Two Rocks Island was far too small to provide permanent habitation for man or decent foraging for any beasts other than the wild cats and goats that had been left there by the crews of passing vessels over the years to either breed or die out.

But the pirate's lair, replete with rocky coves for safe anchorage and sea caves that led far inland, and were thus perfect spots to stash away plundered loot or hide from British men-o-war was large enough to completely hide the Courageous from the view of any other ships approaching the island on a north-by-northwest course heading. And in the thick salt fog that now hung low over the surface of the sea like a briny blanket, the Courageous was doubly shrouded from detection by her unwary prey.

■

All hands were already awake and a lookout manned the crow's nest high on the foc'sle, the sailor's sharp eyes scanning the far horizon for signs of the expected prize of the day. The object of the lookout's search was a Spanish merchant vessel. The name of the ship was Alonso de Palensia, and highly reliable reports bought dear in the seaside scum lairs of old Kingston town in nearby Jamaica indicated that she had put out to sea from the port of Malaga some two days before. Following a northwesterly course that would carry her across the waters of the Mediterranean Sea, around the Cape of Good hope, and then into the Atlantic, the Alonso de Palensia was bound for New Orleans.

The merchant ship's hold bulged with casks of Portuguese wine from Oporto, crates of Caribbean tobacco, heavy sea chests full of African Ivory plus sugar, coffee and other valuable trading commodities. But there were also two chests of finely smelted Libyan gold secreted onboard, and even a single chest of such a prize was worth more than all the other cargo onboard the Alonso de Palensia combined.

■

# DAVID ALEXANDER

In the captain's quarters of the anchored pirate raider, Snakeskin Blake stood bent over his nautical charts.

Snakeskin was a medium tall man, and well-muscled rather than too slender of build. His face was hard and angular, marked by a cruel mouth as quick to show anger as to break into a broad grin at a good and merry jest.

His hard gray eyes were fixed with a seasoned mariner's calm precision on the chart as he stroked the cobra-shaped scar on his left cheek. From his lips jutted a burning cheroot, tipped with an inch of smoking gray ash and redolent of the rich Napoleon brandy into which he had let it steep before drying and lighting it.

Snakeskin was checking for last minute questions that might arise, making certain that the taking of the Alonso de Palensia would proceed as smoothly as clockwork.

That the merchant vessel was carrying the three mahogany chests of pure Libyan gold, Snakeskin took as an article of faith. He had received the information separately from the Spanish brigantine's charted course through an agent in Tripoli who, if not completely trustworthy, was nevertheless smart enough to understand that the money Snakeskin had paid for the information meant that he would pay with his life if the information turned out not to be genuine or if a trap was in the making.

Snakeskin heard a sudden rapping on the shipmaster's cabin door and straightened to his full height of five feet, nine inches. Although he was not as tall as some, his shoulders were broad as the length of an axe from the top of its head to the tip of its handle and his mastery of the skills of Chinese Boxing, learned while serving with Chinese Charlie during the Teipei Rebellion, insured that few men could stand up to him in a fight and that those foolish enough to try would likely as not come out second best.

"Come in," Snakeskin said in a voice as rough as sandpaper.

"Begging your pardon, cap'n," the man who entered replied.

Big Little Jopling wore a leather vest over a striped sailor's blouse. His right eye was patched and a badly healed puckered scar ran down the left side of his face. He was Snakeskin's first mate, and another Taipei veteran who had served with Charlie Gordon's motley assortment of British and American mercenaries.

"But you wanted me to report when the Alonso de Palensia was sighted."

"Show me," Snakeskin said, indicating the navigational chart spread out on the table.

Jopling crossed the cabin and bent over the chart. Placing one thick finger down on the lines describing shipping lanes, he indicated the position of the Alonso de Palensia and said, "She's here, Cap'n, thirty degrees north, fifty west. Just about where we expected her to lie. Nary a mile off course, cap'n. I figure she'll be within hailing distance in fifteen minutes."

"Excellent," Snakeskin pronounced, rolling up the map and stowing it away in one of the polished teak cabinets on the cabin walls. "Tell those scurvy dogs I pay good money to man this ship to proceed to their stations. There's a bottle of unwatered Haitian rum for every stinking cur among 'em if we pull this off -- make sure they know it.

"Aye, cap'n," Jopling acknowledged, his smile at the contemplated pleasures of action and rum-guzzling revealing gapped and broken wolf's teeth in a sinister mouth. "I'll tell the men."

"I'll meet you topside in a few minutes."

Jopling gave his assent and rushed out into the companionway, closing the cabin door behind him. Snakeskin went to his drawer and took out a matched set of .44 caliber LeMat revolvers.

Each of the white ivory handled LeMats (he'd had the handgrips specially retooled by a Singaporean gunsmith to replace the original checkered walnut grips) were equipped with an outsized cylinder capable of firing nine shots in rapid succession and a centerpiece, smooth bore barrel, that was made for firing grapeshot like a rifle.

The formidable weapon had been devised in New Orleans by the Confederacy's leading gunsmith, and it was in the port of New Orleans that Snakeskin had obtained the matched pistol set of the last remaining .44 editions, which took standard cartridges, in a game of Five Card Stud that had ended with the gun's former owner on the floor with an unfired derringer in his hand and a hole in his belly, courtesy of the smoking Colt under Snakeskin's end of the poker table.

Snapping open the wheels of both weapons, the captain of the Courageous checked to see that rounds filled each of the nine slots in their rifled cylinders, as he smelled the odor of oil rising from the well-cared-for firearms. The inspection was performed more out of habit than necessity as Snakeskin always kept his prized guns cleaned and loaded.

Then, jamming both LeMats into the broad and well worn belt of engraved Moroccan leather that encircled his trim waist, Snakeskin followed Jopling's path from the cabin, feeling the blood pound in his ears as every nerve came alive with anticipation.

# DAVID ALEXANDER

And now, like the Courageous' first mate, the captain of the privateer grinned too, savoring what was about to come next.

4. All Hands on Deck

*F*aintly, beyond the creaking of the ship's timbers and the steady cadence of waves lapping at the stony outcroppings of Two Rocks island, Snakeskin heard the Spanish merchantman in the distance as she plied the calm waters off the southern shores of Curacao midway between the Windwards on the underbelly of the Caribees and the shoal-infested coastal waters that lay hard off Baranquilla on the South American mainland.

Snakeskin knew she'd follow a straight course for Jamaica, where she'd turn to complete the last leg of the voyage to the Mexican port of Valparaiso. That course would have her pass within no more than a league or two of Two Rocks Island.

The sun had just risen as though reluctant to light the world and reveal the flagrant sins of mortal men to the eternal vigils of heaven. It was now little more than a faint yellow blotch on the color-streaked horizon. The dense fog insured that twilight still held sway and would for at least awhile longer.

The sailors aboard the Alonso de Palensia would be on guard for an attempt to take the vessel by the cutthroat buccaneers which plied these waters so often traversed by richly laden treasure ships of the Spanish navy. By now the word of the valuable cargo that the merchant was carrying in her hold would have become an open secret. A prize as rich as it would make the Alonso de Palensia an attractive target to pirate vessels.

The crew of the Alonso de Palensia would be especially watchful, Snakeskin knew. And even through the dense fog, the eyes of an experienced lookout could discern the telltale silhouette of a ship against the faintly lit horizon as well as a hen could recognize her brood of chicks. If the Courageous were spotted in time, offensive measures could be taken by the Spanish merchantmen's crew that would not be pleasant -- her cannon were modern breech-loaders manned by experienced gunnery crews. Far better to catch the prize all unwary and take her fast, quitting the area with booty before any alarms she might have raised could bring other, and more dangerous vessels, into the area.

While the Courageous was well armed with its revolving gun turrets and Cosgrove rockets and its crew carried rifles and revolvers in their belts, Snakeskin wanted to avoid any needless confrontation or bloodshed.

The tactics that had allowed him to survive in his treacherous business called for stealth, speed and surprise to catch the enemy unawares, seize the initiative and make off with the prize.

The last thing Snakeskin wanted or needed was a bloody fight at sea, if he could at all avoid one.

In pursuit of this objective, the Courageous had hoisted its mooring anchor slowly and quietly, its cable, capstans and hawse pipe all well greased to avoid making unnecessary sounds and to prevent any fouling of the cable as the great black flukes of old Admiralty iron broke free of the bottom and a ton of dead weight dangling from its cast metal crown began rising slowly off the floor of the ocean.

Blake's buccaneers were forbidden to smoke or to speak as well, and although they looked seedy, they were all professional thieves to the last man. More than that, they were more loyal to Snakeskin than to any other living soul, willing to follow him straight into the gaping jaws of hell itself if he asked them. Every mate onboard the Courageous knew the reason for their captain's orders and would follow them to the letter.

Snakeskin now pricked up his ears, straining to interpret the meaning of every one of the faint sounds coming through the blanket of swirling mists. He knew that he was hearing the sounds of the approaching merchant ship, and that it was only a matter of minutes until the vessel broke through the mists and bore down upon them.

481

# THREATCON DELTA

And then Snakeskin saw the prow of the Spanish treasure ship break through the dense gray fog bank. Jopling had also seen the Alonso de Palensia suddenly loom within range and was watching Snakeskin intently for the signal to heave to from the anchorage just around the leeward side of Two Rocks island. Snakeskin raised his hand just before delivering the signal and then brought it sharply down.

Jopling made circular motions of his own hand to the helmsman who immediately issued the order to apply main power to the ship's engines. There would now be no escaping the sounds made by these operations. No matter how silent the crew remained, the sounds would be audible to any listeners onboard the oncoming merchant vessel, echoing across the sea in the fog.

Snakeskin felt the Courageous lurch as her twin screws churned under the combined force of half of her eight boilers and she swung out into the tide. Within a matter of seconds the pirate vessel had slid past the small, rocky island. Seconds later the lookout in the crow's nest high above the foredeck of the hapless Alonso de Palensia spotted the telltale black silhouette moving like a wraith through the gray shreds of curling sea mist.

He instantly raised the Very pistol loaded with the red flare cartridge that signaled imminent attack by privateers and pulled back the trigger.

# DAVID ALEXANDER

The flare burned like a red star of ill omen above the ship, illuminating the ocean for at least a league all around in its fitful, sizzling glare, and sent the crew of the Alonso de Palensia into violent motion as sailors ran for their battle stations.

The cry of alarm too had roused the captain of the merchant ship to sudden wakefulness as he jumped from the bed, ignoring the imprecations of the East Indian whore who'd warmed him as he slept. Hastily throwing on his black breeches and bright red waistcoat, jamming his loaded revolver into his belt holster and putting his three-cornered and cockaded hat on his closely shaven head, the treasure ship's captain gained the deck and shouted for general quarters to be sounded.

Standing on the afterdeck, the ship's yeoman began to ring the alarm bell to call all hands to action in a frenzy of warning. Seconds later, hands from stem to stern aboard the Courageous were in position to take the Spanish prize.

"First mate -- hoist the ship's battle ensigns. Fly the Jolly Roger!"

"Aye, Cap'n Snakeskin," shouted Jopling in reply, as he went at his appointed task with black-hearted relish.

Her stacks blowing dense plumes of brown-black smoke as her engines made all eight boilers work to earn the coal that fed their furnaces, the

# THREATCON DELTA

Courageous shot from its cove in the lee of Two Rocks island and hurtled toward its prize.

Now Jopling ordered that the privateer's ensign be raised aloft, and the sailor up high on the masts unfurled the great banner of yellow Chinese silk bearing the emblem of a great sea serpent coiled about a whale and preparing to devour its prize with the motto "To the Victors Belong the Spoils" surrounding the bold depiction.

Taking up his binoculars, Snakeskin trained the twin lenses on the Spanish merchantman now looming closer in the distance and glassed her over. He could now see men rushing about confusedly on the Alonso de Palensia's decks.

Swinging up the glass, he could see other crewmembers hurrying to change the vessel's main sail's cant so that she could tack to starboard in order to try and evade the trap into which she had stumbled. The ship appeared as though preparing to turn and make a run for it, having applied reverse torque to her screws. As it did, the Alonso de Palensia faltered before heeling hard about in the direction from which she'd come, and she began to cut a wake in the choppy sea.

"Damn! She's trying to make a break for it," Snakeskin shouted to Jopling, letting the binoculars drop on their leather strap about his neck. "Alert bow and stern turret gunners. Have them fire warning salvos across her starboard bows."

"Aye-aye, Cap'n Snakeskin," Jopling replied, and relayed the order to the crew of cannoneers posted at battle stations throughout the Courageous.

A few moments later, fulminating clouds of cordite smoke rolled and billowed across the Courageous' heaving decks and every plank vibrated as the sound of the automatic cannon fire echoed through the dense fog.

Hoisting up his glasses again, Snakeskin could see multiple stitch lines of glowing green phosphorescent tracer fire belched from the flaming muzzles of the turret guns arc across the bows of the merchant ship's deck.

"She's not changing course, Cap'n," Jopling commented after a few heartbeats had passed. "She'll try to run for it. Maybe lose us in the Windwards and then make for Jamaica."

"Not a bad guess," Snakeskin wagered. "Same as mine in fact."

It was apparent that the Alonso de Palensia had chosen to run from the attacking vessel rather than stand to for boarding by the pirate crew.

"Orders, Cap'n Snakeskin?

"Hard to starboard! We'll cross her bows and punch a few holes in her stern close to her ordnance stores. If we get too close to hitting the magazine it may change the captain's mind."

"Aye-aye, Skipper," Jopling replied, relaying Snakeskin's orders to the helm of the Courageous and to her gun crews in the turrets fore and aft as well as the artillery near the stern.

Snakeskin felt the Courageous heel sharply about as the pirate vessel gave chase to her desperately fleeing quarry. The merchant vessel was fast, but she was no match for the far fleeter blockade runner. Within minutes the Courageous was standing hard across her bows as Snakeskin had ordered, cutting off her single avenue of escape toward the Spanish port of Jamaica.

"Is the cannon gun crew ready?" Snakeskin asked at a shout.

"Ready as a groom with the bride's nighties off, Capn'," Jopling replied, affirming this with a glance at the crewmen to starboard who again stood ready to pull the chains that would ignite the big powder charges to send the .30 millimeter shells arcing across the open water.

Minutes before, under the direction of their skippers, they had strained on the ropes to haul the guns back from the side of the ship where they were secured by heavy tackle and mounted on wheeled recoil carriages. The cannoneers had then loaded the heavy deck guns, rammed the powder charges down the rifled gun barrels to the far end, followed in turn by the heavy artillery shells with their high explosive warheads.

"Order them to fire," was the command Snakeskin next issued as the Courageous' pilot succeeded in putting her starboard bow abeam of the merchantman.

In a second, the big deck guns roared, making the Courageous' deck planks shudder and the air echo with deafening reports. The rounds fired at the Alonso de Palensia from the muzzles of the artillery pieces were jacketed with pellets of pig iron held together within the shell casing in a waxy matrix. This shrapnel, as it was called, would fragment on impact or on fuzed proximity to a target. Well, not quite fragment -- that was too tame a word. For in an age of largely black powder weaponry, rounds might hit with a savage fury that tore limbs from torsos as the rule, not the exception.

Yet while the shrapnel-filled artillery shells could be far deadlier to the crew of the merchant ship than the cannonballs of previous naval engagements (while still capable of tearing the limbs clean off any luckless soul in harm's way), such rounds would still present less chance of sending the merchant ship to the bottom -- an outcome that Snakeskin did not desire.

Snakeskin watched the cannon shot find its targets amidships of the now badly mauled merchant vessel. A sudden explosion at the stern of the stricken craft told him that its ordnance magazine had been struck dead center.

Within a matter of seconds the entire aft section of the Spanish treasure ship was engulfed in flames and awash with dense billowing black smoke. She was riding lower in the water too, indicating that the sea was flooding into breaches ripped in the Alonso de Palensia's ironclad hull by the Courageous' accurate cannonades.

Snakeskin Blake was close enough to hear the screams of crewmen unnerved by the assault and beginning to panic as they'd seen fellow sailors struck by the maiming, limb-tearing, bone-shattering shrapnel. Snakeskin ordered the Gatling-armed turret crews to fire tracer bursts at the masts and shatter them as the Spanish merchantman slowed and her wake flattened behind her.

Finally the Alonso de Palensia stopped dead and Snakeskin knew the Courageous and her crew had won both the contest and the prize that belonged to the victors. The merchantman's captain did not have any fight left in him. To his credit he was wise enough to know that he was beaten and behaved accordingly.

Soon Snakeskin saw the white flag of surrender hoisted high up on the main mizzen boom. The prize was finally his! A great cheer rose up from the Courageous. Blake's buccaneers had won.

Those of the crew who were still alive and whose wounds did not prevent them from feeling it, knew the anticipation of being within reach of valuable booty. The merchantman would have ample provisions and plentiful food, ale and barrel stacked upon barrel of good, stout Portuguese wine and dark Jamaican rum as well, and soon they would be enjoying the plunder of their defeated enemy.

"Bring her hard to," Snakeskin instructed Jopling from his perch on the flying bridge of the Courageous. "And have the men make ready to board our hard-earned prize. We've got her -- and the treasure in her hold."

"Aye, that we do, Cap'n Snakeskin," Jopling replied with a broad smile, and relayed Snakeskin's orders to the Courageous' cheering crew, every man among them eager for grand plunder and bars of Libyan gold.